MISTER NICE

JAMIE JENNINGS

Editor: Hoffman Smith
Cover: Mitxeran

ISBN: 978-0-6453608-9-9 (Paperback)
ISBN: 978-0-6453608-8-2 (EBook)

CHAPTER ONE

The problem for Troy Evans with having a friend who's animated as Quinn Weissman is that she signed as if she was on cocaine. While the average person can sign about one hundred to one hundred and thirty words per minute, she's going at least two hundred at this point with her swift movement and comedic facial expression to go with it.

"So, when I got to the mall, you'd think the day would be better, right? I mean, you know how I am when you put me in a mall with my latest paycheck, but then the girl at the Starbucks gave me whole milk instead of oat. You can only imagine how I felt going to a public restroom and just stuck there for an hour. Then my heels, don't get me even started," she signs with an exasperated look of pure irritation. Well, at least, that's what Troy thinks she has signed. The girl went so fast with her hands that it was hard to follow at times.

"Let me guess," Troy signs back, grinning at his best friend. "Your expensive red bottom heels broke?"

At his question, her shoulders sag in utter defeat with a loud sigh. She nods, tucking her blonde hair back as she stares at him, and continues with signing. "It was worse than just that. I think I saw my soulmate there, and now? The chances are ruined."

It takes everything in him not to laugh, though, in the end, he caves as no one is in their usual spot in the park. A silly smile makes its way to Quinn's face, as it's not often she sees her best friend laughing without a care in the world and not being self-conscious about it. However, she completely understands being born deaf and not knowing what they sounded like.

Troy bumps his shoulder onto hers before continuing to talk with his hands. "That's okay. You're going to find your soulmate sooner or later. Though I can't help but feel bad for the poor fellow who—hey."

He didn't get to finish before she punched him playfully on the arms. From how her shoulders shake, it's a good enough sign that she's laughing before she raises an eyebrow. She chugs her water before cocking her head to the side. "Are you sure you don't need me to go with you to the tryouts for men's tennis tomorrow? As I said, I don't mind calling in and staying with you for their tryouts."

Just thinking of the tryout for men's tennis tomorrow for NCAA Division 1 makes butterflies explode in his stomach. The thought of being part of the intramural tennis team at Columbia University had always been his dream. Still, it finally took two years before he decided to sign up for tryouts after being part of the club tennis as a casual player for a year and watching others play. He even was a former tennis coach for the youth program for two summers.

It's been his long dream to become one day one of the first deaf LGBT professional tennis players and pave the way for others like him. However, the hard part is getting picked during tryouts. As he's not on any sports scholarships either and on a VISA, he didn't know if they would even spare a glance at him during tryouts tomorrow.

Troy tries hard not to show her how nervous he feels inside as he shakes his head before signing once more. "No, I'll be fine. I know you have work, and the last thing I would want is for you to call out. How else will you afford another pair of your expensive red bottom heels that would potentially find the millionaire soulmate of your dreams?"

At his sarcastic question, she flips him off, though both knew they were joking after being together for almost ten years at this point during his first day there. Finally, when he was utterly lost, he decided to gather enough courage and tap the girl next to him before scribbling down with shaky hands if she knew where freshmen orientation would be held.

Much to his surprise, she smiles before signing, "You have terrible handwriting like my brother."

Little did he know that the small stroke of luck was all it took for their almost two years and counting friendship, as they were also both majoring in social work. For the past two years, they were joined to the hips while bringing her bubbly personality everywhere Troy went. So often, he's convinced that she would probably sign better than him if she would just slow it down for a minute.

As it turns out, Quinn learned sign language when she

was younger because her little brother, Raymond, was slowly starting to lose hearing due to Usher's syndrome type-three. Since then, they had stuck together like magnets, and Troy often came over to Quinn's parents' home on the weekend for dinner as his parents were still in Sydney, Australia.

"I have you know," she signs with a huff. "That my criteria have changed. He now must be a billionaire instead of a millionaire, possessive, alpha, and possibly able to give me two babies and one fresh bulldog. Other than that, I don't think I'm asking for too much, do you?"

Troy couldn't help but grin. He knows she has a soft spot when it comes to erotica romance, and if that's what makes her happy, he would never try to get in the way of it. "You? Asking for too much? Impossible, sweet pea."

At the nickname, she narrows her eyes until they are slits. She knew from the moment she brought Troy to their family dinner and realized what her nickname was, she would never hear the end of it teasingly. She throws her hands up at the sky before signing. "Well, you still haven't told me who your dream man is."

The comment makes him press his lips into a thin line; it's a question that often stumps him as a child and even now. But, honestly, Troy has often been too shy in his adolescent years to find himself a boyfriend and hasn't even had his first kiss yet, let alone who his perfect dream person is. In fact, he still had a hard time putting a label on his sexuality as no one had made him feel comfortable to pursue a relationship.

"Someone...nice," Troy finally signs awkwardly.

"Nice?" she questions, throwing a few more question marks in her signs. "Just...nice? Mister nice?"

"Well, I never thought too much about dating or who the perfect person for me would be. My goal and ambitions have always been about sports," he confesses with lazy movements of his hands to drive his point across. "Though if you're asking about dating; if I can find someone who can accept me fully...with my disability—"

He didn't get to finish signing before Quinn captures his hands and then gives him a stern look. He knew from her reaction that she didn't want him to even think about finishing that out loud, solidifying his fears as she immediately went on a spree. "You did not just insult you and my brother."

Trying not to wince, he immediately shakes his head along with his hands. It's not his intention, but it was how he felt when people had categorized him as such his whole life. "No, I'm just saying that I just want to find someone who would not think of me as bothersome; someone who's nice and just gets me."

"You will," Quinn signs sternly before a light-hearted smile makes its way to her face. She reaches forward to grab the remainder of Troy's biscuits set out and pops it into her mouth before continuing. "In fact, I'm willing to bet you'll find one before I find my billionaire soulmate."

"Funny," he signs, grinning as he gets up and looks upwards. It seems the clouds were getting heavier and darker; only it's one of the few things Troy loved. The rain always makes him feel calm, especially standing and feeling the droplets all over his skin, almost like music to his body, as his ears couldn't take it in. "Do you have an umbrella with you?"

Quinn shakes her head before flicking her hands. "It's fine. I have a car, and I'll just dash into my workplace if it starts pouring. Do you have an umbrella since you have one more class left before you're done for the day?"

He shuffles and produces it for her to see before shoving it back into his sling bag. "I'm going to get a drink at the café before going to class. How about I treat you today as good luck you"ll bump into your billionaire soulmate today at work?"

"Haha," she signs, deadpan, before she gets up and brushes her yellow dress. The one thing that Troy noticed from the moment they met was how beautiful his best friend was. However, she's also the most unkempt person who always misses something or trips on air. Her hair is usually down, coming down in waves, and her face is always fresh with makeup as she wears the latest designer clothes that generally don't match her shoes or bag. "Though I wouldn't mind a drink, but I'm paying; it's my turn for our coffee payment, in case you forgot."

"Fine," he signs, knowing it's better just to allow her to win at this point.

She holds out his hands, and they walk to the campus café, just enjoying one another's silence. It's the one thing Troy loved about Quinn. It's never boring or awkward when it's the two of them. So when Troy decided to come to America to study, he certainly didn't expect to make a friend on the first day, much less someone who could sign aside from his assigned roommate, Aston, who was also deaf like him.

Though halfway there, Quinn would let go with a gasp before going on about a story she had forgotten regarding the latest romance book she had just finished. Though mostly, she spiraled in complaining about how terrible the ending was as the rain came drizzling down lightly. By the time they reached the coffee shop, it was full-on raining as Troy quickly pulled open the door for her.

A frown makes its way to his face upon realizing that the floor is slick and slippery at the exit. Luckily for him, he had worn the black rainboots that helped steady him when his feet slid slightly on the linoleum.

"Jeez, you'd think the campus wouldn't want their student not to sue," Quinn signs, rolling her eyes as she makes her way to the counter. "Should I get our usual? Two lattes, one with oat and the other with skim and hazelnut drizzle for you?"

Troy nods just as the counter calls for the next person based on how the other person has already gone to the waiting area. There were only three people, all lost in their own world. Watching Quinn's mouth move and then the cashier, Troy sometimes couldn't help but unconsciously realize that the world is filled with sound, something in which he will never be able to know what it would sound like. He had long come to terms with it, but sometimes, it comes in waves about what the world would sound like along with the rain or voices.

With that, his head slowly turns towards the window,

watching the Earth gradually getting cleansed by the rain. Once they got their lattes, he thanked Quinn with a nod that had slowly become their secret language of thanks when they couldn't sign if their hands were full. It's then he grabs his cup from her hands. Just as he turned to ensure she wouldn't trip before getting his umbrella, someone came bursting into the coffee shop.

The door swings open and he immediately crashes with his cup. Troy gasps, his eyes widening as coffee splashes onto his grey t-shirt as the cup falls onto the ground. Then, out of surprise, Troy is about to slip once more when he feels two strong arms onto him, holding him steady.

It's then their eyes meet, and Troy's heart starts racing at just how lusciously green this stranger's eyes are. It's as if time stops for him right at that moment; the man almost looks as if he stepped out of a magazine cover. He seems just a few years older than what Troy had deduced. His hair is light golden brown and matted from the rain. The way it's sticking up in all sorts of directions made it look as if he's been running through them all day. His jawline is chiseled to utter perfection and a five-o'clock shadow.

Who is this man?

The stranger's mouth moved, but Troy couldn't hear anything but silence. He wished he knew what this person would sound like for the first time. He wonders if it is rough or smooth as butter from all the books Quinn has read.

Troy watches awkwardly as Quinn's mouth moves and then to the stranger, though nothing but silence greets his ears. The good thing would be how well he had picked up on reading body language before he clumsily reached into his large shoulder bag and grabbed his marker and pen. He bites off the pen cap, scribbling a question down before turning it to him: "Are you okay?"

Usually, this would be the part where people often get awkward upon realizing that Troy is deaf. However, if Quinn were there, they often would talk to her, which she would then sign to him. So he was surprised when he slowly reached for the notepad and pen. Their hands brush and goosebumps break out everywhere, along with a flush on Troy's face at how much bigger his hands are.

Troy watches the stranger write before turning the pad over to him: "I should be asking you that."

He's trying to communicate with him the same way he did with the notepad. Troy feels as if he's in some sort of dream-like state as he hands the notepad back before setting his large gym bag that was on his shoulder onto the floor and lifting off his black sweater. The shirt he had underneath rises, and a flush makes its way to Troy's face at the glimpse of his abs. He swears there's a tattoo just peaking out before Troy snaps his attention back up. Their eyes pierce one another as the stranger hands Troy his sweater.

His eyes widen tremendously as he tries to tell him that it is okay, but the stranger only shakes his head before turning to Quinn. She looks just as perplexed as the stranger gives them both a smile, waving farewell when Quinn grabs Troy's hand and leads him out. He opens the umbrella, still baffled by everything, before she turns to him, signing wildly.

"Oh my God, he noticed you, Troy," she signs, her eyes like saucer plates as she goes on as if she was possessed. "I can't believe someone like him. He's so sweet, and he even gave you his sweater because he wants to make sure you make a good impression in your class as it's the first day; I told him you have one class left. It's like out of a coffee shop AU, and I'm so jealous. So when is it my turn?"

"Who?" Troy signs to the best of his ability while balancing the umbrella. Quinn holds it, allowing him to slip on the sweater. It's ridiculously baggy over his body, but the smell of cigar and sweet vanilla. "Is he some sort of celebrity or something?"

"Do you not know who that is?" she signs, much slower this time despite how fast her heart is racing. "He's essentially the star in the tennis world around here. How do I know that more than you when you're part of the tennis club? Wait, no...oh, it's because I've been to their frat parties. He's Jayden Harrington, the star player for our university's tennis team."

Troy tried not to look so shocked at the thought of getting to see him tomorrow during tryouts. However, it was rather nice of him to give him the sweater because he heard he still had class and went to write in his notepad as well rather than relying on Quinn as the translator.

"Oh, cool," he signs, not sure why Quinn has a devious smile on her face before she winks.

"He can also be your mister nice guy dream."

"Haha, as if," he signs, scoffing. At that, Quinn pinches her lips tightly together and eyes Troy before the sweater he had placed on. He holds up his hand in self-defense. "Okay, he gave me his sweater, but that doesn't mean anything. He's just being nice—like a human being would be."

Troy thought with a sigh as if someone like him, who's essentially every woman's walking wet dream, would notice someone like him. On the contrary, though, he couldn't help but wonder if he would enjoy having Jayden's attention on him. Shaking the thought, he decides to walk Quinn to her car before heading to his last class for the day.

CHAPTER TWO

Were all women clueless regarding hints, or was it just her?
Irritation courses through Jayden Harrington's vein
as he tries to keep it together. He knew in his guts that he
shouldn't have come to this party when his best friend and
teammate in tennis for the last season, Trevis Scottland,
invited him.

He's tapping his cup, trying to calm his nerves as he
settles with the fact that it's just her. In fact, he had already
forgotten about his.

However, he can't allow his anger to win as he forces a
smile. The girl was beautiful; Jayden wouldn't try denying it.
She's in a skimpy black dress that just pushes her breasts upwards, egging you to take a peak. On any other day, he wouldn't
have minded taking her home; however, something's been on
his mind, and when it comes to him, the idea won't allow him
to rest until he goes through with it. "Listen, Diana, I—"

"Danni," she interjects. He gives himself credit for
somewhat getting that right, though she didn't look offended by any means. Instead, she brushes her blonde locks

back before batting her eyes up at him. Jayden's eyes twitch in irritation when she leans over, practically shoving her tits into his face. "Do you want to go somewhere a bit more private, Mr. Undefeated?"

Christ did that for Jayden at the nickname he's been given by everyone in the tennis league for never losing even more since he had first started playing competitively for Columbia University. It's always about the title when it comes to him as he shakes his head.

"No," he clips without explanation. The ringing in his ears only gets louder, impeding to explode soon. The day had already started somewhat rough already when he didn't watch where he was going, completely knocking someone's drink before giving his sweater away. Now, it only seems to be getting worse from thereon.

"Oh, come on, I promise I'll show you a fun time," she pushes for.

"I'm not interested," he grits out, grinding his teeth. He can feel he's riding on the very edge, but he can't allow others to see his true self at the risk of ending it all. There's too much on the line as he lets out a shaky breath. "Have a great night, Diana."

"Danni," she huffs once more, anger now laced in her voice when she sees him walking off without another word. He weaves his way through the packed house, trying to find his friend among the drunk partygoers. He sighs, cursing at himself once more. He loves parties and letting go, but he should have listened to his guts, which had been bothering him all morning.

Finally, he sees Trevis crowding around Cassie. As usual, he's the rowdiest of the bunch and in just a pair of black shirts, his chest on complete display and glistening from sweat as he's chugging beer from a tube connected to the funnel. Everyone is clapping, cheering him on without a care in the world. Jayden didn't even want to know the coach's reaction when everyone but him was hungover. His jaw ticks once more at the appraisal as the coach also loved to brag to his parents, as they were relatively close.

Given how much his parents loved to donate to their tennis team, it's not a shock.

He taps Trevis, and before he can say anything, Jayden cuts him to it. "I'm calling it for the night."

"Already? The night barely started," he raises an eyebrow at him, tilting his head curiously to the side before pointing over at Cassie. "You're going to miss out on Cassie getting shit-faced and streaking across the yard while security tries giving chase. That shit was hilarious last year that our coach almost had a heart attack when the pictures came up of him riding our statue mascot."

"It wasn't that bad," Cassie says drunkenly as everyone laughs. But, it was particularly bad, especially when he ended up throwing up on the coach's brand new leather shoes at the start of tryout and making him walk around in slippers that were three sizes too small for him.

"Are you going home with someone today?" Trevis questions with a wink as he follows his friend to the exit to grab another drink. Out of everyone, Trevis is the only one able to read his friend well. Truly, Jayden wasn't sure what he would have done without his friend there when he needed it the most.

"I'm most definitely going back to my place sober and not blacking out," he replies before looking back. "What's with the question?"

At that, Trevis' mouth twitches. "I saw you sneaking off a few days ago at Yvette's party."

"Problem?" he questions, arching up a brow in return.

"No problem here. I just didn't think you'll start trying to corrupt the straight ones," he jokes.

Jayden tries not to roll his eyes at his friend's humor. Any other person saying it, it would have left a bad impression on Jayden, but he knew that Trevis didn't mean it like that. As the only bisexual tennis player, he makes sure to stay on the fine line. If someone were to bring it up, Jayden wouldn't have tried brushing it off into the closet, but he also chose not to volunteer the information as well. However, he did try to be discreet regarding it, especially around his teammates and coach. "So long as he and I consented, I don't see the problem. Plus, when did people say that he's straight?"

In honesty, not many people knew he was bisexual, including his teammates and coaches. He didn't feel the need to tell the world by any means. As he didn't live in a dorm either, most didn't ask about his sexual orientation or the people he left a party with.

Well, so long as you're not nosy as Trevis when his eyes widen. He leans in, clearly intrigued. "Really?"

When he only furrows his brows, Trevis throws his head back and laughs.

"Nah, he was bi-curious, if you ask me," Jayden replies. However, he has nothing against the frat brother for being curious. He supposes that it's the appeal of college and being away from home. It's easier to mess around with someone; you pretend you don't know one another the following day and know how to shut up. It's an easy, no-strings-attached hookup, a blow job, and maybe a fuck depending on their liquid courage before they walk off and pretend he hasn't been eyeing Jayden the whole time. The same would apply to girls.

"They all become curious when it comes to you," Trevis chuckles, shaking his head; however, he could sense the irritation in his friend from the way his jawline was ticking and his eye twitching. A frown makes its way to his face. "So what's really wrong? It's not like you to go home this early, especially when the tryout is tomorrow. You like to just let loose before the new season."

"If I'm being honest, I'm thinking of getting another tattoo."

"Right now?" Trevis questions, and there's no judgment. He's known him well enough to know what kind of double life and façade he's putting on, always at the edge of breaking. "Is there any place still open that's taking walk-ins?"

"My regular place is open for another hour; it's been on my mind that I feel like I need to get it now," he confesses with a long sigh. He tugs at the ends of his hair, pulling at it. "I was going to wait until after tryout, but something feels right about doing it now."

"Impulsive as ever," he chuckles.

That was the understatement of the year. "You have no idea, brother."

"You still coming to tryouts tomorrow and playing?" he frowns deeply.

"I am," he affirms. "If Cassie can come in hangover, then I'll be damned if I wasn't."

"Touche," Trevis laughs, raising his red cup before chugging it all down. "I'll see you tomorrow then."

Jayden couldn't book it fast enough if he even tried. Once he's out of the frat house, a part of him feels like he could breathe once more. A part of him was convinced it was because he's twenty-three now and wasn't into the party scene anymore.

However, a larger part of him knew the truth about his impulsive and reckless behavior, and it was the only outlet he knew how to do aside from playing sports. The need to feel alive and do something only he can do takes hold.

Getting into his car, he drives out from the campus and into the Westside to his usual tattoo shop. A grin finally makes its way to his face when he sees Bo on his phone, looking lax as people wouldn't usually stop in half an hour before closing. He's a man with a pot belly and a long beard. Usually, he comes off as grumpy and rude, but he's slowly started growing onto Jayden since he first stumbled into his shop five years ago.

The bell goes off, and Bo doesn't even look up when he speaks. "We're closed, come back tomorrow."

"You close at ten, and it's only nine-thirty."

At the sound, Bo looks up and arches a brow before

squinting. It only makes Trevis grin even wider in retaliation as he knows what that look on his face means as he props his body onto his usual spot while he places his phone down. He shakes his head, crossing his arms as he gets up with a grunt. "I didn't think you'll be back so soon."

"What can I say?" he chuckles. "I just love your work that much."

"How did the tattoo come out?" Bo questions. At that, he raises his shirt and shows the tattoo he got on his hips just one month ago. It's of a whale he had seen just a few months when he had gone kayaking. Since then, the image has stayed with him until he etched it onto his skin. The same kind of nagging made him leave partying early to get a new ink as he grins.

"Healing beautifully," he informs Bo, who's admiring his own work rather proudly. He then tugged his shirt down, producing a paper from his pockets of the latest sketch he had been working on. It's of a bird he had seen today, flying into the storm just as he got his coffee after giving his sweater away. "I wanted this right on my left thigh. About the size of half my finger, if possible."

"At this point, you're going to run out of places to ink where it can be hidden," Bo grumbles. He had made it known of his displeasure of Jayden only getting inked at places you couldn't see unless you were to raise his shirt, but his conservative parents would have had a heart attack if they had seen the tattoos and things he was doing. However, he goes to grab his pen and gloves, prepping himself up for his latest work before eyeing him. "Are you sure you want to get a tattoo right before the tennis tryout tomorrow morning? You got tryouts, right?"

Jayden glances up at his longtime tattoo artist and lifts a brow. When he came down here with his latest idea after practice, he didn't think he'd be here for a pep talk. But he's not shocked he knew the tennis schedule, being a longtime fan and coming to the games despite him claiming he never did.

"I didn't think you cared that much, Bo," Jayden muses. "Are you finally admitting me as your favorite?"

At that, he grunts before narrowing his eyes at the young man. He pushes his shorts upwards, scoffing as he starts up the pen. "I care when a customer comes just thirty minutes before the shop's supposed to close, Jayden."

However, he doesn't complain, and neither exchange works. For Bo, he had to ensure his work was top-notch, putting all his concentration and soul into it. For Jayden, the stinging of the needle makes his heart beat once more, reminding him that he's in control of his body to some extent once more as he closes his eyes.

The only time he felt this free with this type of high was on rare occasions. It's a break from the façade he had placed, keeping up an act to appease his parent and what was expected of him. With each sting, he feels as if his muscles are relaxing.

The buzzing eases him greatly, and almost forty minutes pass before Bo pulls the pen away from his skin. Immediately, Jayden lifts his head to look as Bo wipes away the excess blood, leaving behind a beautiful tattoo of a white dove, the impending storm in the background and encased in a small circle. It's simple and yet detailed enough as he smiles. "It's perfect."

"Obviously, as I'm the one who drew it," he grunts as he places the bandage over the tattoo. "As I said a few times, make sure to apply the ointment I've given you the last time you were here. Also, make sure not to remove the band-aid or try smudging it in the next few days."

"You got it, boss," he beams, sliding his hands into his back pocket for his wallet. As Bo rings him up, he can't help but eye him after finally realizing that Jayden is in only a black shirt.

"You don't have your sweater?" Bo ponders with a frown.

"Nah, I gave it to some undergrad since I knocked into him at the coffee shop," he informs him. In fact, it was just after he did so that he saw the bird as the rain came pouring down. After signing and offering a generous tip, he shrugged. "It's cool. I walked around the whole day without it. Plus, my car is just parked a street away."

"Good luck tomorrow, and make sure not to smear my fucking work, or I'm banning your ass," Bo calls out as Jayden exits the shop. The cold air licks and settles onto his skin as he looks up at the sky. His head felt lighter as he went to flip Bo off.

Tomorrow will be a good day; he could feel it in his bones.

CHAPTER THREE

"**Y**ou're out!"

At that, Jayden is resisting the urge to smile in amusement when he sees Trevis practically explode as the lineman's voice rings out across the vast tennis court. It didn't come as a shock that the coach called out as he'd been tinkering at the edge already before he threw his racquet in anger. The others are laughing in amusement under their breaths, still a bit hungover from the party last night.

You'd think someone playful and supportive like Trevis wouldn't be like this over a callout, but when he's on the field, he could become quite competitive and brutal to anyone that crosses his path. He goes off for a few minutes before he strides up the umpire's chair and throws his hands up in the air.

"Are you fucking blind?" he growls out. His nose flares as he racks his hands through his hair. "That ball was good and didn't hit out. Everyone who has eyes can see it except that linesman. You're just being an asshole to me, aren't you? Someone bring up the court cams, and let's see it."

"We don't have time," the coach hollers, pinching the bridge of his nose while shaking his head.

"That's fucking bullshit," Trevis calls back, and I don't blame him. Those who have already been apart and returning to intramural tennis for NCAA Division 1 in the past year had an earlier tryout session. With just about an hour, most of them wanted to sit and chat unless you were Trevis.

"Watch your language," Coach calls back, narrowing his eyes. Sometimes, Jayden couldn't help but wonder if the coach liked to complain to his parents during their bi-weekly dinner. He certainly wouldn't when Jayden is at the table, though it didn't mean they wouldn't exchange gossip when he wasn't there either.

Despite it starting as a friendly competition, it soon quickly morphed into something entirely different with Trevis as he picked it up and pointed his racquet at the coach. "With a bad call, Ray now had a break point to win the set because of this."

"Yeah, so get ready to be paying for my lunch this weekend," Ray grins confidently, setting his racquet on his shoulder as he places his other hand onto his hips. He knew provoking his friend would only make him more heated, but he could not care less. Trevis only narrows his eyes until they are only slits at his comment.

"I hope your mom is ready to pay for my lunch this weekend after she —hey!" He didn't get to finish when Ray threw the ball straight at him, barely dodging his face. As he didn't hit the ball back, the lineman clearly wanted to get on Trevis' nerves by not calling out either.

"Seriously, how are you not praying you're not paired with him again in a double, Jayden?" Cassie questions as he turns his attention to Jayden. He's still rubbing his temples in dismay, and in honesty, Jayden wasn't quite sure how he played well enough despite how hungover he should be.

"Who says I'm not?" Jayden retorts with a grin before his other teammate, Isaac, slaps him hard on the back. Sometimes, he couldn't help but wonder if the football was this brute and rough.

"Nah, Mr. Undefeated here has the charm to not only woo people but ensure they win," Isaac grins, and it takes everything in Jayden not to snap at him. Instead, he forces himself to smile, ready to brush off the comment when Cassie frowns.

"What is your score overall in double again?"

"His whole career? Fourteen to seventeen," Coach couldn't help but chime in rather proudly. It didn't surprise Jayden. After all, he practically taught everything Trevis knew regarding tennis when his parents forced him to attend Sunday masses till he turned sixteen. His excuse was to focus more on tennis, which he soon fell in love with. "Single overall in his career? Sixty-seven to twenty-three."

"You should have seen his first year with an impressive nineteen to six in a single play," Isaac beams, his eyes widening. "His earned rank beat even California's No.70 Nabil Hillson and Duke's Benjamin Poe. It was utter insanity."

"God fucking damn," Cassie shakes his head while looking over at Jayden. "If you didn't do a gap for three years before attending Columbia at twenty-one, I can't imagine you not going pro by now."

"Hey now," Coach interjects before getting up. "It's never too late to go pro. So alrighty, sit yourselves down, Ray and Trevis. I'm going to give a rundown of what you all need to work on before the new faces come in for tryouts."

At that, everyone quiets. Everyone presses their lips thinly together as his criticism is still churning in everyone's stomach from last week. However, they knew it was to make them a better player at the end as they sucked it up at his brutal comments that lasted almost two to three minutes each. Then, finally, it lands up to Jayden.

"As for you, Mr. Harrington, keep it up," he simply states. Jayden catches himself in time before a frown can form. He knew for sure that there would be some pointers. After all, he had checked the cams and knew there was room for more improvements. However, Coach would never call him out on it for one reason or another. Once everything comes into wraps, Coach then looks up from his board before checking the time. "Still got three minutes, but I suppose I'll let the newbies in and get them prepared."

"Anyone catch your attention, Coach?" Trevis questions, slicking his hair back. "Aside from us."

"There is," he states in a matter of fact while flipping through the pages of his clipboard. "He's been coming here to play and part of the tennis club. I had hoped he'd apply, and it seems he's finally taking a chance on us. In fact, his gaming is near flawless like Jayden."

At that, it catches Jayden's attention. It is rare that Coach would ever compliment another player so easily. He couldn't help but feel excited and took it up as a challenge to find out who this new player would be. As the coach prepares for the tryout, Trevis sits next to Jayden with an arched brow.

This, he had to stay for.

His teammates start to trickle out to the locker room to take a quick shower or grab their stuff for classes. Thankfully, Jayden didn't have class or work today, so he had all the time in the world to stay and watch. He didn't understand why Trevis didn't leave as he turned to him. "You staying to watch?"

Trevis gives a half-hearted shrug. "I don't have a class for another hour or so. So I might as well see since you're staying as well."

It's then that Coach turns to both. "That's perfect. You'll help spar with the tryout newbies since you're both one of my best players. Trevis, I'm counting on you not to scare new recruits with your anger issues."

"No promises," he laughs before turning to Jayden. "You in?"

"Might as well," he comments before getting up to do a small stretch. "Nothing better to do anyway. It might give them a chance to see what they are truly up against."

"Are you scared that someone young is going to steal your spotlight?" Travis ponders, tilting his head to the side. Trying to hunt down your competitor?"

"I'm not that old," Jayden scoffs, leaning back in his chair. However, he needed to start fixing his sleeping schedule as he noticed it was taking a rather extensive toll on his body. He hasn't been able to sleep well since he moved here from London with his parents, but it didn't mean he wouldn't try.

"By our standard, you technically are," Trevis points out, which is true. "Usually, people who are twenty-three are already ready to settle, pop three babies and wither away by the time they turn thirty. Not be a sophomore in college. So, are you worried?"

"In honestly, nah, I'm not too worried," he shrugs at his question before slicking his hair back. If anything, he was more than excited to see if what Coach said met his expedition as well. "To be frank, I'm excited to see what Coach got going on."

"Cocky, aren't you?" he ponders, putting his racquet back into his gym bag.

Honestly, it was far from it; he's been craving a challenge and a competition for what seemed like eons. Though he had a few close matches, no one else can match up with his skillsets when it comes to playing on the field.

"No, more so looking for someone to test my limit," he finally admits. His hands have been itching already for any sort of distraction in life. He shifts, the stinging from his tattoo from last night reminding him to take it easy.

"Do you want to have a bet to see if we can spot who Coach is talking about?" Trevis wagers.

That didn't come out as a surprise for Jayden as he smiled back, a genuine one all morning. But, of course, he could always leave it to Trevis to not only figure his mood out with ease but give a distraction. "What's in it for me?"

"Loser has to pay for Ray's meal instead," he states.

"Why would I take the bet when you were going to pay his meal for losing the match?" he ponders out loud, arching up a sly brow.

"Fine," he groans. He rubs at his dark stubble, knowing that already, but was hoping his friend would have taken the offer before settling. "Loser has to pay for Ray's meal, but if you win in general, I'll also pay for you tonight."

"Deal."

With that, they shake on it as a smile makes its way to Trevis' face.

"I hope you're ready to pay for the black hole of a stomach that's Ray Milad. But seriously, the man has no stopping when it comes to food," Trevis says, shaking his head. They both knew as one time, they saw that man single-handedly eat a whole extra-large pizza with every topping imaginable and still have room for dessert after.

"Which is why I'm confused as to why you and him made a bet when you know he's going to play dirty. The man doesn't even drink while you're working on a hangover. I wanted to know what was in it for you," Jayden questions.

Trevis gives his friend a sheepish grin. "His sister's number."

There it is as he sighs, trying to hold back the humorless chuckle. "Yeah, that's never going to happen."

"I know she's way out of a league, but it doesn't mean I can't try. I mean, she's a sport-illustrated model. A model, Jayden," he emphasis as Coach finally opens the door to let the regular players in for tryouts. Jayden does a quick scan of the room to see. Some were skinny and nervous, already giving it away that they wouldn't make it. Others are athletically built and confident, which makes Jayden wonder who Coach is talking about.

It's then that Jayden sees him—the boy from yesterday.

Now that the light is brighter, he couldn't help but assess him. He's quite slim, with a bit of muscle. His reddish-blond hair is sticking up in all sorts of directions. While Jayden stands just an inch over six feet tall, Troy is about five feet and ten inches. His gaze slowly catches on his jawline with high cheekbones.

Not to mention, his eyes were grey, just like the storm yesterday. It makes it seem as if he was standing in the eye of the storm. They were the most exotic grey Jayden had ever seen, with stray rain droplets clinging to his eyelashes. Except right now, his eyes weren't focused on him but rather trying to make sense of what was happening as chatter filled the field.

Confusion fills him for a moment when he looks at him, finally recalling his name and one key detail.

That Troy Evans is deaf.

Jayden's frowns only deepen as he tilts his head to the side. Surely, he wasn't here for tryouts.

However, Troy is in polo with shorts alongside everyone else. The confusion only makes Jayden more baffled and perplexed if he's only here for moral support of some sort. From the small exchange he had with his friend, which he remembers is Quinn, he's born deaf.

Seeing the ball wasn't enough to be taken seriously in

competitive play in tennis. In fact, simply tracking the ball with your eyes is insufficient enough. You must hear the ball to estimate its speed and enable a faster reaction time. It's a critical advantage in tennis that even a fraction of a second could mean losing or winning, which is why you need both your ears and eyes.

Someone who's deaf wouldn't be able to do it.

Now curious more than anything else, he had no choice but to stay as he watched as Troy took out his notepad, scribbling in his awful handwriting that almost made Jayden laugh at the hierographic writing from yesterday before stopping himself.

There's not a chance someone like him would be able to make it through the tryout. However, something regarding Troy even coming here to try out despite being unable to hear and would most likely not make it to intramural tennis catches Jayden's attention as he crosses his legs and watch with anticipation.

Let's see what Troy could do.

CHAPTER FOUR

Looking around, Troy couldn't help but feel as if he didn't belong.

In fact, he's the only one who looks like a shrub amongst the others here who are applying to play professionally and is less than six feet tall. Usually, he feels overwhelmed when thrown into a crowd of people that he knows should be filled with sound but is nothing other than utter silence.

Timidity, he pulls at the hem of his polo. It didn't surprise him that he should be the only one with a disability trying out for competitive sports. He takes a deep breath, trying to calm his speeding heart.

When no one is looking, Troy writes down the word 'courage' into the palm of his hands before bringing it up to his mouth and swallowing it. It's a rather silly thing he had picked up from Quinn's little brother; if he writes down the emotion he wants to embody, he needs to write the word and physically swallow it.

Right now, he's praying for courage while he watches the coach's mouth move; he presses his lips into a thin line.

He should have made it clear or even emailed him the fact that he was deaf. Though Quinn had asked once more if he wanted her there for support, he didn't want to bother anyone regarding it. Everyone starts forming a group, and Troy swallows the lump in his throat before walking up to the Coach.

His heart is racing erratically, and his hands grow clammy. When he gets up to the Coach, he timidly smiles before getting his notepad and pen out. Then, as quick as he can, he scribbles out: "I'm sorry, Coach. My name is Troy Evans. I'm deaf. Would you be able to explain to me what is happening? Or should I get an interpreter?"

It's then that Troy sees it, even for a fraction of a second. It's the way their shoulders sag upon hearing him having a disability. Those pity or sympathetic eyes and the creases in their forehead as they awkwardly try to find help by speaking, hoping that he would be able to read lips.

However, it's impossible, as Troy was born deaf.

It's then that he forces a smile as he slowly hands his notepad and pen over to the Coach, who quickly understands what's happening. Troy could feel the judgmental eyes on him, cold sweat just dancing to break out until Coach turned it back to him with the written sentences: "No, you're fine. I'm breaking groups up by last names that they will be trying out. You'll be in group two, and you'll be sparring with one of my two best players, Jayden Harrington and Trevis Scottland, on rotation. I will play here and there, depending."

Jayden?

His heart flutters, though he quickly brushes it off momentarily as he didn't want to waste anyone's time more than necessary. Troy writes down his thanks before clumsily making his way to the bleachers with his small gym and sling bag. He puts his notepad away, and that's when his breath catches for a moment when he sees the man who bumped into him yesterday at the coffee shop.

Jayden Harrington, that the Coach had mentioned.

His eyes widen, flabbergasted. There are butterflies that explode and make him flush for a moment. Now that there's more lighting, he was even more handsome. The perfect chiseled jawline and high cheekbone pair with his dashing light golden brown hair that seems to radiate. In just a pair of black shorts and a t-shirt, it clings to his muscular, broad chest as thoughts start creeping up on him.

Troy persuades himself that it's not just him that finds him handsome. After all, you can be straight while admiring the beauty of the same gender. Jayden's mouth moves as he speaks with the man sitting across from him, who is laughing. Just as he raises his head, Troy quickly looks downwards.

From what Quinn told him, he knew that he was part of the tennis team but didn't think he would see him. He had hoped to bump into him later at the coffee shop to return the cardigan, which he promptly washed and dry-cleaned. Suddenly, he feels somewhat flustered, and he thinks of giving him the cardigan but settles with it after the tryout.

Would he remember who he was?

It crossed Troy's mind before dismissing it. He had to

stay focused on the others to see who he'd be up against. There are only fourteen players and almost fifty people for tryouts. Troy is more than confident that the coach had already picked some from the previous year already.

His phone vibrates. He fumbles, taking his eyes off the court for a moment to see that Quinn had texted him. A smile breaks out of his face as she sends two pictures; one with her fingers splayed, her middle finger pulled inward and touching her chin. The second picture is pointing her hands outward now, the middle finger pointing towards the camera.

"Good luck!"

He shakes his head, trying not to break into a full-blown smile there. He honestly didn't know where he would be without Quinn there supporting him the whole time in everything he did. She could have simply texted him, but going the extra mile always touched his heart. He shoots back a message as thanks before putting his phone away.

Only then does he sense prickling as if someone is watching him. It's something he had picked up, an annoying superpower his parents like to tease him about. He lifts his head, his eyes connecting with a pair of deep green before Troy looks away.

He contemplates if he knew who he was before biting his lips and focusing back on the court just as Trevis makes his way to the side facing the bleachers. As tryouts begin, Troy looks over as each person gets up in the order in which they were seated. The first thing he noticed was the way Trevis plays.

Most of them were perfect aces, serving it near perfectly that the opponent couldn't even touch the ball with their racquet straight off the bat. It seems that Trevis isn't going easy; his backhand and forehand are near perfect. In fact, he didn't hold back at all.

Troy watches in amazement that they are on a different level altogether. He was a tennis coach for the youth program, and even then, he didn't think he'd be able to match their skills. However, how Trevis moves around the court had Troy gripping the edge of his seat in anticipation, his eyes drinking everything in to see how he moves and swings. It's almost as if the racquet is apart from his body rather than just an extension. Even the serves are grace and elegance, despite how it gets a tad sloppy when he gets overconfident and leans towards his right leg.

Before long, the first group had finished, and Troy would feel his nervousness and anticipation starting to kick in. He was seated at the first end, which means he would be up against Jayden. A part of him is rather excited to see how someone playing competitively would be different, much less someone like him that Quinn had been gushing on the whole night through video call.

Disappointment makes its way to Troy's face when he watches Trevis take his seat as Jayden throws a towel in his direction. He thought he would be facing off Jayden when Coach placed his clipboard down instead and headed over to the court while saying something in the direction where Hayden and Trevis were sitting.

Unbeknownst to him, Jayden couldn't help but feel the

same disappointment as he expected Coach to ask him to play with the second group. He narrows his eyes ever so slightly, bouncing his legs while Trevis chugs a bottle of water before wiping off the excess. "You good?"

"Yeah, I'm fine. I thought I would be playing. It's half the truth, which causes his friend to laugh. He swings the towel over his shoulder after wiping his sweat.

"We have five groups. You'll get your turn," he informs him. Little did he know that Jayden wanted to go against Troy, as Trevis continues. "I'm not impressed with the first group, by the way. They all sucked and lacked the proper stance."

Jayden scoffs, raising an arched brow. "Says the one who did not go easy on any of them."

"I'm only making Coach's life easier," he retorts while slumping into his seat. "I'm betting Coach was not looking forward to any of those players I just went against. Let's hope he gets someone actually good, or we're screwed this year. It's been a while since I see Coach playing, so let's see if the old man still got it."

"You better not say that in front of his face," Jayden chuckles, bumping his shoulder onto his before he sees Troy getting up from his seat. For some reason, his movement reminds him of a newborn duckling. He couldn't help but wonder if he'd surprise everyone or be a disappointment. Jayden bites his tongue, amused when Troy stumbles out with his own racquet, which he brought with him, just as Coach takes the stage.

He watches as Troy takes a deep breath, and Jayden can

practically feel his nervousness. It's hard to imagine that he was the same at one point in his life. Coach bounces the ball once on the floor, relaxing his stance before serving the ball across the net without missing a beat. It's a rather dirty play, Jayden noticed as he had gone all out just as Trevis did. It wasn't like Coach to go all out like that on a newbie, and he's more than sure that Troy will miss serving it back.

Instantly, Troy sets off, diving straight to serving it back without missing a beat either.

For the first time, goosebumps ricochet all over Jayden's arms at the grace in which Troy moved. He's able to make up for what he lacks quickly by not only tracking the ball and calculating but much more than that. He realizes that Troy focuses intensively on what the other person is doing, how they're moving and swinging their racquet, how the ball looks when it's coming over the net, and timely decisions based on it.

All within three seconds or less.

He's rather impressed.

Jayden hasn't even realized he's learning over at this point, wholly memorized by Troy's movement.

In fact, he's never seen someone move with such confidence and power that it awakens something deep within him. The way he plays on the field is a mix of utter agility and grace in his timing; as a result, he's able to create something Jayden has never seen before, timing his body to move fluently.

No matter how hard he tried, Jayden couldn't look away or dare to blink for fear of missing even a moment. An advantage of hearing is also being able to hear how hard someone hits a ball. Though you may not be able to tell how many miles per hour it's traveling, you can hear and guess it. If they hit it hard and flat with their net, it makes a loud popping sound. It's the first thing you know before seeing it. You must hear the ball to play it to your advantage, which Troy didn't have.

However, the passion in his eyes shines so brightly—something that Jayden had forgotten about.

It's almost as if he was a completely different person than the guy he met at the coffee shop; there's nothing but confidence in each step and each swing like it's a work of art. But, of course, the coach wasn't going easy on him either with his groundstroke and overhead passes.

"Holy shit, he plays like a fucking pro," Trevis mumbles, impressed. "I've never seen anything like him since…well, since you, Jayden."

For some reason, Jayden held back from telling Travis the fact that he's deaf. He wanted him to look at him like any other average person, as he knew firsthand how fast people jump to a conclusion. But, in honesty, Jayden couldn't believe that he was deaf.

Not with the way he moved, as if he was using all his senses perfectly.

Jayden didn't even realize that he was gripping onto his seat, utterly captivated by the single-point game as if his life depended on it. He couldn't remember the last time he felt like this, as if he was hypnotized. Troy serves it right onto what's known as no man's land in the area right before the baseline and behind the service line.

Many don't want a territory as if the ball hit at a player's feet or behind, you will be struck, falling backward and off-balance. Essentially, you are completely defenseless if you stay there too long. However, Troy had managed to push Coach there in just a few turns before diving once more and serving a forehand stroke that earned Troy the point.

It's then that it hits Jayden. It's the reason the Coach didn't want him to play. His eyes widen as his heart thumps wildly in his chest. It's as if there's something stirring in his chest, and he feels his blood kicking into overdrive. "It's him."

Trevis turns to him, baffled. "What?"

"The guy that coach was looking forward to."

CHAPTER FIVE

Troy looks over to where the two-star tennis players are, chattering and laughing happily from the looks of it as his heart thumps erratically. Tryouts had just ended, and people were slowly shuffling out of the courtroom with their newfound friendship while he tried to comprehend what had just happened. Then, finally, he wagers to go up to the coach once more and ask him to summarize in writing or send him a message.

Perhaps he should have requested an interpreter or even asked Quinn to tag along.

Columbia College had assigned Troy an interpreter for classes since he first applied to attend after providing the DSS coordinator with the necessary documents and class schedule. He has been more than grateful, and since he didn't know if he'd attend tennis tryouts until yesterday, he didn't want to notify the DSS as the chances of getting an interpreter within twenty-four hours were near impossible.

Timidly, he gets up and is ready to make his way to the touch when there's a tap on his shoulder. He turns, blinking a few times as he takes in the man who's standing up. Standing already six feet tall with shaggy brown hair swept to one side and lush green eyes with two deep dimples, it catches Troy's attention.

For a moment, Troy realizes that he's kind of cute before brushing the thought away. He couldn't help but smile, a bit taken back and confused until the stranger pointed to the notepad next to him that he used to speak with others. Immediately, Troy scrambles to give it to him alongside a pen.

Rather curious, he watches as he writes for a moment before turning the notepad towards him: "Hey, sorry—my name's Benjamin Minton. In case you're wondering, coach said he'll post the results outside the tennis court tomorrow. I really liked how you played earlier, by the way. A lot of people were impressed."

Troy's face becomes somewhat flushed at the compliment in the last sentence. He didn't think he'd make a friend here, let alone get a compliment, as Benjamin returned the notepad and pen. Quickly, he scrambles to write a response before turning it back: "Thank you for telling me; that means a lot. I'm Troy Evans. I hope that I'll see your name tomorrow when making it."

He smiles, his dimples making Troy feel somewhat flustered as he only takes the pen. Finally, he pushes the top of the pen and bends forward to write again on the same page. Troy tightens his grip on the notepad as he writes just one word: "Same."

Benjamin only nods his head before putting his fingers

upwards to bid farewell. While watching him, Troy wonders if both of them would make it past the tryouts. He hadn't noticed him playing before as his mind had been too focused on how Jayden, Trevis, and the Coach played to gather more information on their technique and playing styles. But it certainly seems that he'll have a friend at the very least if everything goes well.

Grabbing his bag and slinging it over his shoulder, he grabs the sweater from his schoolbag. He's been working up the courage to walk up to Jayden that Quinn has been setting him up to during their talk on video chat.

They even watched a few videos posted on their tennis Youtube channel, which was why he had been looking forward to it. However, Troy was slightly disappointed when he saw how Jayden played with the other recruits. In fact, he's been quick to notice how he moves.

In particular, Jayden would lean and put his weight more on the left side if possible. As a result, many of the near misses that he could have served back with ease that could save him time were avoided altogether, which Troy couldn't understand why.

Snapping out of his train of thought, he glances over, and his eyes pierce with a pair of drawing green eyes. Troy's heart starts pounding recklessly in his chest as he realizes that Trevis is looking as well while waving at him.

Troy awkwardly waves back and finally commands his feet to take him down the bleachers. He tries to recall just how long he's been spacing out, completely living in his head that everyone already left already except for the three of them. As a greeting, he tucks his thumb near his palm and brings his hands straight onto the side of his forehead and away, almost like a salute.

Getting in front of Jayden, he realizes just how beautifully handsome he is in the light now without the gloomy weather. His grey eyes stare straight into Troy's soul, having a grip onto him that he's never experienced before as he bites his tongue.

Trevis' mouth moves, only to fall on deaf ears. Troy couldn't help but wonder what he is saying as he continued to babble and why Jayden hadn't tried to inform him that he was deaf either. Rather, if only he knew it was because Jayden is rather amused as Trevis goes on a spiraling rampage in appraisement for his tryout play against the Coach.

"I mean," Trevis continues to throw his hands up in the air. "That ace move? It was so fast that even the coach wasn't expecting it. The way you're able to push him behind the service line without trying and everything."

In response, Jayden chuckles in amusement, agreeing with every word before Troy ultimately reaches for his notepad and turns it after scribbling profoundly fast onto it: "Sorry, I am deaf, so I apologize for the inconvenience."

"What the hell?" Trevis says, his body cringing backward in shock for a moment.

At his response, Jayden's jaw twitches in irritation. His annoyance had started the moment he read what Troy had written and apologized for something he considered to be a hassle that he had no control over. He's ready to elbow his friend before his following statement is directed to Jayden.

"Damn, I wish I knew sooner so I didn't look like an idiot. I mean, how is that possible? The dude is next level even without hearing then; no wonder the coach was getting his dick wet over it," he exclaims in wonder before taking grabbing the notepad and pen, holding up one finger as he starts writing down what he wants to say.

"I hope you're not writing about him wetting Coach's dick," Jayden frowns deeply in response.

"No promises or filter. I said it once out loud; I gotta treat it as such, even in writing."

At that moment, Jayden couldn't help but be proud to have a friend like Trevis that didn't have any sort of judgment for those who were disabled. "Just don't come crawling to me if he files a harassment because of you, as I already warned you."

"Nah, impossible," he snorts. "Did you know, though?"

At this point, Jayden doesn't find a reason to hide it anymore as he nods. "I did."

"Really? How?" Trevis ponders, glancing up at him for a moment before continuing his writing.

At that moment, Troy fumbles for a moment and pulls out his sweater almost timidly. There's a small thank you note on top and an explanation that it was washed, too. Then, taking the sweater from his hand, their hands brush alongside one another, and it causes Troy's breath to hitch for a moment at the electricity before bashfully looking away.

Then, he gestures to the two words on top before placing his right hand straight. Finally, he places it onto his chin and extends it outwards as thanks, and in response, Jayden went to put his thumbs up. For a moment, Troy wonders if it's a coincidence that it's one of the two signs in ASL that could mean you're welcome.

Except, his train of thought was lost when Trevis hands the notepad back to him. He's taken aback once more by everyone's kindness, much less someone like him who wrote in a ramble of everything he liked about his playstyle.

Lost in reading what he had written, Trevis nudges Jayden with a sly grin. It didn't take a genius to discover his thoughts as he scowled. It only gets bigger when Trevis places one hand on his shoulder as support. "What, Trevis?"

"You slept with him, haven't you?"

"No," Jayden deadpans, scowling as he tucks the sweater beneath his arm.

"So...the sweater isn't yours?" he questions, though he already knew the truth. After all, it was his favorite that he had received from his parents. He looks over to see Troy still taking his time reading what appears to be the Bible at this point.

"It is," Jayden replies with a shrug without any elaboration.

"Really? You're just going to leave me like that?"

"I bumped into him at a coffee shop yesterday," he finally answers while taking a step away, causing Trevis to stumble before regaining his balance. "In case you were wondering, it's the reason I didn't have my sweater on the whole day as well."

"Sounds like something out of that rom-com my sister watches," Trevis laughs, causing him to punch him in the arm. It's not hard enough to hurt, but enough to get him to wince before going to rub his shoulders.

"Shut up," Jayden growls.

Scribbling, Troy finally turns his notepad back, his chicken scratch writing making Jayden hold in his chuckle of amusement as he repays it with everything he enjoyed watching Trevis play. Likewise, it makes Travis laugh, puffing out his chest proudly in response.

"I like this dude," he grins, turning to Jayden.

"Great, so tell him," he states.

"Nah, you can; I got somewhere to go," he says, flashing him a cheeky smile before taking out his phone.

"I thought you said you didn't have anywhere to be," he points out, frowning.

"My FWB just texted me, so now I do."

"F…WB?" Jayden parrots, tilting his head to the side in confusion with the new acronym being thrown his way. Though he's only twenty-three years old, being older by a few years,

"Friends with benefits, get with the program, grandpa. Anyway, I got to shower before meeting her," Trevis informs him. With that, he quickly takes the pen, scribbling that he'll see him tomorrow before leaving for the locker room first.

Troy watches with admiration, hoping that what he says is true and that he'll make it through tryouts. Not wanting to leave without saying farewell either, he quickly flips it to the next page and writes: "It was nice watching you play, Jayden."

At the compliment, that seems almost disheartening after seeing the block of texts Troy had written compared to the one he's given to Trevis. It shouldn't bother him, yet he wants to ask if he did something wrong as a player-to-player.

However, he didn't want to push it before realizing someone was opening the tennis court door. Jayden recognizes it as Troy's friend or girlfriend from yesterday as he points to her. It causes Quinn to wave back in response as Troy turns to her and grins.

The girlfriend then, Jayden settles with.

"Hey there again," Quinn laughs, nodding at Jayden. "I see you got your sweater back."

"I did," Jayden muses before Troy tucks his notepad away to sign. "Feel free to leave at any time. I'm just going to pack and get out of here, but there aren't any drills today from the Coach, so there's no need for a rush."

"Thank you," Quinn chirps before focusing her attention back on Troy, who still looks shocked.

"What are you doing here, Quinn?" Troy signs, completely blindsided to see her here without classes.

"I had to talk to my advisor at the last minute about dropping a class, and I thought we could get lunch together. So I texted you, but you weren't picking up," she huffs loudly, moving her hands quickly while rolling her eyes. "I'm assuming you're done with tryouts?"

At Quinn's question, Troy nods before signing. "Just finished fifteen minutes ago."

"I know, you stink," she giggles. "Did you have fun?"

"Very much so," he agrees with a smile through his sign.

"Do tell, did you play against Jayden Harrington?" she grins, winking. As he slowly packs his sweater back into his gym bag before turning to see them interact. Jayden watches the two of them interact; the way they moved was so fluent, almost like it's a form of art. He notices that while Quinn signs as if she's running high on sugar, Troy is calmer and more fluid in his movement.

"I didn't," Troy signs in response.

"You don't look that disappointed," Quinn questions.

"I don't know, it doesn't..." he trails off for a moment, stopping his signing as he tries to think of the right words. He steals a glance over at Jayden, not liking to be talking about someone's flaw in front of them, before deciding on his word. "Focused?"

"Focused?" she ponders, cocking her head to the side as she signs the word once more.

"Yeah, his movement is a bit lackluster," he signs with a sigh. He replays back the way Jayden serves in his head, and even down to the strokes and movement is slower than usual. He leans too much on his right side for support and wasn't in a proper position to maximize his play either. "It's difficult to understand. Should we get lunch now or should I go back to the dorm and shower first?"

"Nah, I want a date just me and you without your roommate," she confesses with a sheepish smile before quickly continuing with her hands erratically. "I mean, I like Aston, but it's funnier with me and you at the end."

"You mean he complains too much when you drag me to the mall with you," he grins back.

"Quickly," she shrugs as she signs the one word before linking her arms with him. "Now, let's go."

Troy watches as Quinn turns to Jayden, presumably to say goodbye to both; he prayed that he would be able to see him tomorrow or even make it to come back for another tryout if anything came to be. He knew that the Coach seemed to have high expectations once more when they were playing, but to take in someone deaf that would get along with the team always nudges at the back of Troy's head.

He didn't want to be any inconvenience to anyone more than necessary.

With that, Jayden waves bye with his hands as a slow smile makes its way to his face. Troy's eyes widen ever slightly, his heart picking up. He knows that he's reading too much into his wave of goodbye as if he's signing goodbye to him.

Not to mention, Jayden seems rather irritated from the way his jawline clench, almost as if he knew what Quinn and Troy had said—almost as if he knew and was angry about what Troy had picked up with his gaming style.

It had to be a mere coincidence, just like before.

CHAPTER SIX

When he opens her eyes, only darkness surrounds him once more. Her knees are drenched in black globs of mud that seem to hold, making it hard to walk around. At first, he thinks he has somehow lost his eyesight until he looks down at the familiar t-shirt he's wearing alongside a pair of shorts.

Yet…something was off about it that he couldn't quite place.

Once more, Jayden lifts her head and looks around, finding everything pitch black from his surroundings to the sky above her. He couldn't make anything out of the horizon that seems so far away, where the sky both ends and begins with the land. There's only terrible, insurmountable darkness that holds him down.

I'm dreaming.

The knowledge came to him naturally without thought, as most of his dreams and nightmares did. Dreams rarely made sense as they were mere fragments of imagery conjured by the sleeping, tired mind that warps around your conscious thoughts. The same went with his nightmares that replayed his torture for the past few years since he moved here with his parents when he was just *a troubled teenager from London. Though most of it was true, the mind would often morph into new details.*

After all, the twenty-three-year-old knew dreams well… and nightmares, too.

Then, it all happens so quickly that it startles him. First, he was all alone in the expanse of the dark void, and the next second, someone was there. Then, finally, he could see someone walking in front of him, a light illuminating around the person.

Jayden rubs his eyes and looks once more to realize that the person isn't walking towards him—

They were walking away from him.

Without a second thought, he fights against the sludge clinging him down as he runs to that person. He didn't know what compelled him, but he had to. His legs moved, albeit slowly, to catch up to the figure that was walking away from him. He's running with all her might, and the brown-haired person was just walking.

So why could he never catch up to him?

He realizes soon that he's not an adult but a boy once more. He's in a densely wooded area once more, the sound of yelling and blinding light starts to show through the thick shrubs. He turns his head, realizing where he is, before turning back to the person.

"Weston, wait!" Jayden calls to him, and that's when he remembers who he is.

How could he have forgotten?

Move faster, legs.

As a child, he was pretty thin and twig-like, which didn't help his situation. His lungs feel like it's on fire as mud cakes onto his shoes, weighing him down like cemented bricks. Still, he had to try with all his might to save him.

To go home this time with him, hand in hand.

At this point, he wanted to cry out in frustration as he thrusts his arms outwards in hopes that Weston would stop for him. It's been so long since she saw Weston that, for a moment, emotions swelled inside of him that he thought he died the same day he had.

It was until Weston spoke again. It's quiet, dreary, and almost like the woods have gone silent to hear the two exchange. He turns to him, his eyes dull and lifeless. "It's useless, Jayden. Just go back."

His voice is scratchy and foreign to Jayden's ears. There's something unnatural and eerie to him, causing him to stop for a moment as he tries to remember as to why it feels so off and inexplicable. Still, his question makes him swallow the lump in his throat. "What do you mean it's useless?"

"You'll never catch up to me," he states, turning as his identical green eyes pierce the same green ones that belong to Jayden. For a moment, he has never seen him look so expressionless that it stuns him to silence before he continues. "You'll never catch up to me, Jayden."

"W-why not?"

"Go back to mom and dad already," he deadpans, and it feels as if his heart was shattered all over again. Then, suddenly, it was his mom's face in front facing him after he blinked. Tears are streaming down her face in rapid session as dad holds him back. Her body is shaking as she screams.

"Why," he sobs. "If only you kept your mouth shut and not run away, Weston wouldn't have died."

Then, suddenly, the darkness behind his brother lashes and pulls Weston into it. Snakes coil around his legs, hissing as it *slowly drags her into the puddle beneath him. He watched in horror as Weston didn't even fight back as she simply closed her eyes and sighed almost as if in relief to be free.*

"Wait, Weston," he pleas, falling onto her knees as he claws at the darkness. "Please, don't go. I'll go to your place instead, okay? Please don't do this. I can't do this without you by my side. You know that you're the better."

It's then that he smiles, breaking more of Jayden's heart as he holds up his hand, signing something to him. His eyes widen as he opens his mouth to speak once more; it gets him nowhere, no matter how much Jayden digs at the ground. "You can't. So, the question now is, how will you live out your legacy without me?"

Then, he watches in horror as his brother is dragged under. The darkness that was upkeeping Jayden this whole time suddenly turns liquid-like. He gasps in surprise before the inky black water drags him down without a moment of hesitation. It's freezing cold, and as hard as he tries swimming upward, there wasn't any use.

It's then he realizes that her hands are covered in dark blood, his eyes paling when he sees his white shirt now filled with blood as well. At the bottom were dead weeds and carcasses that seemed to be trying to grab him. He couldn't move as his body sank lower to the depth, and air left his lungs.

He recalls thinking that it was the end for him here.

Then, something grabs onto the back of his shirt and yanks him back forcibly as he wakes up gasping. Instantly, air fills his lungs, and he feels a tad thankful to learn that he's still alive and breathing. Taking a look around, he realizes that he's back in his apartment.

It feels strange.

The sensation of drowning is still fresh in his mind. In fact, the nightmare feels far too real, and he can still feel her heart pounding against his ribcage. So many emotions swirl in his mind as he looks down at his hand.

Of course, they weren't covered in blood anymore, and he knows that since he stopped taking his prescribed pills or his sedatives either, it made him too groggily and unfocused when it comes to playing.

However, he would never tell his doctor or his parents that either.

Glancing over, he realizes that his alarm is set to go off in just ten minutes, so there wasn't a point in going back to sleep. Yawning, he shuffles out of bed after turning his alarm off, racking his hair back. The good thing regarding having your own apartment compared to living at his parent's home was not only having your privacy but not having consistent nightmares that reminded them of that night.

Each time he comes home to visit, the night that is reminded that he should have been him.

Shaking the thought away, he makes his way over to brush his teeth, getting ready for the day. His one-bedroom apartment didn't consist of much, but it's something he affords while balancing college life and his road to becoming a semi-professional tennis player.

He hopes to get recruited and sign with an NCAA Division 1 program soon.

Opening the closet, he shuffles for a while until settling in with a pair of his university sweatpants and grey shirt before throwing on the sweater that Troy had given back the previous day. The smell of cherry coke and cinnamon fills him as he stares down at the note still resting on the desk for a moment, before grabbing his necessities for the day.

As he lives just a mere fifteen-minute drive away from college or a leisurely thirty-minute walk, he opted for the latter just based on how pleasant the weather is. As it's already Friday, he's already mentally preparing himself to call his parents. His hands were already growing clammy at speaking to both, especially mom, but he didn't want to worry them.

Hell, they're still trying to persuade him to come back as they only live a mere one-hour drive away. It didn't make it better than he's due soon for a family dinner gathering soon once things start settling down at the new semester.

Deciding that he needs a cup of coffee before classes, Jayden makes his way to his usual coffee shop before doing a quick glance. He didn't know what compelled him to, but he figured to say thank you and sorry for bumping into him the other day when it was raining.

His shoulders slump for a moment before he orders his usual black cold brew.

Getting to the tennis center, he's not surprised to find himself the earliest there by almost half an hour. He feels a moment of peace in that moment of pure silence. What had started as playing as a distraction became his absolute passion. The roaring in his ears and how his mind could only focus on his heart pounding and the rush in his head.

The tennis court has cushioned six hard courts, ideal for their team. With a painted blue surface, it makes your eyes to catch onto the ball's movement faster alongside the lightning no matter the weather outside as well. Top with the state-of-the-art video system and scoreboard, it's every tennis' player's team come true.

Making his way over to the board, a frown makes its way to his face. He'd expected Coach to have placed who passed the tryouts there already. Given he didn't have to till eight, but he had expected someone who likes to prepare to have done it.

He walks to the locker room, passing by Coach; he seems completely lost in thought, and he probably hadn't realize Jayden passed him. It makes him a bit concerned. Changing to practice, he decides to drop by with a knock.

"Morning, Coach," Jayden greets, stifling a yawn as he makes his way to court.

"Jayden," he says, almost relieved to see him as he waves for him to come. "Please, I need your opinion on something. Close the door because I've been thinking about this all morning, and I'm about to lose the remainder of my hair at this point."

"What's up?" Jayden ponders, his brows bumping together as he throws himself into a seat.

"Do you remember yesterday's tryout regarding a certain player named Troy Evans?"

He did remember and won the bet as well with Trevis as he nods. Not only did he know him, but they kept bumping into each other since their encounter at the coffee shop. "Yes, the guy from group two that you played against. He had a good ace; I'll tell you that much."

At that, Coach sits up, nodding in agreement. There are creases alongside his forehead, giving away the fact that he's rather stressed as he places his pen down, where Jayden quickly realizes the tryout sheets stating who passed. "Well, I want to tell you the fact that he has a hearing impairment. Born deaf, from what I've gathered. While Columbia College certainly is not the type to discriminate by any means, I do want to make sure that Troy feels comfortable and not alienated should he be recruited after a second look."

The last part stumps Jayden for a moment. "Wait, you want him to come back for another tryout?"

"I do," he affirms. "Well, I want to, which is why I want to ask for your opinion."

It didn't make sense from what Jayden is hearing. He's never seen someone with skills as raw as Troy on the field that he's more than confident that Coach would have placed him to pass without trying. Baffled, he knits his brows together and tilts his head to the side curiously. "Why?"

"I want to make sure that he has the abilities to play like a pro," he says before wincing at the poor choice of wording.

"It is because he can't hear?"

"Well, that and because I would like for him to bring an interpreter as well. He's used a notepad and pen, but I want to move forward with him getting a feel of things and reassess him once more after creating a level playing field," Coach tells him. "Though I would like a second opinion as I'm wavering between the two options right now."

"Let me ask you this," Jayden begins. "If he isn't impaired, would you have recruited him?"

"I would," Coach murmurs, not wanting to lie. "He does have talent; I'll give him that much. Hell, maybe he'll go on to be one of the first professional deaf tennis players. I have never seen someone so focused and with his bloodlust since you came along."

"I say put him on callback," Jayden finally settles with after consideration as he pinches the bridge of the nose of this. It leaves a bad taste in his mouth, especially in recollection of Troy apologizing yesterday. He never understood why those who deem themselves to be inconvenient at all. "Though perhaps talking to him separately and reach out via email to see you privately regarding it. Actually, if we see him during practice, then you can talk to him regarding how he would like moving forward."

"An interpreter takes two weeks in advance to get," Coach points out.

"He has a girlfriend that can sign. She went to pick him up yesterday after tryouts and we talked for a bit," Jayden explains. However, he knew that getting her to go out of her way and translate for something she may not even understand could be difficult.

At that, Jayden gets up. He didn't know to this day as to why he felt compelled to help as he drew a shaky breath. His fingers twitch, every inch of his body feeling as if it's seizing alongside his dream from last night from Weston. He didn't know why he even said it, as no one is forcing him, and he's been keeping it disassociated from himself for so long.

How will you live out your legacy?

"If it comes to me, then I'll assist."

He knew how shocked Coach would be and he didn't want to stay around for it either. Despite him knowing, Coach never pushes for anything more or his history, which he greatly appreciated. So, for him to spring it out of the blues only baffled both of them before he opens the door and heads to the court.

What the hell is he doing?

CHAPTER SEVEN

"You got called back?"

"I did," Troy signs back to Quinn in excitement and worry at the same time. He watches with amusement as Quinn is jumping up and down on the other side of their video call in excitement, probably making a commotion in her household and waking her parents up on a Saturday morning when they're all late risers. Although Quinn only lives a short drive from campus, and her parents offered her a whole college experience, she didn't want to be away from Raymond. Troy loves the Weissmann family like his own, and he wishes sometimes he has the money and time to fly back to see his parent in Sydney. Still, his heart is pounding erratically fast; his face is completely flushed. He flails his hands quickly in signing his following worries that come just as quick as his excitement in motions. "Though I'm not sure if I should just go today since it's a Saturday and there won't be anyone, or Monday before my classes begin."

"Definitely now," Quinn quickly decides for him, using

her hands to repeat the last word over and over. She shifts till she's on the edge of the bed, still in a pair of pajamas, as she props the whole up. "You don't have any classes or anything to do today, right?"

"I don't," he confirms in sign as he thinks of what he had planned for the day before receiving the email. He leans back on his chair, thinking for a moment. "I was just going to catch up on reading for History. The professor already started to assign bulk work."

"Ew," she signs, scrunching her face upward to drive home her point. Then, fiddling with her hair, she shrugs. "Well, you might as well get it done with and be on the team already. How many spots are left to fill?"

"No idea; I think I'll find out when I get to the tennis center as there's going to be a bulletin board there," he informs her before staring up at the email once more and releasing a deep breath. "Though, I have to make an appointment for the time."

"When's the earliest?"

"Seems to be in an hour," he signs after checking. There are quite a few spots opened throughout the day today compared to the one on Monday, where most are already unavailable. "The next one is going to be at noon."

"Knowing you, I know you won't be able to rest until you got it over and dealt with," she scolds him, which is nothing more than the truth. Troy has a lousy habit of overanalyzing and stressing things that haven't happened yet. "Sign up for the one in an hour."

"But—"

Troy didn't get to finish his sign before she held up one hand, stopping him from finishing.

"Oh, don't start with me, Troy Evans," she signs sternly, her brows pulled together. Quinn pulls herself upward, growling already in irritation. "You are doing this or so help me; I will not let you see my parents or Raymond again. You can say goodbye to tomorrow's brunch date, and we have mom's famous blueberry pie too."

"You're going to hold seeing them over my head?" he signs, flabbergasted though there's already a grin he can see his best friend trying to fight off. "Not to mention your mom's famous blueberry pie as well? That's just the devil's work."

"You know it, and when you ask for fashion advice, I'm going to lie about it," she signs proudly.

"Like you did about those blue khakis I wore a year ago?" Troy brings up, making them shudder in horror. But, honestly, he didn't know what he was thinking wearing those out to a party Quinn wanted him to accompany her.

"I can't say anything if they were sent from your mother, that's like...a rule," she settles with.

"Even if I was a fashion mess?"

"A rule, even if it killed me internally," she signs with a shudder before refocusing onto the elephant in the room. "Now, Troy...you're going to be fine, and you're going to get into the team. You hear me? Well, you see me sign, technically. You're the best tennis player my father has ever seen, and he plays a lot."

"I think he plays golf way more than tennis," Troy points out.

"It's still about the same thing," she signs with a huge grin. "Now, did you make the schedule?"

"Yes, mom," Troy signs back, rolling his eyes.

"Ew, not anytime soon, until I find myself a rich and loving husband. Did I mention the rich part? I can't survive without being spoiled to death," she signs, her hands flying at her passionate cry. "Why can't my story be a romance erotica?"

"Okay, ew," he snorts, making a gagging face at the thought of his friend living out an erotica novella he had once read out of boredom from her house. But, unlike her, it was definitely not something he would want to lie around.

"Have you told your parents about tryouts yet?" Quinn signs curiously.

At that, he shakes his head. His parents knew how passionate he was about sport but never wanted him to step out of his comfort zone if he didn't want to, including going to apply for a sport that they all knew he'd be the only one deaf. "No, not yet. I don't…want them to be disappointed if I don't make it through tryouts today."

"Oh, don't be so negative on yourself," Quinn aggressively signs out. "You're going to be amazing. Trust me. Have I ever been wrong about anything? Well, aside from not being able to predict 2000s fashion coming back. I'm not entirely sure what's going on here, but who am I to judge people with their see-through bags and mom jeans."

"I'll tell them after this," Troy promises, holding out his pinky afterward as Quinn does the same. It's a tiny little thing they picked up from Raymond before they both sign.

"You make a pinkie promise; you keep it. If you break it, you'll be thrown into ice water, and the cold will freeze off your fingers, so you don't lie again."

It's a somewhat twisted thing to sign, much less where Raymond learned it, but it has stuck to since then.

"Already, I'm going to get ready to work," she signs, letting her head fall back in what Troy presumes to be a loud groan. "Someone needs to pay for the next season's collection. I'll talk to you later, Troy. You'll let me know all the details then."

Signing bye to one another, Troy decides to get ready. Pulling on a pair of sweatpants and a shirt, he pulls his reddish-blonde hair back and takes a deep breath. He texts his parents the usual good morning and if they were fine today with their usual weekend talk before grabbing his keys and gym bag filled with his tennis equipment.

Would Jayden be here today?

The thought makes him flustered at the beauty of seeing him play, albeit not at his best from what Troy noticed. The way his muscles flexed, and his eyes that filled with nothing but determination sparked something deep inside of him—

Troy wishes to be the first LGBT tennis player.

Though he brushes it off as nothing more than admiration for Jayden rather than anything more.

As he passes by his roommate, Aston, he looks up in confusion before signing. "Where are you going?"

"Tryouts," Troy signs back to him. He's rather thankful that he got lucky with Aston Zhou as his roommate since freshmen. Not only is he hard-working, but he is probably one of the best roommates Troy can ask for.

Aston stands close to six feet, born and raised in San Francisco. As a computer science major, he's often seen up at all hours of the day, helping Troy with technology as he's terrible at it. Unlike Troy, who was born deaf, Aston had lost his hearing due to a fever. Aston pushes up his glasses curiously before signing in return. "I'm going downtown to catch a movie with some friends, lunch, then hitting a house party. Do you want to tag?"

"No, thank you," Troy gives him an apologetic smile before continuing. He loved how Aston always tried incorporating him into his life and was quite thankful as well. Though, parties are not really his scene either. "I already have a ton of homework. Can you imagine?"

"I told you not to take Professor Yvette; the dude is shit on RatemyProfessor," Aston grins.

"You're just lazy when it comes to writing," he signs back with a playful grin of his own.

"Why written ten pages when it could easily be summed in three pages?" he retorts, signing lazily as he yawns. "Well, good luck then on your tryouts. You're going to kill it. If you change your mind, you have my number."

"I'll be back in about an hour or two, so I'll let you know if I change my mind," Troy signs before leaving first. As he leaves his dorm room, he takes in the fresh air as it had rained the night before, and it instantly soothes him for a moment. When he lived in Sydney, his parents always loved going to the beach.

It's been far too long since Troy had gone there, and he makes a mental note to go when his schedule clears up, perhaps even today. It's one of his favorite places since coming to Chicago and away from his family and friends. It reminds him of home whenever he feels alone or overwhelmed while watching the receding shorelines and seagulls. His favorite part had to be when the sun was just setting and allowing his feet to soak in the sand.

He shuffles his bag, taking in how there are fewer people around than the busy weekday on campus. Of course, there are just a few people walking, but it's the thing he enjoys about the weekend on campus or at the beach.

How does he know that it's supposed to be quiet, like his brain can finally comprehend it's supposed to be silent. It made him feel…normal and not an outcast. Troy wishes that he could turn off his doomsday brain at times. Even after twenty years, he still has a hard time coming to terms with the fact that he'd never be able to hear.

That he'd always be the odd one out that isn't labeled "normal."

He shakes away the intrusive thoughts, tightening his hold onto the strap of his gym bag. It's something that comes up at times that he's never told anyone, especially his parents, as he's scared it might worry them.

That's the last thing that he would want.

A cool breeze passes by, settling onto his skin as he makes his way to the tennis center. He scans over the list, seeing that there are still five more spots to be filled, with about twenty to thirty people needing to come back for tryouts. A small smile made its way to his face when he saw Benjamin Minton making the tryout spot on the first try.

Except when he checks out the bulletin board for what appears to be the fourth time, Troy soon realizes that he's nowhere on the callback tryout list. His brows furrow together in confusion as he fumbles for his school's email again to confirm that the Coach had emailed him to come back with the appointment time in ten minutes.

Yet, if it wasn't for tryouts, what more can it be?

Troy's hand grows somewhat clammy as his heartbeat picks up. He shifts from one foot to the other as he tries to recall if he has done something wrong. Wavering at the front door, he knows that there's no time like the present to find out and calm his churning stomach.

Once more, he finds himself writing the word courage onto the palm of his hand and swallowing it in hopes of manifesting that exact feeling. Finally, he straightens his back and makes his way inside. He has assumed that Coach would be there, but when he sees Jayden there as well, his eyes widen for a moment.

They're in a midgame, and compared to yesterday, Jayden is moving with much more precision, even diving into serving it back. He couldn't help but be curious as to why he wasn't playing well yesterday or perhaps he has stage fright of sorts.

They were so in the zone that they didn't even realize Troy had come in, which he respects. Each of his swings isn't just powerful but held with calculation and determination of where he would like it to go.

It's a relatively tight match, even making up for what they like by going after one another's weaknesses. However, Jayden pushes through at the end, making Coach grin at him before seeing Troy hanging out near the entrance. The coach waves at Troy; he quickly tries to take his notepad and pen out. As he takes it out, his eyes pierce Jayden for a moment, and Troy can see how nervous he is as he stares at the door. It's almost as if Jayden is expecting someone like Quinn, who has been there the few times they bumped into one another.

Perhaps Jayden wanted Quinn there, as they did seem to get along. Or does Jayden not like him?

For some reason, those questions didn't sit well with Troy.

"I hope I'm not too early," he quickly writes before showing Coach, who shakes his head. Troy could feel his cheeks burning as he felt Jayden's watchful eyes and how sweat is trickling down his face as he's only in a tank top that wraps around his muscular body perfectly before quickly scribbling again. "I realize that I'm not on the board for the callback. Is something wrong?"

Troy watches anxiously as Coach and Jayden look at one another; they speak to one another, looking rather grim and severe. He wishes more than anything that he understands what they are saying. Unfortunately, it only serves as a stark reminder of the fact that he's an outlander.

Finally, Jayden turns, taking a deep breath and closing his eyes. Troy tilts his head to the side, seeming somewhat wary of what's happening. He lowers his notepad rather awkwardly as Jayden's eyes pierce his, stealing his breath away before the next thing he does.

"That's because you're not here for a callback," Jayden signs as Troy's eyes widen like saucer plates. He can barely even comprehend what is still happening, and his eyes are still trying to process everything as he finishes his signing. "You're here for a proposition."

CHAPTER EIGHT

Troy thought for a moment that he had utterly lost it; his eyes feel as if they are moments from popping out, almost like a dream of sorts. He's staring at Jayden, flabbergasted for a moment as his mouth opens and then closes it like that of a gaping fish on land.

For a split second, he feels as if…he's normal.

All the while, despite how nervous Jayden has been feeling inside, he's fighting the one of amusement. It's been so long since he signed, but it's no different than being bilingual to him. Though a bit rustic, it still comes relatively easy to him.

In a peculiar sense, he also feels quite free to use what he knows to help someone else after his dream. Weston's question still plaguing him of how Jayden will live out his legacy going forth without him. Secretly, he had hoped Troy's girlfriend would have been there with him, so he wasn't given the two options of choosing.

Even Coach had given Jayden a choice right before Troy in their debate as he knows that it might change up his life going forward, primarily because of how nosy his teammates and the university are. Most regard Jayden as an up-and-coming pro-tennis player.

It's not a big deal, Jayden knows, but explaining why he knows sign language in the first place brings up a whole other can of worms at the same time. He doesn't like talking about it. Even Coach, who knows, never asks anything regarding it either, which he's thankful for.

In the corner of Troy's eyes, he can see Coach laughing from the way his shoulder is shaking before Jayden scowls at him. He can't help but wonder how close the two seem to be before Troy lifts his hand, which feels rather heavy. He quickly goes to tuck his notepad below his arms as his hands bring up the shock of his voice. "You…you know ASL?"

Jayden closes his first at his question, shaking up and down as a sign for 'no' before continuing. "Yeah, it's the reason why Coach wanted all of us to talk in private to make this whole process easier. You don't have an interpreter with you at all, correct?"

"No," Troy shakes his head in affirmation, biting his lips before signing back. "I was coming just to try out as I last minute decided to with some help. I thought of getting an interpreter, but there wasn't enough time. Is that a problem?"

Once more, Jayden repeats the sign for no. "Not at all; Coach wanted you to feel part of the team. Are you okay if we go to his office to explain what we have as a proposition and see what you'd like going forward?"

"Going forward?" Troy repeats in, signing in utter shock. "As in…"

Jayden gives a slight grin before signing once more, which only confirms to Troy that he actually knows sign language. "Yeah, you passed the tryouts with flying colors. The Coach was even looking forward to playing with you upon seeing your performance on the cams, but don't tell him I told you that."

For the first time all morning, a smile breaks out of Troy's face at the information he's given. His heart raced in the excitement of knowing that even the Coach had seen potential in him. He fumbles, trying to sign comprehensive sentences. "Oh, that's amazing. So may I ask why I am here exactly?"

"Coach was actually looking forward to having you on the team, but we don't want to put you on there yet without speaking to you regarding how you would like to move forward being on the team," Jayden informs him while chuckling. "Are you okay coming with us to talk this through? I'll be your interpreter, but if it's something personal, you're more than fine writing it down and telling Coach privately."

"Yes, that's fine," Troy signs before looking over at Coach with a timid smile.

At the same time, Jayden does and nods at Coach. "Okay, everything should be good. I've explained to Troy what's going on. Whatever you want to say, I'll be the translator as long as it's not too personal."

"You're amazing," Coach sighs in relief before turning to Troy and giving him a thumbs-up. He then turns first, leading them both into his office before taking a seat. After that, there isn't much needed but to see how both would like to cooperate going forth. Leaning forward and putting his elbow onto the wooden desk, he tilts his head to the side. "Alright, are you ready?"

"Ready as ever," Jayden informs Coach with a façade smile, which Troy catches on right away, despite not knowing what he just said to Coach. It's an intuition that Troy catches on right away that he doesn't seem to enjoy signing, making him frown. However, he didn't want to push to know either.

For the next half an hour, they went into detail regarding Troy's life a bit more and how the team might be able to incorporate him into matches going forth as the only deaf person. Each time Jayden signs, he makes sure to speak out loud for Coach to follow along. Upon seeing how nervous he is, Jayden quickly adds that his teammates are rather talkative, and he shouldn't feel tense joining the team. Oddly enough, Troy believes him right away, especially after seeing Trevis play just yesterday and how friendly he seems alongside Benjamin as well.

"Already, last question, and you're both free after this," Coach laughs as both sigh in relief once Jayden informs him through signing. Coach then goes to clear his throat and arch up a brow. "Now, you can discuss this with yourselves for as long as you need, and please do not feel pressure either, Jayden. I want you to think about it first. Would you like Troy to have an interpreter, or would you like to be one for him unless completely necessary?"

It's a rather heavy responsibility; Jayden already knew that.

It's not as simple as just becoming an interpreter, but possibly being on the same team with him going forth. He cocks his head to the side at Coach. "If that is the case, would I be paired with him going forth?"

"That is up to you, but his playstyle is on par with you in terms of style skill sets, and I'm not just saying that," Coach replies, which is true. From the beginning, Jayden has already been impressed with Troy. When playing professionally, most players pick a friend, someone they like playing with, and definitely someone who isn't a threat to their singles career. Ironically enough, Troy didn't qualify for those as they had just met.

"Right," Jayden murmurs under his breath, causing Troy to become curious about what the conversation they were having was about as he fiddles with the hem of his shirt. Finally, Troy nods. "Well, so long as you access us accordingly and not become biased when making teams for the matches, I will not mind being his interpreter if he would like that instead of one assigned to him by the school."

"I'm not going just to pair you up because you can help interpret only, especially to a future as bright as you, Jayden," Coach states, a bit offended before he smiles. "Though, thank you so much, Jayden. You really are Mr. Nice, as everyone calls you, huh?"

This time, Troy sees the way he flinches ever so slightly, his eye twitching at whatever Coach said before he chuckles. Even if Troy can't hear, he can see his body language clear as day more than anything else as whatever he said, he didn't like in the slightest. So, when Jayden forces a smile, it only tugs at Troy's heart in the slightest before he turns to him.

"The Coach has one final question to ask," Jayden tells him through sign rather slowly. For some reason, it makes Troy anxious, given the look on Jaden's face just before. Troy has never been the one to prey, knowing firsthand how intrusive it is, but it's the first time he's ever been so curious.

"Okay, what would it be?" Troy questions timidly, signing before playing with the hem of his shirt again. For once, Troy realizes that Jayden's mouth isn't moving either, which means whatever he wants to sign next would be rather important.

"Would you like an interpreter?"

"Well, I presume that it'd be necessary, I would think, right?" he questions, arching a brow. "Well, I don't mind using my notepad, but I think it would be best for something major. I'm more than fine making the appointments for it."

"No," Jayden shakes his head, signing it at the same time.

"I don't understand," Troy confesses, his lips pressing onto a thin line for a moment.

"Yes, you're getting an interpreter regardless, but…" he trails off, and it only adds to Troy's worries before he takes a deep breath and continues signing where he has left off. "Would you like for me to be your interpreter? Or would you like Coach to file one on your behalf based on the schedule for our plays and tours?"

There's a beat of silence, and for once, Troy knows what absolute silence is right now. It's almost as if the universe wants to shock him into an induced coma, as never in a million years would he presume Jayden to know how to sign, much less ask to be his interpreter, either.

"You?" Troy signs, his brows are reaching the ceiling.

"You don't have to look like that," Jayden fights a chuckle and nods.

"No! That's not what I meant at all," he quickly signs, throwing in more exclamation points before continuing. "I mean…I would never want you to take time playing just to translate to me. Nor do I want you to change your routine for my sake either."

"I do not mind," Jayden signs.

"Not minding is not the same as meaning if you want to," Troy points out, shaking his head. He didn't mind many things in his life, but some don't mean he wanted it either; he just didn't mind it too much. "If you wish to not, I completely understand as well."

"No, I want to, but only if you're comfortable as well," Jayden goes more in-depth. "I don't know if we'll be paired in the long run either, but something like drills and Coach giving pointers, I do not mind in the slightest interpreting for you."

"Are you sure?" Troy questions, taking in his body language as an indicator. "I don't mind getting an interpreter at all. Maybe…we can do some sort of test run and see if we even get along before doing something like this?"

Jayden arches up a brow but takes in what he's saying. It does make a lot more sense than both going blindly into this only to realize they are not compatible in the slightest, either. "Okay, I'll let Coach know. What about a one-week trial of sorts? See if we can get along, and also test our playing styles too?"

However, it's an unspoken thing between them that they both know that they play perfectly in sync on the field, maybe even matching one another in their skill set. Jayden hums before nodding in agreement. It'll also give Jayden time to adjust and allow his teammates to get over the shock of it as well.

"Deal," Troy signs with a smile as Jayden turns to Coach and explains their plan in action.

Coach grins from ear to ear before getting up, holding out his hand for Troy to shake as he welcomes him to the team going forward. He will be shooting him a schedule that Jayden signs to him. It almost seems like a dream come true to Troy as excitement runs through his veins.

Once they make their way out, they both walk the same way back into the tennis courts, where Troy watches as Jayden grabs his things from the bleachers. Troy didn't want to leave awkwardly either, and he's been itching to head to the beach and process everything before telling Quinn, his parents, and everyone else. Hell, he's still trying to comprehend everything, and a small part of him is curious why Jayen even knows ASL.

"So…" he signs before trailing off, still trying to calm down his speeding heart and how fast his heart is racing at the same time. It's then that he's able to think through the haze that his eyes widen exponentially. His conversation with Quinn in front of Jayden is still fresh in his mind. Now that Troy figured out that he knows sign language, it only makes things so much worse as he'll be working alongside him. "I am so sorry."

Jayden only arches up a brow in surprise at his apology before signing. "At...what?"

"Yesterday during tryouts," he signs manically, his flush growing bigger as it reaches his shoulder. For once, he feels like Quinn signing like his life depends on it without even considering how fluent Jayden is in ASL. "I...I didn't mean to say you were not focused on your plays."

"Oh, that," Jayden smirks playfully at him while walking with him out the front door of the tennis center. "No, don't worry about it; you were completely right, my playing was off that day. What was that you signed? My movement is a bit lackluster, right?"

"I don't—" he signs, ready to explain himself, but is cut off by the twinkle in Jayden's eyes. It's yet a new emotion he's never seen before, full of mischievousness and deviltry. For some reason, it seems to fit Jayden much more than the nice personality.

"Do you want to know why?" Jayden signs.

Before Troy can sign back that he's not going to pry, he lifts baggy shorts. Troy's eyes widen for a moment, another blush coming on strong when he takes in just how muscular Jayden's form is. However, he focuses more on the small tattoo on his left thigh. It's not that large, possibly about half his middle finger or so height and across. It's a black and white tattoo, with the painting encased into a black circle. There's a brewing storm in the distance in grey clouds, tiny speckles of grey dots representing rain. In the middle is a white bird flying straight into the storm without looking back.

Just like when Jayden smiled before at the Coach with whatever he had said to him before asking if he wished to be his interpreter, it tugged at his heart for an unknown reason. Troy blinks several times before tilting his head to the side as he signs. "It's…somewhat sad."

His interpretation of the tattoo causes Jayden to become shocked. "Is that right?"

"I hope you're not offended," Troy signs back. It's only been ten minutes, and the last thing he would want is for them to get off on the wrong foot over something so whimsical. However, he couldn't help but speak his mind when he first laid eyes on it.

"No, art is supposed to be subjective," Jayden smiles while he signs to him. In fact, it feels pretty nice at the end to speak to someone more than willing to be honest, much like Trevis. "I'm the one who actually designed it."

"Wait, really?" Troy signs as his mouthparts for a moment.

"Why would I lie?" he muses before they get to a split on the campus road. For a moment, Jayden debates in his head, yet he doesn't want to stop talking to Troy just yet and to learn more about him. Not to mention, once he started signing again, it's like he didn't know when to stop. "What are you doing after this?"

"Nothing much; I was going to the…beach," Troy confesses awkwardly as he's more than certain no one in the right mind would go right now, yet he finds himself confessing such. "Then grabbing something to eat before returning back to my dorm."

"By yourself?"

"Yeah," he nods.

"Your girlfriend's busy?" Jayden questions as he thinks back to the girl, Quinn, who has been with him.

"My…I don't have a girlfriend," Troy signs quickly, baffled as his cheeks start burning. He quickly realizes that from an outside perspective, as Quinn and he have hung out often, people may have categorized it as such. "Quinn is a friend."

"Well, why don't I tag around with you then?"

"Huh?" Troy blinks a few times, causing Jayden to laugh at how easy he is to read.

"We can get the whole get to know each other now during our trial period."

CHAPTER NINE

The closer they get to the beach, Troy becomes more self-conscious as reality sets in. Perhaps this is a magical spot to him, and he has never brought another person before. In fact, a small part of Troy is somewhat nervous about what he would think of coming here just to stare at the water more than anything else.

A million questions start flooding in his head from every angle without a satisfactory answer to help as they silently sit on the bus to Montrose Beach. If Jayden did know ASL, Troy is more than confident that Quinn would have said that right off the bat. Not to mention, Jayden had looked somewhat awkward signing to him with mild discomfort as he forced himself to do it.

Oddly enough, as they sat there in silence, it didn't feel awkward in the slightest.

"This is it," Troy lamely signs to him, pressing his lips into a thin line as seawater smells fill his senses. He watches a flock of seagulls flying overhead and a decent amount of people spread out playing in the water or kicking sand.

"There's a perfect place here that not many people know about, and away from the crowd I usually go."

"Is there now?" Jayden signs, arching a brow.

"Do you want…" Troy signs halfway for a moment before continuing. "To come look?"

"If you would like," Jayden replies.

"It's up this small narrow area," Troy signs before gesturing to the hidden winding path that leads up to the base of a small cliff area. He walks a few steps in front of Jayden, leading the way past the narrow passageway. Upon seeing just how dangerous this place can be at night, a slight frown makes its way to Jayden's face.

After all, he had already tripped a few times, even for someone like him. So, it didn't sit well with him to see Troy navigating his feet through the wet stones. Jayden's hand starts growing clammy, his heart kicking into overdrive as irritation builds inside him; he always has his hand ready to catch himself from slipping into the water and Troy's.

Once they ascend to the top and very edge of the cliff overlooking the ocean, Troy's mouth breaks into a smile. After such a hectic day, it's nice for him to know that there's something that will never change—

The beauty of the ocean and how it soothes his very soul as he turns to Jayden.

"Do you come to these parts here often?" Jayden finds himself signing before he can stop himself, unknowingly cutting Troy off from asking if he likes this secret place. Troy also notices the small disapproving look on his face and the way his brows are bumped upward.

At that, he takes a hand and makes a first before bobbing it back and forth to confirm his question. When Jayden's frown only becomes deeper, Troy tilts his head to the side before Jayden signs again.

"Alone?"

"Yes, since I moved to Chicago for college and accidentally discovered this place," Troy nods and places his fingers onto his forehead while bringing his hand forward before down, making sure his palm faces him. "Why?"

"I don't know," he signs before looking over at the scene in front of him. He did agree the place is beautiful, but not with the danger that may come with it. He wavers between keeping it to himself or making it known before taking the ladder. "It seems dangerous if you were to ask me, especially at night when dumb people want to drive through that narrow passageway while you're walking it."

"Luckily enough, I won't come here at night, nor did I ask you," he signs with a teasing grin.

"Touche," Jayden chuckles. "I'm starting to think there's more to you than meets the eye."

"Isn't that most people?" Troy signs to him. He then sits, his eyes fixated on the border where the sky meets the ocean. He loves that it goes on for miles, the wind caressing his face and hair like it's trying to take away all his worries. So it surprises him when Jayden takes a seat next to him as he looks over, his heart fluttering slightly despite not knowing why.

It's just that Jayden looks almost picture-perfect right now, straight out of some sort of designer magazine. His hair blows and falls almost perfectly onto his face as his stormy grey eyes fixate on sight before him. He convinces himself it's the same look he gives to a person he admires rather than finding attractive.

Jayden didn't even realize Troy had been staring at him as his eyes were locked over the edge, the call to the void holding tightly to him. It's then Troy catches the wildness in his eyes, seeming to ride on the surface almost as if he wants to do something reckless like jumping off the ledge and into the water below. But, instead, there's some sort of calculation in his eyes. It's not a far jump per se, but it's definitely not something Troy would do.

There's so much that Troy didn't realize about this man sitting next to him who will be playing close with him for the remainder of the season starting in a few days. Unfortunately, this probably means he may be unable to return here for a while. Troy didn't know how long he and Jayden had been watching the ocean crash onto the beach and then recede before turning to him.

"Can I ask you a question?" Troy finally gathers enough courage to sign after a long period of silence.

Jayden tries not to go rigid at his question. He should have known that for sure; Troy would be asking questions regarding why he knows sign language. He tells himself that he should be expecting this, especially with his teammates and others knowing since rumors spread like wildfire.

He knew going into this, but he didn't expect it so soon.

"Yeah, sure," he signs, trying to compose his body from giving away the truth.

"What does the ocean sound like? Or the shoreline

receding as well?" Troy questions as his eyes fall back onto the water. He puckers his lips, letting his hand fall onto his knees before continuing to speak with them as he turns to face Jayden. "If you can describe the sound in your own words, how would you describe it?"

The question surprises him, as that's the last thing Jayden had expected to come out of his mouth. However, the more he tries to explain the ocean's sounds, the more Jayden finds himself stumping over it.

How can you explain sound to someone who probably has known nothing but silence?

"The sound of the ocean, huh?" he signs, taking a deep breath before releasing it.

"Quinn tells me it sounds like crashing," Troy signs with a slight frown at the words she had used to describe the sound from what he has learned. "Though, I don't think that makes sense as a car crashing sound, huh?"

"Yeah, most definitely not," Jayden replies with his hand, shaking his head all the while.

"Or a soda can being crushed?"

Jayden holds up two fingers and his thumb and closes them while swiping. "Nope."

"My parents told me that it sounded like a roar when I was a kid, but I soon realized it's not the same sound as a lion's roar either," Troy explains with a small, meek smile. "How and why is there one word to explain different sounds?"

"Humans aren't that creative," he joshes with a grin.

"I've always heard that the sound of crashing waves on

the shore is the most relaxing sound on Earth, so I wanted to ask, if you don't mind," Troy quickly throws in. The last thing he wants is to make things awkward or off to a rocky start when trying to make a quick conversation.

There's a pause that stretches out as Jayden looks outward at the ocean. For the first time, he doesn't feel the need to do something reckless that he always suppresses, like leaping into the ocean. Instead, he allows his mind and heart to take in the sight in front of him, the sound, and everything to it.

Rather than giving him an answer, he turns to him.

"Well…what do you feel when you look at the ocean?" Jayden questions.

Troy looks over to the ocean for a moment. "I always felt drawn to the ocean for as long as I remember, and my mother concluded it's because I'm a Pisces," he smiles warmly at the memory of the way his father would then roll his eyes as he didn't believe in these astrology signs. "I don't know; there's just something about the ocean that calms me. I feel…not just relaxed but relived and refreshed."

"Refreshened?" he repeats with his hand curiously.

"Well, it's like washing away my worries when I watch the ocean waves. It crashes forward, taking away my stress and worries," he signs in clarification. "It's why I always wanted to know if that is true and wish to hear the ocean rather than just seeing it."

"If you ask me, sometimes…" he stops signing for a moment to put into action what he's trying to convey. "I suppose the best thing in the world can't be heard or seen but felt in the heart. What we connect most with that stays with us rather than any other of our senses," he clarifies. "What do you feel right now looking at the ocean? Hearing or seeing it won't change how your heart feels."

As their eyes connect, it rocks something deep in Troy's very core. His heart thumps erratically fast for the first time, and honestly, he can get lost in them. Not once had he ever thought of it like that, and much have someone else bring it into light. As they continue staring into one another's eyes, he becomes more lost in them while his face starts feeling rather hot.

Am I blushing right now?

What is this feeling?

That's the only two questions going through Troy's head right now upon realizing his face is growing rather flushed. His eyes only widen, and his heart kicks into overdrive when Jayden frowns, his lips puckering together as he places his hand over his forehead before signing.

"Are you okay?"

"I…" he stops midsentence before retracting his words with a meek nod. "Yeah."

"You should wear my cardigan before it gets cold," he signs before shrugging it off and placing it over him. The last thing Jayden wants is for him to catch a cold right before the semester and the season for their games begin. "Sorry if I offended you or looked like a preacher."

"No, I never thought of it like that. It helps a lot," Troy signs in return. "Are you from the states by chance?"

"My parents and I are from England."

"England?" Troy repeats before his lips pull into a deep

frown momentarily. Something about it just isn't adding up as he tilts his head to the side curiously before continuing. "You're...signing in ASL rather than BSL, though."

"I moved here when I was thirteen. Luckily enough, about thirty per cent of the signs are the same, so it's easy for me to pick up and learn ASL," he explains. "I'm probably not as good as you are, but I'm coming around. What about you?"

"I'm from Sydney, Australia, but I'm here on a VISA. I learned ASL in middle school when I showed great interest in attending Columbia, where my father graduated from," he explains. "It was hard in the beginning."

"Let me guess," he signs back with a chuckle. "Transitioning from the two-handed alphabet to one?"

At that, he nods with a smile of his own. "How long have you been playing tennis?"

"I think I was playing before I even learned to read, but it was more so as a hobby or something to pass the time," he admits. "I became more serious later in life and realized I have a talent at the very end for it, so I'm hoping to become a pro. You?"

Troy didn't know how long they played twenty questions, learning more about one another. Interestingly, Jayden enjoys the whimsical questions, finding that they have a handful of things in common.

"Do you have any siblings?" Troy questions before he sees Jayden going rigid completely. There's almost an underlying darkness in the simple question. He wishes nothing more than to take it back, especially seeing how Jayden leans his body closer to each other.

"Yes, I do," he replies through gritted teeth, and the urge to leap off the ledge is stronger than ever before. He had fun with whimsical questions, and his guard was completely down when the question came. "A brother."

Once more, Troy finds himself having many more questions than before.

What is with that look on Jayden's face?

Why did he know sign language so well?

Did something happen to him, which is why he had started it with such anguish?

"Do you want to jump over the edge right now?" Troy finds himself signing blindly before he can think it through. He wanted nothing more than to change the topic but didn't know what else to sign next aside from that.

"Kind of," Jayden says in amusement. "How did you know?"

"I can see the wildness in your eyes," he admits. "Are you going to?"

"I would love to," he signs with a grin before getting up. He slowly holds his hand in front of Troy, arching a brow. Troy takes it as a sign to take it, their hands clasping onto one another as electricity zaps through every inch of his body, just like when their hands touched back in the coffee shop. It's something he never felt before that he could recall, especially realizing just how firm and rough his hands are before he pulls away to continue signing. "However, I don't want to walk around the city with my whole body wet. Now let's eat; I can hear your stomach from here for the past ten minutes."

Troy goes entirely still for a moment before his mouth falls open. His eyes widen, his face growing even more flushed at the new discovery before he signs with horror. "Wait, you can hear when I'm hungry?"

"Yeah," Jayden confirms. "It makes a growling, roaring sound of sorts."

"Like…an animal? My God," he signs in complete horror. "How come no one ever told me that?"

Then, Jayden ultimately doubles over, completely losing himself in his laughing fit. It's the first time in what seems like forever that he has ever laughed like that, especially with the look on his face. His shoulders shake uncontrollably as Troy watches, completely memorized. But, unlike his curiosity to hear about the ocean, he decides for the first time to enjoy what his heart is feeling upon seeing him laugh as Jayden composes himself before signing.

"I'm sorry; I'm not laughing at you if that's what you're thinking."

That Troy already knows but decides to play along. "Really now?"

"Yeah, you just…remind me much of my brother."

The softness reaches his eyes, and it only stumps Troy even more of what happened between him and his brother. Before, when he admitted to having a brother, there was nothing but anguish; now, it's nothing but sweetness. Still, Troy didn't wish to pry as they slowly returned from the cliff to get some food in the city.

After all, everyone has their secrets.

CHAPTER TEN

"**I**'m sorry, can you repeat that? Yet, much slower with your hands?"

Troy does so again at Quinn's request in front of his best friend and roommate, looking as if he had indeed lost his marbles. It only confirms to Troy that no one seems to know that Jayden did know sign language in the years he had spent there, which confuses him greatly. "Jayden Harrington knows sign language."

"As in, what we are using to talk right now?" Aston signs, completely flabbergasted from the look in his eyes that Troy has never seen before. It certainly is shocking, to say the least, as Troy gives a confirming nod in response. "Wow, that's insane. Was it known he can use sign language?"

"Not that I know, and I know all things gossip for the most part," Quinn signs back in shock before her eyes go relatively wide. "Fuck. Does he know that I've been throwing provocative words at you behind his back?" she signs quicker than probably the Flash himself. "Oh God, he does, doesn't he? Did I blow off my chance of scoring the one rich man who could give me the world when I snap my fingers?"

"I thought you'll never go for rich sports jocks because they have a tendency to cheat in your words," Aston points out with a teasing smile on his face before signing. "What did you say? Two out of ten men cheat on their partners, right?"

"A girl can dream about bagging a rich man that's loyal," Quinn signs while puffing out her chest.

"Wait, Jayden's rich?" Troy questions with a relatively deep frown. The word he's signing already bothers him, but it seems everyone knows but him. Really, he feels as if he's been living under a rock of sorts, given how well known he appears to be around the campus if he thinks about it.

Rich.

Nice.

Tennis player.

Knowns ASL, BSL, and can speak perfectly.

"His parents are huge donors," Quinn signs with over-the-top emphasis. "As in, mega-rich loaded. I think they have a class building on the campus named after them or something along that line. Of course, everyone wants a piece of him, but personally, he's only a four to me."

"Are you serious?" Aston's eyes widen as he slowly signs. "A four out of a ten?"

Even Troy did as well. By all accounts, Jayden is a perfect ten in everything. However, he recalled that his best friend seems to have a rather unique taste for men, which there's nothing to be ashamed about.

"I'm into older men; excuse me for knowing what I like," she signs in clarification, not seeming that much offended before winking at Troy. "Yeah, he's cute like I'm not blind, but not my type; though, I can totally see Mr. Nice with you, Troy."

"What? Me?" he signs out with a rather flushed face. He hopes neither realizes the redness spreading like wildfire over his rather pale complexion. In fact, Troy is more than confident that they would tease him about a crush, which is not the case.

It's nothing more than admiration for him.

"Yeah, you guys even went to eat pizza together," Quinn signs with a rather sly smile. "Jayden paid."

Thank goodness he didn't tell them about their time spent together at the beach either.

At that, Aston's brow furrows together. "Did they?"

"You didn't tell Aston?" she questions with her hand.

"It's not that important," Troy signs, leaning back onto the adjacent seat. "I said I'll pay, but he said he's ordering more, so he insisted," he clarifies. He didn't even realize how much Jayden could eat in one sitting. "Nothing more to read into."

"That and you promise to treat him next time, which means there would be more to come," she signs, wiggling her eyebrow at Troy before grabbing her cup of tea. She takes a small sip before getting more comfortable on the sofa. "It seems like something out of a cute romance BL novel."

"B…L?" Aston arches a brow, signing the alphabet slowly to ensure he's getting it right.

"Boy's love," she clarifies before fanning her face for a moment before continuing. "There's just something about boy's love that gets me going if you know what I mean. Any reason why that is by chance?"

"Okay, that's way too much for me to know, gross," Aston's nose crunches together in disgust.

"You can leave if you would like, Aston," Quinn signs and points toward the front door.

"It's my dorm room, may I remind you," Aston rebuts, causing them to grin at one another. "Speaking of which, can we order something to snack on? I know it's ten, but it's technically not Monday, which means I will enjoy my last two hours of freedom before the dreaded first week of classes. Does anyone have cravings?"

"I think only fast-food joints are open at this time," Quinn signs, doing a slight stretch. "So long as I'm back home by my curfew at one in the morning, I'm fine with anything. I know I shouldn't be, but why not have a cheat day then."

"I'd like a burger," Troy informs them. His phone vibrates in his pocket as he takes it out to check who's video calling him so late at night, though he already has a hunch. It's confirmed moments later when he sees it's from his parents. He had already made a mental note to call them tomorrow after his classes about the good news, but he supposed that his parents had free time today. He looks over at both of them. "Parents."

"Take as long as you need; we'll order first," Quinn signs, with Aston nodding in agreement before heading to his bedroom. He makes sure to lock the door before sliding the answer button, and immediately, a smile emerges on his face when he sees his mom beaming at him.

"Hi, sweetheart," she signs in excitement. "I hope I didn't call you while you were sleeping?"

"No, not at all; it's only ten here," he signs once he props his phone onto the small standing desk. He does a mental calculation to find out that there is currently one in Australia. "Hi, mom. Where's dad, by the way?"

"Oh, he's right there," she signs before dragging her husband onto the screen. "So…?"

"I got in," Troy signs proudly with a grin.

At that, they give little jazz hands to resemble clapping in a silent applause. Pride and happiness are written on their faces, and there's nothing Troy wanted more at that moment than to hug his parents, who's halfway across the world.

"That's amazing, Troy!" Mom gushes out with a beaming smile. "We know you would have gotten in."

"Do you want us to fly in to celebrate?" Dad questions, tilting his head to the side. The funny thing is that Troy is more than confident that they would do it in a heartbeat. "I would cancel my classes; I'm sure my students won't mind for three days."

"I can take my vacation days," Mom chimes in, shoving her husband to the side so she can sign.

"That's too much," he signs in return, shaking his head.

"I think we have enough miles for us," Mom huffs, narrowing her eyes. But, just like any proud mom, there is nothing she wouldn't do in making up an excuse to see his son. "Dad can just stay behind."

"Using my mile points?" Dad signs back, causing her to laugh. Her whole body is shaking as she covers her mouth. It's then that Troy sees the way dad's face softens tremendously, almost as if he's captivated by her laughter.

For a moment, he thinks back to when he and Jayden had been at the beach. The way he laughed just as the wind was blowing and the sun shined onto his face, outlining his perfect features. Troy wonders if that's how he's stared at Jayden.

Would Jayden ever look at him like that?

His eyes widen slightly at his own thoughts. The flush on his face began to spread like wildfire once more as he didn't know where that thought even came from. No, Troy has looked at Jayden out of admiration—

Obviously.

"I love you, Troy. We're so proud of you," Mom signs proudly once more to his son, switching to Australian sign language almost naturally. It snaps Troy entirely out of his daze of Jayden to realize tears are brimming in the corner of his eyes.

"I love you both," he signs, completely transitioning to Australian sign language before giving Mom a warning stare. He's more than sure that if she cries, he might as well see her this emotional. "Mom, please don't cry."

"You know I can't help it as a Pisces myself," she signs with a pout. It earns an eye roll from her husband, who doesn't believe such a thing as Mom composes herself.

"Speaking of which, have you been seeing your therapist weekly still?"

Even though Quinn and Aston are in the living room while Troy is in his room, he's glad his parents have switched their sign language. It's not something he's particularly interested in sharing with anyone, much less his close friends.

"Mom," he signs, shaking his head sternly and throwing in a few exclamation points at the end to emphasize his point. He knows his parents, especially his mom, are worried about him, but it's a thing he wants to put in the past. "I don't want to talk about it. I'm fine."

"I'm just concerned," she signs back slowly.

"He knows," his dad signs in return, and he can see the stern look on his face. Troy takes a deep breath, not wanting to upset either of his parents, without wanting to go into too much detail. He rakes his hair back before continuing.

"No, I don't need to. The nightmares went away," Troy says honestly.

"Are you sure?" his dad signs, arching up a brow.

At that, he places both his index fingers up before crossing one over the other and tapping it twice firmly. He knows his parents can see right through his lies as he nods firmly. Positive. I cross my heart that I haven't had one in months now."

Oddly enough, there hasn't been one yesterday either when he thought he would be stressed following the news of joining the tennis team. It's usually during big changes like the new semester or during testing season.

Perhaps he had a relaxing day yesterday at the beach and then grabbed pizza with Jayden.

"We're just worried, is all," his mom signs.

"I only have nightmares when things become too stressful," he reminds them both.

"Have you been stressed? Maybe you should make an appointment now that you're balancing—"

"Mom, I'm fine, really," he signs, trying to clear up the tense atmosphere and make it evident that he is fine. Giving a small smile, he continues. "I know you're worried about me, and I love you both, but I honestly feel like I'm turning over a new leaf."

The small amount of tension leaves mom in the process as a genuine smile breaks free. There's nothing that makes your night like seeing your mother smiling so brightly because of you. "I'm glad. Oh, before I go, anything…like meeting someone recently that I should know about?"

"You know I'm not looking," he signs, rolling his eyes. Dating is the last thing on his mind right now with college and then focusing on becoming the first deaf tennis player to go pro. Instead, he wants to show that there's more than meets the eye when it comes to disabilities.

After all, the best thing in life is felt in the heart, right?

Once more, he tries to understand why he's thinking of Jayden once more. Those words still reside deep inside Troy even now. Jayden really is a force Troy has never expected. He's nice, and yet there's also another side to him that Troy noticed:

His *reckless* side, like getting a tattoo last minute and wanting to hop off the cliff despite the dangers.

"I'm just saying," mom signs with a wink. "I met your dad there, and—"

"I'm going to hang up," he cuts her off, his nose scrunching together. He didn't need to hear this story a thousand times without gagging at their love story. It was rather romantic the first time, but after hearing it for the hundredth time, he practically memorized the story and was able to tell it back with his hands while his eyes were closed.

"I'm just saying," Mom pouts while signing. "Well, we'll talk to you soon then. I don't want to keep you up too late when you have practice and classes. If it gets too stressful, please take it easy or see Katie, okay?"

"I know. I love you guys," he signs.

"We love you too," his dad signs before hanging up. He continues to stare at the black screen for a moment, taking a deep breath before releasing it. Though he loves his parents deeply, he did wish that, at times, he didn't become such a liability by letting them worry about him.

He tries not to burden them any more than he has thought in his head as he focuses on the positive.

Tomorrow is when everything changes going forth—he can feel it in his bones.

CHAPTER ELEVEN

"**Y**ou fucking know sign language?"

It didn't matter how uneased Jayden felt all morning in telling his teammates because they were going to figure it out today anyway during their first official meeting now that tryouts are completed. He figures it's best to just air it all to Trevis first before the others today. With the roster out with their first play against Princeton next week, he needed no distractions or stress.

The last thing he wanted was to do something reckless to calm his nerves, like getting a new tattoo, driving at over eighty miles an hour at night, or getting shit-faced at a bar a few towns over before dragging himself to class the next day.

Or jumping off that cliff that Troy had taken him.

He figures he'd break the news first to Trevis before the others come.

Glancing over, a small chuckle escapes Jayden's lips at how Trevis is staring at him with his mouth completely open, his eyes bulging out in utter shock. In the almost two years that he has known him, he thought nothing much would shock his best mate.

"Yes, sign language," he confirms, stripping his shirt in one fluid motion and throwing it into the locker.

"Like, talking with your hands?" Trevis asks, waving his hands in shock. "Something like this?"

"A rather crude way of putting it, but yes," Jayden nods in confirmation, his mouth twitching once more.

"Dude, what the fuck?"

"Why are you more shocked about this than when you found out I was bi?" Jayden questions, arching a brow with a deadpan expression. Honestly, he had presumed Trevis would have taken it worse than right now, pressing to ask why he knows and so forth.

Though, when you've spent your whole life hiding something, it would seem bigger than life.

Travis snorts as he slips his tennis shoes on, pointing up and down Jayde's body with his racquet. "I mean, with the way you dressed? I *knew* there was something about you that you don't scream one way," he laughs before slightly pausing. "No homo."

"You didn't say no homo, when you threw yourself on me last year at Isaac's birthday bash," he teases with a laugh. It's almost like all the worry he's been holding slowly disappears, significantly, when Trevis shudders at the thought.

"My dude, you know damn well it was because that freshman was coming up too strong and didn't know how to take no. She only backed off at the end because I had you kiss me," he groans, banging his head onto the closed locker a few times before giving him a pointed look. "Plus, you vowed never to bring it up."

"Yeah, in front of others," he laughs at the distinct memories, winking playfully when he scowls in return. "Though don't worry, you can be my dirty little secret that not only did we kiss, but you were also terrible at it, dude."

"God, please don't say that. I swear I saw her last Spring on campus, and she couldn't even look me in the eye," he shudders, only causing Jayden to laugh harder. "However, I still can't believe you didn't tell me. Are we even brothers?"

"I don't know," he rebuts, slamming the locker closed as they make their way to the tennis court. "Have I ever *called* you my brother? Though if you go around kissing your brother as well, I'm a *tad* concerned."

"Fucker, you know what I mean," he chuckles, elbowing him hard before cocking his head to the side curiously. "In seriousness, that's pretty cool that you know sign language. When did you learn, if you don't mind me asking?"

Humming for a moment, Jayden shrugs. It's been a while since he had thought about it, much less talk to another person about it. In fact, only a small handful of people knew, so he raked his brain before taking a close guesstimate. "When I was around...I would say five or six?"

"Why didn't you tell me?"

"It's not something that's important enough to tell people, is it now?" he arches a brow.

"Yeah, that's true," Trevis nods in agreement before his brows bump together as they get to their usual spot for a quick match for the day. Now that Jayden's tattoo has healed, for the most part, he's able to move more freely as he grabs a ball, bouncing it a few times first. "So…why are you telling me now?"

Ah, the million-dollar question.

Well, better to explain it now anyway and ease the blow of everything later. He figures it'll be better to ease Trevis in first before the other guys, who'll figure out once they start showing up for practice in less than half an hour as he nods across the net. "Remember that bet I won?"

"I wouldn't say won," he calls back, rolling his eyes. When Jayden stares at him deadpan while placing a hand on his hip, he throws his hands up in annoyance. "What? It's true, I was going to say Coach Winter was excited to play against him, but you beat me to it."

"Uh-huh," he nods, not looking an ounce convinced. "Sure, you were."

"What was his name again?"

"Troy Evans," he answers.

"Anyway, what about him?" he huffs in annoyance. "Are you going to serve or stand there, Harrison?"

"He's actually deaf," Jayden articulates right before serving the ball. It's a cheap tactic to serve after delivering relatively shocking news, which causes Trevis to miss the ball by a hairline, even if he had been diving for it.

Falling rather ungracefully onto the floor, he points his racquet at him with a snarl. "You were waiting to do that, weren't you?"

"You said to serve, *Scotland*," he teases, tapping the

beam of the racquet on his shoulder with a smirk. "Unless you want me just to stand there as well, I can do that for you."

Trevis only flips him off before getting up to retrieve the ball before it processes just what he had said. Whipping his head, his rather long hair hits him straight in the face. "Wait, seriously? *Him*? As in…completely deaf?"

"Yep," he confirms, and he can see the wheels turning in his head.

"What? How?" he questions, looking somewhat perplexed. Thinking back on the way he moved with ease and accuracy that matches Jayden's, Trevis did have a hard time believing it. "He certainly doesn't *play* like he can't hear."

Something about his comment rubs Jayden off the wrong way. The anger he usually feels simmers at the surface, and before he can suppress the thought, it comes spilling forth. "Well, you certainly don't seem like the type to play tennis with how you look, but here you are."

For a moment, Jayden is rather surprised by how unkempt he had been just mere seconds ago. It wasn't like him to lash out like that, unable to keep his emotions in check. What the fuck is wrong with me today?

That was all he could think of. Even Trevis is relatively surprised, arching a brow at his friend.

"Dude, chillax," he consoles, tilting his head to the side. "Awfully protective."

"Fuck, sorry," he sighs, combing his fingers through his sweat-drenched hair for a moment before it hits him as to why. Troy reminds him so much of his younger and quieter brother that he accidentally projected. "I got to speak to him, and he's really nice."

"Nah, I'm not offended; I think it's part of my charm to get me recruited," he waves off the comment as he bounces the ball a few times with a wink. "Though, you're right. Plus, I'm starting to get the full picture of why you're telling us now."

He didn't wait for his reply before serving the ball. Jayden runs towards it without missing a beat, easily swinging the racquet and the ball back. He knew that Trevis was completely serious when his jawline clenched, submerged in the game, much like Jayden was.

However, there's a reason why Jayden outshines the rest, and it's his utter focus. It's the reason why he even fell in love with the sport to begin with. When he's playing, his mind doesn't *wander*. Rather, the voices in his head finally seem to simmer down, and nothing matters more than getting that score.

It's almost as addicting as when someone first wakes up. It's when your mind is still full of cobwebs as you try to even form coherent thoughts of consciousness. It's where nothing seems to make sense yet, and you can focus on nothing more than the comfort of just waking up—

Well, unless you were Jayden with his endless nightmares, then this was close to it for him.

Moving with precise and calculated movement to save his energy, he was able to beat him in three games. Heaving, Trevis places one hand on his knees to catch his breath, panting out, "One day, I will beat your ass."

"Dream on, Trev," he chuckles. "Good game, though; I see you're getting better at your upswings."

"Work in progress," he comments. "Now, does that mean Coach paired you up already?"

"Nah, you and I know he's not the type to do that," he flicks off the comment. "In fact, I didn't get the chance to play with him personally either, though I'm itching to play against him. In the meantime, I'll be his ASL translator."

"Who's ASL translator?"

They turn in time to see Ray and Isaac striding in, with Isaac following behind with a yawn. Trevis jogs up to them, doing their usual handshake before filling them in. "Did you know Mr. Nice guy over here knows fluent ASL?"

"Shit, seriously?" Isaac frowns. "It's like he's trying to bag all the ladies with his multilanguage, huh?"

Jayden tries not to breathe a sigh of relief that no one attempted to pry regarding his past, of knowing as he thought they would. Most people are naturally curious by default, especially if you weren't born, to begin with, as Jayden flips him off. "How's this for nice?"

"Cute, though you're not fooling anyone," Ray comments. "I mean, my sister is learning ASL in her prep school rather than taking Spanish, so it's nothing new. Though, who's translator are you going to be? What did we miss?"

"You'll hear all about it soon from Coach," Trevis waves it off. "Trust me, so might as well save Jayden's breath from repeating it a thousand times when practice is about to begin soon."

"Awfully nice of you after getting your ass beat," Jayden

points out, causing his teammate to laugh. They played another match, exchanging thorough strategies and suggestions between points while they awaited for Coach and the others.

It didn't take long, and strangely enough, it was that moment when Jayden lifts his head towards the bleacher that he instantly finds Troy with ease. Though it's not too hard with his rather distinctive reddish-blond hair. What he didn't expect to see was him smiling rather widely at what appeared to be another new recruit to the team.

Dimples.

That was the first thing Jayden noticed about Troy's smile that didn't show in the few interactions they had. The second was that he's never seen Troy smile that widely before. Frequently, he's rather jumpy or flushed, his smile never taking up his face to show those deep crevices on his cheeks.

The third thing Jayden noticed was how cute he looks, though he would never admit it.

If there's one rule he has, it is to not fuck a teammate. It'll only complicate things, especially if they'll be playing in teams of doubles. Another rule was that dating was entirely out of the question, as he had already known himself well enough that he couldn't date. He was too emotionally stunted in his belief.

Even if it did to appease his parents, it'll be a woman at the end of the day—someone that can give them grandchildren they so desperately have been hinting at, especially his mother. However, Jayden can't seem to keep his eyes off him, his frown only deepening in the process.

It wasn't as if Troy was his type by any means. Through his series of one-night stands with no strings attached, they often weren't shy but adventurous. They didn't turn red at the drop of a hat, nor did they go on long walks to the beach and rather spend their time with one close friend. In the end, he settles that it is all in his head.

Seeming to sense Jayden's eyes on him, Troy turns in time and locks eyes with him.

Dull grey against livid bright green.

Jayden wishes there is a word to truly say how vibrant Troy's eyes are. It's unlike anything he's ever seen from the moment they had bumped into one another. They're utterly hypnotizing, seeming to shimmer when the sunlight hits them when they were at the beach.

It's lush green like the forest.

Just like—

Instantly, Jayden is snapped out of his daze when sees the way Troy flushes again; glancing away that Jayden notices he has a notebook with him, communicating with the person he's sitting next to with it. Another frown makes its way to his face as he hasn't thought about his past before, not when he was fully conscious. The person seems to turn, looking puzzled for a moment before smiling.

Jayden offers a façade, friendly smile as he makes his way over to where his friends were sitting with just a few minutes to spare. A scowl makes its way to his face when he realizes that while all his teammates were laughing and joking around, Trevis seems to be grinning him ear-to-ear, wagging his eyebrow, which usually means nothing good.

Taking his phone off the bleacher, he sits down next to him and resists the need to punch him when he wraps his rather sweaty arm around him, holding him in a chokehold as he whispers, "I can't help but notice you staring at a certain someone. A certain someone that you played a knight in shining armor protecting him before."

"Not a word," he grits out in warning. "Even if I was, though I'm not, it doesn't matter."

"Whatever do you mean?"

"You know what my two rules," he deadpans. "I'm not sleeping with a teammate no matter what, nor will I date anyone either. Shit's too complicated once things end, and I don't want to get involved in all that jazz."

"What about the power of love?" he teases, batting his eyes. Opening his mouth, he was cut off by his phone just as Coach Winter came in with his clipboard. He let out a curse, forgetting to put it on silence this morning as he hurries to mute it before practice begins.

What he didn't expect was for his father to be calling him.

Instantly, his mood sours tremendously, and his heart drops straight down to his stomach.

CHAPTER TWELVE

Shit on a fucking stick.

Of all the damn times they had decided it'll be a good time to call, it just had to be now. Instantly, his skin starts to prick. The feeling threatens to take hold of him, choking him alive until he can't even breathe. This feeling of helplessness and anxiousness takes hold of him like every Friday when he had to go over for dinner—

Even at the sound of their voices.

It makes it worse that he never did call his parents back either with a proper explanation of why he had canceled dinner on Friday night. Though he didn't want to pick it up, the last thing he would want is for his parents to come to campus. Even the mere thought made him wince before he bites his tongue for even thinking so.

After all, his parents had done everything for him, so the least he can do is suck it up—

Play up as Mr. Nice, even if it's for a few minutes.

He didn't want to tell them it had been because of the nightmare he had that morning, the same one he had since he was a child that he kept hiding from his parents. After helping Coach decide to be Troy's interpreter as well, he didn't have the strength to go back home.

So, he *lied* despite it killing him.

He lied, saying he didn't feel good and would call back without explaining much regarding it. However, it completely slipped his mind to call, following everything that had happened with Troy. For a moment, he thought of sending it to voice mail, but it would only make matters worse.

His father knew he had practice because he stayed on top of all his games with Coach. So, it must be important. Instantly, his back straightens, and his heart kicks into overdrive for completely different reasoning altogether.

Did something happen back at home?

Once more, the feeling of being lost of control completely grips him and spirals him into madness.

Had mother finally—

His stomach churns and he refuses to waver on that thought. He slowly gets up from his seat, causing Trevis to look over at him with a frown. "Where are you going? Coach is going to set us in pairs soon and match us up based on our play during tryouts."

"I know," he murmurs, forcing himself to remain calm. "Though, I have to take this. Parents."

"Ah," he nods, completely understanding. "Yeah, I'm sure Coach would understand. I'll let him now."

"If Troy is looking for me, let me know," he says. "I'll be in the locker room."

When Trevis gives him a devious-like smile, he slaps

his friend hard on the back in thanks, causing him to grunt in pain. Winking when the smile turns into a full-fledged scowl, Jayden jogs out of the room and into the locker room for some privacy. Ensuring that the room is completely empty, he takes a seat.

Taking a deep breath, Jayden presses the green button and presses it to his ear and, preparing for a battle. He didn't even get to greet his father when he speaks first. "Well, look who finally decided to pick up."

The stern and judgmental tone on the other line made him bite the inside of his mouth, allowing the metallic taste of metal to somewhat keep him at ease. No matter what, the feeling of dread and guilt never seems to leave whenever Jayden speaks to his parents.

"Hey, Dad," he says, quickly adapting a rather preppy façade no matter what he's feeling on the inside. "Sorry about not being able to come Friday night for dinner or calling over the weekend. I completely got sidetracked with tryouts; I'm sure Coach will fill you in soon."

"Yes, he already told me everything," he clips.

Of course he did, Jayden thought.

Really, there's nothing that happens inside of Columbia University, especially inside of Harold Harrington Tennis Center, without his father knowing. After all, he had been the one to donate close to six million dollars to construct the whole dome. On top of that, the equipment and other generous donations. It's the reason it was named after his father, a blinding reminder to Jayden every time of what his parents had done for him.

Despite what he had done.

"Is everything okay back at home?" he finds himself asking.

"Your mother has been worrying immensely, relapses if you will," he states on the other line. Jayden flinches, knowing it was because of his not showing up that had probably set her off. "Currently, she's back on medication, especially with the...anniversary coming up."

Even now, it's still an unspoken incident they never touched upon

Fuck.

Instantly, he feels nauseated and sick to his stomach at his father's words because he feels responsible for what happened. Still, he thought it'd be better now as it's been close to a decade since the incident that changed their whole family.

He thought that he could just not come to at *least* one dinner.

"Should I come back home?" he questions, waiting with bated breath. Every fiber in his body aches, and it's like he's thirteen all over again. His throat burns, and the compulsive need to do something with his anger overrides him.

"No, you have an important game coming up in two weeks; your mother knows that," his father acknowledges on the other side. "However, I will not stand you upsetting her either. She's already been through a lot, Jayden."

"I know."

God, he knows better than anyone else which is why he wants to prove to them he changed. He's different since they completely left their past in London the same year to start again as the Mr. Nice Guy.

He's the man the neighbors love. The men who held doors open for all his dates and the golden boy with perfect grades and a bright career in tennis. He's the guy who offered women his shoulder to cry on and brought them flowers for occasions.

Not the reckless, obsessive adrenaline junkie that cost him—his parents—everything.

He only drank in moderation and has little one-night affairs and tattoos when things get tough. He was fine hiding between a mask, displaying the image he tried to project most of the time and the level he'd been striving his entire life to live up to—

The façade he worked so hard to maintain.

Christ, if only people knew the truth.

How hard he worked to be this dependable, police nice guy that everyone could rely on.

How badly he fought to actually suppress those wild urges that arouses more often than not. How frustrating it was to dutifully play the part of the rich, prodigal son, good friend, and everything in between.

Like most people, he wasn't perfect, having slipped up a few times. Sometimes, the need to truly let go couldn't be ignored. He had to ease it however he can and used tattoos and other reckless stunts like fighting to ease that. Jayden had heard that people often used sex or violence as an outlet for release, as a way to feel alive and in control.

Hell, he can't even deny that as he often fought to soothe the dark restlessly part of himself he hid.

Sex, on the other hand, didn't achieve the same result.

"Then you know what to do," his father comments, snapping Jayden back to reality. "I'm only able to call you because I just dropped her off at Dr. Schnitz. I advise you to call her tonight and pretend you don't know. I also expect you to be home this Friday for dinner at the very least, after class and practice."

"I will," he murmurs.

"I heard also you're working with an impaired player? As his translator? What's that about?"

Fuck.

Pressing his lips for a moment, he lets out a small sigh. There's no point in trying to sugarcoat or hide things either. "Yeah, his name is Troy Evans, just three years younger than me from Sydney. I'm sure Coach already told you, but he seems to have a lot of potential from his playstyle."

"Hm," he hums on the other side. "Still, you didn't have to do it."

"I know," he answers, lowering his head. Even at twenty-three years old, he hates how small he felt when he spoken to his father. Even with his mother, he had to dance around most of the sensitive topics in fear of triggering her anxiety. If you were to ask Jayden, he wouldn't be able to tell you when they last had a genuine talk.

"You don't owe him anything."

I owe you both everything.

He stops himself from speaking, balling his hands into

a fist. He hated for even thinking that. His father had everything in Syndey with an amazing start-up and rocketing his new company in being a billion-dollar company. His mother loved it there as well. They were the perfect family until they weren't because of him. "I know."

There's a long pause before his father speaks. "Will this distract you from the games?"

"No, it's nothing I can't handle," he admits, which is the truth. "I'm just translating what Coach said."

"Still, you don't owe him anything, much less doing this for free, Jayden."

"If my performance starts to waver, I'll let Coach know," he clarifies before asking the million-dollar question that had been on his mind since his father told him what happened. "How's...mother since Friday? It's nothing too bad, right?"

"She's doing...better now," he settles with. "Though I was rather upset you canceled dinner at the last minute and didn't call as you had promised. She said it's not like you and showed signs of relapse of her depression and hysteria which is why I drove her there."

"Yeah, I'll make it up to her," he says. "Thank you, Dad."

"Come Thursday for dinner."

"I will."

With that, he hangs up, and it takes everything inside Jayden not to snap because someone might hear. He rakes his hair back, counting to ten in hopes of easing the impulsive desire to erase how he's feeling threatens to spill—

The need to feel alive and do something only he can do takes hold that reminds him *he's* in control.

Calming himself down enough and not wanting others to pry, he makes his way out to practice again. Luckily, it seems the new recruit had taken in using a pen and notebook to communicate with Troy. Though Coach glanced at Jayden, he didn't push in, asking why he was out either.

Jayden was more than thankful that Trevis had been busy in his competitive nature to notice his mood dipping since he came back from the call. The last thing he wanted was for anyone to figure out the façade he had worked hard to compose.

While he thought no one noticed, someone *had*—a certain man with lush green eyes.

It wasn't until after practice that Jayden swings the corner of the locker room and completely bumps into someone. Instantly, his hand goes out steady the other person by the arm before glancing down to see who it was.

"Really now, Troy," Jayden signs with a smile, arching his brow playfully after making sure Troy was steady enough before continuing. "It seems we bump into one another everywhere we go, huh? Is everything okay?"

Staring up at Jayden, Troy could *sense* something was rather off with him since he came back from the locker room, though he didn't know what nor did he want to push it either. The look of anguish and kept wrath Troy knew *too* well.

Troy knew pain when he saw it, and for some reason, it gnaw away at him until it was all he could think about. It's almost as if he fears what he'd do next which is why he had followed him to the locker room when everyone had left.

In fact, he even had this grand speech he was going to sign up for until now.

"I should…be asking you," Troy slowly signs back, pressing his lips together as he feels the tip of his ear growing red. It wasn't what he had in mind, but it seems his hands had a mind of their own. When he sees Jayden quietly staring at him, he quickly continues. "It's just…your play has been off today. So, I was worried. With pair-ups coming up soon, I was hoping to play with you."

Once more, Jayden is surprised. Never once had someone noticed. Still, he shakes it off.

"Yeah, everything is fine," he signs, nodding at the same time. "Did you need something from me or did Coach say something you didn't understand either? I apologize for not being there earlier. Some emergency came up, though I'm willing to play against you tomorrow during practice."

"Oh, no, you don't need to apologize," he fumbles in signing. "My friend, Benjamin, helped."

"I see," he smiles again. "I'm sorry I let you down, though that's nice you had someone."

Something about his smile makes Troy's heart dully ache, and he knows he needs to do *something*. Troy wanted to tell him that he didn't let him down and that he was worried by the look on his face. However, he didn't seem as if it was right either.

What can he do?

He had to sign something—anything.

"Actually, do you want to go running together before practice tomorrow to make…make it up?"

CHAPTER THIRTEEN

What Troy would have traded right now to be back at his dorm, sleeping his Wednesday morning away.

The sand is rough and rugged against his feet, packed down by the pebbling rain that had been plummeting Boston all morning. It somewhat helps with the heat wave, which Troy was relatively glad about. He welcomes the chill in the air as it settles onto his skin, hoping it will help the scorching heat in his chest—

Which prompted to soon spread to his cheek when Jayden strips off his shirt casually while continuing to run ahead of him. Despite this being the second day of running, Troy hadn't realized how out of shape he was until he realized that Jayden could make four miles of running look like child's play.

By the time they reach their destination, Troy feels as if his feet are moments from falling off from tracking in the sand. Up until this exact point in his life, Troy had prided himself in thinking he was quite athletic and fit.

Though now?

He's starting to think otherwise, especially when

comparing himself to Jayden, while trying not to stare once he turns to him. It's a bit hard, too, especially with the sun starting to come up. His body is coated in sweat, showcasing his six-packs and glistening muscles.

God, even his tattoos are near perfection.

It's almost too much, especially when his cock starts to harden as he turns his attention to the ocean. It doesn't help when he realizes moments later that Jayden walked up to him, cocking his head to the side playfully before squatting down to where Troy is now completely sitting in the hot sand.

"Tired already?" he signs with a humorous grin.

"I'm convinced you're a robot," he signs in return, narrowing his eyes when his shoulders shake. An indication of laughter that Troy has longed forgotten of being able to hear but wants to do so at that moment.

"We really need to work up your cardio," Jayden states through his hands, getting up and burying his feet into the sand. "If you're going to be my partner, you should be in sync with me if we want to be partners and get scouted to be Pro after college."

"Do you not want to go pro?" Troy questions curiously. Some tennis players want to go pro, while others do it just for fun and attend college for free. However, Troy can't help but feel it would be a waste of his talents.

Rather than answering, he turns the question around. "I mean, do you?"

Without thinking twice, Troy nods eagerly. It's been his dream for a long time as he remembered seeing his first game when he was only seven. It wasn't about fame or fortune but proving to the world that having a disability wouldn't define or slow him down.

He wants to prove to others it's possible.

"Yeah," Troy nods. "I want to become the world's first deaf professional tennis player.'"

"First, huh?"

Troy knows that Jayden didn't mean it in a harsh way. It's the same way his family had asked if he had a Plan B to fall back on; however, he knows he's always been a dreamer over a realistic, dreaming until it's reality.

"I have to dream big," he grins, puffing out his chest. "It is bad to dream?"

"Well, you also have to consider what's realistic, as my parents have told me," he signs, and Troy swore that once he signs the word 'parent,' something in the atmosphere changes around them. "Do you have a Plan B or C?"

"No, not in particular," he signs, shaking his hand before quickly aiding his choice upon Jayden arching a brow. "I mean, if I do, it means I'm not believing myself of this working out first, right? I know it's dumb to probably think that way, but I don't know...something feels right to me about it."

"What about your major?" he asks with a slight frown. "Are you not a social work major?"

"Oh, I'm quite passionate about helping others," he signs in confirmation. "However, it's more so that I needed to have a major chosen by sophomore year for my continuation at Columbia and scholarship requirements."

"Do you think hard work alone would get you through

it?" Jayden asks through his hand, trying not to show how bitter it sounds. He didn't know why he was even asking, showing this side of him that seems to slip out so easily when it's him.

Perhaps it's because he reminds him so much of—

"No," Troy signs, his eyes piercing his. "Working hard alone doesn't assure that you'll achieve your dreams. Actually, there are many cases that you might not happen, but…even so…working hard, trying, and achieving something is some consolation at the least. I want to live with no regrets, after all."

Jayden swears he stopped breathing at that moment.

To live without any regrets.

How much those words meant to him more than anything else upon knowing how short life can be.

"So what's the plan to become pro?" he questions curiously, and there isn't any judgment either. He has seen rather just curiosity when speaking to Quinn about his goals and ambitions. "How will you catch the eyes of recruiters?"

"I'm hoping my rankings in games would help, especially seeing I can play solo or with a team," he explains with his hands. He buries his feet into the sand until it's up to his ankle. "Given that I had only chosen to finally chase my dreams recently with Quinn pushing me alongside my parents to try out for recruitment, what do I know what would have happened if I applied to tryouts my first year."

It's something Troy has learned about in one of his classes—Atychiphobia.

It's the reason why some people who are so passionate

about something never take the jump. It's not because of laziness but rather their fears holding them back. So long as they don't try, then you can never really fail.

Something he can relate to deeply.

What if this didn't work out?

What if he realizes how bad he was?

What if other scouters brushed by him because he's deaf?

"It's better to not focus on the what-ifs…just focus on what-is," Jayden signs, breaking Troy out of his thoughts. A small smile appears when Jayden signs the quote, memories flooding in. A sense of peace washed over him for the first time since his dad had called. It's strange just how similar they are without trying, and perhaps that is why he always allows his façade to slip when near him.

At least, that's what he tells himself.

The smile, paired with the quote, makes Troy's heart skip a beat.

Focus on what-is.

It's almost as if Jayden could read his muddled mind, giving him the encouragement he needs.

What is right now is that he made it through tryouts.

What is right now is that he's giving it his all.

What is right now is that he's the first deaf student to try out, which is a feat.

"I like that."

"What are partners for?"

"We're…partners?" he signs, his mouth falling for a moment. "You want to be my partner?"

"Well, did you think I would go running with you out of whim?" he questions, adding a few question marks. "Your playstyle is rather unique where even Coach was intrigued to playing with you, so I figure we can be paired up for the season."

"Are you sure?" he questions with wide eyes. "What about the trial period?"

"Positive," he nods. "We might as well be paired for a duo match first and go from there. We've had a practice round yesterday, and I think we'll do well together, based on our playstyle. No one put me up to it if you're wondering."

"How did you know I was going to ask?"

At that, he shrugs. There's not a chance Jayden would tell him how easy it is to read him. The last thing that happened was with Weston only. "I just had a hunch, and the answer is no; I just like spending time with you."

"So are you suggesting we go running every morning together then?" he signs, still trying to even his breathing and the blush creeping on his face. Truthfully, Troy also enjoys learning more about Jayden but doesn't have the guts to confess it with ease as he did. A glimmer of hope passes in his eyes, especially of being able to see Jayden every day. However, Troy tells himself it's because he admires him.

Nothing more, nothing less.

"If you want," he signs. "You need to work on those muscles if you want to go pro."

For a moment, he remembers that Jayden has never told him if he wants to go pro but gets distracted when he holds his hand to help him up. Troy clasps his and then hoists him up. Clumsily, he almost crashed into his chest due to his loss of footing in the sand if it wasn't for Jayden. With ease and precision, he steadies him with one hand on his arms, and electricity runs through every fiber of his body.

It's the most bizarre sensation ever, and his breath hitches when he stares into those bright green eyes.

"Sorry," Troy signs apologetically, though every part of him seems to die on the inside for embarrassing himself once more. Really, he never seems to be able to catch a break when it comes to not making a fool of himself in front of Jayden.

"You should be careful regarding your footing," he scolds lightly, assessing him. "Are you okay?"

"Yeah," he nods as a confirmation. "Quinn is convinced I'm the only person on Earth able to trip on air."

"I wouldn't be surprised," he shakes his head after signing. Once Troy finally catches his breath in time, they start their light jogging back to where they had started. Luckily enough, Jayden had slowed down tremendously.

Paired with how they even ran into the water to help cool off, it helped greatly.

Perhaps one day, Troy would learn how to swim. It still baffles him why he didn't learn, given how much he loved the water, but it's always one thing or another that has stopped him from doing it.

"So are we meeting tomorrow at the same time?" Troy asks, circling back to the question from earlier. He hoped it didn't come off too clingy either, but he hoped to have a partner like his playstyle. "Since we might have a better chance of being paired for matches?"

"Oh, yeah, but actually," Jayden signs, pressing his lips into a thin line. For a moment, he seems to be wavering between telling him or not before jumping the gun. "I won't be able to go running with you tomorrow morning, though."

"Why?" he asks curiously, quickly retracing upon realizing he might be prying. If there's one thing he hates, it makes anyone uncomfortable, especially knowing firsthand the hardship that comes with it. "You don't have to answer if you do not wish to do so."

"No, it's fine," he signs, though it looks rather forced. While his hands are saying one thing, Troy notices that his facial and body expression are saying otherwise. "I'm going to visit my parents tomorrow to meet up for last week's weekly dinner, so I won't be able to. I already got a sign-off with Coach, though he wasn't happy with it."

"Right, I forgot they live so close," he signs. What Troy would give to have his parents live so close if it wasn't for his education and the scholarship he received. "That must be nice to see them every week, huh?"

"Yeah," he replies. Something about his clipped and short reply before shoving his hands into his pocket catches Troy off. It's the same look from two days ago, and it guts him again to see that anguish on his face.

Perhaps he doesn't have a good relationship with his parents.

The thought makes Troy freeze up, especially if it is because he caused his bleak mood.

"That's okay. So, what are you doing after this?" he quickly signs the first thing that came to his head. He tries to keep up a rather friendly smile, hoping he won't do anything crazy. "I'm going to shower first thing back at the dorm since Quinn and I are planning to meet up for brunch in about two hours at the city square if you want to join."

He prayed he'd accept because seeing him like this didn't sit well at all.

"I'm going to hang here for a bit first since I'm not really hungry," he answers before using his hand to brush his hair back. Troy knew he was an adult who could care for himself, but he didn't want him to do something crazy.

"Are you sure?"

"Yeah, I'll text you later then," he states. "Enjoy your day with Quinn."

Then, he watches Jayden making his way over to the almost eighty-meter rock groyne that stretches out into the ocean. Without missing a beat, he follows; though a bit wobbly due to the wet rocks, he still manages to follow behind once he finds his gripping.

He should have reached for his shoes first, but he couldn't stop himself either.

Over the crashing waves, Jayden must not have heard him coming. He didn't even know why he was running for him. It wasn't as if anything would happen to him, but he couldn't help but wonder what would happen if he slipped and bumped his head.

What then? It's not as if Troy would be able to go after him as he can't swim.

He didn't want to be a nuisance, and certainly not the reason for upsetting Jayden either to do something crazy. He knew firsthand how it felt and the burden one might carry as well with it; he has seen it the night everything changed for him.

No, he couldn't allow it to happen.

Troy is able to reach halfway, trying to quickly close the distance between them and make up an excuse again to hang out a bit longer because every fiber in his body tells him to do so. Only for him to lose his footing on a rock. His eyes widen in shock, and his mouth parts, though not a word slips out his mouth.

Then, he hits the water.

CHAPTER FOURTEEN

Jayden can only recount two times in his life that he had been terrified in his twenty-three on Earth.

The first time happened when Weston went missing, and so did the events that followed.

The second time was shortly after his mom's first mental breakdown and the pills in her hands.

Now?

It was as if he was living it all over again—of Weston and watching the outcome—before he quickly dives into the water after Troy when he realizes he was sinking. If he had realized Troy was following after him, he wouldn't have come.

Why did he follow him?

What was the point?

"Fuck," he curses, throwing his wallet, car keys, and phone onto the rock line before jumping in without a second thought. As it was only shy of eight in the morning, there wasn't anyone who might call for help either.

Why would Troy follow him when he can't swim?

The cold water is frigid on his skin, and his stomach churns by how eerily it feels to his dreams, which are a fabrication of his living hell. The water feels like heavy braces, his demons wanting to weigh him down after what happened that night, but he had to fight away the nightmares at bay.

Right now, it's not about him.

He paddles his legs downward, forcing his eyes to open while ignoring the stinging in his eyes from the salt water. Memories assault him like the water, but he brushes past them as his eyes focus on Troy's body.

At that moment, he's all that matters.

Upon getting a firm hold on his body, he makes his way back up while holding Troy's body close. Once he can break through the water's surface, they both take a large intake of air as he paddles to a low rock groyne.

The air filling Troy's lungs immediately sends him into a coughing fit, water spewing forth before looking over at where Jayden is sitting. He has never seen Jayden so distraught, and guilt eats him up when they get to the rock's shoreline.

His eyes are still blurry as he looks at Jayden, his lips pressed into a thin line.

Jayden is yelling, but nothing but silence greets Troy's ears except for a ringing. The veins on Jayden's neck are raised, and his face is also turning red. He had thrown his hands up in the air, pacing on the small rocks. Despite not hearing a single thing, it made him flinch, the vibration and heat in his body telling him everything he needed to know about how upset he was.

Then, upon composing themselves a bit more, he goes into a tangent with his hands, signing faster than Quinn, which Troy didn't think was possible. "Are you out of your mind? Why would you chase me out into the ocean where you could have fallen and died? You shouldn't have done that, especially knowing I can't hear you over the ocean. You are never to do that again, do you understand me?"

"I…I'm sorry," Troy lamely signs, pressing his lips thinly together to be scolded like that. He didn't mean to fall in, either. However, it sort of happened because of the layout of the rocks, paired with it being wet from yesterday's rain and the crashing of the ocean water. "I didn't…mean to."

They then stare at one another, unblinking and soaked from head to toe.

"Why did you follow after me?" he signs out, his eyes narrowed. "When you can't even swim?"

"You looked…upset," he finishes, albeit a bit meekly after what happened.

"So?"

"I wanted to make sure you're okay," he informs him. He didn't want to go into detail regarding how much it had bothered him either. "I didn't mean to fall; I'm sorry for causing trouble."

Jayden's nose flares at his confession and how genuine it sounds. It's how his brother…

God, he can't even think about it without losing control once more. He had been yelling rather than signing because he didn't think he could capture everything he wanted to say in the heat of the moment.

A small part of him didn't want him to even sign afterward of the anger he felt, but he had to.

"You don't need to apologize. I know you mean well," Jayden signs with a loud sigh, shaking his head. He had calmed down tremendously since then, and now his heart had stopped speeding like that. "Can you promise me never to do that again?"

"As long as you promise not to throw yourself in front of danger either," he signs in return.

"I would have been fine because I can *fucking* swim," he grits out through narrowed eyes. Again, something about this side of Jayden seems so much more genuine to Troy. "I didn't realize this was a bargain either."

When Troy only chuckles between another cough, Jayden only clenches his jaw while Troy takes up his hands to clear the misunderstanding. It's not his comment that he had found humorous, but something else entirely. "You should be like this more."

"Concerned and angry?"

"No," he shakes his head. "Honest and just...*you*."

Again, they stare at one another—grey again green.

If only Troy knew the effect his statement had just now on someone like Jayden, who had worked on ensuring he never allowed his façade to slip. He had worked hard to become who he is, and in just a week since Troy, it came crumbling down.

He didn't know what he should be doing with that information either.

"Let's go back to the shores," he commands through

his hands. He bends down to grab his belongings before returning to where Troy is still sitting on the rock. He stares at the shore for a moment before their eyes meet. "Can you stand on your own?"

"Yeah, I think so," he says and manages to get up. Still reeling from earlier, his knees grow weak right before Jayden reaches over and grabs his hands into his. His eyes widen, his blush spreading like wildfire but quickly shaking it away.

No, he's holding your hand to make sure you don't fall, Troy scolds himself.

He shouldn't be acting like some sort of lovesick puppy. Staring at his hand around his, Troy realizes how rougher and larger they are. Squeezing his hands, they slowly make their way back every so slowly.

Something touches Troy's heart when, occasionally, he turns to ensure he's okay while pointing at some unruly rocks that might be hard to walk on. A small part of him couldn't help but have a rather heavy heart that they were in this situation *because* of him.

Once they reach the shoreline, Jayden lets go of his hand. Instantly, coldness seems to settle over, and a feeling of loneliness. It's a feeling he's never felt before, but he shakes it off while watching Jayden grabbing their shoes.

"Thank you," he smiles.

"Put your shoes on; we're going back to my place," he states once they get back onto the shores.

"What?"

"It's closer to my place than back on campus. Plus, probably better than walking around to your dorm drenched from head to tail," he signs. "You can shower there while I throw your clothes into the shower. I'll let you borrow my clothes."

"Are you sure you're okay with that?" he signs in shock.

"Yeah, it's not a big deal since it'll be faster and less of a hassle," he says as Troy follows behind him. It's been a while since he had invited anyone up there. Most of the time, it would be just him, or he would be crashing at the place the team members had rented out. "I live just a few blocks anyway. Do you want to do a light jog there?"

"Okay."

By the time they got into the apartment's elevator, it suddenly became very real what was happening. Nervously, Troy bites his lips, trying not to show just how nervous he is. It's a rather big step because the last time he was alone with another boy, something unimaginable happened.

The reason why he had been trying to deny the past and everything that it brought with it.

However, something about Jayden puts him at ease as the scent of his apartment floods him. It's a relatively small place, but perfect for someone in college with one bedroom. Awkwardly waddling in, he looks around the living room. Black and white framed photos decorate the walls and a bunch of papers on the coffee table.

Upon closer inspection, Troy is taken aback by the sketches. They were beautifully adorned, full of detail that stole his breath away, just like the tattoos on Jayden's body. He resists the urge to pick it up, eagerly drinking everything in.

Did he design these?

"On the left is the shower," Jayden says, jolting Troy out

of his daze as he turns his attention to him after cracking up the heat. "You can go first since you have somewhere to be, and I don't want you to catch a cold either. In the meantime, I'll find you something to wear."

With that, Troy makes his way inside after signing thank you.

He really did owe Jayden for doing all this. After showering, he pokes his head out to see clothes waiting for him outside as he puts them on. It's only after he realizes they're too close to his sizing actually to be his.

Something about whose clothes it is makes his stomach twist, a frown readily appearing on his face.

Jealousy.

He can't even remember the last time he felt jealous and wonders why. Still, it's not his place to ask; he should be thankful for their friendship. Opening the door, he returns to find Jayden on his phone while standing with a towel on the floor.

It doesn't make it better that he's just in his boxers.

Troy goes on to bite the inside of his cheek, hoping it'll stop the flushness that wants to spread. He shouldn't be gawking at his tennis partner, especially when there are a million more reasons why it'll be wrong.

However, his stupid heart just didn't know how to listen and for once, he wanted to accept what he had denied this whole time. Swallowing the growing lump, he closes the distance while trying to keep himself calm and collected.

"Thank you again for letting me use your shower," he meekly signs with a small smile.

"It's not a big deal. Do the clothes fit okay?"

"Yeah," he replies, and despite pinching his own hand, it's not enough to keep his body from signing. "Are these your clothes by chance?"

"No," he shakes his head. "I think it's Trevis' when he was crashing at my place one time after too many drinks, and I had to haul his ass here because he was too drunk to drive. I have to say, the girl he was planning to take home? She was not happy in the slightest."

Trevis.

Raking his mind for a moment, Troy remembers that he was his friend who played during tryouts. Strangely, that's enough to settle his busy mind, and even though he shouldn't be relieved about it, it still did.

"Oh," he only signs. "Yeah, they fit well."

"Your clothes won't be able to dry in time for you to meet with Quinn, though," he replies. With how much sand was also inside, he still needed to dump most out before throwing it in. "If you want, I can drop it off tomorrow when I drive home from my parents."

"That won't be necessary," he shakes his head. "You can give it to me Friday in the morning."

"I also was able to check your phone, and it is still working, luckily enough," he states. "I hope you don't mind that I picked up your facetime call before. I didn't tell her anything but that you needed to shower because sand got everywhere. Quinn said she was off class early and could meet you at my place soon."

"I don't mind," he smiles. "Really, I don't know how I should thank you."

"You don't *ever* do that again," he signs, arching a brow. Troy can see how tense he is, especially when he strides toward him. His stormy grey eyes widen even further when he backs him up against the wall, caging him in. "I mean it, Troy. That's how you can thank me; you can't do anything like that again, you hear me?"

Meekly, he nods, and his cock thickens slightly at how his eyes look. They're so vibrant and luscious, his movement so commanding that he's wholly swept up now. Staring at one another, it almost feels as if there's been a spell that's been cast over. Neither one of them can say anything. It's like there's a magnetic force despite both knowing they shouldn't be doing this.

More than anything else, Troy *wants* Jayden to kiss him.

It wasn't like him at all, but there's something to Jayden that doesn't make sense. It's from the way his body reacts all the way down to how he had saved him. Their lips are inches apart when the intercom rings, signaling that Quinn is already here. It snaps both out of their daze as Jayden backs away.

"I'm going to shower first so you can close the door behind you when you leave. It locks," he signs before walking off first. Troy buries his head into his hands for a moment before tugging at the end of his hair.

What the hell was that about?

Honestly, he wasn't entirely sure how he would survive seeing him two days before practice for their run. Not to mention, they're going to be seeing each other every day because their partner will be so much worse.

Hopefully, Quinn might be able to be a distraction from these budding feelings inside of him. Though he should have known better than his best friend would make it so much worse by teasing him the rest of the day.

God forbid she finds out about the almost kiss and how much Mr. Nice really isn't what he said he is—

Not to mention how much Troy *wished* to see that side of him more. The side that Jayden had hidden behind being Mr. Nice, which was only revealed to him alone and the way his heart sped wildly. He still couldn't wrap around that not only did Jayden save him…but they had almost kissed.

What did I sign up for? Troy questions with a heavy sigh.

CHAPTER FIFTEEN

From the way Quinn had been jabbing a finger on his cheek for the past hour, Troy was more than surprised it didn't cave in as he let out a sigh. Honestly, he didn't even know how to answer his best friend's question, much less comprehend it himself.

Shooting the hyperactive girl a glare, she only pouts in return.

"You can't keep it a secret forever," she pouts, signing with tenseness. She even went as far as to cross her arms like a child for a moment, leaning back into the diner's leather couch for a moment before shooting back up. "It's not as if I'm going to judge you or anything."

"I think my hands are going to cramp by how much I've been signing it," he signs, rolling his eyes. "Nothing happened between Jayden and me. We went running, I accidentally fell into the water, and he saved me. These are one of his teammate's clothing."

He watches in the way her eyes narrow. "Why were you flustered than when I came up for you?"

"It's because of the run before," he signs after taking a long pause to drink his cup of coffee. With that, Quinn's pointer and pinkie fingers extend and thrust the hand forward to signify the word he knows all too well.

Bullshit.

For a moment, he feels as if they're high schoolers again while letting out another exasperated sigh. However, she had another thing coming if she thought he would tell her the actual reason. It was already quite a surprise that they almost kissed.

Or was he imagining it?

Hell, the whole morning seemed like a fever dream since he was saved

The way he dragged him out of the water.

The way his face had gone completely red.

The way he looked so heart-wrenched and *gutted*.

Not to mention the way his heart skipped a beat and, more than anything else—

He not only found himself wishing to hear it all but wandering what would have happened if Quinn hadn't interrupted the moment. The revelation of his wishes startled him more than he'd like to admit out loud.

As he was quite out of the loop when it comes to who's dating who on the college campus, mainly choosing to keep to himself and his small group of friends, he didn't know that Jayden might swing both ways.

Why did that make him *happy*?

Troy had to hold his tongue from asking Quinn if she knew of his sexual orientation, convincing himself that it didn't matter. There were a hundred reasons why letting whatever he thought would happen was a bad idea.

The most obvious was that they were teammates.

He knows it'll come to not only bite him in the ass, but it's a recipe for heartbreak. However, he couldn't stop thinking about this morning and the events leading up to now. For all he knew, this could be the work of the suspension bridge effect, where he had confused the feeling of fear from drowning with excitement and love for him.

After all, what more can it mean?

Sure, he had this reckless side of him that no one seemed to notice aside from Troy, and he was sweet when he wanted to be; it didn't make any sense. He was good-looking but barely conversed enough for it to be anything more.

Right?

"Honestly," he finally signs out, his hands feeling rather slow and heavy. He supposes it was better to confine in someone to help his somewhat murky mind this morning. "I don't even know what to make of everything."

"What do you mean?" she signs, and her brows bump together. Her mouth parts as she immediately leans in, going on a tangent. "Did he do something to make you uncomfortable? If he did, you let me know because I'll—"

Troy immediately reaches out to grab her hand, shaking his head furiously and defensively.

"No, nothing like that," he affirms, looking around the deserted diner with slumped shoulders. If there was one thing Troy was terrible at, it was keeping a secret above all things, especially to Quinn and his parents. "Do you promise not to utter a word?"

"With my mouth and hands, yes," she joshes.

"Morse code with your eyes?"

"You know damn well I don't," she signs, batting her eye ferociously with breaks here and there to pull on his legs. He rolls his eyes, composing himself for a moment before going onto a tangent regarding what happened.

Even the almost kiss that he wasn't entirely sure what to make of it either.

The only thing he left out in-depth was that the whole Mr. Nice Guy persona might very well be a façade, alongside his rather impulsive nature, like getting tattoos and wanting to jump off ledges without thinking twice.

By the end, he was relatively amused that his chattery best friend was completely quiet, her hand entirely still with her mouth hanging open and then closed. Troy finishes the last bite of his corned harsh before signing, "Eart to Quinn? Did I short-circuit your brain?"

"Kind of," she admits, looking up at the ceiling for a moment. "I mean, can you blame me?"

"I know, it seems like something out of a TV series," he signs, unsure if that was good or bad. He watches as she calls for the waiter to get a check while Troy shuffles for his wallet as it's his turn to pay. He's thankful at the very least, they didn't eat out every day, or he would be completely broken by the blackhole that was Quinn's stomach.

"Or an MM romance novel," she grins after signing, putting her cheek rather dreamily for a moment. After paying, they leave their usual diner to take the train line towards the mall. "So…Jayden has a little crush on you if that's what I'm getting at then."

"Are you insane?" he signs wildly, his eyes widening as his heart skips a beat. Even if he did, which Troy convinced himself that is not the case, it still wouldn't make sense to dive right into any relationship when he is on his way to becoming a pro player. "We barely even know each other."

"Physical attraction is what usually starts it off into something more if you catch my drift," she replies before wiggling her brows playfully, making a rather inappropriate gesture before laughing based on how her shoulder shakes. "I mean, I see the way he stares at you, and if I were a guy, I'd totally go for you."

He squints, his lips puckering. "You would?"

"Well…okay, no, I'll go for someone like Jayden," she confesses rather quality. "No offense; you're cute, but you know I'm a sucker for broad man. Luckily, he swings both ways, though now? I'm totally rooting for the both of you."

"I thought you're into older guys?"

"It doesn't mean I can't look at the menu," she answers with a pout.

"So…he is…" he trails off, not wanting to ask the question but wanting validation to know if that accidental almost kiss was all in his mind or if was it true. Even now, he's trying to understand just how he's going to face him the next day during their morning run or even practice afterward.

"There are rumors he's bisexual, leaving with guys or girls from parties, so do what you will with that information," she signs with a shrug. "Though when it comes to these things like him having a thing for you? I'm never wrong with my keen eyes as a cupid."

"So you're Cupid now?" he teases with a grin.

"Always have been," she signs, tapping her temples while puffing out her chest rather proudly upon boarding their train. "My senses tell me that if he got that worked over you, it has to mean something at the very least. It's like Spidey-Senses, you know?"

That, Troy wasn't *too* sure about; the way he looked so gutted and heartbroken as Jayden pulled him out of the water told Troy that there was another layer of Jayden that he kept buried. In fact, it was much more personal than that.

It's the same with the tattoos and the façade he keeps on that Troy doesn't understand.

The more he tried to understand Jayden, the more questions that arose.

However, Troy knew without a doubt that if he kept this up, he'd only be running himself dry at some point and completely snap. He knew firsthand the effects of storing everything inside of himself. If he could even help one person, he would do so in a heartbeat; perhaps that's why he also felt drawn to him simultaneously.

Yeah, nothing more.

Even if there was anything more going on, he didn't think he'd ever want anything more.

He couldn't.

"So what is your keen observation telling you, *Cupid*?"

he signs the title with emphasis, finding a seat across from her on the relatively deserted train heading to the shopping center around this time. He supposes the one thing he loves about the first month of every college semester is how relaxed the professor is with classes, especially when you're no longer a freshman.

"The first and foremost? How dense you are," she points out without missing a beat with her hands and without hesitation. Appalled at her directness, Troy places a hand on his chest for a moment, offended, before continuing his signing.

"Excuse me?"

"Yeah, you don't even know when people are hitting on you," she comments, rolling her eyes.

For a moment, he stares at her in disbelief before squinting. Well, that was certainly new to him, and no matter how many times he racked his brain, he couldn't come up with what she meant. "Wait, what? Who flirted with me before?"

Playing with the hem of her shirt for a moment, she bites her lips and looks around.

"Do you promise not to utter a word?"

"With my writing and hands, yes," he teases, copying the exact words she had signed before. His phone buzzes for a moment, though he disregards it as it's probably the small group chat with his roommate and their small community of ASL club. "Though I draw the line when it comes to morse code like you."

"Touche," she grins. "Well, you're usually living in your own world, which I'm all about sometimes. However, I feel like you don't know when someone is clearly showing interest right in front of your eyes like some sort of mating dance, like Aston, for example."

"Aston?" he repeats, blinking a few times. Well, she certainly had to be wrong. "Like…my roommate?"

"Do we happen to know another Aston?" she ponders, crossing her legs. "Yes, Aston Zhou."

"You're insane; he does not," he signs firmly, waving it off. He didn't want to appear as if he was fishing for attention, so he stopped himself by saying there are many people who are a better catch than him on campus. Aston never hid his sexual orientation from the get-go, but he never made a move on him either.

Yes, Aston had invited him often to outings like movies and dinner.

Yes, Aston had helped him study several times as an academic genius and programmer.

Yes, Aston usually would tag along like right now, meeting them at the mall, just to hang out.

Though what's what roommates do….right?

Great—now even Troy is growing confused and doubting everything, but it wouldn't make any sense. While his roommate is rather outgoing and friendly with everyone, Troy usually keeps to himself and prefers alone time.

"He does; you're just too blind to see it," Quinn grumbles, rolling her eyes in the process before continuing her signing. "It's why I usually don't want to three-way because it's too much for me and sees poor Aston failing so miserably. That's the problem with you, Troy."

"What do you mean?"

"When will you realize that you're worth it, babe?" she signs, and suddenly, he doesn't feel like talking about this anymore. As his best friend, he didn't keep any secrets from her, even if it meant showing her his ugly past of what almost happened at a freshman party nearly two years ago. "When will you stop blaming yourself and know you're worth it and deserve more?"

Quinn was right, and Troy did know it.

"I don't ever want to feel...*helpless* again," he confesses with his hands—the same hands he had used to fend for himself because he couldn't speak. The night changed everything, making him skeptical and fearful ever to let his guard down. He's only snapped out of it when Quinn reaches forward to place a hand on his.

Squeezing his hand, she pulls away. "What happened that night wasn't your fault."

"I know," he signs, though his body posture must have said a different story.

"Have you spoken to your therapist about it?"

"Here and there, but it's in the past," he confesses. He does have occasional nightmares, but nothing too bad either. It's been two years, and all he wants now is to move on with his life. It seems so bright ahead, especially now that he made it into the tennis team after debating for years.

"I know, and I don't want your past to hold you back," she replies sternly. "I'm just saying to not focus on the what-ifs in your life, but what is, as your parents have said before. Live your life the way you want to, and everything else will follow naturally."

He smiles, feeling touched by how caring she is. "I will; you don't have to worry about that. Though, let's not talk about Aston right now since I don't want to make it weird, especially when we're seeing him in less than four stops from now."

"You're right," she agrees. "Let's talk about what you will do when you see Jayden tomorrow?"

"Pretend it never happened," he snorts while replying with ease.

"What do you want to do? I should have rephrased it as," she reiterates. "Do you find him attractive?"

"It doesn't matter anyway," he replies, finally going into his bag to fish his phone out since it had buzzed once again. He's thankful, at the very least, that his phone is still working after it took a dive alongside his wallet. With brows bumped together, she positions her finger right next to her face, wiggling her middle finger three times in confusion.

"Why?"

"It'll be awkward," he signs as if it's the most obvious thing. "We'll be traveling together."

"Sharing the same bed as well? I love that trope," she winks.

"No, most *definitely* not. Everyone has their own hotel room when we do travel," he explains. Most of the tennis competitions held on the weekend didn't require much traveling except on rare occasions to the other states as they moved up in ranks. "Plus, we didn't even have our first competitive double-team match yet."

"When is it?"

"In three days," he signs, balancing his phone onto his knees. "It'll be here, so no traveling."

"May I jinx you, and somehow you end up in that situation when you have to start traveling to play competitively," she signs, wiggling all her fingers with a mischievous look on her face. "I come from a long family lineage of fortune tellers, you know."

"How about you do something good with that power, like winning the championship and me going pro?"

"Hey, I am," she pouts, and when Troy looks rather confused, she laughs. "You'll need to move up the ranks to accidentally be in a one-bed trope situation, right? So, technically speaking, I'm doing something good. Do you still have your V-card?"

Gapping, he can feel his face heating up as he signs out quickly, "Quinn, you can't ask me that in public!"

"As if anyone is looking," she signs while giggling, waving her hand to demonstrate as such. Thankfully, Troy still has his V-card intact, but he was going to tell her that. "So, should I start thinking of ship names? How do you feel about…Troyden? Jatroy?"

"Be serious."

"I am; let's just say, if this is anything like a novel, you're in for a long ride, babe," she replies, taking her phone out and holding it between her lap. "I'll do Aston a favor and text him for the both of us that we're almost there, then."

Burying Quinn's predicaments comment from earlier alongside; he unlocks his phone to realize the text wasn't from Aston as he had predicted before. His breath hitches for a moment, completely forgetting that he and Jayden had exchanged numbers back in case they ever needed to reach out to the other.

> Jayden: Sorry about earlier. I didn't mean to snap at you.

> Troy: No, it's okay; I deserved it. Thank you for saving me and giving me a change of clothes as well.

> Jayden: You never have to thank me for that. We can catch lunch, but shoot me your schedule when you're free. Have fun with Quinn, by the way. I'll have your clothes delivered tomorrow when we see each other. 😊

The smiley face at the end catches Troy off guard, but not in a bad way, either. Maybe it wouldn't be as awkward tomorrow as he suspected, and his shoulders eased. With that in mind, he can feel the tension he's been feeling the whole day slowly start to dissipate.

Funny how many different emotions that man can invoke in him without even trying.

Troy wasn't entirely sure if that was good or bad yet.

CHAPTER SIXTEEN

Swinging the bat as hard as he can, Jayden tries to keep his eyes focused on the ball being served back rather than wanting to look over at his teammate. It wasn't like him to be so distracted when he was playing, and yet, here he was, trying not to look over at Troy during a warm-up to see each other's play styles and servings while thinking of yesterday.

The way he had allowed his anger to win him over.

The way his heart was thumping so fast when trying to retrieve Troy's body.

The way they had almost kissed if it weren't for Quinn.

The way his heart pounded recklessly and more than anything else, he wanted to slam his lips onto—

He grits his teeth, prying his eyes away as he darts to his designated spot right at the baseline, barely able to serve it over the net to where Cassie and Trevis are. His tennis shoes squeaked loudly as he quickly moved back to position.

Fuck, he needed to get his head out of his ass.

Hell, even this morning had been more than miserable

for the twenty-three-year-old when they went running. Even after his classes, he couldn't focus up until practice at two. Unconsciously, his eyes follow to where Travis has now wiped the sweat with the sleeve of his shirt, licking his lips with his brows pinched together.

Seeing him this serious when it came to playing was a complete one-eighty to the usually shy man.

Despite the disadvantages in life, his confidence and determination were unlike anything he's seen before. Even after a longer-than-usual cold shower this morning before meeting with Troy, it didn't do much, especially now.

Jayden was about to break one of the few rules he had set for himself but didn't know what came over him. He didn't know if he should be upset or not that Troy didn't bring up the almost kiss either when every nerve in his body screamed to finish what had been started, which took him by surprise.

Usually, he would easily cave into his impulses, but when it comes to Troy, he couldn't.

Jayden didn't know if it was because he was a teammate member or *what*.

It's then that he sees Trevis setting himself close to the net for volleying, which is typical of his offensive and aggressive headshot for a point. The fucker knew Jayden wouldn't be able to get there on top, though right at the nick of time, Troy does a head dive for it, making the ball bounce up for Jayden to smash it down, and Cassie wasn't able to dive for it in time.

It was fantastic gameplay by any means, but the seasonal players knew the truth.

"Where the fuck is your head, Harrington? Let me tell you that it's certainly not over fucking here," Trevis shouts across the net, holding his hands up in the air while throwing his racquet onto the ground. "Is that enough to wake you up?"

"Come here and say it to my face, Scottland," he snaps before jogging up to where Troy is now sitting on the floor, wiping his swear with the wristbands. Feeling somewhat guilty because that was technically his serve, he bends down on one knee before signing. "Are you okay?"

"Yeah," he signs back with a grin, his heart still pounding from the intensity of it. It's different from playing with casual players in that it completely caught him off by surprise with the huge jump. "I didn't realize how intense competitive tennis is."

"You'll get used to it," he replies, holding out his hands.

"I'm thankful for the runs than in the morning," he signs before reaching to take up the offer of Jayden's hand. Electrical current zaps through every inch of his body in a straight line, but if only he knew that Troy had also felt it.

Clearing his throat, he makes his way over to where their bottle of water was, tossing it to him.

"Thank you," Troy signs.

"Hey, what are teammates for?" he signs back, giving a small, forced smile.

Right.

Teammates.

Something about it makes Troy's shoulder sag at the process, though he doesn't know why. Chugging their water,

Troy looks over to realize they've been practicing already for about three hours which is the NCAA standard, with the Coach giving pointers and exercises in shaping them up for their first match in two days.

One in which Troy is rather nervous and excited about at the same time.

"Quick, teach me to sign 'good game' by chance, like GG," Trevis eagerly demands, going under the net. "Unlike you, he was actually fully focused on the game, and I want to say he was amazing at the last part."

"Wow, thanks," he snorts as he watches someone jogging up to Troy to chat. He squints at the shaggy brown-haired man with a notepad in tow, and even Troy looks happy to see him. It must be a new recruit, but a feeling of uneasiness settles over him when he sees them conversing happily.

Another new feeling is foreign.

Glancing over to where Troy is now scribbling onto the notepad to converse with the newest recruit while, Jayden arches up a brow. Racking his brain, he couldn't quite place his finger on it, which was a first.

What was his name again?

It's then he sees Troy's face light up from whatever he had written to whoever he was, and it took everything in his strength not to rip the damn notebook and check what they were even speaking about.

Why the fuck did he care?

"Did I lie? You were everywhere with your swings, man," Trevis says, making Jayden tear his eyes away to face him. He had hoped that maybe his best friend wouldn't see it, but it was already too late as he was arching a brow, and it was no surprise for Jayden what he meant. "Ah, I get it now."

It took everything inside Jayden not to wipe the damn grin off his face in front of everyone.

"Ah, get what?" he grits out through narrowed eyes.

"Are you really going to make me say it out loud?" he ponders with a wicked grin.

"I don't know what you're talking about," he seethes, only making it worse when Trevis pats him on the shoulder. He makes it away, narrowing his eyes, and it takes everything inside him not only to slam his fists into his cheek but maybe even break the racquet over his head.

"Uh-huh, sure," he smiles. "Though your secret is safe with me, Harrington."

"There is no secret," he growls, still refusing to say anything more because there is no *secret,* and *nothing* is happening. Sure, they almost kissed, and he couldn't stop thinking about it, but it was because of the rush of adrenaline saving him.

Yeah, that was it.

"Sure there isn't," he sings.

"I mean it, Trevis."

If only he knew how hard it was not to look over at Troy either. His eyes want to do it naturally, almost like it was the most natural thing in the world, which only irks him even further. It had started off because he felt drawn to him with being mute.

Now?

He wanted to know if Troy was as soft on the lips as it looked.

"Like how you're going to bend your own rules soon, probably?" Trevis ponders, crossing his arms rather skeptically. Though Jayden wasn't the type to live by the rules, there certainly were a few things he wouldn't overstep—especially the rules he had made *personally,* and he only has two in life.

One, never break his parents' hearts and hope for retribution for his mistakes.

Two, never date a teammate for any reason or sleep with them.

"As if," he snorts, rolling his eyes.

"Do you want a bet, Mr. Nice?" he wagers, upping a brow challengingly. At that, the idea did sound rather intriguing and would help solidify in Jayden's head why it would never happen. With his rather competitive nature, he can't help but smile.

"What's on the line?"

"Cleaning my toilet for the house for the year," he states, his grin going even wider. The whole tennis had opted to rent a place aside from Jayden, as he liked having his own place to call his own. Acting as Mr. Nice around his teammates was already too much.

He couldn't bear doing it for heaven knows how much more.

"If I win?"

"What do you want?" he replies.

For a moment, he falls quiet. It wasn't as if his place was a snob as it was a person of one living there compared to a team full of full-grown men who also liked to run wild parties that matched their fraternity brothers, too.

"I'll get back to you in a week," he offers because he doesn't know what he wants.

Hell, he just wanted to have the title of finally beating the unbeatable.

"Sure."

"Will the whole team know it'll be on the scoreboard?" Jayden asks, referring to the whiteboard that shows who's betting with who currently alongside a scoreboard. Though he isn't the type by any means to keep up the façade, Trevis has never once lost.

Until now, and he's more than confident about that.

He'll finally get his bragging rights taken.

"You know it," he nods and holds out his hands. Without missing a beat, they shake on it.

"You're on," Jayden nods.

"Oh, invite him over to our party after our game Saturday; it'll be fun," Trevis grinned, and it didn't take a genius as to what he was thinking of. After all, alcohol and winning a game usually went well hand-in-hand.

"We didn't even win yet," he points out. "Let alone play."

"Let's be honest, we've won against Knoxville every year for the past four years, and this is going to be no different, especially with you two. You have chemistry on and off— fuck!" Trevis exclaims when Jayden decides to punch him on the elbow. "You fucking bitch."

"Thank you," he grins. "I'll see after Saturday if he wants to go."

Something told Jayden that he might not be a party type but would extend an offer in case he did alongside Quinn. He makes a mental note as he now glances over to see whatever his face is with Troy still, but a few of his teammates went to converse with him. He's rather proud that his teammates and friends were natural extroverts by nature, and something about it eases him more now that they're not alone.

"Though I have to say that you're lucky the Coach had to step away for a moment because if he saw that you're not a hundred per cent into it, the whole team would be punished for it," Trevis points out, and they both shudder how bad it was the first year when they were getting punished daily through drills.

"The same could go for you throwing your racquet before," he muses.

"God, I hate and love our nationally ranked NCAA D1 program for that reason," he sighs. "Thank God we don't have conditioning today, or I would have killed myself. I swear the only places I know that experience group punishment is communist countries, the military, and college sports. Now, are you going to teach me or hug Troy to yourself, *mate*?"

Chuckling, Jayden flattens his hands out to tape them on his chin before putting both hands into a fist with his thumbs pointed upward. Then, he bumps his fists together with the thumbs still pointed up in the air twice. "GG."

Eagerly, Trevis mimics it in front of Troy after tapping his shoulder though missing by a margin, when he taps his chin and lets it fall to the side before bumping his fists together twice with his thumbs upward and one thumb up in celebration.

"GG," Trevis smiles wildly. Troy's eyes widen at the gesture as his face completely lights up like a child. To see him so happy over something so minuscule tugs at Jayden's heart in a way he's never felt before as he clenches his jawline.

Get a grip, man.

He watches him grab Trevis's hand, helping him correct his sign language before he tries again, with Troy nodding eagerly. He always figured Trevis would get along well, and again, a slight sense of pride in knowing how Troy would easily weave into the team would be better from there on out as Cassie and Benjamin also joined in to sign with Trevis.

Luckily for Jayden, Benjamin waves bye and exchanges pleasantries with them as if they're great friends. Not being able to help himself anymore, especially when Troy looks over, Jayden cocks his head to the side.

"You know him?" he signs.

"Yeah," he signs before pressing his lips into a thin line to explain himself more. "Well, sort of. He helped me get around the first day I came here, but I found out he's also in my Literature class recently. His name is Benjamin Minton."

"Got it," he nods with a small smile. Again, he wanted to ask more but stopped himself because it didn't matter. He can talk, date, and sleep with whoever he wants. They're nothing more than teammates at the end.

He took a bet, which meant nothing would ever happen no matter what.

Especially because it'll break both the rules he had set out.

CHAPTER SEVENTEEN

Is it possible to feel so nervous that you're about to puke?

Troy certainly thinks anything is possible at this point.

Taking a deep breath, Troy then opens the palm of his hands, writing down the word "courage" before slapping the palm of his hands into his mouth to swallow the words to embody that particular emotion for the remainder of the day.

In this case, the next hour or so.

It's superstitious, but something he didn't dare to question the legitimacy of it all at that moment as their game was less than half an hour. He needs a prep talk from Quinn now, but he's more than confident that she's trying to find parking or already seated as their university's first double-team tennis game of the season.

While everyone looked eased off the game against Knoxville, Troy was bouncing his legs rather nervously, his hands clammy, which wouldn't help when he's playing later. It doesn't make it better that he never thought of getting this far already, much less playing the first team of the six.

Getting up, he makes his way towards the vending

machine to steady his heart as his teammates give him a few nods and smiles. Troy certainly enjoys the way they try including him in such things by means of using their phone's app to communicate or sticky notes Trevis started to carry around.

It honestly felt…*nice.*

The coach even went ahead before giving a small little speech with his rundown on a paper for Troy, which he found sweet of him. The least he can do is not embarrass the team or drag down Jayden, who's been so supportive.

Though, can he?

This is entirely different from playing against your teammates because it matters if they'll advance. Not only that, but his dreams and ambitions of being the first deaf tennis professional, too.

He lets out an exasperated sigh, banging his head on the vending machine for a moment. He did so several times in hopes it would get him out of whatever funk he was on before picking up his head in time to see a familiar pair of dark brown eyes greet him. Meekly, Troy smiles at Benjamin while working on schooling his flushed face.

Troy is more than confident he saw everything. His eyes travel to where there's a notebook in his hand, flipping it over so he can see what was written. Benjamin then tilts his head rather curiously when Troy reads the one word: "Nervous?"

Troy takes the small notepad, scribbling his response. "Beyond, if you can't tell, aren't you?"

"Well, not exactly," he writes back, and when Troy's

brows furrow together in confusion, he shrugs before continuing his rather cursive writing. "Columbia won against Knoxville four years straight. I'm more than confident we can kick their asses within the first team, which is you and Jayden."

"I wish I had that confidence," Troy writes with a heavy sigh, his shoulder sagging slightly. He can't help but wince at the self-pity party going on, especially right before the game, of all things. Yet, he had so much going up against him currently.

"Don't you since you're going out of your way and making it this far? Give yourself more credit," Benjamin writes with a frown, punching in a series of codes on the vending machine. Then, much to Troy's surprise, it drops out two drinks. The boy with shaggy brown hair only winks. "My brother played tennis and taught me that trick. If you win, I'll totally show you how."

That earns an airy chuckle as Troy grabs the bottle of water. He chugs it, letting the cool water help ease the fiery nervousness that's been budding inside before writing: "Thank you for that, actually. I needed it."

"Are you going to the party?" Benjamin asks, cocking his head to the side while Troy furrows his brows together in confusion. He racks his head, and no matter how hard he tries to remember, it comes to a complete blank. Rather, he takes the pen to circle around the two last words, followed by two question marks. Benjamin presses his lips into a thin line before writing: "Were you not informed of the party after this?"

Troy was ready to shake his head in response when Benjamin's eyes went from him to whoever was standing behind him. Given the way his body shivers lightly, Troy knew who it was without even turning.

When he does, he realizes the way Jayden has his eyes narrowed slightly. It's so small that you could barely see it if you weren't paying attention. Shoving down the way his heart flutters on seeing him, he meekly signs, "Jayden, hi,"

"Hey," he signs, his hands clipped as his eyes dart between the two. "Am I interrupting something?"

"No, not really. We were just…talking," he professes, shaking his hand and watching how his jawline ticks meekly. He wasn't entirely sure why he felt as if he had done something wrong as he tried not to fiddle with the end of his shirt for a moment to recollect his thoughts. Benjamin taps him, giving a small wave before leaving the two. Jayden looks on edge, and it only makes Troy's mind jump to different conclusions about his irritable features.

Was this nothing more than a plot to isolate him from his group of friends?

Did Jayden not want Troy to know about the party because he didn't fit in?

Why…did it hurt so much?

Did Jayden help and humor him because he felt sorry for him, of all things?

The thought made his eye sting, and it didn't make it any better when Jayden held onto his chin, making his eyes pierce his. Troy's heart skips a beat for a reason he doesn't understand. His brows are furrowed together, his lips pressed into a relatively small pout in the utmost concentration.

Making sure his eyes are trained on him, he finally pulls his hands away.

"Are you okay? I looked everywhere for you."

"Yeah…no…well, I don't know. I'm nervous about the game," he fumbles out with his hands, hating how his heart is beating so erratically fast. He tells himself that Jayden looked everywhere for him since they're the first up in less than fifteen minutes, but it doesn't mean his heart would listen. Honestly, ever since learning more about him than the exterior he puts on, he's been staring at him more than he'd like to admit.

Why?

A question to which he doesn't seem to have the answer.

"You got this, Troy. I've seen how you've been practicing that we'll blow them out of the court," Jayden signs, bringing him back to reality. "There are really two reasons you don't want the Coach upset by not living up to the standards he had in seeing you play."

"Why?" Troy asks, playing along to distract himself.

"Let's just say he'll make sure you won't enjoy the after-party."

Was this supposed to be out of mockery?

"Yeah, I know," Troy clips with his hands. He didn't want to go to a college party anyway since it wasn't his scene, and yet he didn't know why it hurt to be uninvited. He thought everyone treated him equally, yet clearly, he seemed it was all in his head.

"Yeah, it's usually coupled with a few other fraternities. Honestly, not that fun," Jayden found himself admitting before realizing the charge in his mood in that instinct. "What's the matter? Did I say something wrong?"

"Nothing," he lied. "Let's just get ready for the game."

He tries to brush past Jayden, who only grabs his wrist, giving it a squeeze. When Troy started to struggle, it only irritated him as to what was wrong. Knowing he wouldn't get him to listen to the old fashion way, he tugged him up against the wall, pinning him with the vending machine on one side, his hand on the other for a moment.

When he's confident he's not going to dash, he lets out an exasperated sigh.

"Troy, come on, not before the game," he signs before he narrows his eyes until they are slits. His body goes rigid as his mind finally reaches a conclusion. "Was it Benjamin? Did he say something to you?"

"What?" he signs in disbelief. "No, of course not."

"Then who?" he angrily presses on, his nose flaring. He's on the very brink of losing it since he lost sight of Troy, distracted by his teammates, and at this point, he can care less about keeping up the damn façade. "Tell me, damn it."

"I know about the party happening tonight," he exclaims with his hands, and it was certainly not what Jayden expected by turning this whole thing on its head. He blinks several times, trying and failing to understand just what Troy meant.

"What about the party?"

"I wasn't invited," he lamely professes, his flush deepening at how stupid this probably sounded as he shrugs before finding the right words to convey. "I know that I'm probably the odd one out, but it certainly stings—"

"That wasn't the reason, Trevis told me to invite you a few days ago," he confesses, pulling away before pinching the bridge of his nose. Honestly, it had crossed his mind a few times, but he didn't know why he didn't want him to go. Perhaps it was because he knew firsthand how wild the party would get and didn't want him there.

This…protective side seems to know no end, and despite wanting to bed Troy, he couldn't lose the bet.

He couldn't break his own rules.

He couldn't break his parent's hearts.

He couldn't break his *own* heart.

"Then…"

"That's because I didn't think you'd want to come, especially how crazy things get. It has nothing to do with my teammates not wanting to invite you," he deadpans. "In fact, if anyone ever gives you a hard time or singles you out, you come to me if I didn't make that clear."

"What are you going to do?"

"You don't want to know," Jayden signs while huffing out a laugh. "Did…you want to go?"

"Honestly, not really," he confesses, dropping his hands for a moment. "Are you going?"

In response, Jayden only shrugs, which Troy takes as a no.

"You're not?" he asks, his eyes widening in surprise. "Why?"

"It's not exactly every week I want to party," he sighs, which technically is the truth. It's a great distraction, but the loneliness that comes when the silence hits and the alcohol leaves isn't something he's particularly fond of either. "Though, I'm sorry it slipped my mind. It's been hectic, but it's not an excuse. You're more than welcome to do so. I know Trevis and the others would love having more people."

What Jayden didn't expect is for Troy to actually look to be contemplating going. His eyes twitch at the thought of someone like him being surrounded by a bunch of drunk guys, and he surges forward. In Jayden's mindset, it seems he can't help but look at him.

After all, who else would do so?

"Would I be able to bring someone if I were invited?" he signs warily.

"You're going?" he finds himself asking, irritation coursing through his veins. Jayden knew he had every right to go, so he couldn't pinpoint why it *bothered* him so. Perhaps it's because he knew what would happen at those parties, and he didn't save him from drowning by throwing him in a tank of sharks.

"Quinn always wanted to go to these parties but can't seem to get in, so I'll go for her sake," he signs with a smile. Although he was still a bit wary of whether he was telling the truth regarding being invited to the party, he did want to find out for himself, too. "She's here as well to watch my game, so it's the least I can do for her."

Truly, Jayden didn't know if he was a great friend or irresponsible for putting himself at risk for a friend.

"Okay," he signs, letting out a small sigh. "I'll accompany you both then."

The invitation to do so slips out before he even thinks about it, and it confuses him. He's been looking forward to actually sleeping in for once and putting aside his reckless impulses. Troy's eyes widen, his mouth parting for a moment. "Why are you going? You just said you didn't want to go."

"I just shrugged," he corrects. "I'm going…just because."

"Because?"

"I felt like it," Jayden signs before pulling away and walking ahead. The last thing he wants is to ask more questions he can't answer. "Plus, someone must be the designated driver to make sure you both get home safe, especially our parties."

Really, what was he talking about?

He's never actually done something like this before because it's usually Trevis looking out for him.

"Really? Are you sure?" Troy asks, a bit skeptical.

"Yes, and that's *if* we win this too that there's something to celebrate," Jayden reminds him and for the first time, he really wants Knoxville to kick their asses before he shakes the thought away. "Now, are you ready to win this and make history?" he asks, his eyes darting to where the clock is. He's more than confident Coach is about to have a search party if they're even a minute later.

"As I'll ever be," he signs, letting out a small laugh. "How are you so confident?"

"It's because I have you as a partner. You'll be fine, I believe in you," Jayden chuckles with a wink. He smiles, patting him on the shoulder. Already, Troy couldn't help but feel the rising flush in knowing such a fantastic player was praising him. "Now, let's do this."

CHAPTER EIGHTEEN

It was over before it even started, as Jayden was more than confident that would have happened.

Being the first team to go and winning four to nothing against Knoxville really did set the mood for how the rest of the game set was headed. Troy was a bit tense in his movement when they first entered the stadium.

Once the game started, he was so natural that even Jayden was surprised by his fluent movements, impeccable speed, and ability to pinpoint where he had to position himself on the field next.

One would never have believed he was deaf by *any* account.

Strangely enough, Jayden couldn't seem to wrap his head around how perfectly in sync they were, better than any partner he had ever teamed up with. They also seem to move as one, picking up what one might have missed and even spotting him when he was in a tough spot.

Needless to say…Jayden really feels as if he has found a great partner.

Now, if only he can stop gawking at his most definitely off-limit teammate—the one he's staring at right now as he looks around the crowd in utter amazement while the team is celebrating. It's another thing Jayden quickly picked up regarding Troy.

He didn't want the fame or fortune many strive for in winning.

No, he does it because he loves it and for the feeling of it.

Though Troy may not hear the cheers, he can certainly feel the vibration from the stadium as he basks in winning. His head is still reeling as he catches sight of Trevis, who grins, putting his thumbs up for a moment before signing, "GG."

"GG," Troy signs back, giving two thumbs up in return before turning his attention to Jayden. No longer is he covered in sweat like they had given an hour had passed since their first game. Needless to say, he looked charming with his hair sticking up in all sorts of directions and a towel draped over him.

"How was it?" Jayden chuckles while signing, nodding his head to the crowd. Some people were already leaving, mainly those coming to cheer for Knoxville, while others went were friends and family. When was the last time his parents came for his game?

He shakes his head, knowing it doesn't matter, as his attention focuses on Troy, who is smiling widely.

"It was…amazing and so fun," he signs before looking up at the stadium. His eyes catch on Quinn, who's waving furiously, and he waves back. Taking everything in, he shakes his head almost in disbelief. "I can see why this becomes addicting of playing in the spotlight. Once you start, it's like…nothing else mattered but winning that match."

"You were a natural," he replies with his hands after he has turned his attention back. Honestly, it was the first time he felt so alive playing again. The feeling of raw excitement was there, like when he did something hazardous and reckless.

In fact, he can't remember when the last time he had been smiling so much while swinging his racquet was. His heart was pounding, and for once, playing wasn't just a means of appeasing his parents for his wrongs, but he had fun.

It was thanks to *him*.

"I can't help but wonder…" Troy signs, taking in the stadium once more. Now that many people had started to leave the tennis center in rapid session, it was the silence that Troy had always been used to. "When the crowd was yelling and cheering after the game…what exactly does that sound like?"

The question slips out so easily of genuine curiosity, and yet a small part of Troy was envious all the same as what it meant to be part of the human experience. It's something that many take for granted as Jayden places a hand on his shoulder and squeezes for a moment.

"The best and most beautiful thing in the world can't be heard or seen but felt with the heart," he signs thoughtfully, and though he can't see it, Troy's breath hitches at his words. "I suppose I would never know how to explain the sounds to you, but to me....it's the same as what you've felt when looking around the stadium."

Something about his comment makes Troy elbow him playfully, though his heart skips a beat of his words, and how insightful they sounded at that moment. "Wow, I didn't know you were a poet as well. What else are you hiding?"

"You're hilarious," Jayden signs with a huff, deadpan, just as Trevis and the others run up to smack him hard and congratulate him. He can't help but notice that some of his teammates were also trying to communicate with Troy using "GG" that Trevis must have taught them or through a sticky note and pen.

"Dude, is Troy coming to the party tonight?" Trevis asks, cocking his head to the side curiously. He puts him in a deadlock, just loud enough for the two to hear, though everyone seems to be riding on the winning high. "You *did* ask, right?"

"I did," he snorts before signing, "Trevis is asking if you're coming to the party tonight."

"I am," Troy signs, nodding in agreement. "Is he okay with me bringing a friend?"

"He wouldn't mind," Jayden answers before nodding at Trevis. "Yeah, he is."

"Yeah, I can fucking see," he muses, pulling away to follow the rest of the guys into the changing room. "Cool, give him the address and make sure you're on your best behavior, Mr. *Nice*. Remember what you said about your so-called rules."

Jayden only flips him off, making everyone laugh as they

first head to the changing room. He turned just in time to hear a loud squeal, and the next thing he knew, Troy was almost being knocked over by Quinn, who jumped onto his back.

"You were amazing!" Quinn gushes with her hands, her eyes darting from one Troy and then to Jayden. "It was the coolest teamwork I've ever seen. GG, by the way. I'm not sure what the last move was where you shot the ball up in the air for Troy to hit, but it got me on the edge of my seat the way you guys had us by the edge of our seat."

She's talking so fast that even Troy had a hard time distinguishing what she was signing, much less Jayden. When she shuffles for her phone out of her pocket, Troy's eyes widen like saucer plates.

"You video-called my parents during the game?" he signs in horror, his face flushing. He wasn't entirely sure how he could be feeling currently, especially with Jayden standing next to him and fearful of accidentally saying something embarrassing.

At that, Quinn only shrugs, not seeming to regret a thing, as she holds the phone vertically.

"There's our champion!" Dad signs, clapping his hands together in excitement. "Look at you, I've never seen you play like that before, and I didn't even recognize you for a moment. Oh, I wish I was there to give you a hug."

"Hey, Dad," Troy signs awkwardly as he watches mom butting in, squinting her eyes.

"Oh, is that your partner I've heard so much about?" she signs, wagging her eyebrows before getting closer to the screen. "Well, he's certainly handsome up close. Goodness, has he thought of becoming a model?"

"Mom," he signs, horrified. "I'm hanging up."

"What? I still have eyes," she huffs, rolling her eyes. "What's his name again?"

Not being able to help himself anymore from standing around and wanting to converse since he didn't know Australian sign language, he gave a small wave. It catches Troy's parents, who then turn their attention to him in excitement.

"It's nice to meet you," Jayden signs, hoping they knew *some* American sign language. However, they look utterly baffled for a moment before clearing their throat and speaking with his hands once again. "Do you mind if I speak to your parents?"

"No, not at all," Troy says, and Jayden turns his attention back to see their rather shocked expression.

"It's nice to meet you, Mr. and Mrs. Evans," he greets. "I have to say your son is amazing in tennis."

"You…know sign language?" Mr. Evans asks, his mouth still hanging wide open at the news.

"Not Australian sign language, but American—yes," he grins. "I'm surprised he never told you."

"You're also his…partner in tennis, right?" Mrs. Evans ponders out loud.

"I am," he chuckles. "It's nice to meet you. I hope I didn't slow Troy down much with my movements."

"Oh, it seems we have a jokester," Mrs. Evans laughs, and for some reason, Jayden can't help but bask in the appraisal of another parent. "I didn't know you knew ASL as well. Where are you from originally, Jayden?"

"London," he answers. "Though I moved here at thirteen, so I was able to pick up American sign language quickly. I have to ask, though, if either of you are a tennis player because Troy is a natural pro on the field."

"No, not this life," Mr. Evans concurs. "He's always been amazing with tennis as a child. Perhaps we can meet one day down the road, especially because we've been thinking of surprising Troy in one of his games."

"That would be awesome," Quinn chimes in, turning the phone towards her for a moment. "Mrs. Evans, can I get some oatmeal raisin cookies? I tried baking it with the recipe you sent me, but it's not the same."

"Yes, Dear, I'll never forget about you," she laughs, and again, Jayden can't help but ask when was the last time his parents had tried to speak with his friends. Hell, he can't remember if they met Trevis either, whom he considered one of his closest friends. "Well, I'll get out of your hair; I'm sure you all want to celebrate. Let me say goodbye to my Darling."

With that, Troy bashfully says goodbye to his parents before Quinn tucks her phone away. She cocks her head to the side curiously before signing. "So, what are you all doing after this? Well, aside from a shower, of course. We should celebrate."

"Actually, we are," Troy signs; a smile edged on his face of surprising his best friend. "A party."

"Wait, you got into a party?" Quinn says, her eyes widening.

"Not just any, but those fraternity ones you like so much," he signs, huffing his chest. Despite him being rather nervous as he doesn't have good memories of parties, he figures it's time to conquer his fears. So long as he didn't drink and kept an eye out at all times, he should be fine.

At least, that's what he kept telling himself to not feel as nervous overall.

He did want to go as a means to get to know his teammates better, and he did get upset earlier about not getting invited. So the least he can do is go through with it for the sake of his best friend, who always wanted to go but stopped herself after the freshman accident.

"What? Are you—"

"Yes," he signs, cutting her off with a small smile. He hopes Jayden didn't catch up with his rather keen eyes of the tension shared between the two as he swallows. "It'll be fun and a nice way to celebrate too."

"Okay…" she trails off, biting her lips to withhold her excitement. "Which party house is it?"

At that, Troy had no choice but to look up to Jayden for help, who then signed, "Kappa Delta Rho."

Quinn squeals so loud that Jayden can't help but wince, not entirely sure as to why she would be so excited to go to a fraternity party. Though then again, he's been going to one practically every other week that he's more than tired of it already.

So why the hell did he say he'll go when Troy said he was going less than two hours ago?

He wasn't in the mood to keep up an act of Mr. Nice in front of his friends tonight, especially during the rather awkward dinner at his family's weekly Friday dinner yesterday with Mother bringing about the death of his twin brother as if he didn't exist.

Yeah, that'll always bring anyone down in their mood.

Yet, he tells himself it's because he didn't want Troy to be thrown in the tank of hungry sharks that can smell newbies from a mile away. Not to mention, he did notice an exchange between the two earlier when speaking about attending the party that caught his attention.

Quinn is jumping up and down, obvious to how tense Troy looks as she turns to Jayden.

"Yes, we'll be there. When is it?" she asks, her eyes filled with glitter like a child on Christmas morning.

"In about three hours," he signs, looking down at his watch for a moment. "I'm going to shower back at my apartment first and get ready. I presume this is your first frat party? Or first time going to a party in general?"

He knows he's fishing for information but can't help it.

Once again, Jayden sees how they share a look that there's more to the story before Troy signs, "First time in a while, but first in a frat party for sure."

"Okay, that's not a problem. Should I meet you at your dorm, and we can go together?"

"Wow, you really are Mr. Nice," Quinn signs, giggling. "Okay, we'll text you then. We can't wait. Now let's go, Troy, you can shower back in your dorm, and thankfully, I have some clothes there shoved in the back of Aston's closet."

"You did what now?" he signs in disbelief. As he watches them leave, Jayden can't help but sign, raking his hair back of just what's in store for him tonight at probably one of the biggest parties of the season with the winning and the start of the tennis season.

Somehow, Jayden knew this was going to be a rather long night.

It didn't make it better he wouldn't be able to bring anyone home tonight either.

CHAPTER NINETEEN

Troy didn't need to hear to comprehend how different college parties were compared to the one he had gone to in his small town back in Australia. The neon flashing light, paired with the copious amount of people and alcohol, made him wonder how no one had called the cops yet.

Not to mention, they were standing outside of the fraternity house.

He can't even imagine the hecticness that goes on within—much less how they do this every weekend.

Standing there, he tried to make sense of everything.

Honestly, he wasn't sure if he should cry or laugh because he didn't know why his heart was pounding so fast. It could be the energy and adrenaline of being surrounded by so many people despite the silence or because of the incident he's thinking back of.

Well, it's better than sweaty palms and the inability to catch one's breath.

However, would that come about later tonight?

Would he be able to handle the embarrassment and shame when his teammates potentially find out?

What if he were to puke or even worse?

What if someone from his small town, as luck would have it, was also attending Columbia University?

What if—

A light tug on his sweater pries his eyes away from the house and onto Quinn, who already has concern swirling in her eyes. Tilting her head, she puckers her lips outside as she signs, "Are you okay? We can leave if you're not comfortable. I know Jayden said we can go in first because something came up, but we can wait for him if you would like as well?"

Personally, he had been a tad disappointed when Jayden had messaged him regarding heading to the party first when they had agreed to go together. Except, he didn't want to feel as if the main reason he even came was to spend more time with him.

That would be ridiculous, after all.

"No," he quickly signs in return. "I'm fine. I'm just... taken aback by everything."

"Are you sure?" she signs, adding a bunch of questions and exclamation points with squinted eyes, which he didn't blame her for. Still, they had already come all the way here, and he had even made it a big deal before when he had presumed he was being singled out.

The least he can do is prove to not only Quinn and himself but everyone that this was going to be okay. Despite not knowing his teammates had actually invited Jayden to tell Troy about the party in the first place.

"Trust me, I'm about to get a ruptured eardrum by the time the party's over," she speaks through her hand with the widest smile Troy has ever seen, with excitement gleaming in her eyes. "You're lucky you're deaf at times like this."

At that, he decides to stick his middle finger as they laugh.

Even to this day, Quinn is one of the few who doesn't mind these sorts of jokes because she knows she didn't mean it in a negative sense. I mean, life is too short to be so serious all the time. So if you can't laugh at yourself, you can't have fun.

"I guess you'll be joining me soon," he signs back, bumping his shoulder with hers.

Sticking her tongue out, she loops an arm around his before a smug grin appears on her face.

"Now, should we go in and find your boyfriend?" she signs.

"My boyfriend?" he parrots back, squinting. "I have no idea who you're talking about."

"Oh, come on, you obviously know I mean your little tennis partner," she mischievously replies. At the sign of his name, he can feel his heart revving up once again, something he's still trying to work out the details as to why.

"He's not my boyfriend," he huffs, trying and failing to slow his speeding heart.

"Not yet," she signs back with a wink. "Now, let's go!"

With a strength Troy didn't know his best friend possessed, she eagerly dragged him through the people loitering outside and into the house. If he thought it was noisy-looking from the outside, it certainly was like a fend for yourself ball-pit on the inside.

Troy doesn't even have a clue as to how people were able to navigate themselves through the packed place in the first place in the way they're packed like sardines. Despite being unable to hear the music, he can feel the vibration coursing through every inch of his body alongside the number of people holding red cups and laughing.

"Wow," he signs, completely taken aback. He had expected it to be rowdy and hectic, but certainly nothing of this sheer size. While not a natural extrovert since he was a child, he dabbles at times just because of Quinn.

"I hope that's an exciting wow," she replies before grinning. "I think the best thing about sign language is seeing each other speak quite literally."

"You'll be right on that one," he muses, looking around somewhat awkwardly. Everyone seems to know everybody already, while Troy is already wondering just how this night will end. The last thing he wants is to drag Quinn down from having fun, especially with her wanting the whole college experience.

"You okay, though?" she signs, almost reading his mind.

"Yes," he says before waving his hand in front of his face. The house reeks of cheap booze and bad decisions already waiting, but he didn't want to swell on that—at least for tonight. He wanted to be the one in charge of his own future. "You don't worry about me, Quinn."

"That's like telling me not to breathe," she quips.

He only rolls her eyes, causing Quinn only to giggle.

However, as a firm believer of action speaks louder than words—or, in his case, signing—he was practically on a mission to do just that. Looking around the party, he follows her, not even surprised by how fast she is at making new friends and blending seamlessly into the party. Though he saw some of his fellow teammates, most would raise their cups before returning to what they were doing.

Thankfully, no one seems to question why Troy wasn't drinking.

For the most part, and gratefully enough once again, it wasn't too awkward for him when people tried to strike up a conversation with him only to find out he was deaf. He was never ashamed of it, but seeing the inconvenience it caused was always awkward.

Strangely enough, most people were too drunk or in the party mood to even try to make new friends, for the most part, tending to stick with their peers. It was about an hour in that suddenly, Troy felt like there was a change in the room.

As if someone had just entered and had been *staring* at him.

Goosebumps ricochet through every inch of his body from head to toe when he turns, and his eyes lock on lushes of forest greenery amidst the crowded room. Troy didn't even know how it was possible, but when it came to Jayden— it feels like nothing *ever* made sense.

Ever since he had saved him from drowning with that look in his eyes.

Ever since he had offered him support right before the game this morning.

Ever since he had been feeling nervous whenever they were alone as if—

A nudge on his arm jolts him back once again to break whatever hypnotizing gaze had surrounded them earlier. He didn't expect to see Quinn's wicked and mischievous smile that stretches so wild that it reminds Troy of a Cheshire cat.

"What?"

Weirdly, he watches as she takes a step away from where she is standing. His brows bump together in confusion when she goes to set the red cup on the table before signing, "Troy, keep it together; you're eye fucking him."

It suddenly then hits him that she didn't want Jayden to see what they were talking about. A blush immediately blooms across his face while he bites down hard on his lips, his heart pounding wildly. However, he didn't know if it was because of the strange energy in the room or what.

Something about him being surrounded by nothing but the untamed craziness of other partygoers and alcohol made Jayden look more…masculine and primal, as if he was in his zone. Lately, something has been growing inside of him that even Troy didn't want to admit out loud yet.

Ever since the younger gentleman had visited his apartment.

Something…growling.

It was gnawing at him.

"I was not," he finally signs back, though his movement was so slow and careless that even he wasn't convinced. Suddenly, for the first time tonight, he wanted a drink to help calm his nerves down despite knowing what it might lead to.

Who might take advantage in his drunken state.

It's strange that once upon a time, he wouldn't have minded going to parties back in high school despite his disabilities. However, he soon realized the danger that derived from drinking with others. How dangerous it was to—quite literally—not have a voice to say the simplest word:

Stop.

"Mhm," she giggles, jolting him back to reality. Judging from the look on her face, Troy quickly deduces it seems almost as if she knows something her best friend didn't quite understand yet. "He seems to have his eyes on you since the moment he came in, so why not take this opportunity go say hi?"

"Go…say hi?"

"Yeah…you know…since you're friends at all," she winks, giving much emphasis and stress in the third to last word by extending her pinky. Troy was ready to roll his eyes when Quinn was already waving over to Jayden right behind his back.

Ignoring her statement earlier, he signs, "Are you sure you'll be okay alone, though?"

Truthfully, he's more than confident she can handle herself—but there's no harm in asking.

"Positive, I'll be fine," she waves off before fishing out her phone to wave in front of him for a moment. "If anything, we have each other's number, now go. Have fun and celebrate your team heading to the next round!"

Chuckling to himself, he decides to turn to find Jayden.

He didn't even know why he seemed more excited about

speaking to him than the whole party. Perhaps it was because they could communicate, but another part of him somehow knew it was more than that. However, what he didn't expect was for him to see Benjamin amidst the crowd waving at him. Something that almost feels like disappointment passes through Troy's heart for a moment, which is soon turned to shock when Benjamin signs, "Hi."

"Hi," he signs back, though right before he can ask, Benajmin quickly takes out his phone.

"Sorry," he writes sheepishly on his notes app. "That was all I learned so far, actually."

"No, I'm happy you're trying," Troy writes back with a smile. He still finds it strange and quite sweet just how far Benjamin was willing to go to make a conversation with him. While his other teammates were quite nice—they didn't go out of their way, unlike Kayden and Benjamin.

Well, Trevis is one of the rare exceptions.

"I'm glad you were able to make it to the party," he communicates through his phone. "You were amazing today playing, by the way. Really, I think we're going to the semifinals at this point with you here."

"Honestly, I should thank you for calming me down before the game," he types back. Benjamin shakes his head before biting his lips nervously. Troy can't help but notice just how nervous he seems right as he turns his phone:

"Was the girl with you your girlfriend?"

Instantly, he shakes his head. Why does everyone presume otherwise?

"No, just a close friend," he writes back, and imminently,

he watches how he practically lights up. Some people came up to greet them while Benjamine waved and chatted with some people before grabbing a red cup and handing it to Troy, who shakes his head. He continues to type, "I'm not too fond of drinking."

Even if he were, it'd only be around people he trusted.

Taking the phone back, Troy watches as he bites down onto the ledge of the red cup, typing away. A small part of him did feel guilty and a sense of urgency which wasn't like him. His eyes shuffle quickly, yet with the sea of people, it was hard for him even to find Quinn.

Much less Jayden.

Nevertheless, he quickly spots his best friend mingling with some girls, allowing him to sigh of relief that she is having fun. Finally, he returns in time to be greeted with what Benjamin had written: "Do you want to hang out together? If you want, of course."

Ah.

On any other occasion, he wouldn't have minded, but since his eyes locked onto Jayden just before, he had wanted to strike up a conversation with him again. He clears his throat, pressing his lips into a thin line for a moment before shaking his hand and writing quickly, "Maybe next time; I hope that's okay?"

"No sweat," he states before tilting his head to the side just as he does the same to his phone. Except for his next written question, he can feel the blood rushing up his face. "Are you looking for someone by chance?"

Was it that obvious?

"Yeah, actually. Jayden," he inscribes, causing Benjamin to arch a brow.

"You guys are awfully close," he retorts, causing Troy to chuckle. It did make sense for them to be close, given that they are running friends and were paired for the remainder of the semester. "I know it's not within my rights, but you should keep your distance from people like him. I heard some rumors about him and the things he does for fun with his teammates; you should be careful."

He blinks once and then twice.

Troy didn't know if it was the alcohol talking, but he was quite surprised by Benjamin's statement. It's no surprise that Jayden did have a somewhat reckless streak, which he quickly picked up on. However, to confidently say that Troy should keep his distance simply because rumors rubbed him the wrong way.

After all, as an outsider, Troy doesn't think we can truly judge someone without a full picture.

Rumors are just rumors, as he has experienced firsthand.

"Thank you, but I have it handled. I know…about the rumors," he writes, and once again, he feels a tad awkward with where this conversation was even headed. He didn't wait before pretending he had spotted Quinn, though somewhere amid everything, he had already lost Quinn in the crowd shortly after, which was what Troy had wanted anyway.

He wanted her to enjoy herself more than feel the need to babysit him, and no matter what, his best friend said she was okay with it; he wanted her to experience the college she always craved. Who was he to try stopping her?

Giving Benjamin his phone back, he shuffles away and feels as if his mood has dampened.

Despite it being a celebration of their win, it did feel as if it was anything *but*. However, what he wanted to do at the moment was get a drink to calm his nervous tic. Puckering his lips, he finally grabs the red cup and brings it to his lips.

Just one drink.

One and nothing more.

One drink to ease himself and celebrate rather than getting sucked back into the past.

Without a moment of hesitation and despite how bad he was at handling alcohol, it had to beat whatever was going on inside of his head at the very end of the day. The taste of alcohol burns down his throat as he jerks his hands down from the cup.

Coincidentally enough, someone bumped into him, and immediately, tremors rock through his body. Whipping his head, Troy's hand grows somewhat clammy as the red cup spills onto the front of his shirt. The guy was much bigger than him, his eyes narrowing until they were nothing more than a slit.

He's saying something angrily by the way he's scowling with his brows bumped up—but not a single coherent word greets his ears. His lips moved once again as he towered over him, but Troy heard nothing but a faint buzzing.

His knees almost buckle with the memories.

Of *him* grabbing the collar of his shirt and dragging him.

Of him forcing him down onto the bed roughly with a wicked grin.

Of *him* saying if he didn't want it, then he should have said something.

Said something.

How would that be possible?

It's then Troy is snapped back to reality when the man slowly reaches for him, and he completely freezes. His stomach churns, and every inch of his body is already in-flight mode, but his feet wouldn't listen either.

Suddenly, the memories he had repressed—the ones he thought he had moved on—comes to spring forth. It's enough to practically suffocate him as his heart kicked into overdrive as if he was drowning all over again.

This time, no one was there to save him.

Someone.

Anyone—

Help me.

CHAPTER TWENTY

Why the hell am I here again?

In his rather foul mood, Jayden downs another bland and almost stalled beer from the red cups. Every inch of his nerves was jumping, and the urge to do something to exert that excessive energy generally made him even more on edge.

He's not entirely sure what's causing his shift in his mood, but he has been like this since walking into this damn party. Perhaps it was because he didn't want to come here today, wanting nothing more than peace and quiet.

Especially after the shit that he had gone through half an hour ago.

Just as he was going to meet up with Troy and Quinn, his father called him out of the blue; he almost ripped his whole apartment down when his father stated that being paired up with someone who was dead might drag him down later.

As if his dead twin brother wasn't deaf.

As if Jayden would ever think someone like Troy would ever be a nuance.

Why is it that it's always those who have impaired the ones having to apologize?

During the call, he had no choice but to grit his teeth and pretend to listen like the obedient son for the sake of his family for what he had done. While his father was on board in the beginning with him being paired with Troy, it seemed watching them play through the recording made him realize differently despite how well their playstyles were.

"It's fine now," his father stated on the line in a rather condescending way that made Jayden roll his eyes. "However, it'll only be a matter of time before something happens, and your play streak will be ruined because he can't hear."

It's strange how parents always thought they knew best.

Luckily, he was able to persuade his father otherwise from speaking to the coach about switching partners. In fact, Jayden realized he was one of the few people aside from Trevis he got along with. Shortly appeasing his father, he did end up asking about his mother, knowing if he hung up too early, his father would cause another commotion.

He didn't even want to get started on the aftermath of speaking of the new medications his mother was now on to not only help her sleep but cope. Which begs the question of why he was even here surrounded by drunken idiots.

It was for the sake of Troy and Quinn that he had settled with the knowledge of.

Now, he feels like an animal about to break from its loose leash; after all, if he had been accompanying Troy and Quinn over, then Benjamin wouldn't be trying to make conversation with him.

Without even realizing it, his eyes drifted over to Troy for what seemed like the billionth time for the night with a scowl. He hates how easy it is for him to find Troy in the crowd with ease, and he seems to certainly hate seeing him with *Benjamin* even more so.

Was it because he had seen Benjamin all happy-go-merry with Troy?

Why does he care?

Once again, his eyes twitch in annoyance.

The alcohol wasn't helping either, alongside the blaring headache. Usually, at parties, it was his way of not only relaxing but allowing him to forget when he could drop his persona. Right now, every fiber of his being wants to blow off his steam somehow.

Someway.

"You look ready to set the Kappa Delta Rho's house on fire."

At the voice booming next to his ears over the loud music, he turns to force a chuckle. He didn't even need to turn in recognizing Trevis's voice as his other teammates raised their red plastic cups in greeting.

"I'm surprised I haven't yet myself," Jayden muses, grabbing another red cup. Gulping it down, his nose scrunches in pure disgust once again as he faces him. "You'd think they'll have better shit than lukewarm beer at this party."

"Hey, they're free, so can't complain though…" he trails off for a moment, giving him a wicked grin. Jayden only scowls in return, shrugging off Trevis's arm as he sings, "Someone seems to be in a bad mood."

"I'm shocked you're not given your slip-up on the second half of the court," he counters, trying to rub salt in his friend's wound. At that, Trevis scowls when their other teammates nearby laugh while slapping him hard on the back.

"Honestly, the couch was ready to blow a lid; how you missed it," Ray chimes in loudly.

"Dude, I was ready to fucking beat his ass myself if he had missed it," Cassie agrees, nodding over at Jayden. "Actually, you mind switching with me and taking Trevis off my hand for Troy? Even he can play better than this idiot."

"Shit, I can't believe he's deaf sometimes," Isaac remarks in astonishment. He finishes his drink before throwing it right on the floor to join the other trash, continuing with a slur in his tone. "His movement and attention to detail on the field is unlike anything I've seen before, dude. Sometimes, I wonder if it's Trevis the one with the issues."

At that, Trevis shoves his rowdy teammate roughly as he tumbles, laughing all the while even when he flips him off. Once again, Jayden was already counting the hours until this shitshow was over. "Fuck you."

"You wish you could," Isaac winks playfully.

"I mean, I won, so who's the real one? Plus, the fucker was trying to trip me up, but he can suck my dick because we won," he pridefully states, flipping the others off. He scowls when their drunk asses have already moved on to something else, like checking out girls. Rolling his eyes, he slung an arm around Jayden and out of earshot from their drunken friends. "So...which begs the question...what crawled up your ass since you came? Quite literally."

It wasn't what per se.

Rather—who.

"Wouldn't you like to know?" he rebuts.

Still, there was no way in hell Jayden would ever confine in something like this with a friend, especially one that was the holder of their bet. Shoving his hands into his pocket, he was ready to tell him to fuck off when he saw Troy once again.

It seems his eyes naturally always drift over to a certain someone.

Sure the house was completely overrun with teenagers, with barely any light coming in except for the flashing neon lights here and there, but it wasn't that hard. I mean, it wasn't hard per se either, especially with his reddish-blond hair.

What Jayden didn't expect was to see the serious look on Troy's face at whatever Benjamin had written down on his phone, which had been their method of communication. From what Jayden could make out, Troy's face was pulled into a frown, his brows bumping together almost in disappointment.

What were they talking about?

"Oh...I see what's going on."

The smug tone really did make Jayden want to sucker punch his best friend as he snaps his attention to him. Pretending to play innocent, he cocks his head to the side. "What are you going on about this time?"

"You're jealous."

Jealous.

Yeah, as if.

Jayden didn't have time for relationships, much less jealous of someone speaking to him. After all, they're nothing more than friends and partners at *best*. In his opinion, he only got well with him the best because he was so much like his twin brother.

So much like Weston.

From his meek and kind demeanor to always wanting to take on more than he could handle.

The bravery behind it—despite the world being so cruel.

At the thought of his dead brother, paired with the crushing guilt, he grabs another drink and downs it. It's going to take a lot more alcohol to drown out the day he had, and really, no one was making it any better, either. When Trevis doesn't look as if he's ready to drop it any time soon, he decides to humor him, "You really think I'll be jealous?"

"Aren't you?" he counters. "I can't help but notice the way you're staring at a certain someone,"

"You're being an idiot," he snorts.

"Maybe…or I'm about to win a bet," he sings, pinching his cheek playfully.

"Hilarious," he deadpans, rolling his eyes. "I'm only looking after him because I'm his partner, and I was the one who invited him over."

"It's not like he can't take care of himself," Trevis counters before his eyes widen. "Oh, it seems Benjamin just kissed him." At that comment, Jayden almost snapped his neck from how fast he had turned, only to see Troy giving back Benjamin's phone. Scowling, he turns back to see a Cheshire-like grin on Trevis's face. "Got you."

Never being shy of showing his brute strength to keep him in check, he snarls before punching him hard on the elbow. He grunts loudly in return, rubbing at his elbow for a moment with his eyes pinched closed. "You're not fucking funny, dude."

"I never claimed to be, but I did want to prove a point," he chuckles upon regaining himself. However, his face soon drops shortly after as he tilts his head over to his side. "Hey…is that Victor by chance next with Troy? I thought Kappa was banned from coming after his last fight."

"Do you honestly think I would fall for that after what you pulled less than two minutes ago?"

"No, really," he hisses, and before Jayden can say anything, Trevis practically turns his whole body. At the sight, his blood runs cold at the scene before him. Troy's face was pale as a ghost, his body seeming on the verge of collapsing while Victor was towering over him—yelling profanity so loud that even a few partygoers were staring.

Instantly, before Jayden can think twice about anything else, his body is already moving just like when he had jumped into the water to save Troy. Shoving past the number of people, he feels as if he's moments from losing it, especially when he sees Victor already reaching for him.

Before Victor can even lay a hand on him, Jayden beats him to it as he grabs Victor's arm roughly, squeezing so tightly that he sees how he winces. Instantaneously, the smell Jayden greets and calms Troy down quickly, much to his surprise.

Jayden.

His heart flutters in the way he had almost read his mind, coming to aid him quickly when he had called for help inside his head. Jayden's back was turned to him, his whole body rigid as he placed himself in front of Troy.

Once again, he had come in to save Troy, and his heart skipped a beat.

"Fuck Off," Jayden snarls darkly at Victor, who is intoxicated. He snatches his hand back for a moment, pointing at Troy, who flinches roughly. Something about his reaction only angers Jayden even more as he takes a step back, allowing Troy to grab onto his hoodie.

"He was the one that shoved me and didn't even offer an apology," he snaps.

"You can say that to everyone else at this party," Jayden shoots back, narrowing his eyes.

"Think you're hotshot, buddy? Just because you play tennis? Fucking faggot," Victor throws back, and just as he tries grabbing for Troy again, Jayden beats him to the punch. Without missing a beat, he takes a swing at him, a chorus of gasps filling the room when he falls onto the floor with a loud thud. Everyone seems to quickly sober up nearby, putting a distance space from getting mingled in the crossfire.

Hell, even his teammates were in shock because he had come to aid others before but never made a move to punch first. For a moment, no one can mutter a word, their mind not entirely processing his brute strength and the way he had moved with swift precision.

Instantly, despite the music still raging in the background—everyone was in shock and disbelief at the scene unfolding in front of them. Mr. Nice, who had never laid a hand on another person, had done just that.

If only the other knew the reason Jayden had even held back was because of Troy fisting the back of his sweater. If it hadn't been, he's more than confident he would have caved into the desires of relieving his strength and sending his ass to the hospital.

Break his parent's hearts.

Still, when he hears Victor calling Troy that, he can't help himself.

He allowed his emotions and impulses to win in front of everyone.

How the hell do these people still exist with that mindset?

"Do you want to say that again?" he snarls darkly, a tremor running down the back of those who had heard the venom in his voice. Victor could barely stand back on his feet with how intoxicated he was, but even more so when Trevis came with some of the other Kappa members who realized what was happening amongst the commission.

"Last I check, you're kicked out from Rho's place, Victor," Trevis starts, standing in front of Jayden.

"You want me to get him?" one of the Kappa members suggests, and instantly, Victor freezes, knowing he won't be able to take them all on. After all, Rho had made it very clear that the last time he had come to his party, he would personally kick his ass.

"The party's shit anyway."

With that, he starts cursing to himself while stumbling his way out. Luckily enough, the party goes back into full swing shortly after, everyone minding their own business per usual, just as Jayden turns to Troy. Raising his hand, he signs, "Are you okay?"

"Yeah," Troy signs back, though, from the shakiness of his hands, he wasn't entirely convinced either.

Turning to Trevis and the others, Jayden clears his throat. "Can you find Rho and let them know I'm going upstairs to calm Troy down? Explain the situation and if you find Troy's friend, Quinn, text me and explain it."

"Got it," he nods.

With that, Jayden turns his attention back to Troy, who is still staring around rather meekly, clearly confused and overstimulated by everything. It tugged at Jayden's heart more so than he'd like to admit. In fact, he wanted nothing more than to find the fucker again and beat him for even scaring him. Still, he had to compose himself as he signs, "Let's go somewhere quieter until you can settle down."

He didn't wait for a reply before taking Troy's hand into his and going upstairs.

CHAPTER TWENTY-ONE

What the hell?

What the hell was *that*?

There's a roaring in the back of Jayden's skull, his heart thumping wildly while his blood boils. There's a ringing in his ear, something he often feels when he does something irrational, thrilling, and daring that is adrenaline-seeking.

Street racing at one in the morning.

Jumping off a cliff into the waters without precautions.

Ice swimming in Lake Michigan and, once, even walking across it.

Knowing the danger that might come in brushing upon death was something he longed for.

It goes without saying that the more Jayden puts himself in the probability of the unknown, the more he feels like he's living again since the death of his twin brother because of him. Feeling anything was better than the anguish and nothingness of losing his best friend.

Yet, he had always separated the two because he couldn't fathom the thought of disappointing and worrying his parents again. He knows in his mind that he owed that much to be the perfect son to make up for what he had taken.

Going as far as to impersonate everything his younger twin brother was—perfect, meek, intelligent.

Going as far as agreeing to their father's dreams and ambitions he put on Weston now pushed onto him.

Going as far as allowing their mother to call him Weston and pretend whenever he visited that he was alive.

That the one dead was him when he ran away into the woods in the middle of the night.

At times, he hated how he started to resent his twin brother, who had died, making him take everything that he should have done. While Jayden loved playing tennis and how it distracts him, it wasn't something he enjoyed doing growing up.

Unlike his brother.

In fact, it was one of the rare sports aside from cricket that his chess-loving twin liked to partake in. Jayden knew that he owed his parents that much for putting up with him when he should have faced worse for being the reason their perfect child was dead.

So, something like punching another person and potentially ruining the reputation he built for his family?

It was something Jayden never thought he'd do in front of witnesses.

Everything thriller-seeking he has done to date had been done alone or sometimes with Trevis.

Yet, he can't say he regrets it either, strangely enough.

He had worked for his reputation as Mr. Nice around campus, but right now, he wanted to curse everyone out who just stood there and watched rather than trying to help. So when they get into Rho's bedroom, he slams it shut, but it doesn't help settle his nerves in the slightest.

He had presumed that putting a physical barrier would do something, but at this point, Jayden is somewhat convinced that what would help is finishing the job. Perhaps he should have knocked some of his goddamn teeth out and broken his fingers for—

A small, animal-like squeak jots Jayden back to reality.

He whirls his head to see Troy looking down at where Jayden is still gripping hard onto his wrist. Though he didn't struggle to free himself, he looked down at their joint hands with a flushed expression.

Fuck.

Immediately, Jayden let go of Troy's wrist. He had forgotten he was holding on, and his stomach churns when he sees how red it is. He swallows the lump in his throat, guilt eating him up before signing, "I'm sorry."

"It's okay," Troy signs, shaking his head, but Jayden knows it isn't.

Why did he have to lie?

Just like his brother when Jayden accidentally hit him too hard as a kid and made him bruise.

Weston said it was okay but heard him crying. When he excused himself to go to the bathroom, he cried.

He hurt him, and he said it was okay, and now Troy was doing the same thing.

Just like when he had apologized for being deaf, it only made Jayden's mood worsen.

Why did he have to apologize? Why did he have to say it's okay when it isn't?

"It's not okay," he signs out tensely, narrowing his eyes at his wrist. "I hurt you."

"It's nothing, really," he counters, and Troy really does mean it. Yet when Jayden still didn't look convinced, he smiled gently. "Jayden, I'm fine. I appreciate your concern, but it's barely anything, I promise. Though I should be thanking you for saving me back there."

He presses his lips into a thin line before he sighs, going to sit on the edge of the bed. Feeling rather awkward for just standing there, Troy takes a seat next to him as well but keeps a relative distance while looking around the room absentmindedly.

Troy did feel bad for imposing on another stranger's room, but given what happened downstairs, he also wanted a chance to calm down. His phone is still in his back pocket on vibrate, and since it's not ringing off the hook, Quinn probably hasn't caught wind of the situation yet.

Somehow, that makes him feel a tad better because he'd hate to ruin her night because of him.

Not to mention, it was him who wanted to come to the party and got upset when he had presumed he wasn't invited. It was confusing, and the alcohol wasn't helping him in the slightest with sorting out his rather conflicting feelings.

Plus, a small part of him withers that he had accidentally dragged Jayden into his mess again because of his disability.

It seems from the moment they've been paired that he's been doing so much more than Troy knew how to repay. He swallows the lump in his throat, staring down at the hem of his shirt before turning back to Jayden, who begins signing.

"Where's Quinn? Should I go get her?"

"No, I don't want to bother her," Troy quickly signs back, shaking his head furiously. "If anything, she can call me, or I can call her. But, please...I don't want to inconvenience her right now...or you. You can ...go back to the party. I'll be fine; I'm sorry."

It takes everything in Jayden not to lose his temper and flip Rho's room inside out as he takes a deep breath. There were so many things with what he had said, and it only upset him that he didn't even know it.

Why is he apologizing?

How can he think he's an inconvenience after that rather traumatic experience earlier?

"You're not an inconvenience to anyone, and don't apologize," he signs, trying to school his expression, but it only seems to be getting harder and harder. When he agreed to come to the party, he certainly didn't expect the night to go like this. "If anything, it should be me apologizing as I should have been with you from the start."

"I can't force you to babysit me," he sighs, brows bumped together, feeling quite offended.

"You're not forcing me to do anything, much less babysitting you; trust me on that one. I should have looked out for you and Quinn because you're my friends," he clarifies, raising his pinky to give more stress to the last word. Plus, it wasn't like Jayden wanted to even be here tonight, but he wasn't going to make Troy feel guilty because Jayden wanted to come because of Troy anyway. He's already thankful he decided to because he's certain no one would have jumped in. "There's nothing more to it than me wanting to because I just do. Why is that a hard concept to understand?"

But *why*?

The question wavers in Troy's hands, the tip of his fingers twitching because he wants to ask, but he doesn't want to seem as if he is fishing for something, either. After all, his parents and Quinn look out for him because they love him as a person—as a son and a friend in Quinn's case— and he's more than thankful for them.

However, it's not as if Jayden and he weren't teammates first and foremost...right?

Why was he willing to do so much for him in the first place?

Why does he know sign language?

Why does he get so heated when it comes to him?

There's still so much that Troy feels like he doesn't understand when it comes to Jayden.

"You...really are a nice person, Jayden," Troy finally ends up signing, completely at a loss for his words. He isn't even sure if it's the alcohol finally in full swing, but he can feel his whole body heating up. Perhaps it's just too hot in the room with all the windows closed. "I'm glad you consider me a friend."

Troy then glances at him shyly, greeted with one of his rare smiles that shows off his dimples. Despite the younger student being around his older upperclassman before, those smiles were relatively rare. It's almost like a persona he had put on.

Troy had seen more than he'd like to recall.

Why?

He's jotted back from his curious, swirling mind when Jayden suddenly gets up from the bed, taking Troy by surprise. Jayden then places a hand on top of his forehead with a frown before signing: "Stay here, okay? I'll be right back."

"Yes, why?" he signs, baffled.

If Jayden wanted to return to the party, Troy would never try to stop him. However, he didn't think it would be right to hang around a stranger's room and in the pits of his stomach; he didn't like the idea either.

So, is that the reason why a small part of him was rather upset about being left here?

"What do you mean by?" Jayden questions, and suddenly, Troy realizes how rude it may sound.

"No, I just wanted to know, but if you wanted to go have fun first, I get it," he fumbles, his hand growing clammy. "I mean, this is a party, and it's probably not fun just hanging up here when the life is downstairs, so—"

"I'm going to get you water to drink and help clear your head, but I'm worried someone might try coming up here," Jayden articulates before opening the door and turning back, "Just in case, lock the door. Your phone is on vibrate, yes?"

"Yes."

"I'll text you when I'm coming up. Until then, lock it."

With that, he turned to leave first, and something about

him being so protective and concerned about his safety did something funny inside his heart. He gets up from where he had been awkwardly sitting on the edge of the bed, locking it.

Though not a minute later, Jayden texts him that he's back at the door and returns with two bottles of water. Upon closer inspection, Troy realizes he also had a bottle of vodka, canned beers, and a box of pizza as well.

Coming in, Troy closes the door again just as he settles everything—including himself—onto the rug in the middle of the room. He decides to follow suit, not getting to ask before Jayden beats him to it by handing a bottle of water to him first.

"Here, have some water. Your whole face is flushed."

If only Jayden knew that it was not just because of the alcohol, but Troy would never admit it. Instead, he took it, chugging it down, and didn't even realize how thirsty he had been. Swiping the back of his hand, he smiles at Jayden. "Thank you."

"How much did you drink anyway?"

Troy racks the back of his head at the question for a moment. "Honestly, about a cup."

He was on his merry way for a second cup to help ease his mind and anxiety when he bumped into that guy. Of course, it goes without saying that everyone then found out where that led to. After seeing his answer, Jayden cocks his head to the side. "You're not much of a drinker, huh?"

"I'm not much of a party person," Troy confesses, twiddling his thumbs. Most people his age loved partying, from what he had read online, and talking with Quinn. It's all about letting loose, connecting with people, and just having fun for two years before sobering up with your major classes.

Perhaps it's because he grew up rather sheltered, but he much preferred reading a book, playing video games, or just binge-watching a series of shorts with buttered popcorn. In addition, just being around people was rather draining.

"Yeah, it was the reason I didn't want to invite you in the beginning, if I'm clarifying. It's not wanting to seclude you by not inviting you purposefully or thinking it's a hassle because you're deaf. It's because inviting you would maybe put you in a tough spot between thinking you have to because you're part of a team versus going to the party because you want to," he explains.

Then, he downs his own water. Again, it's an excellent opportunity for Troy to think of his response, and again, he finds himself surprised at how much Jayden had already thought about this. If it hadn't been for Quinn, there's a high possibility he might have shown up just for a bit before leaving.

After all, aside from Benajmin and Trevis, he didn't have anyone else to talk to. The last thing he wants is to also cling to them either. With a sigh, he signs, "I thought it would be fun...I mean, it is...up until that part."

"Why did you want to come then? To be closer to the team?"

"Well, it's not just to feel like a part of the team by any means," Troy disputes because the team has been more than kind and accommodating. They even looked happy, just smiling and waving at him, while others would write in his notepad whenever they wanted to talk to him about a certain technique. "I know how much Quinn wants to experience the full college life, and I figured if I could repay her kindness, I should as her friend."

"She didn't look after you though—some friend," he quips with narrowed eyes, and Troy quickly jumps to defend Quinn. Troy did know where he was coming from, but at the same time, it's not like it wasn't him who told her to have fun.

"No, it was my fault. She told me I should say hi to you, and I wanted to—"

"You wanted to talk to me alone?" Jayden questions, and currently, Troy wishes the carpet would open a hole right there. He fumbles hastily for the water, gulping some more down in hopes it would help balance out his drunken state, even to be blabbing something like this in the first place, and then shakes his head.

"No."

"Hm, I find that hard to believe," Jayden signs, the grin widening as he leans onto the edge of the bed.

"Really!"

Troy watches as he laughs, and again, he finds himself wondering just what it would sound like. From what Quinn had said, usually in her romance novels, it's deep, sexy, and seductive. For some reason, Troy feels like that would match Jayden quite well. A small amount of time passes before Jayden rubs the back of his head, almost gathering courage before tilting his head to the side.

"Well, what about Benjamin then?"

Benjamin?

Where did that come from?

"What about him?" Troy signs, lips puckers.

"You both looked as if you were having a good time."

Raking his brain once more, Troy only becomes more confused. "No, he was just being friendly."

Friendly was the least of it, but Troy wasn't looking to cause a problem. He didn't dare that at that moment; it almost looks as if Jayden is relieved by that statement. It's the way in which his shoulders drop momentarily before he follows up with his next question.

"Do you want to tell me what happened?"

CHAPTER TWENTY-TWO

Just like that, Troy's mood dropped ever so slightly.

Troy is confident that he has already heard it from that person, but he still decides to recount it from his point of view. "I was drinking, and someone stumbled into me. Unfortunately, I accidentally spilled some on him, and I wanted to apologize, but…I completely froze."

It was more than just freezing, but Troy didn't think it was even appropriate to bring up his past, which only four people knew, consisting of his parents, Quinn, and his therapist. When that stranger started yelling, all Troy could hear was white noise, his anger and drunkenness reminding him so much of *that* person that he couldn't think.

He couldn't even move.

Something told Jayden from that far-away look in his eyes that there was more to it than that by how terrifyingly pale Troy looked at that moment. Not wanting to push it but didn't want him to get overwhelmed by his own thoughts, he sighs, "Troy, it's not your fault."

He lets out a small huff. "I...I should have...I don't know, did something."

Every time he signs, he *hates* it because it almost serves as a reminder.

That he was different.

No matter what, he will always be faced with these disadvantages that were not of the "norm."

He should have accepted it long ago, but he sometimes wonders what it would be like if he wasn't deaf. If he could be a normal person and not have his parents worrying about him. His toes curl in his beaten-up white shoes before working up the courage to look at Jayden, who gives a stern expression. "Don't blame yourself; he was an asshole."

"Still, I did spill my drink on him, so I can't say it's exactly his fault," he quips weakly with his hands.

"Even if you did, it doesn't mean he should get violent just because he didn't understand the whole situation," he throws back, his hand signing faster to give emphasis. Jayden could feel himself getting angry on Troy's behalf, mainly because he looked dejected and skeptical.

"I mean, if I weren't so useless and incapable, then maybe there wouldn't be this issue," he bitterly signs. Troy is more than confident it's the alcohol talking at this point, but he can't stop. "Sometimes, I wonder why I was *born* if it'll be this way. Why am I even here when I'm causing nothing but pain to everyone?"

His parents had to give up many aspects of comfort to accommodate him.

Quinn always gushes about the latest movie, fashion trend, or parties on campus but doesn't go.

He knows it's because she's a great friend and he has the best present, but he feels like a burden.

Frustrated tears prick at the corner of his eyes, and he knows how inconsiderate it sounds, but he can't help it. He wanted to enjoy the party and not feel as if he was being babysat by Quinn, who probably had missed out on many things because of him.

Still, it eats him up from the inside, gnawing and gnawing on his insides until this *very* moment.

The next thing Troy realizes is that Jayden cups one side of his face and forces him to look at him. The younger gentleman's breath hitches, especially when he sees the seriousness in his expression. He definitely has to be drunk because he can't recall Jayden being this beautiful either that it entirely steals his breath away.

When he releases them, it takes everything in Troy not to frown at the cold and empty it feels. Rather, he focuses on his hands as he slowly signs, "Troy, do not ever talk to yourself like that again. Do I make myself clear?"

"You can't say it's not tr—"

Much to Troy's bewilderment, Jayden grabs his hands and clasps them between his. They're so much bigger and more wonderous, but what caught him off guard was for him to settle Troy's hands between Jayden's knees and lock them together.

Essentially shushing him.

It's something Troy finds amusing for some reason

because he's never been quieted this way before. It had been just signing over him for his parents and even Quinn, but something about this feels...more intimate and personal that Troy didn't know what to make of it.

He had to physically silence him to know that Jayden was so serious about what he wanted to say.

"I know I'm coming from a place of privilege when I tell you this, but I am more than sincere that you are perfect the way you are. Your struggles do not define you, but they should refine you. You're stronger than you give yourself credit for even to get this far, chase your dreams, and play tennis," he starts. "People who can hear can't play as good as you. Your talent should define you, not your disability."

Both of his hands twitch from where they're being squished between Jayden's knees as he stares at him. He can barely process his words properly, feeling the tip of his ears reddening and his eyes getting rather watery.

Not to mention, his heart skips a beat at Jayden's words because...because what the heck?

How can he say the words that seem to make everything all right?

Like everything is going to be okay?

His parents and Quinn had comforted him before, but it was to reassure him that he was not a nuisance to them at all and that they loved him regardless of everything. It's enough to make him shy because he's never had someone so passionate in comforting him before, but it seems no one can match when it comes to Jayden.

Except, he wasn't done talking yet.

"It's not your disabilities but your abilities that count. Let me tell you that you're one of the best players that Coach and I have ever seen because you don't let your disabilities characterize you. You train yourself to be better than any other players I've gone against before competitively," he signs, and Troy is confident he stopped breathing. "You're going to be an inspiration one day, Troy. You don't need to be fixed or dwell on ifs—focus on what is. Don't look at your disability as one but something you can use as an inspiration and accept yourself. One needs to be accepted for who they are, and that starts with you believing in yourself."

It didn't take long before the alcohol came full swing, and Troy's lips started to quiver. He quickly rubs at the corner of his eyes, his heart feeling so full and content with his statement that he didn't even know where to start.

Don't focus on what ifs, but on what is.

Be an inspiration for those in the sports world who are inspiring players, who want to give up before trying. The only reason he even gave it a shot was with the support of his parent and Quinn. He wants to be the one heartening others to chase it.

To not let a disability define them.

"Thank you," Troy signs, at a loss for words because, more often than not, it's Jayden helping him more than the other way around. To have someone who isn't deaf understand his struggles is amazing, and again, Troy wonders why he knows sign language. "Really, I don't know how I can repay you."

"That's what friends are for," he replies. "I mean it, don't ever talk yourself down like that again."

"Yeah, I won't," he nods in agreement before deciding they need to cheer up the mood. This is supposed to be a night of celebration for moving forward in the next tournament, not having a pity party. "So...what's all this?"

The grin appears on Jayden's face, and Troy's heart does those weird skipping again.

"Well, who says that the life of the party has to be just downstairs? I managed to find Quinn; who knows I'm with you, and I heard you like pizza, so..." he trails off towards the pizza box, popping the cardboard open, and the smell wafts through the room. Instantly, Troy's mouth watered, and he didn't even realize just how hungry he had been. "Let's have our own private party. I told Quinn she's invited up here at any time."

"Isn't this someone else's room?"

"He owes me," he signs with a half-shrug, opening a beer.

"Is that right?"

"With how I helped him be a wingman? Yeah, he does," he answers, and then they indulge entirely in their own little celebration party for the next hour. It was better than any party, in Troy's opinion, and strangely enough, he felt comfortable enough to not only be alone with him but drink with him as well.

Something he didn't think would be possible with anyone of the same gender after that night.

Troy supposes it's because he had been to Jayden's apartment before and didn't try anything.

Plus, he didn't seem like the type to take advantage of someone.

Though then again, neither did *he*.

Troy had no idea how many shots or cans of beer he had neither, their hands becoming increasingly incoherent, but it felt so nice. The more he talks with Jayden, the more he sees these other layers of him that he has never shown anyone.

Troy notices how much they're getting closer every time they talk. It doesn't make it better that the room is getting even hotter now as Troy sways from side to side. The more he looks at Jayden, the more he really does recognize just how gorgeous he is.

Ever so slowly, Troy's eyes drift down to Jayden's lips, and he grins.

"You have crumbs all over your face," he remarks. Rather than trying to find tissues, he'd figure it would be easier to use his hands. Except, what he didn't expect was how magnetizing Jayden's eyes would be and how close their faces were.

God, why did he have to look so kissable?

Neither one of them said anything, nor did the other pull away either. There's a light buzzing in the back of Troy's mind, but he can't even form coherent thoughts. All he can think about is how Jayden's lips would feel against his.

Why the hell not?

Don't focus on what-ifs; focus on what-is.

At this moment, what is true is wanting to kiss him.

Gathering all the courage he can muster, it's then that Troy does the unthinkable.

He leans the remaining distance and takes the initiative to kiss Jayden first.

At that moment, Troy had no idea if it was because he was completely wasted, but everything seemed to explode. Just like all those cliché romance movies and books that Quinn gushes on about that Troy is sure it's nothing more than crazy claims.

How wrong he feels now.

A big bang of sorts that was groundbreaking.

Sparks were flying, almost like a thousand fireworks were going off at once.

Butterflies explode from the depths of his stomach, almost like they're threatening to spill.

Honestly, it wasn't what he had expected at all to kiss another person—of the same sex, no less— but in a good way. For one thing, his fantasies of kissing Jayden failed to account for just how soft his lips are, almost like a rose petal, or the pounding of their hearts back onto one another with the smell of fresh spring showers and morning dew.

How is it possible for another to smell this good?

In fact, Troy felt like his heart was about to explode out of his chest when Jayden cupped his cheek and deepened it before parting his mouth, gently guiding their kiss deeper. It certainly feels much different than those pecks he had given to his middle school girlfriends or the girl he had taken to prom.

After what feels all too soon, they pull away from one another, and Troy looks at those brilliantly bright green eyes.

Troy's head is completely muddled as he lifts his hand to say something. Yet the next thing he knew, the world spins.

His brain lurches and a sense of dread settles at the bottom of his stomach.

He didn't mean for himself to get this drunk while talking to Jayden to pass the time. He had only wanted to drink enough to celebrate their win and advance to the next game. Not to mention to forget the disaster that happened downstairs about an hour ago.

He didn't want to black out.

The last time something like this happened, he was almost taken advantage of. Bile builds in his throat, and soon, he remembers hitting something muscular and so warm that it made his panicked mind settle just a *bit*.

This man that he had kissed only confirmed what he already had known.

This man who makes him feel a certain way he's never felt around anyone before.

This man who keeps saving him time and time again in more than one way when Troy needs it.

Jayden.

For some reason, he feels like he can *trust* this man who has protected him many times before.

Yelled at him, too, when he had tried to save him but ended up being the one drowning instead.

Who ran with him every morning and made him feel included since joining the team.

The last thing he recalled was that a pair of arms soon wrapped around his smaller, which was so comforting.

Then… everything went black.

Yet, he didn't seem to worry in the slightest because it was him.

Once he falls right into Jayden's chest, the man is left completely baffled for a moment before concern and worries overtake his system. He gently pulls Troy away and sees he's still breathing with a light flush spread across his face. His nose twitched, and it seemed he had completely blacked out.

Upon that realization, he lets out a groan.

Cruel.

Too cruel, Troy.

How can someone be so trusting like this?

Then again, this is the same person who chased him out and almost drowned.

The last person who did so was his brother, and look where that ended up.

Yet, Troy is the same person who came to his apartment despite his nervousness.

Something inside of Jayden's heart aches, and he finds himself growing enraged at once for Troy's carelessness. Had it been anyone else, they might have taken advantage of the situation in his blacked-out state.

Is he like this with him or everyone?

Why does the thought of him potentially getting into trouble bother him so much?

He tells himself he sees his little brother in the small things that Troy does, and he feels the urge to protect him from the fact that he's deaf, which first drew him in, to his personality and his being so caring and passionate about everything he did.

Sure, he was cute and quite good-looking—Jayden wasn't blind.

However, he had told himself he would never sleep with someone from the team.

When Jayden thought about just sleeping with him, his face scrunches together at how wrong it feels. From the amount of time that he had spent with Troy as his tennis partner, Jayden already deduced that he deserved so much more than he'd let himself believe.

Someone willing to take him out on regular dates.

Someone willing to give themselves to Troy and care for him.

Someone whose parents accept his sexual preferences rather than say that it is a *phase*.

Woah, dating?

The thought quickly makes Jayden frown, with his brows bumped together in confusion.

It's not as if he hasn't drunkenly kissed someone before or had a one-night stand, so for Jayden to still be thinking about what Troy deserves at the kiss itself struck him as odd. He had to admit it was different from what he had imagined.

It was awkward, almost innocent, making Jayden question if that was even his first kiss. It's not as if he would ask anyway because it was clearly an "in the moment" kind of situation. With how much he had drunk, Troy would probably not remember any of this by tomorrow morning anyway.

Again, why did that bother him?

Why did a part of him want Troy to remember?

Why did his lips still tingle with the smell of berries and rosewood? Why was he still *thinking* about it?

The more he tried thinking of a proper answer, the more frustrated he got before he took out his phone with a grunt. There's no way he'll leave Troy completely defenseless right now in a frat boy's room, just in case.

With that, he takes out his phone and makes a call.

All the while, his lips still tingles, and for the first time in his life—his heart was pounding.

Yet, he wasn't doing anything thrilling to have caused it except an awkward drunk kiss with Troy.

CHAPTER TWENTY-THREE

"**S**o…did you do it?"

Jayden could feel his eye twitching in annoyance at Trevis's question—something he had long been expecting since the party two days ago. But frankly, he was surprised it even took him this long to bring it up.

It had to be Monday morning during their practice before everyone showed up.

Of course, it also happened to be right when he was getting his ass kicked at thirty to love—

Also known as zero.

Fortunately, or unfortunately—Jayden isn't sure yet which is it—Troy couldn't meet for their daily morning jog before practice. Hence Jayden is even entertaining Trevis, of all people. He knows he's trying to rile him up but refuses to fall into his trap.

"Do what?" he deadpans, arching a brow.

"What do you mean, you sly fox? Obviously this," he grins, making a circle by connecting his thumb and middle finger. Then, using the butt cap of his tennis racket, he moves it into the space he created with his fingers while wagging his eyebrows suggestively.

Sometimes, Jayden really does want to throw his damn racket at him, but he remains composed.

Instead, he bounces the tennis ball and catches it several times to recollect his thoughts and breath. When he and Trevis played, they didn't hold anything back. It was precisely what he needed; this time, it was no exception either by the sweat trickling down his face.

"One, do you think I would *ever* have done anything in *Rho's* bedroom?" he begins, ticking one finger down before continuing. "Second, may I remind you that even though a certain *someone* had drunkenly done just that last year, it doesn't mean everyone would have a bad judgment?"

"Hey, I treated Rho out for a month after!"

Third," Jayden continues like Trevis didn't just talk. "Fuck knows how many microorganisms are growing on his bed and how dirty his sheets are, especially since that guy doesn't even know how to change the damn things."

It's enough to make him shiver because he sat on it.

At the very edge of Rho's bed, it still counted.

"Wait, you're supposed to change them?" Trevis gawks in shock. When Jayden's face scrunches in pure disgust at his comment and takes a step back despite them being on opposite ends of the court, he quickly retracts his words. "I'm joking!"

"Are you?" he drawls out.

"Yeah, I change it every six months!"

Christ, Jayden makes a mental note to stay on his bed when he goes over. He can't even find it in his heart to try correcting him as he continues his last point. "Lastly, when I brought Troy down, he was completely unconscious. Do I have to remind you?"

"Maybe sex with you is so good that he fainted," he remarks casually.

Was he serious?

At this point, Jayden questions why he is friends with this man. From the look on his face, he does think it's a possibility. He tilts his head to the side and squints his eyes, thankful that no one else is here yet for practice.

"Seriously?" he questions expressionlessly.

"What? That's the rumors going on about you; I have, you know," he exclaims, huffing out his chest with his eyes closed like a proud peacock. It's all the opening Jayden needed to serve the ball without any warning. But, unfortunately, by the time the echoing sound of the ball encounters the tennis racket's net process, it's too late.

Trevis misses it by a nick of time before pointing his racket at him. "Hey! You're a fucking cheater!"

Just like that, the game ends forty to love.

"Didn't Couch touch you anything, *love*?" he emphasized, grinning widely at the double representation. When Trevis goes to flip him off, he rolls his eyes, letting the racket rest on his shoulder. "I may be bisexual, but I am *never* going to fuck you."

Not just because he has vowed never to sleep from the team but because Trevis is his friend.

Though most importantly, he wasn't his type in the slightest.

Something which Trevis looks actually offended by. "I just brought up the rumors, not that it was a suggestion that I want to sleep with you! May I also remind you that you kissed me rather than the other way around?"

At that, he snorts since the full detail was that though he suggested it to get rid of a girl hounding his ass, he also didn't dare to go through with it. Jayden makes his way back to the bleacher to grab his drink, and once he's parched, he arches a brow.

"You sure do bring it up a lot now that I think about it," he comments.

"Fuck off," he retorts, grabbing his own water bottle and jogging it. They slump onto the seat once they can breathe properly, and he looks at him expectedly. "So, what happened at the party?"

The question makes Jayden stiffen back up, completely forgetting the conversation.

What happened? Fuck, where would he start with that if he wanted to?

He resists the urge to think back to the kiss, something that he can't stop thinking about nonstop, which is a rather large concern. It was just a simple, drunk kiss initiated by Troy, and yet, Jayden's mind seems to hover over that particular memory repetitively.

However, he wasn't going to tell Trevis that.

For one, Jayden knew deep down that he'd be tormented to death by the constant teasing. The second and bigger reason was that he didn't even know why it had been on his mind so much. So rather than telling him any of that, Jayden leans back, giving a slow half-shrug. "We ate and drank after we got up at Rho's."

Trevis throws him a somewhat skeptical and astonished look. "That's it?"

"Why do you sound surprised?"

"Hm…" he trails off momentarily and then shakes his head. "Nothing."

"Spit it out," Jayden scowls, bumping his knee onto his rather harshly. When Trevis usually says it's nothing, he doesn't want to share it unless it's beaten out of him or threatened. Jayden certainly wasn't in the mood to fool around, either from his hangover last night or his lack of sleep paired with Troy canceling this morning. "Trevis, I swear if you don't say it—"

"Okay, okay, damn," he interjects, holding out his hands in surrender before sighing. He rubs the back of his head, looking around the court. "Since no one is here yet, I just want to say that what you did…the way you reacted was shocking not only for me and your teammates but everyone else there."

"Yeah, I figured as much," he replies, following behind Trevis in sighing a moment later.

"You never laid a hand on someone before like that, at least…not before trying to de-escalate the situation," he continues, his expression completely serious now. "You didn't stop, and some of the guys thought you might have been given some sort of drug in your drink to react the way you did."

"The fucker had it coming; let's get that clear," he scowls.

Just thinking about it is enough to get his blood boiling once more.

"Oh yeah, for sure. The fucker knew what he did was wrong, which is why we haven't heard a peep since," Trevis nods in agreement. "However, you wouldn't stop, which prompted me to ask—from one friend to another—are you Troy doesn't mean anything?"

"You'd like it to so you would win the bet, right?" he quips.

"Or I'm trying to be a good friend and make you stubbornly come to the realization that maybe you do find him more attractive than you're willing to lead on," he retaliates. "Look, I know that has it been anyone of us, you would step in but not attack him like you had when it came to Troy. Am I on the right track?"

He is, and Trevis hated it.

Had it been Trevis in Troy's situation that night or anyone else, he would have stepped in.

Just not act the way he did when it came to them, as when he saw the terrified look on Troy's face, it made him utterly ballistic. He never lost himself like that, letting his emotions and wants out in front of others.

It was freeing addicting, as much as it was horrifying.

Why?

What was it about Troy that made him lose control this easily?

Is it because Troy reminds him so much of his little brother?

Or was it because it was his tear-stricken face?

Something told him it was the latter, and it was entirely new that Jayden didn't know what to make of it. So, he decides to glare at his friend through narrowed eyes. "So? What's the point you're trying to make?"

"Something more happened that you're not telling me, right?" he ponders, and instantly, Jayden is thrown back to the party over the weekend. He's received many kisses over his lifetime, and it wasn't him bragging by any means, just a fact.

Yet nothing shook him up the way Troy's kiss did, and it was a small *peck*.

He feels his heart doing something funny, and he shoves Trevis. "Fuck off."

At that, he chuckles before his expression becomes serious once more. "Word of warning that if you want to pull out at any time, you better do so if you don't want to get hurt. I would hate to see you or Troy hurt. He's pretty nice."

Hurt? As if.

There's a reason why he doesn't do relationships, much less try to get into one with a man.

He was going to keep up the façade for the sake of his parents until the day he died.

Win this year's championship, get scouted, and sign with a major league.

Accomplish winning all four major championships.

Make his parents—his brother who was supposed to be living *this* life—proud.

Jayden didn't get to say anything more when the metal

doors leading to the courts groaned loudly, and numerous chatters loitered in. Their teammate is rowdy as ever in complaining about how fast the weekend went and needed to get ready before Coach makes them do some grueling training as punishment while heading into the locker room.

Cassie is the first to holler at them as soon as his eyes sweep over them.

"Hey, look, it's Jay and Trevis. You should have told us you were already here practicing!"

"Should have used your hands and looked in," Trevis hollers back, getting up to join them.

However, Jayden doesn't move from his seat in the slightest—his eyes are practically fastened onto Troy, who is talking with Benjamin via a notepad. Jayden is more than confident he could have burned a damn hole into his body from how intensely he stared at him.

Hungover? Troy seemed just fine, and not only that, but he seemed happy talking with Benjamin.

What were they talking about? Why isn't Troy looking at him? Why does he care?

It is only when they get to the halfway point towards the locker room that *finally*, Troy glances his way. Their eyes connect, and for Jayden, it did feel like something had changed since that drunken kiss. He wasn't sure if he remembered it, and it's been eating him up.

Though, just as swiftly, he looks away before speeding off to change with Benjamin in tow.

Something in him, vile and ugly, churned inside of his stomach.

Did he fuck up that badly?

Did he remember what happened and how Jayden didn't try to stop him?

The uncertainty gnaws at his insides, and he has no idea how he'd be able to make it through practice. It doesn't make it better that they're partners as well. Sitting on the bleachers, he bounces his legs while tugging at the ends of his hair.

Fuck.

His worst fear does come true less than fifteen minutes later when practice officially begins, and Troy refuses to meet his eyes aside from their usual greeting. When Jayden then asked how his head was, he gave an awkward smile that Jayden could tell it's fake before signing that nothing water couldn't solve.

Even their usual teamwork and synchronization when it comes to playing was off-beat.

It didn't make it any better that, by the minute, the pressure and anxiousness only added fuel to the burning storm inside of Jayden's mind. When they lose once again, Jayden can't take it anymore. He looks up at the ceiling temporarily.

Ah, to hell with this.

"Coach, I need ten," Jayden calls out. From the look on Coach Winter's face, he looks ready to beg for them to work out whatever the hell is going on between them. When Jayden looks back at Troy's confused face, he signs. "Can I speak to you privately for a moment?"

Instantly, he sees how Troy tenses which only upsets him even more.

After all, the answer was more than clear about the fact that he remembers what happened that night. Not just that, but it informs Jayden of where Troy stands regarding that drunken kiss. He watches as Troy then swallows the lump in his throat to sign. "Okay."

With that, Jayden makes his way toward the locker room first before holding it out for Troy. Once inside, Jayden doesn't see the point in beating around the bushes anymore. He decides to jump right into it.

"So about…last Friday," he begins, his hand movement slow and somewhat uneasy.

Inwardly, Jayden finds himself inadvertently cringing, but it grows even more when he sees the way Troy practically recoils a bit. It gives Jayden all he needs to know about how Troy felt about it, and the last thing he would ever want is to make him feel pressured.

"Jayden—"

"I'm sorry I kissed you," Jayden signs, cutting his sign off. "I know my words may not mean much, but I really am."

After all, it seems that if he doesn't want to bring it up and acts uncomfortable the entire time, then it means it was just a silly mistake. Of course, he made many mistakes when drunk, so who was he to think no one else would?

Troy blinks several times, almost baffled, before he finds the right words with his hands. "You…what?"

"It was out of line for me," he signs back, and while Jayden wanted to say it was a drunken mistake and he could forget it, truthfully, he *couldn't*. In his life, he regretted *many* things that he could think of at the drop of a hat.

Running away from home as a child got his twin brother—the better one—killed.

He was unable to do what he wanted for the sake of his parents to repay them.

Yet the kiss? He didn't, but he would never say it out loud.

"Wait, you...kissed me?" Troy reiterates, his brows bumping together in bafflement.

It really was the other way around, but he didn't want Troy to take the blame. Jayden is more than certain he didn't recall much, so he'll take the blame if it means accepting the responsibility. He nods, brushing his hair back before signing. "Yes. It was a mistake, and again, I'm sorry. If you want to switch partners, I'm more than fine with it and—"

"No," Troy signs quickly, shaking his head furiously. It shocks Jayden by his moment of outburst as the flush blooms across his face. "I mean, no, it's okay. I'm sorry as well; I didn't know how to...I mean...about what happened—"

"It's okay," he cuts him off, trying to save Troy from further embarrassing himself. "I get it. Are you...fine? Like really? With everything? If not, I do understand I don't mind switching if that's going to make you feel more comfortable."

"You do make me comfortable," he blurts out with his hands and then fumbles with his hands. "I...what you did was very sweet, and I just didn't know how to thank you for everything you've done up until this point."

"We're friends," he retorts. "Aren't we?"

"Yeah," he signs, but Jayden notices the pause before he has signed that one word, albeit a bit stiffly too. "Yeah, we're…friends. If that's it, I'm going to call it a day first since…my head is still killing me. Can you please tell Coach?"

He didn't wait to finish before heading towards the showering area first while Jayden stood there. Then, without missing a beat, he slams his fist onto the locker, the sound echoing across the room, which would go unnoticed.

How the hell was he going to make this better?

CHAPTER TWENTY-FOUR

"I_t was a mistake."_

Those words rattle at the back of his brain like a broken record since Monday as Troy lays in his bed staring at the ceiling. It's been six days, and true to Jayden's promise to him, he made it seem as if everything that happened that night didn't transpire.

In fact, when they went on their morning run and during practice, Jayden did an exceptionally well job at moving the conversation along as if that night didn't happen at all. However, it was all that Troy could think about within these past six days.

Despite blacking out, he recalled some bits and pieces like a puzzle.

Like—for example—it really was Troy who took advantage of the situation and kissed Jayden.

Not the other way around.

Troy knew he should be happy that Jayden had been so understanding and calm about the ordeal. Yet instead, whenever he thinks back to it, something in his heart dully aches, making him want to rub at it. It didn't sit right with Troy.

Unfortunately—or fortunately—it also appears that Jayden didn't seem to think the incident was a big deal of Troy kissing him while drunk less than a week ago. In fact, not only did he not bring it up since, leading Troy to wonder if this sort of thing happens to him frequently, but he acted as if everything was perfectly normal.

It's worrying that he seems so unfazed, as if people drunkenly throwing themselves at him and kissing him was common at parties. But, peculiarly enough, it only made Troy's stomach churn unpleasantly at the thought of Jayden kissing another person.

How common was it?

Did he push those people away or go home with them?

God, Troy still can't believe he completely blacked out shortly after.

Yet another pressing question soon arises of what would have happened if he hadn't.

Would they have gone further in his drunken state?

The most arguable question perplexing him is why he wouldn't have minded, even thinking about it now. After what happened two years ago at a party, almost being sexually assaulted and unable to even scream for help made him wary.

Conscious around people, especially other men.

Yet every time Jayden looked or touched him whenever he fixed his posture during practice, Troy didn't mind. So when he awoke and everything came crashing down that

Jayden asked Trevis and Quinn to bring him back to the dorm and ask Quinn to stay with him; it made his heart do funny little flips.

Not just that, but he can't find himself to stop thinking about the kiss either.

Gingerly, Troy touches his lips while looking up at the ceiling.

Then, he feels his shorts tightening across his crotch area as he tries to clear his mind, but to no avail. In fact, it only seems to get worse as his mind seems to have wandered off to remembering how gorgeous his abs were whenever he casually lifts the hem of his shirt to wipe the sweat during practice.

Kill me now.

Troy awkwardly adjusts his shirt and curls onto the side of the bed, desperately trying to find something else to focus on. All his life, he liked to believe his upbringing wouldn't make him have such an inappropriate thought at the flick of a switch.

Yet these new budding emotions he had never felt for anyone continued to blossom.

Much like the area between his legs.

He lets out a loud huff of air that no matter how much he closes his eyes and tries to distract himself, temptation seems to be everywhere. They're practically following him around, and he can't stop the improper thoughts floating in his lately empty brain.

Still, what was so different about Jayden to which Troy could find himself relaxing around him?

Was it those words he said that very night?

Was it because he saved him when he was drowning that day?

Was it because he treated him no differently from the get-go?

The more Troy thought about it, the more he knew there was no point in denying what he had always known. It was something he had dismissed shortly after his assault, locked away, and brought back to reality all within the last week.

It probably wasn't any shock that—

Suddenly, a hand brushes his forehead.

It snaps Troy straight up from the bed, his heart almost barreling out of his chest as his eyes catch onto familiar pale blue eyes and strawberry blonde. Quinn immediately jumps back and starts signing the same word over.

"Sorry, sorry," she fiddles with her words. Troy lets out a sigh, narrowing his eyes playfully as he continues to rub his chest. Thank goodness his lower half was under the blanket, as that would be embarrassing. "I wanted to check if you were okay because you're curled, and your whole face was red."

"Ah…must be hot in here," he excuses. "Why didn't you text me?"

"I did," Quinn replies, holding out her phone and then grabbing Troy's, which happened to be at the edge of the bed. She presses it on, and sure enough, he's met with about ten messages and two missed calls. "Did you forget we promised to meet today? It's your turn to decide where we eat for dinner; by the way, now come on."

Shit, just how lost was he in his own thoughts?

"Ah," he signs awkwardly. "Sorry. Right."

He had forgotten entirely about the time, much less what day it was. Classes and practice went by in a complete daze altogether. Even Coach had to bring them to the side to lecture them about their forehand swings.

He was terrified that he might be dragging Jayden down sooner or later.

Or, worse yet, ask to switch.

This whole kiss was riling Troy to the point where it was disrupting his plays. He knows it can't go on like this, yet the young man wasn't sure what he could do either. He watches as Quinn sits on the side of the bed, tilting her head. "You okay there?"

Was he okay?

It's a simple question, yet it holds so many opportunities to be open.

He tinkers momentarily at the thought and then draws his knees up to his chest before trying to convey his thoughts properly with his hands. "No, I…I'm not sure, but I think something might be wrong with me."

She quickly tenses. "What?"

"Not like physical," he quickly jumps in to clarify with his hand gesture before Quinn can freak out. He can feel his face doing a strange thing, twisting and scrunching up as he feels his ears and face burning red. He swallows the lump in his throat while his best friend observes, examining his every move. "Okay, well…I'm going to let you in on a secret."

"Okay," she leisurely signs. "Go on…"

"I'm…I'm trying, but I'm not sure where to start," he professes, his hands slowly in his signing as he tries to come around on the idea properly. To sign it out is no different than speaking, making your thoughts a reality which can be hard for just about anyone, especially Troy right now, who had always tinkered with the idea.

Yet he never admitted it.

There's no point in denying it anymore, especially after that kiss, after all.

"That's okay, take your time; we're in no rush," Quinn says soothingly with a gentle and encouraging smile. "To be honest, I figure something had been on your mind. I know you're the type that needs some time to process, so I didn't want to push you. So let me guess; it's about whatever happened at that party, huh?"

At that, he meekly nods.

More specifically, a certain man from the party.

He takes a deep breath before another as his hands start to fumble.

"Uh…so like…it's like… I might have a tiny crush," he blurts out with his hands quickly and then retraces his steps. It's a bit more than that, as he hyper-fixated on his hands so his brain could process his own words. "Actually, I think I might be gay. No, rephrase, I am gay."

His expression is completely serious, and it's almost like a huge weight has been lifted to get those words out. It wasn't as Troy never knew about his own sexuality or the gender he was attracted to. However, he had been in a state of denial. Yet he felt he had no other choice, backed into a corner with his thoughts and needing someone to confide in.

"Oh?" she signs, arching a brow with a grin, much to his surprise. "May I ask if that crush is a certain man with those luscious green eyes and golden-brown hair that looks like he jumped off a Taylor Swift music video?"

Huh.

Well, that certainly wasn't the reaction Troy was expecting.

He had always known his best friend was rather accepting of all, but could he handle it *this* casually?

When his brain plays catch up with her last comment, his eyes widen as he shoots up to where she is.

"You absolutely can't tell him," he quickly goes on, throwing his hand in front of his chest to stop how rapidly it's thumping and then continuing to sign. "You absolutely cannot tell Jayden! I know you're both close, but you can't even hint that I like him because we're partners, and I don't want things to be awkward and—"

"Wait, hold on, hold on. Let's do this one thing at a time," Quinn interjects. She goes to grab his hands, squeezing his hands gently. Only when she neatly folds them on Troy's lap does she sign, "I'm confused. You said you were going to tell me a secret, right? So what's the secret?"

He blinks. "What do you mean? I—"

"Okay, let's back up for a moment," she interjects, her hand movement not wavering in the slightest as she rolls her eyes before giving him a small, calm smile. It's one he's reasonably familiar with whenever he's freaking out over something that she has to center him again. "I don't know what gave you the impression that I don't already know that. I've been known and everyone else but wanted you to come around to it."

Wait, *what*?

"Everyone else?" he parrots with his hands slowly. "Who's everyone?"

She rolls her eyes. "Your parents, my parents…man, Aston. Aw man, your roommate is going to lose his marbles to find out your heart is accounted for before he has a chance. Well, actually—oh wait, maybe not because he was with someone that night I brought you back with Trevis, which is why I was able to stay over. I totally saw him a few days ago with a cute boy."

His roommate had a thing for him? Seriously? Are they still on this topic?

"Wait, back up, what? He does not," he snorts, rolling his eyes, to which she grins.

"He does, but that's a topic for another day of how guileless you are to the bigger picture," she muses, wagging her eyebrow with signing quickly. "Oh, right. Second of all, I already know you have a crush on Jayden. It was quite obvious that night."

Troy's cheek burns the color of a tomato.

In love? Maybe a crush, but certainly not in love!

"In love with J—I'm not…Quinn Weissman!"

"Also, you being gay doesn't mean anything wrong with you either; let's get that straight," she comments, ignoring the flustered look on Troy's face. He watches her shoulders shake, a sign of laughter as she continues signing. "Get it? I say get it straight, but you're not?"

"Can you please at least pretend to be surprised?" he groans before burying his flushed face into the palm of his hands and rapidly shaking his head. He continues once he recomposes himself where he feels like he can face Quinn again. "This is humiliating for me! Do you realize how hard it was for me to finally come around in telling you?"

"Was it?" she remarks with a curious look. "You know I wouldn't think of you any differently."

"I meant with Jayden," he clarifies before trying to school his features. He supposes it would have been quite evident in his opinion, especially because while he tried to deny his sexual orientation, it wasn't like his actions weren't a large indication.

Oh God, did Jayden know?

Was that why he had been acting strange and giving him a way out?

"I mean, as I said before, it's quite obvious. Though honestly, I don't blame you either with a Greek god," she comments with a wink. It certainly didn't make him feel any better while he watched Quinn settle comfortably. "So?"

"So? What do you mean?"

"I mean, what are you going to do with that revelation?" she reiterates.

"Uh…keep it to myself until I'm dead?" he answers with a deadpanned expression. There certainly isn't a chance he'd bring it up again, especially when Jayden had gone out of his way to draw a line to their relationship.

"What?" Quinn signs, her eyes bulging out like a gaping fish. "Wait, are your parents…?"

Oh, she thought he was referring to him being gay.

"No, no, they're quite supportive," he says before pausing upon a particular memory. Now that he thought about it, there were a few times his parents would nudge and tease him about a particularly cute guy. They even seemed somewhat shocked too when he brought a girl to prom as he buried his head momentarily in the palm of his hands before signing. "Actually…they might actually have known for a while."

"Told you," she signs with in an exasperated movement.

"Does everyone know but me?"

At that, Quinn wags her finger before answering.

"Eh, denial is the first step, but you're doing quite well running through all the other stages straight toward acceptance," she answers with a grin before her expression becomes serious once more. "So…you're not going to try pursuing it and see if maybe it might be something more?"

"I'm not sure if that's the best course of action right now since I have to focus on my education and my career right now," he remarks, unsure if it's obvious the larger elephant in the room. Since he brought him back when he blacked out, Quinn had stated that Jayden had been quite concerned.

He even reached out to Quinn several times, and it's enough to make his heart flutter.

Not that he can admit out loud as to why; it makes sense.

"Yeah, but can't you do both?" she asks, her lips puckering. "I know many people find the love of their life in college and still be able to focus on their education and career. Additionally, he's your partner too! Can you imagine being called the first gay and deaf professional tennis player and with a boyfriend like him?"

It was enticing of a title; Troy can't even lie.

Still, there's a slight nagging at the back of his head. "What if we break up?"

"You will with that attitude," she retorts. "Why focus on the thing that didn't even happened yet rather than what's going on right now? That has to be a taxing way to live, you know. Plus, you should have seen the way he was acting that night."

Wait, what?

"What do you mean?"

Instantly, there's a glitter in her eyes as she gets more comfortable on the bed. It's the same look she often has whenever she's gushing about her new celebrity crush of the week or her newest monthly obsession over a series.

"Shit, I forgot to even tell you," she signs in a maniac matter. "He was fuming, Troy. He came barreling down, yelling for Trevis and me at the top of his lungs over the music, which no one knew Mr. Nice could even do. I didn't even know you were being harassed, which again—"

He grabs her hand, shaking his head before signing, "It's not your fault; I didn't look for you. Drop it."

"Fine," she pouts after freeing her hands. "Anyway, he was carrying you like a damn princess in his arms, and he looked so concerned even though he knew you had blacked out. Even when we returned to the dorm, and I said I'd stay for the night with you, he was practically blowing up my phone. It was chiming every ten minutes. Which leads me to now ask…what happened at the party?"

Troy stiffens in a groan, knowing it's better to tell her everything now. So, he recounts it but leaves out the more uncomfortable and harrowing part regarding how he almost had a panic attack. While Quinn knew, it wasn't something he liked talking about regardless.

Then, he ends it with, "I kissed him before blacking out."

Quinn, who had been silent the entire time, almost tackled him onto the bed in complete shock.

"What?" she signs, adding a bunch of questions and exclamation marks. "Shut up."

"I don't even know how to face him the last few days, but when I did, he beat me to the punch. He apologized and said he was sorry for kissing me, but I was the one who kissed him first. I recall that much, at least."

"Back up; he took responsibility and said he took advantage and kissed you?"

"He did. He knew that I knew, but…he was stern on taking the blame and giving me a way out."

"Well…shit," she signs, her mouth agape. "So…he just basically suggested to forget it then?"

"Yeah," he nods, and now, he doesn't know what he *should* be doing.

He stares at Quinn as she signs, "Well…what do you want to do? What do you want, Troy?"

Leave it to her to read him without even trying, and he quietly stares at his best friend. He would have never thought that at twenty years old, he'd be faced with such a dilemma and to someone he should most definitely not be crushing on.

What does he want?

He thinks back to the kiss, and he can feel himself flushing.

Troy was a stranger to these emotions fluttering inside of his stomach, but the last thing he wants is to make things outlandish between him and Jayden—especially if they were partners. If he were to pursue something like this, it would definitely be off-season when things don't get awkward if things went haywire.

After all, they did have great chemistry on the field and off, but he wouldn't dwell on it.

"For one," he signs awkwardly and gives a half-shrug. "I think I want to see where this goes first and foremost. These are still really new to me, and after what happened at the party, I didn't want to rush into things blindly."

"Then it's decided," she grins and gets up from the side of the bed. Afterward, she does a stretch before nodding her head. "Let's go eat then because I'm starving and gawk together at Instagram photos of your man. Find out more about him because if there's one thing women are good at, it's online detective work."

"He's not my man," he signs, rolling his eyes as she winks.

"*Yet*," she emphasized. "Still, he has my approval because it seems you really trust him, Troy."

Trust, huh?

Well, that much is true and something that still baffles him when he is moments from blacking out.

Rather than freaking out, his body completely relaxed in knowing that he was with Jayden. By the way that Quinn had signed it with that twinkle, Troy wonders if there is a slight chance for them to do so in the future—especially with how he reacted when he was unconscious. Though even if there *was*, he first needs to sort through all his emotions and determine if this is what he truly wants.

Especially pursuing someone like Jayden, who was his partner for the next few months and teammate for years. Not just that, but I also respect Jayden's wishes too after the disastrous party he still can't remember without cringing.

However, the bigger question remains: Where does one even start in mending an uncomfortable circumstance that the other party doesn't notice?

CHAPTER TWENTY-FIVE

The following two weeks went off without a hitch.

Well, the best two teammates—one who realizes he's severely and cripplingly crushing on said teammate, just came to terms with his sexual orientation but also feeling guilty about what happened at the party two weeks ago—can do without going insane.

It makes it so much worse since the guilty conscience really is about to eat the younger man alive regarding Jayden taking the blame. Truthfully, Troy didn't know if he should be thankful or lean into becoming irritated as he sighed while picking up his salad.

How should one begin to apologize for something two weeks ago that had been "deemed" to be solved?

Did he want to undermine the work he had done?

Wouldn't it just make things more awkward?

It didn't make it better that it seemed *only* to be eating him up, too.

Their gameplay has been nearly spotless.

In the two games they played against the other

university's team, they barely even bat an eye and set a new score on behalf of Columbia University. So much so that the Coach even made a standing ovation to, which Jayden had to transcribe as Troy had no idea what was even going on.

Rather, he was so focused that Jayden is finally conversing with him without that weird tension that all he could focus on was him—until it was all over. Yet, Troy tells himself it's all in his head. Even during their morning runs, everything seems perfectly normal. Well, he thinks it's been a tad quieter and more awkward than usual, but at this point, Troy is almost certain it's all in his head.

Right?

He stabs his fork right into his salad and lets out a long exhale.

This really can't go on forever, and yet, he's never exactly been a fighter when confronting any issues or concerns. It had been the reason why what had happened years ago at a graduation school party in Australia had been swept under the rug.

He didn't want to be an inconvenience already on top of being deaf.

He was only *almost* sexually assaulted.

It was his fault for drinking.

His fault.

His fault.

He didn't tell his parents because he had convinced himself it wasn't a big deal.

Until it wasn't.

Until he had woken up with panic attacks.

Until he couldn't even get out of bed without throwing up.

Until his parents took him to get evaluated when the truth came out.

Troy would often downplay his problems or hide, not wanting to face the reality of his disability despite also wanting to become the first professional deaf tennis player. It was a strange relationship, much like his sexual orientation.

To think that if he made it pro, it would mean becoming the first openly gay, deaf tennis player.

A tapping-like vibration followed by a shadow being cast overhead snaps Troy back to the present day. He looks up from the salad that he had stabbed a few dozen times at this point to meet a pair of familiar dark brown eyes.

Benjamin.

Troy blinks momentarily and fights the wave of disappointment that it isn't Jayden.

He recalls they have the same interlude every other day and have even bumped into one another a few times, ending with them having lunch. Secretly, it was something Troy had enjoyed immensely, seeing one another more outside of practice.

Getting to know one another.

Yet, since the party, Jayden hasn't been coming to the university's cafeteria at all.

Coincidence? For Troy's sanity, he hoped it was just a coincidence.

Benjamin waves in greeting before pointing at the seat next to him, to which Troy quickly pats it in invitation.

He tips his baseball cap in greeting before setting his textbook, notebook, and laptop down. Troy watches curiously as Benjamin opens his laptop and launches a Word document.

> "Hi, sorry, I didn't want to startle you. I figure typing might be faster than writing. Is that okay with you?"

Oh!

That is actually quite considerate, and Troy nods before quickly typing back a response.

> "Yes, that's fine by me! No, you didn't startle me at all; who taught you that knocking on tables like that?"

> "If I'm being honest, I do this with my grandma, who is hearing impaired. What are you doing? You've been staring into space, so I wanted to check in with you. I thought you'd be happier, seeing as you and Jayden are the reason that we have a chance of getting into the Conference Championship. Is everything okay?"

Troy stares at the blinking cursor momentarily; his eyes fixated on the last question.

Is everything okay?

A simple question and yet, enough where it stumps him enough to think of his answer and if he should be honest or come up with a simple white lie. While Troy can confine Quinn regarding his dilemma, he has heard that getting a different outlook might help him break through in terms of clarity. Not to mention, Troy hasn't exactly enclosed everything after coming out as he was a tad worried his best friend might not be able to keep her mouth shut out of concern for him and confront Jayden personally.

Good intentions, but horrible execution.

Still loved her like a sister, nevertheless.

Given the choices presented in front of him right now and how Benjamin has been as a person from the moment they met, He went out of his way to try conversing with him from the get-go and even sought him out often to say hello.

Troy figures to go for it. He takes a deep breath, trying to find the right words before settling.

> "What would you do in my shoes if you messed up with a friend and you don't know how to make it up?"

Benjamin doesn't even blink before quickly answering.

> "Did you get into a fight with Quinn?"

Here goes nothing.

> "Jayden, actually."

If you were to ask Troy why he feels so nervous about it, he wouldn't even know how to answer. He's never felt so desperate to mend and fix their rather fragile and soured relationship—even if Jayden would not outright say anything in the last two weeks.

Troy's eyes are completely trained on Benjamin as he

reads over his response as soon as he slides the laptop back over. He can feel his palms growing exponentially sweaty at the question Benjamin had typed.

"Something happened at the party two weeks ago?"

"How did you know?"

Was it that obvious?

"Everyone was talking about it, given how Jayden was acting. So? Do you want to tell me what happened?"

"I accidentally did something I didn't mean to."

"Let me guess—you kissed him or vice versa?"

Troy unconsciously whips his head to him so fast, and by the time he catches himself, he already realizes that his actions essentially answered his question so long for wanting to keep that a secret for a tad longer.

Yet two weeks have been more than enough time for Troy to not only digest his own sexuality but understand just what he wants as well. He didn't want to hide it, but he didn't outright want to shove it into anyone's face.

It should be normalized, shouldn't it?

When Troy finally recollects himself, he types out his response.

"I'm starting to think you're a mind reader."

"No, you're just very easy to read, but I get it. Is that why you've both been acting standoffish the last two weeks?"

That earns another wince.

"Was it that obvious?"

Benjamin nods, giving a sheepish smile before his face becomes entirely serious, and he types away at his laptop. It was the first time he had taken so long and typed so quickly that it somewhat made Troy a tad anxious. He turned it back only a few moments later, and Troy realized it was a thoughtful response to his question earlier.

"While I can't offer you the best advice, I can only speak from my own experience— so please take this with a grain of salt. Don't leave the topic hanging in the air, especially if it's still bothering you and him. It's going to cause nothing but miscommunication and headaches down the line. I'm not going to pry nor pretend I know the full story, but if it were me and I was in Jayden's shoes, I would be bothered as well if you're both still hung up on it. From what I've seen, it seems like it is from how you both talk and interact. Talk it out with him."

Troy reads it over once and then twice.

Suddenly, it does feel as if a weight has really been lifted off his shoulder to be given such a piece of thoughtful advice. It also serves as an affirmation of what he already knows he should do as well. It may take him out of his comfort zone, but he feels like he needs to correct what was wrong.

Hopefully, that would get their relationship back on track.

Hopefully, it would also stop gnawing at the back of Troy's mind as well.

He doesn't dare to hope for his wishful thinking regarding Benjamin's second to last sentence, which also bothers Jayden. In the past two weeks, they have been playing well enough, and yet, they barely spoke if it didn't pertain to tennis and their gameplay.

Could what Benjamin pointed out be true?

When Troy realizes he has been staring a tad too long with the response, he quickly types one out. Alongside that, he feels as if he needs to be more honest with himself after Benjamin has gone out of his way to do the same.

> "Thank you, I needed it. I hope I didn't make it uncomfortable as well regarding my sexuality. Me being gay, I mean."

Troy tries not to cringe at the last part, but as they're essentially live chatting, it's not exactly as if he can waver on his comment. Though frankly, it makes him feel good to make it known out loud to the world what he has already known and denied after almost being sexually assaulted.

He feels freer.

Even more so of Benjamin's next response.

> "Why would I be uncomfortable? It's the 21st century; love whomever you want."

Love whomever you want.

It's beautifully woven together, making him smile as he turns over to sign, "Thank you."

He knows everyone on the team knows that much. Travis has not only gone out of his way to converse with him but has even taught a majority of the team basic sign language from Troy. He really can't ask for better teammates.

Afterward, Troy's eyes drift toward the stack of looseleaf paper and the textbook sprawled out. He curiously tilts his head to the side before the distressed look on Benjamin's face and then types out his question.

"What are you doing anyway?"

Troy takes a deep breath before exhaling, often a sign he learns to be associated with stress and anxiousness. Benjamin looks over at his question before running a hand through his hair with an exasperated look on his face.

"Unfortunately, statistics. I have a test this coming Monday, and if I don't pass this, Coach is coming for my ass."

Ouch.

He can only imagine the stress that comes with that.

Thankfully, a majority of his core and major classes this semester have been easier than in his freshmen years. His eyes take in the papers and the formula. At the top of his head, he recalls tasking himself in solving these equations before.

"Do you want me to tutor you, by chance?"

Benjamin's eyes practically bulge out from his socket.

"Really? You know how to read this witchcraft?"

"Yeah, I think I still have my notes, and I had taken advanced statistics back just last semester, so I still remember most of how to solve these equations. I can ask Quinn to come over tonight if you're up to it; you've met her before, right?"

"You're a damn lifesaver if you do."

"It's the least I can do after all you've done."

That comment earns a frown as Benjamin writes back quickly.

"Troy, I do it because I consider you a friend and not asking for repayment."

Really, just how sweet is this man?

"I think you're an amazing teammate and friend as well. I'll text you my dorm room tonight?"

"Yeah, I'll come with pizza then—no arguing. It's going to be a long night, and I need you all not to fall asleep so I can pass this class before I get kicked

off. Is your roommate okay with me coming over
and staying until an ungodly hour, by chance?"

"Yes, I think he's out tonight anyway. So
I'd just be you, me, and Quinn."

Quinn often likes to hang around anyway until the ungodly hours and sometimes even crashes over too.

In response, Benjamin gives a thumbs up, and Troy
smiles in return.

It's only at that moment that Troy's eyes catch onto
a particular person just as he looks up. His heart thumps
when his eyes land on Jayden just as he walks through the
entrance. It's strange how there are almost a hundred to two
in the college's main cafeteria, yet Troy can find Jayden with
ease quickly.

He's in another one of his many hoodies, strikingly
beautiful, gorgeous, and handsome as usual. Now that Troy
has come to terms with himself, he finally accepts what he
has always noticed but doesn't *dare* to admit.

Jayden is probably one of the most handsome men he
has laid eyes on.

His soft brown hair tousled as if he's been running his
hand through them.

Now that he thinks about it, has it always been this
messy, or wasn't it more recently in the two weeks?

His eyes then drift over.

It's then that Troy realizes that Jayden isn't alone or with
their usual teammates, either.

Rather, a beautiful girl in a cheerleading outfit is glued to his side. She's completely sticking to his arm like Velcro, and based on the way he didn't push her away, it meant he didn't mind either as they made their way through to their destination.

All the while, Troy couldn't look away.

Especially the grin on his face at whatever the girl said. Who is she?

What is this feeling bubbling in his chest?

Jayden is too preoccupied even to notice Troy. It's something that makes his chest ache and his stomach twist as he pries his eyes away. Only to see Benjamin frowning before pointing towards his laptop to see a whole paragraph written out that only makes him feel worse.

> "Look, I know I stated I wouldn't stick my nose where I don't belong, but as a friend—I feel like I should make it known regarding the gossip surrounding Jayden. As I told you two weeks ago at the party, and just in case you might not recall, Jayden is known to hook up with girls and guys—and nothing more. I wouldn't want you to accidentally play yourself without realizing what you might be getting into since you've both shared a drunken kiss. Hence, I stated that you should make it clear to one another before *you* get hurt. Talk it out, but don't get your hopes up or think it's anything more for your sake."

The last comment hurts more than Troy would like to admit, and now that he recalls it, Benjamin did bring it up at the party right before everything went downhill. A large portion of himself wants to defend Jayden, saying that Benjamin doesn't know him well.

Yet, what about him?

It seems that his friend isn't trying to motivate Troy and Jayden to be on the same page per se but to talk and make it clear where the line is drawn. Rather, it's to ensure they don't do anything that can jeopardize their playing as teammates and their chances of qualifying for the conference championships.

Troy knows he needs to get control over his crush soon.

Regardless of what he had told Quinn, he's come to realize it's very well near impossible to pursue in a man like Jayden. He had thought if he were to pursue something like this, it would be off-season when things don't get awkward if things went haywire.

Yet right now, he knows just how hard it would be to get over a man like him.

After all, Jayden wants nothing but to be casual while focusing on tennis—something Troy knows deep down he doesn't want—and he certainly wasn't going to try changing the man either. No matter how much it pained him, it wasn't his place and would never be anything more.

Unless he does feel the same, deep down.

Why else would he jump to your aid like so?

He shakes away that little thought and flicker of hope and, instead, decides to focus on replying to Benjamin. From the in-depth response, Troy can only presume that he had gone through something similar before for him to be this keen on knowing.

For him to go out of his way to caution Troy only makes him feel more appreciative of him, too.

"Yes, I know. Thank you for looking out for me."

He tries not to show how affected he is by the comment but rather gives a small, gentle smile and nods once more just as his eyes dart up again. His breath soon hitches upon encountering those luscious green eyes.

They hold one another's gaze for just a second.

His eyes then flicker over to behind Troy, and immediately, it's almost as if the temperature around the cafeteria dropped—much to Troy's utter confusion as to what had upset him. After all, there is no one else sitting behind him other than Benjamin. Soon after, Jayden turns into a café with the girl and is out of sight of them—as if his existence didn't matter.

In an instant, Troy's stomach drops at the confirmation.

Why did it feel as if the rift between them was only getting wider?

Not to mention, just what exactly is this dull ache in his chest?

CHAPTER TWENTY-SIX

"You taste so fucking *good, Troy.*"

A shudder runs down his back as Jayden signs those words before settling between the man's inner thighs, setting off goose-bumps like wildfire across his body. He can't believe how scorching hot he feels wherever Jayden peppers his lips as his body arches, searching for his lips onto his leaking cockhead, begging for attention.

He chuckles, Troy thinks, from the slight vibration he feels against his skin before he feels him swiping his tongue on a small junction of his inner thighs that makes him choke in unkept, ravenous hunger. When Troy finally manages to pry his hazed-filled eyes open to look at him through his long lashes, his chest is heaving from what he's doing while lying at his complete mercy.

"Jayden," he sighs weakly, his arm feeling like gelatine. "Please."

"Patience, my love."

Love.

What those words can do to a man like Troy.

Then, Troy can feel Jayden kissing across his public bone right before lapping at the base of his cock against his bulbous head that is leaking a copious amount of precum. Both of them groan, their sounds filling the room.

Almost as if Troy's groan—if that's what he's doing by the slight vibration quivering in his throat that makes his Adam's apple bob—fuels Jayden to continue, driving him crazier. He lapses at the precum as if it's fine wine, and his fingers slowly make their way down toward his puckered back entrance.

Rather than feeling nervous, there's something about Jayden's finger that excites him more.

More, more—especially so when, at long last, Jayden swallows his entire length just as he can prob one finger into him. Never in Troy's life had he come that fast before, squeezing the intruder tightly while he was hoping it was something else entirely.

Something much bigger and girthier.

Troy's pants grow heavier, his heart pounding harder when Jayden concentrates on not only the bulbous cockhead but also on working his fingers into him. He's not sure if the sound he's making—if he is—sounds strange or off, but for some reason, he doesn't find himself embarrassed or shy.

As if he can trust Jayden and be himself around him.

Soon, it didn't take long until the younger man bucked his hip up to his face, barreling towards the impending implosion just around the corner. He's never had anything—or anyone— touch him back there before, but it feels so right with him.

The way the little stubbles prick gently on his balls as he plunges two slick fingers into him makes the man almost lose it. With tears pricking at the corner of his eyes, he forces his eyes open as he signs, "Jayden, please."

"Do you want me to fuck you, love?" he signs upon removing his fingers, nuzzling his cock all the while, and the sight makes Troy's cock pulse and ache terribly. He doesn't get to answer when suddenly, Troy is now on his knees, towering over him as he tugs his boxers down.

When his cock springs free, Troy is more than confident he stops breathing altogether, especially more so when he practically bends him so that the bottom of his feet is up towards the ceiling and then rests him on Jayden's massive shoulder.

Soon, he's pressing his member into his tight opening.

His eyes are entirely trained on Troy the entire time as he slowly signs:

"Are you ready to give yourself to me, Troy?"

Troy's body jerks from the bed with a jolt, sweat chilling on his skin as he kicks off the sheets to realize that not only is his heart thumping erratically fast alongside his ribcage, but his boxers is damp with copious amounts of precum.

He can't believe it.

He can't believe that not only did he have a damn dirty dream just after his gay awakening, but also...

He didn't have a panic attack.

For the first time in two years, he didn't dream about the attack that forever changed the projection of his life. No, it was replaced entirely by something else that made him moments from completely ruining his bed sheets, and just like the drunken kiss he had shared with Jayden, he wanted more.

Fuck.

His heart is beating ferociously in his chest, and he's more than sure his cheek is more than flushed red. He's more than thankful that he's all alone, something he'd never thought he would ever be appreciative of. While Troy did offer them a place to sleep over, Quinn ended up taking up Benjamin's offer of a ride back home, as he was heading towards the city anyway since he lived off campus.

Something he's immensely grateful for right now.

God, how am I going even to face him today?

It almost feels like a middle finger from the world, mainly because he was set on trying to make amends with the same man that not only he has a crush on—which he shouldn't—but just had a provocative dream about him, too.

Just how am I supposed to confront Jayden today?

After Benjamin's prep talk, Troy set out inside himself to set things right.

Yet how will he even look this man straight in the eye without blushing after that dream?

Once he can steady his heart enough, he looks over and almost succumbs to a second heart attack when he realizes the time. Not quite believing what he's seeing, he quickly reaches over to his phone, and his stomach lurches.

Of course, he would have forgotten to charge his phone after the fiasco of the night he had tutoring Benjamin with Quinn there. It should be no surprise that once Benjamin got a hold of the steps needed to solve the formula and understand the concept, Quinn was the first to say that a celebration was necessary.

By means of binge-watching a movie and shoving pizza down their throats at midnight.

Troy had presumed it would have been a tad awkward, but he should have known that she would have been friends with Benjamin within ten minutes regarding his extroverted best friend. As it turns out, they had already been a tad familiar with one another from the party, and Benjamin recalled seeing Quinn a few times.

Troy somewhat regrets not eating now, as he feels a smidge hungry.

However, he'll just have a bigger brunch since he has an hour in between his classes right after tennis practice. He takes a deep breath and knows that if he were to run out in the next fifteen minutes, he might be able to make it.

Throwing off the covers, he goes and quickly plugs in his phone, as five percent is better than a dead phone when he leaves the dorm. Troy then rapidly goes to brush and tries taming his hair; of all days, he should have known it'd be a mess today with the back ends sticking upward.

He didn't even want to talk about the bags under his eyes while running on just two hours of sleep.

When he gets out of the bathroom, he throws on a random shirt—he's almost certain he wore this yesterday, but he can't even recall right now—and shorts before grabbing everything he'd need for the day; he slips on his shoes and darts out.

By the time he jogs to their usual meeting spot, he makes it just as he sees Jayden walking up with headphones.

Troy immediately gives a small smile, trying to ignore the slight frown on his face all the while.

He's probably reading too much into it.

Talk it out with him.

Benjamin's words ring at the back of his mind, and Troy realizes it's much easier said than done. He swallows the small lump in his throat as they place their items down, just as Troy decides to break the tension first.

"Good morning," he signs, trying not to stare too intensely as he anxiously tries to chase away the provocative dream he had this morning with his costar just a few feet away from him.

"Morning," he replies in turn. The tension is so thick that Troy is confident he can grab a knife and cut through it. Troy can't even start to comprehend why things seem to be getting worse and worse; he knows it can't carry on. Just as Troy is working up his courage to bring up the issue, Jayden beats him to the punch. "Are you ready to run?"

"Oh, yes," he signs while nodding.

Perhaps he'd find a way to bring it up then since he did get up and leave in such a rush.

It would be awkward to bring it up now and then run in awkward silence.

With that, they begin their usual morning routine.

All the while, Troy is trying to see the best approach to this situation.

How should he even bring up this rather heavy topic without it getting even worse?

However, it doesn't seem all that necessary as if only he

knows that Jayden has been in a state of chaos, rage, and prickliness since two weeks ago. The amount of time the older man has flipped on Trevis, one of his other teammates, or a random person was uncanny.

Even more so yesterday when he saw Troy with Benjamin.

In fact, he wants nothing more than to completely punch Benjamin square in his face for the look he has given him— as if he's nothing more than a crook. He didn't understand his problem, but he was more than sure he had something against him since the party.

Then, the way he slowly places a hand behind the top cap, as if he's displaying where he stands.

It made him absolutely enraged.

Jayden had nothing wanted more than to stride up to him.

Yet, he thinks back to the kiss and how things have been since then.

He had not only shown a side to him he never wanted anyone to know at the party, but he was more than confident he made things impossibly awkward and uncomfortable for his teammate. Aside from Travis, who had kissed because that said friend needed a quick way out of a situation, he had never laid his eyes or hands on anyone of his teammates.

However, things have been up in the air whenever Troy is involved.

From the moment they bumped into one another—quite literally—something inside him shifted.

Even more so when Jayden saw the raw talent the man possessed.

At first, Jayden knew his eyes caught on him because Troy reminded him so much of his brother.

He was deaf yet still persevered with a bright future.

He was sometimes a little ditzy yet in the most wholesome way.

How he's able to light up the room without trying because, despite his disabilities, he doesn't allow it to define him. He's also quite clumsy in acting before thinking, like putting Jayden first and almost drowning. Really, the man never thought there was another person who would put himself in danger for someone else.

Someone similar to his brother; it's uncanny.

Perhaps that's why Jayden continues to enjoy his company, but also, he realized a part of him recently regarding himself. It's a feeling he's never experienced with anyone else but rears its ugly head whenever it involves Troy.

The possessiveness and bile that come with wanting him since the kiss despite knowing his own rules.

Never date or sleep with a teammate.

Not just that, but wanting more, and he's come to acknowledge it fully yesterday when he felt a prickling-like feeling at the back of his head. When he turns in that direction, his eyes immediately catch Troy.

No matter where he is, he can spot him easily.

Even in a crowded party, as showcased two weeks ago, too.

However, everything comes to a halt when his eyes drift to where Benjamin is. Just like that, he's no longer in the mood to accompany Miranda or entertain her as was his original plan. He never did, to begin with, but she practically threw herself onto him as they just so happened to be going to the same place.

What exactly had been that feeling?

By the time they finished their jogging at their usual spot, Jayden had been so lost in thought that the only reason he had even snapped out of it was the sound of what appeared to be a growling stomach. He blinks, realizing that he has now caught his breath from running as he wipes away the sweat to look over at Troy, who's frowning slightly.

It's at that moment that Troy has his own dilemma.

As he hasn't had time to have breakfast this morning and wasn't exactly in the mood to scarf down a greasy pizza at midnight right before sleeping, unlike Quinn and Benjamin, he realizes he hasn't had a full meal. Even his salad went untouched yesterday during lunch.

Troy can feel his own stomach not only gnawing, but moments later, he realizes the conversation he had with Jayden a few weeks prior. As it turns out, stomachs make loud gurgling-like noises closer to growling, as Jayden pointed out.

Damn it, then that means Jayden can hear it, can't he?

It's confirmed moments later when Jayden wipes away the sweat on his forehead before signing.

"Do...you want to get something to eat?" Jayden asks, watching the way Troy's brows knit together.

Well, that's...unexpected.

"What about practice?" he questions in return, and Jayden does a half-shrug in response.

In his almost two years on the tennis team, he had never

once skipped or even thought about it. It's a strict regime he had, despite knowing Coach wouldn't exactly rat him out to his parent so long as it's not consistent either, and he could also shoot the team a message to inform Coach he wouldn't be able to come today.

No matter the hangover, nightmare, or lousy night he had.

It was like an unbroken regime ingrained into his system.

Yet here he was, standing here and suggesting just accompanying Troy for breakfast before he could even think twice once he had heard his stomach grumbling. At this point, Jayden wasn't even shocked anymore as he came up with a justification for why they should.

"I'm sure Coach won't mind seeing as we won thirty to love in the last game and are on our road to a new record of wins in our team's conference with this weekend's match; we deserve a skip day," he answers with a straight face. "Plus, I don't think you should practice on an empty stomach, either."

"Yeah, that's true," he agrees, and when Jayden squints his eyes, Troy gives a sheepish smile. Somehow, he already knows what question is coming next, but it doesn't mean he wants to answer it either when it comes exactly.

"Please don't tell me you hadn't eaten this morning before we agreed to run," he signs.

Instinctively, Troy curls his toes inside his running shoes to be scolded. He resists the urge to play with the hem of his shirt and, instead, gives a rather sheepish smile before signing, "I believe I have the right to plea...the fifth?"

"You know working on an empty stomach is terrible for you, right? Especially for someone who also has tennis practice right after as well?" he quips, and Troy tries not to wince that he's being scolded and then meekly nods.

"I'm sorry, I didn't realize."

He sees the way that Jayden's shoulder scrunches together before letting out a breath.

"Why didn't you eat this morning?"

"I woke up late," he answers, and when Jayden shoots up a brow for a further explanation, Troy continues signing. "I stayed up all night with Benjamin and completely forgot about charging my phone. Once I realized the time and that I had overslept, I ran here to meet with you as fast as possible."

It's almost as if the temperature around them drops to freezing in the blink of an eye.

"What?" Jayden signs, flatting his palm towards the sky and giving them a little shake.

Once more, it's that chilling look of complete wrath and turmoil.

Jayden's body is completely rigid, his nose flaring.

Yet why didn't Troy feel scared in the slightest?

More so confused as his brows bump together.

Was it because it's usually toward his safety every time he's angry and directed at him?

Like when he fell into the ocean or when he saved him at the party two weeks ago?

Yet...what about now?

For a moment, the immediate change is enough to make Troy freeze completely as he racks the back of his brain.

He gives a sheepish smile when it feels as if he might have missed something because of the heat or running too much with the lack of good in his system.

"What?" he questions, repeating the same gesture Jayden has done before while tilting his head to the side. He didn't exactly say anything wrong that he knows, so he adds on, "I'm sorry, I'm a bit confused. What do you mean by that exactly? Have I said something wrong?"

"When did you both become so close?" he signs with his jawline clenching.

Close? Benjamin and him?

Troy becomes more confused, feeling his eyebrow about to hit his hairline in confusion.

They're certainly friends, but he didn't think he was that close.

"Uh, we aren't exactly," he finally signs, albeit a bit confused and perplexed, as Jayden then storms over to where he is. It's at that very moment that Troy's mind decides it's the perfect time to think of that intense look Jayden gave him in that dirty dream less than an hour ago.

His member thickens, and he tries to think of anything else just as he's less than a foot away.

Though the next question Jayden makes into existence through his hand is enough to kill it instantly.

While Jayden is trying not to bow a damn lid on the outside, his inside is churning and violently shaking him at the thought of someone touching Troy. He knows it's none of his business, and yet he feels compelled to be enraged by the news.

That no one deserves this man, not even himself.

It's something he would certainly never think of why, either, as Jayden angrily signs his next question that spins this whole thing onto its head.

"So why on Earth would you *sleep* with him?"

Troy blinks and he's more than certain is jawline almost hits the damn floor.

What?

CHAPTER TWENTY-SEVEN

"**S**o why on Earth would you *sleep* with him?"

The words echo, and just like a movie scene, it keeps looping at the back of Troy's mind like a broken record. Jayden's words and his hand's movement are only more apparent because, in ASL, you can't precisely misread something so obvious.

Dizziness bleeds into Troy's head much like spilled ink, and he must blink a few times.

Did the heat finally get to his head from all that running?

Or was it the lack of sleep?

Is he still dreaming?

Jayden still has a thunderous expression, but Troy has seen many different sides of him before. He's seen Jayden stand up for him and save him, but none of Jayden's moods have ever scared Troy. This time is no different because it seems to be out of concern.

Yet, what exactly did he mean? Sleep?

Surely not...sleeping in terms of *sex*, right?

If not that, then what else can it possibly mean?

A blush blossoms and spreads like wildfire, but he refuses even to humor that it could be what he meant.

So, the younger man rakes his head in a desperate attempt to fill in the missing piece of the puzzle of where they had lost one another. In the end, Troy comes up wholly baffled as he squints his eyes at Jayden while trying to find the right words.

"Sleep?" he signs back, with his brows knit together. He defuses the situation and clears the air by first understanding what Jayden means. At this point, it always seems as if they're taking one step forward only to take three steps back. "I don't...understand? He didn't stay the night after I was done teaching him."

A pause follows, and this time, it's Jayden who's confused.

"Teaching?" he parrots.

"I guess it would be considered tutoring?" Troy finds himself correcting, pursing his lips momentarily. "He didn't understand a problem in his statistic class for his test coming up today. I recall learning how to solve the equation and invited him over with Quinn. The last thing I want is for him to get in trouble with Coach because of his grades."

Troy watches how Jayden's shoulder sags ever so slightly, and he doesn't dare to wonder what it might mean. The older male lets out a heavy sigh, racking his hair as he looks up at the sky before signing. "You..."

He didn't even have the right words to cover the rollercoaster of emotion he'd never felt with anyone else before. In the beginning, when he thought Troy had slept with Benjamin, he almost felt like he might blow a lid.

Even though he knew he didn't have the right to be.

When it comes to Troy, he is a mess regarding his feeling; it's something that falls on uncharted territory, and it makes him alarmed as to why that is. He told himself it was because of many similarities between Troy and his dead twin brother.

Weston.

From their caring and trusting nature to the way they're both mute.

It was the reason Weston even ended up getting killed—because of Jayden's recklessness.

A budge lunges at Jayden's throat at the thought that Troy, who is standing just a foot away and how he, could have drowned, and no one would have even known. Again, because of Jayden's recklessness and the reason why Jayden even felt compelled to help Troy.

Yet what about this?

What about the jealousy that almost boiled over because he thought Troy was sleeping with Benjamin?

Not to mention, what about that relief of knowing he had been wrong when he never cared?

Was it because Jayden only wanted to sleep with Troy? Or something else entirely?

Troy, who doesn't understand Jayden's situation or inner turmoil, only tilts his head to the side. He had patiently waited for Jayden to finish what he had been saying earlier, but it seemed forgotten now. When Jayden finally refocuses his attention, Troy's hand moves ever so quickly. "What were you going to say? Did I do or say something wrong?"

"No, you did nothing wrong," Jayden remarks, shaking his head to give emphasis.

However, he can't exactly tell the truth now, can he?

The water crashes nearby fills the silence; before Jayden can make up some excuse for what he had meant, Troy decides to ask what he had thought Jayden meant before, albeit a tad awkwardly. "Did you...actually think I...slept with him?"

Another pause follows, and for the first time, Troy realizes he understands the saying that he's never heard silence quite this loud. He resists the urge to pick at the hem of his shirt while he watches Jayden, who lets out what appears to be a sigh and nods.

"I did."

At least he's honest, but it doesn't mean it didn't exactly hurt; it's just a pinch for Jayden to think Troy would want something like that. Yet a smaller side of him can't help and be a tad woozy for him to be this heated.

Even though he knows he shouldn't because of what Benjamin had warned him about.

Jayden only plays around and partakes in one-night stands, nothing more.

Suddenly, his mood changes again as he debates what to say before settling.

"Ah...well, thank you for the concern but...I'm not exactly looking for something casual," he remarks.

"You're not, huh?"

Troy doesn't know if he's reading too much into it, especially because Jayden's hand movements in his response are a bit laxer, as if he's actually happy about that answer. He shakes his head, and it feels like the rift between them closes ever so slightly, just as Troy feels his stomach growling once more.

He bites his lips, looking at Jayden rather awkwardly as Jayden smiles.

"Let's go run back and get our stuff. I actually know a good bagel spot near here," he offers, and they make their little jog back with that. This time, Troy feels like a heavy weight has been lifted from his chest.

When they returned, they quickly grabbed their bags, hiding just in the shrubs, and headed North towards Gold Coast. On the way there, Jayden had already contacted Travis to let Coach know he wouldn't be coming in today alongside Troy.

What he was sent back is enough for Jayden to make a mental note to punch him later.

He had no doubt there would be chatter amongst the team, but as long as it didn't pass to his parents, he didn't care. Coach Winter wouldn't reach out to his parents either, so long as he didn't do it that often or raise other flags.

So long as he continues to play well and keep up the perfect little façade that everyone loves about him.

Mr. Perfect.

The man who can do no wrong.

Mentally, he's already dreading dinner tonight and re-living this façade dream for his parent's sake.

For his mother's, really.

While the end of the week is often considered the most

relaxing, it was slowly becoming his most stressful. The façade had been starting to crack for a while now, but with each passing week, it only seemed to grow worst.

The long, silent dinners.

How much more can one keep it up?

The way his collared shirt would dig into his throat, almost choking him alive.

The way Dad would go about how amazing Jayden was, and he couldn't wait for him to go pro.

The way Mom would call him by Weston's nickname, and Jayden knows she's seeing his perfect son.

Not him.

No one ever *sees* him.

No one ever *asks* him anything.

Jayden is so completely lost in his thoughts that he hasn't even realized it until he feels something tugging lightly at his shirt. He immediately turns to see Troy looking at him with concern and anxiousness in his eyes.

No one ever *sees* him.

"Are you okay?" Troy questions quietly with his hands.

No one ever *asks* him anything.

Once more, Jayden could feel something in his chest-thumping erratically—

Something he had never felt before.

Are you okay?

Jayden can't help but notice just how many times they've come to ask one another that exact question.

From the very moment that they bumped into one another at the coffee shop when Jayden had been having a rather rough week—that was the first thing Troy had asked. Then, from what he recalled, it had always been Jayden from when Troy tripped on air or what went down at the party.

Up until this very moment when, again, he was just about spiraling.

Coincidence?

He wouldn't be able to say for sure, but Troy does do amazing with timing if that was the case.

"Yeah, sorry," he signs back, giving him a slight grin. "What were you saying?"

He's met with a slight pout, and for some reason, Jayden finds himself grinning even more.

"I was asking how far the bagel shop is," he ponders.

Strangely, he had been perfectly fine with just not eating and having a heartier breakfast despite his hunger. Yet right at this moment, after clearing up the miscommunication from earlier, Troy is rearing to have some food in his system.

Actually, he hadn't had an appetite since his huge quarrel with Jayden. Yet his reaction earlier, when he had thought he had slept with Benjamin, made him an utter mess on the inside. He dares to believe that, to some extent, it means that Jayden and he can work something out.

Maybe.

He knows it's more than likely his lack of sleep and active imagination running wild.

Yet, at that moment, he didn't care but to bathe in it for a bit longer. Even if he were to know, it would never work out with someone who only wants something serious and another who cannot be bothered by such things.

"Oh, don't worry about that. We're relatively close, actually. I'm not that cruel to starve you to death before then," he replies with a playful chuckle. It's far different from how they've acted since the party, making Jayden relax ever so slightly.

He didn't realize how much he had missed just talking to Troy normally.

Aside from Quinn, Troy had always felt he didn't have anyone he had connected well with in college thus far. Sure, he got along with his roommate, Trevis and Benjamin, but it's not exactly the same. From the moment they started to converse, he felt this instant connection with him, unlike anything he'd ever felt before.

Needless to say, in just a small amount of time, they fall back to the lull they had always been used to.

When they finally arrive at the promised bagel shop, Troy can already feel his mouth salivate as Jayden holds the door open. Seeing as they're pretty far from campus and the city center, there aren't many people, so they didn't have to worry about finding a table either.

Staring at the menu for a while, Jayden allowed Troy to have a moment to look over what he wanted. He came here quite often since he accidentally stumbled there one drunken night. One lox bagel later, he knew this was the best spot in Chicago for bagels.

After a few minutes, Jayden turns to Troy and signs. "Have you decided on what you want yet?"

"I'm thinking of a bagel with cream cheese and jelly. Then, a large, iced coffee, two sugar," he replies.

"Wait, a bagel with cream cheese and jelly?" he parrots with his hands, squinting his eyes as he's never heard something like that before. He even gave emphasis on the usage of a few more question marks when signing, which earned him a large grin.

"You have to try it; it's my favorite type of bagel. I swear you won't be able to go back," he comments rather confidently. It catches Jayden's attention as someone who's usually rather stubborn with his belief. Not only that, but something inside him wants to try Troy's favorite bagel and see if it does hold water. "What about? What are you getting?"

"Lox bagel, black coffee," he replies. "Have you ever had? Smoked salmon with cream cheese?"

Troy taps his chin for a moment. "I heard from Quinn that it's like…a Philadelphia roll? I like that."

"I can't even look at you right now," he replies, raising his nose to the air. Jayden is more than confident he's never been quite this offended in some time now. "Want to do a bagel split, then? You take half of mine, and I take half of yours?"

"Okay," Troy signs, nodding enthusiastically.

"Great, I'll go order for us then. Do you want to get a seat first?"

"Yes, that works. Hand me your bag," he signs, already holding out his hands, to which Jayden passes it towards him before making his way to the cashier in order. Troy picks a spot near the window, and once Jayden makes his way back to stand next to him while he waits for their order, the one sitting starts to take out his wallet. "Thank you for ordering. How much do I owe you?"

He flicks his wrist as if to dismiss it and then confirms it when he signs. "It's fine, my treat."

"What?" he signs with his brows scrunched together. "No, I can't—"

"You can get me next time," he interjects, then looks away, rubbing the back of his head. "Plus, it's the least I can do after…offending you this morning. I didn't mean to get defensive like that, and it's not my business with who you are with either…but just…I was worried about you since…I know you're not the type to do that either."

Ah.

So, he does feel somewhat guilty.

It still makes Troy's heart flutter just a tiny tad to know that Jayden is concerned about him. There's also another part of him that's excited that there's a slight chance they can also do something like this again if he says Troy can pay next time.

However, there's still a bigger issue hovering and breathing down Troy's neck that he had wanted to bring up for a while now with his last topic. It wasn't until Jayden grabbed their items and sat across that Troy, once more, gathered enough courage.

As his parents have stated, going to bed angry at one another is no good.

Given that it applies to people in the relationship, the same can technically be used here. It's better to deal with the problem now and be on the same page than allow it to simmer and get even messier. What happened just before was a good icebreaker, at the very least.

So the chance to grab hold of the issue and amend it has no better timing than this very moment.

If their relationship had been somewhat rocky up until what happened at the party, then the best way to deal with the issue is to go headfirst into it. Except, Troy is more than keen on finishing his much-beloved bagels first because he is absolutely starving.

He goes to devour his bagel cream cheese and jelly first and lets out a small sigh.

Did food always taste this good?

Or was it because he was eating with Jayden sitting across from him?

Troy didn't realize how messy his eating had become with how much cream cheese and jelly they had given him until he saw Jayden grinning across from him. When the younger man arches his brow questionably, Jayden decides to spare him from embarrassing himself by signing.

"You have a little cream cheese smeared on your cheek," he signs while holding out a tissue.

Oh.

A bit mortified and self-conscious of making a fool of himself in front of his crush that he's still working on getting over—and mending the burning bridge simultaneously. Hastily, Troy places his bagel back down and wipes the napkin across his lips mindlessly, hoping he has gotten it.

Once finished, he looks expedited at Jayden for confirmation as he puts the tissue down.

"Sorry, what about now?"

What Troy doesn't expect is what Jayden then signs next. "Here, let me do it."

His heart flutters when Jayden gets up and then leans over before he can mentally prepare himself. Given that he was wearing just a tank top as workout clothes, Troy could very well see the inside of his shirt at his perfectly packed six-pack.

He can also remember his dreams this morning distinctively, with a particular main character being the same main character across from him.

It takes everything in him not to freak out despite feeling his face thoroughly heating up entirely. He's confident he stopped breathing as Jayden then goes to swipe the excess cream cheese with his thumb, which is already causing Troy heart murmurs.

Even more so when he licks it clean as their eyes find themselves connecting.

Troy finds himself pressing his legs tightly together, his member pulsating terribly.

As he had now come to terms with his sexuality, it was like opening Pandora's Box. He didn't have to deny himself and his feelings anymore. Yet, at the same time, it feels as if everything is much more intense regarding this man's effects on him.

Damn it all.

Troy knew at that moment why Jayden had so many people crushing on him.

He knows he didn't even do it on purpose either, and somehow, it makes it all the more erotic.

He really is out for his damn heart.

This is why, because Troy refuses for the remainder of his heart to leap right into Jayden's open arms, he sprints through with the first thing that had been on his mind headfirst without thinking things exactly through.

"About the kiss," he fumbles with his hand, almost knocking over his iced coffee in the process. He sees how Jayden tenses, but before the other man can say anything, he quickly finishes the rest of his senses. "I think I should be the one apologizing!"

CHAPTER TWENTY-EIGHT

Just like that, it feels like everything comes crashing down, which Jayden knows was always destined to happen. The older man even knew that leaving things like this would only create even higher mountains that, sooner or later, no one could climb it.

He had prepared for it to come, but now that Troy had brought it up, it certainly didn't prepare him.

Seriously, what is it about today?

Just as he was perfectly fine with things finally moving forward, life decided to fuck him in the ass and send him five stops back. Jayden can feel his heart kicking into gear, and his hands grow clammier. It only happens when he's doing something daring and downright reckless.

Never like this.

The cream cheese and bagel—a delicacy he didn't think he'd *ever* like of how sweet it is—was delicious.

Up until this very moment.

There's a lump in his throat as he thought about how he came to take the blame two weeks ago so Troy wouldn't feel bad about what happened. At the back of his mind, he already had a hunch that Troy might have already known.

That might be why he wasn't just awkward with him but looked extremely uncomfortable as well. However, he didn't want to bring up something that would open another can of worms. Just like with his brothers, lock it away.

Put a band-aid over it and carry on like nothing's wrong until the new normal settles.

It was why he certainly didn't think Troy would bring it up at all, given his soft-spoken nature.

He places the bagel down and signs, "Troy—"

However, he doesn't get to finish when Troy beats him to it.

"I remember I was the one who kissed you, and I shouldn't have done it, so I apologize but...but I'm not sorry for kissing you," he fumbles out, and then he quickly retraces his step with his face as red as a tomato. "W-well, I am, but only because I shouldn't have thrown myself at you without your consent because that's wrong. However, you should know I wouldn't kiss... kiss anyone randomly, either...drunk or not! Or sleep with them!"

Much less drink, but that wasn't uncharted territory Troy didn't want to dive into today.

It was the fastest Troy had ever spoken with his hands in his life. Even his fingers felt as if they were slightly cramping. Quinn might be rubbing up on him, and he's more than confident he might have broken the world record by how fast he signed.

Did something like that even exist?

However, Troy knows himself well enough that if he didn't act upon speaking what had been on his mind, he might very well chicken out, and things are going to be awkward again. Today, just before, was the closest to feeling like how they were before the incident at the party.

If Troy didn't try bringing it up now, who knows *when*.

Speaking to Benjamin last night had given him the push he needed to sort out his feelings. He'd get over his crush eventually, but he greatly valued his friendship with Jayden over anything else. Neither of them dares to move—to make a physical interaction of any sort known between them—while they digest one another's words. For Troy, he had hoped he conveyed his feelings enough that he wasn't someone who would just drunkenly kiss anyone.

Sure, he wished he hadn't thrown himself onto him in his drunken state, as it made him no different than what happened back in high school. But in the end, he didn't regret the kiss because he really *couldn't* from the bottom of his heart.

He couldn't, no matter how guilty it also made him feel, so he needed to apologize and convey his feelings properly. Yes, Troy had just gotten his hopes up in the process regarding the kiss, but at the same time, it was what jumpstarted it all for him to come to terms with his own sexuality. He can't deny that Jayden wasn't the most handsome and generous man he had ever seen.

Yet, he also knew he couldn't exactly go after someone who only wanted to sleep around. Tragic at it that tugs at his heartstrings, he knows he can't dwell on it, but he also wanted to make it clear he didn't regret it either.

As for Jayden, he's having his own dilemma once more.

His head whirled as he played back what Troy had signed in complete disbelief of where this was going. Not only did Troy admit he didn't precisely regret kissing him, but he didn't see it as a mistake. Something that Jayden thought had been the main reason why he was ignoring him up to this point.

Then does that mean...

"Has...was this the reason it bothered you the last two weeks?" Jayden finally questions, their eyes connected the entire time. Troy has been so tense because he felt guilty he had drunkenly thrown himself at him, rather than what Jayden had presumed, which was that by taking responsibility, he was now scared of him.

It made him feel...reassured ever so slightly.

Even more so when Troy nods.

"It...has," Troy signs, interjecting Jayden's train of thought. Why wouldn't it?

Yet, needing more to his theory, he continues. "It's because...you had *drunkenly* kissed me?"

"Of course," he signs. He didn't exactly want to open up about his almost sexual assault right here, nor did he want to see the pity in his eyes, so he gave him half the truth. "I... it doesn't make me feel good that I had taken advantage of you like that."

No one should be placed in that position.

It would be different if two parties had wanted and expected it after both converse and drank together.

Yet Troy knew Jayden certainly didn't expect to be kissed out of the blues suddenly after the events that transpired. Jayden's next question baffles the other man even more. "So… you don't regret the kiss itself if we disregard the fact that it was done due to liquid courage?"

Seriously?

This time, Troy can feel himself blushing because he just happened to want to focus on that of all things. He leans back on the booth and swears he can see the mischievous, teasing nature in the corner of Jayden's eyes.

A sign that for the first time in two weeks, they're on the same page again—possibly.

"Are you really going to make me say it? Really?" he signs with a huff, sending a glare into his eyes.

Troy already knows he's too deep, so there's no point in returning now. Plus, Troy knows without a doubt that since Jayden is bisexual, he probably has friends who compliment him daily regarding his appearance.

He thought he was having his legs pulled, except for the seriousness in Jayden's eyes while he signed.

"Please? It's important."

How?

Instantly, just as quickly as that question pops up, he realizes the meaning behind Jayden's question. Knowing they can both be adults about it and not exactly wanting to hide it either, he pierces his lips together for a moment.

"Yes, and also…in fact, it wasn't clear, I'm…gay. Though I promise I won't make it weird between us," he professes, wincing as he hoped he wouldn't. "I had kissed in my drunken state because…well, I got caught up in the moment after what you did for me and…thought…you were my Prince Charming?"

Smooth, Troy.

Very, very smooth.

Silence soon follows once more before Jayden signs. "You really know how to surprise me."

Troy didn't expect Jayden to put his hands over his face, then push his tray away before slumping his head down onto the table. Immediately, Troy is on high alert, and Jayden picks himself back up just a few seconds later to see Troy frantically signing.

"What happened? Are you not feeling well? Should I go to the counter and ask her to call for help?"

Jayden shakes his head, trying to recollect himself and all these different emotions currently coursing through his veins. "No, it's just…I thought you'd been trying to think of a reason to let me down softly of why we couldn't be partners or friends anymore."

What?

Troy stares at him, baffled momentarily.

After all, shouldn't it be the other way around?

"What? Why?"

"I had a hunch you might have known something didn't add up when I took the blame just as you brought it up two weeks ago," Jayden explains with a skittish smile. "I mean, I wouldn't look at or judge you any differently just because you're gay. I think you've already heard I swing both ways anyway, so I'm the last to judge, but…I thought you were avoiding me because I had been lying, or maybe…you thought I was too violent."

It was what his parents always hated most about him.

The outbursts he now vents in the form of extreme daredevil stunts.

Troy's train of thought trails off for a moment, contemplating if it would be considered rude to ask, and yet, he knows if he didn't, it'd probably eat him up. "Wait, has that been bothering you the entire time as well?"

"Yes, why would it?" he signs back, his brows bumping. "You are an amazing partner and friend as well. Just like you didn't regret the kiss, I also didn't exactly regret confronting that fucker who made you have that look on your face, but I didn't want to scare you either."

Why did that make Troy's heart flutter to know they were bothered by the same thing?

That they both want to be friends badly, where they didn't know how to bring up the issue?

"You didn't scare me when you came to save me in the slightest. In fact, why did you think I said you were my Prince Charming," he quips, feeling the tip of his ears starting to redden once more. "I would never be scared of you, Jayden."

If anyone were to make that claim, Jayden wouldn't have believed them.

However, it makes him genuinely smile because Troy has seen him through better and worse from how much they have spent time with one another. It's a rare occurrence, but something Troy can bring out with ease as he leans back into his chair.

"You know, Troy, I don't know if anyone has ever told you, but you're really brave," he praises.

The sudden change in topic confuses him. "What do you mean?"

"I'm saying I would have never brought something like this up," he confesses as he reaches for his cup of coffee. He takes a sip, recollecting his thoughts before going on. "The kiss and what happened afterward, really."

"Why?"

Jayden shrugs, rubbing the back of his neck for a moment before deciding to be honest because they're already talking about it. "Well, I was scared I'd make things awkward between us, but I've realized this was a much better option."

"The tension was getting to you as well, huh?"

"Hell fucking yeah, it was," Jayden signs and then raises his cup of coffee. The latter instantly understands and raises his cup of coffee to cheers. They then chug their coffee before Jayden adds on. "Oh, and Troy?"

"Yeah?"

"Don't feel bad about what you did—drunk or not," Jayden replies, taking a bite of the cream cheese and jelly bagel he dares to believe actually tastes better than his beloved lox bagel. He never thought that day would ever come. "You have no idea how often this happens. Not kissing per se, that's a first, but throwing themselves on me."

Troy squints his eyes. "Are you just boosting at this point?"

"No, not in the slightest. I don't like people throwing themselves around me, but..." he trails off momentarily, allowing his hands to hang in the air as he grasps the right words. "I don't regret you kissing me either if it makes you feel better. You'd be surprised that you're not the first person I kissed on the team; it was Trevis."

The jealousy that bubbles quickly disperses as Troy stares at him with wide eyes. "*Trevis?*"

"Don't tell him I said anything, but he had a code red where someone didn't know how to get off," he reminisces, the grin on his face widening because he loves to fuck around with Trevis, who detest it had come to that with every fiber in his being. "He practically begged me to kiss him, and now, it's my number one way to torment him."

Hearing the story, Troy's mouth almost falls. "You're actually quite mean, aren't you, Mr. Nice?"

He watches the way Jayden's nose scrunches. "I don't even know where that even came from."

While he had worked on just being a nice person for the sake of façade, it somehow manifested and took a life of its own beyond his wildest dream. Before he even realized it, the nickname made its way around the campus.

As Coach was quite close with his parents, it wasn't as if he could stop the façade he had either.

"Yeah, you're more Mr. Handsome and Reckless," Troy agrees, and Jayden is more than glad he wasn't eating or drinking because he's confident he would have most likely choked at his honesty. Seeing this more relaxed and playful side to Troy is shocking and refreshing as he arches a brow.

"Handsome, huh?" he signs, cocking his head to the side, to which Troy would then roll his eyes.

"Is that all you got out of it?" he grumbles, finally taking a bite from the lox bagel.

Much to his utter surprise, he dares to believe it tastes better than his cream cheese with jelly.

"Can you blame me?" Jayden replies nonchalantly.

"You know, I think you should be called Mr. Cocky," he answers before using his hands to completely start devouring the bagel Jayden had given him to try. He's confident that Quinn is a liar because it tastes much better than the Philadelphia Roll.

"You should be Mr. Cutie," he replies with a wink, and Troy is thankful he's chewing so that he wouldn't have to answer just yet. Nonetheless, a sudden thought makes him almost stop chewing midway, watching as Jayden devours the cream cheese and jelly he seems keen on not liking before.

Are they...

Are they flirting? Or was this something Jayden does with his friends?

Is it safe to presume he might even feel something towards him?

No.

He doesn't date.

He only has casual sex, which wasn't something Troy wanted either. With the mix-up with Benjamin, Troy had even outwardly stated just before that he isn't the type to have casual hookups. Meaningless sex wasn't something he was interested in without the intimate connection—especially when it would be his first time as well.

So long as Troy can work on smothering down that feeling, he'll be fine.

Yet why did it feel nearly impossible by the way Jayden was teasingly grinning at him?

CHAPTER TWENTY-NINE

"**C**oach informed me a few days ago that you and your partner are quite compatible in your playstyle."

Jayden tries not to wince when he accidentally puts too much pressure on his steak knife, slicing it through his dinner so quickly and hastily that it screeches piercingly through the empty house. He should have grown used to it since Weston's death a decade ago.

After all, he was the light in everyone's eyes.

Just like any other formulaic twin, he was everything that Jayden wasn't—

Charismatic, funny, caring.

Well-behaved.

Perfect.

He swallows the lump threatening to choke him alive, but breathing in this household is still near impossible. It hasn't changed since his little brother's death, as if the house itself is stuck in a part of time when things were perfect.

He didn't think it was possible to move into Chicago—something he had foolishly thought was to start anew—only to be still trapped in a moment of time when things had been perfect. Photo frames of the four of them but never over a certain age, with trophies and metals lining the shelves with Weston's name, from his spelling bee competition to his junior tennis trophies.

Still polished and well-kept as a preservation of a time they can't get back.

As if he was still alive and would walk through that door at any moment to brighten up the mood because he was always able to do that with ease, mending what was broken. However, he can't do that anymore, and the price to be paid would never be enough.

Not to his parent's eyes, no matter how much Jayden tries.

He takes a deep breath and nods, trying not to bounce his legs. It's a habit he never seems able to break, and only comes out on Friday nights. "Yes, I've never seen someone who can play the way he does. He's talented."

Father hums lowly for a moment. "What was his name again?"

"Troy. Troy Evans," he answers, and he wills himself not to question why he wants to know.

His father bringing this up wasn't random or trying to make conversation to fill the silence; however, speaking up would only upset his mother because Weston never questioned them back. She is listening, but you would have never thought of so with her head hanging downward as she picked her vegetable.

She lost weight again, the bags under her eyes informing

Jayden she was not taking her medication properly. However, Jayden can't even bring it up upon the immense other topics for fear of triggering her episodes.

"How is he as a person?" Mother asks.

How is he?

He's everything that Weston is, but also not in the slightest, either. Aside from their consideration for others, their love of sports, and that they're mute, they're two vastly different people. Truthfully, he's gentle and thoughtful of others but also clumsy and scatterbrained at times.

He's...strangely cute in his own way.

Oddly enough, the thought almost makes him smile, but he works on keeping a blank expression.

However, it seems that isn't necessary for his father's next question.

"He's...deaf, isn't he?" he ponders out loud.

He should have known that's where it was headed.

"He is," he replies, trying his hardest not to give any of his emotions away of why that matters. Weeks ago, Father had been the one who stated he didn't need to hold himself back for the sake of a disabled person and should consider switching.

It still leaves a bitter taste in his mouth as he places another cut steak into his mouth.

"A deaf player with such a talented streak," father comments, the first time Jayden had ever seen him sound so awed over a person since his twin. "I've seen some of his play since you're teammates. You would have never thought he was deaf."

He should have known his father only cares because he's a deaf player with *potential*.

His jawline ticks, but he finds himself more upset on behalf of Troy for them comparing him to his brother than seeing him as his own person with accomplishments. He's okay if he's comparing him with Weston, but when it comes to Troy—

It seems to be a different case.

"It's almost like it's meant to be, like Wessie is still here," Mother whispers and Jayden almost drops his fork. The tension is so thick you can cut it open with a knife. He's thankful he swallowed his steak as he takes a deep breath in and then out to keep his emotions in check.

Conceal them so he doesn't explode.

I'm here too.

He stares at his half-eaten steak, which he doesn't even like much compared to his mother's baked lemon salmon she had made almost a decade ago, but he can't say that. The whole family is still a fragile ticking timebomb. Thankfully, Father had jumped in.

"Coach also informed us the team's performance this season gives him high hopes of potentially being in the top five for the conference championship based on your team's game performance," he continues as if Mother hasn't just brought up Weston.

Right.

Truthfully, he is actually looking forward and would give it everything to pass. It's not because he's precisely a fanatic about going pro in his tennis career. No, if the team continues to be qualified for the conference championship as they compete with other neighboring colleges, he'd have an excuse not to come home on Fridays, as they'll most likely have to travel to other universities to compete.

Hell, he's already counting down the minutes until *this* is all over.

"We'll be cheering for you," Mother chimes in, lifting her head from where it had been hanging. Jayden can feel him gritting his teeth so hard that he swears his head is throbbing from that rather than trying to keep it all together.

"Don't disappoint us. It's been your dreams, after all," Father maintains, and it takes everything in him not to snap. Jayden knows a broken family can't be repaired deep down, especially when they refuse to acknowledge the issues when they first arose, and for them, that's a decade ago.

Even now, they refuse to see him for *him*.

They look at him and see the son they loved and cherished more than the other.

They don't understand or seem to care that it's not his dream to go pro from the beginning.

It was Weston's dream, and even that statement is pushing it.

They were just kids; how did they know what they wanted to do for the rest of their lives?

Weston had only wanted to play tennis because that's what his father liked, and he wanted to be more like him. Yet, it's not something he can bring up without possibly sending his mother back to the emergency room, only to then come back out without proper treatment because neither of his parents wanted to admit something was wrong.

"Thank you," he murmurs, and it should be no surprise that the conversation ends there.

No asking how his classes were.

No asking how his week was or what he did.

I'm not asking about the tattoos or the healing bruises on his face that were more noticeable last week.

It didn't matter to them, aside from him potentially becoming a pro player like Weston had "wanted."

He reaches for his cup of water, and the silence resumes except for the clattering of plates. He glances over at the plate sitting next to him across from Mother, empty but there as if there's a possibility of his return.

Recently, he's been feeling more exhausted from getting up this façade more than anything else.

Ever since he had gotten into that fight—no, it was before then.

When he dove in to save Troy when he almost drowned, the act he had been upkeeping for years had slowly come apart at the seams. It was then that everything started to change around him, and he felt himself becoming more honest when it came to him.

For some reason, he's the only anomaly that could make him act out like that.

Jayden then places his cup of water down and puts another piece into his mouth. It's flavorless and bland, but most things tasted like that since Weston's death, if he was honest. If it wasn't for him being an adrenaline junkie to get his blood pumping, he is more than confident he didn't have a heart of any sort.

His likes and dislikes.

His hobbies and disinterests.

His favorite food and drink, he had pushed aside for the sake of making it up to his parents.

He had no preferences because it never did matter what he liked.

However, he remembers just last week when he had taken half of Troy's bagel. It was so overly sweet and creamy, but he found himself liking it despite hating sweets. It wasn't just flavorful; something about eating alongside him made him have an appetite.

If he's being honest, that did sound good right now.

Why was that?

It's one of many questions he still can't quite understand, and another is how he's barely even hooking up anymore with random men or women who showed him interest. His cock wouldn't even stir, but being near Troy is an entirely different story.

However, sleeping with his teammate—especially with the bet in place—is a huge no.

He deserves the world—even if the thought of him with someone else makes him see red.

Still, he pushes it aside.

Fortunately, he survives another night of weekly dinner without imploding or accidentally lashing out. It happened on the third anniversary of Weston's death, and it only ended with his mother being sent to the hospital for having a mental breakdown right in the middle of their living room.

Shortly after, they packed their bags and moved here, only to be sent to a psychiatric ward when she noticed Jayden's tattoos, as that's something her *son* would never get. It's as if she only had one. The next time she returned, Father made him promise to always wear long sleeves or pants during dinners so as not to upset Mother.

For a moment, he tickers about returning to his apartment, but then the idea of being alone in his thoughts threatens to eat him alive. He thinks about going to the nearest bar and getting hammered because it sure as hell sounds better than being sober right now.

It's not as if he had anything going on this weekend, and most of his classwork is durable.

As he takes out his phone to navigate towards the nearest bar, he doesn't know why, but he thinks about asking Troy if he wants to meet up. He goes as far as to waver over his thumb over his recent contact, not exactly realizing until this moment how much they call one another.

He supposes it makes sense, given that they do run every morning.

Usually, when he's in a foul mood like this very moment, only two things get him out of it; either doing something that gets his blood pumping—ranging from cliff diving in the middle of the night, spontaneously getting a tattoo, or scaling something like a building without equipment—or drinking.

There has never once been an option to reach out to another person to talk.

So why now?

Shaking away the silly thought, he searches the nearest bar only a few blocks away and makes his way over; as soon as he went in, the bass pounding into his head instantly overpowered any unpleasant, upsetting thoughts he had building up the entire night, serving as the perfect distraction.

The neon flashing lights of red, blue, green, and white blare and cover his vision entirely, but give or take, there are at least a hundred or so people on a Friday night. Chattering and laughter help drown out his thoughts just as he makes his way over to the counter.

He quickly orders two shots, letting the alcohol burn as it travels down his throat.

Just as quickly, he slams the shot glass down for the other. Jayden then messages his parents, saying he got home safely, as the last thing he wants is for them to call and inadvertently mess up everything he had built before tucking his phone away to order another.

It's not often he finds himself drinking.

In fact, he's become numb to his parents' antics, yet something about today got him on edge. If he had to pinpoint it, it was when they got Troy involved. The thought makes him feel down, as lately, his emotions have only become unstable and disorderly when it comes to him.

As he's about to order another, he sees a woman starting to approach him with a sultry-like smile. A stunning red dress that leaves little to the imagination by the way it wraps around her curves and that lowcut, she is precisely the type of woman he would have gone home with months ago.

Yet right now, his cock didn't even stir the slightest, and he wasn't in the mood to keep up the façade.

"Hi, are you—"

"Not interested," he clips, and just like that, the smile drops as she scowls at him.

"You didn't have to be an ass," she grumbles as he works his fourth shot in less than fifteen minutes. He's starting to feel better now with the alcohol coursing through his body, but he doesn't know why and wants to hear Troy now more than before.

I mean, that's what teammates and friends do, right? They talk on the phone.

Jayden is too plastered to think about this logic doesn't then apply to Trevis or any of his other teammates. He takes out his phone and sluggishly takes out his phone as he squints his eyes towards the time.

He should be up; it's only midnight...right?

Without another thought, he presses his number.

CHAPTER THIRTY

Troy can't believe it.

Almost ten hours later, lying in bed, he still thinks it's a dream.

Their team qualified for the playoffs—the conference championship.

After coming down from that shellshock of the news that he was one step closer to his dreams of being the first deaf *and* LGBTQ+ player, he called up his parents. It went without saying that the video call left his phone clinging at fifteen percent of battery when it started at around ninety and his hands and fingers cramping by the time they hung up.

It's a feat that wouldn't be possible, but shuffling between his parents, who then decided to call his relatives and everyone else in their vicinity, he supposes that'll be possible. He didn't even want to get started regarding Quinn and her parents since he had gone over to dinner before.

Even if they wouldn't be eligible for the national tournament—something his parents and Quinn told him not to think so negatively about— he's still happy he was able to make it this far in his first year and with the best teammates that he could ask for.

After returning to all the messages from people he didn't even realize he knew, he finally collapsed onto the bed. He glances over at his roommate, who looks completely immersed in whatever game he's playing, and messages what Troy presumes to be his boyfriend.

He's not precisely tired but more exhausted mentally as he slowly closes his eyes to rest them.

That is until his phone vibrates intensely next to him a few seconds later, and he puckers his lips in confusion. It's already close to midnight, so he isn't quite sure who would be calling him unless it's his parents because of an emergency.

He turns over, reaching for his phone, and his stomach flops as he instantly shoots up from the bed to why Jayden is calling him so late. The sudden motion catches Aston's attention, and he looks over from his game in surprise.

"Sorry, it's nothing," he signs, and Aston gives a thumbs up before giving him the privacy.

He takes a deep breath, trying to seem calm and collected as he answers it.

Only his expression soon twists into a frown when he sees the rather dark screen and the color of different flashing lights. His stomach twists as he tries to understand if something is wrong or if he had called by mistake when suddenly, Jayden comes into view.

Alarm bells start to go off at the back of his mind.

"Troy," he signs with a giant grin on his face. He grabbed an empty glass he found that someone had left behind, propping his phone up so he could interact with him better. "I'm sorry for calling so late. Were you about to sleep?"

Even if he was a smidge tired, it's completely gone now. "No, don't worry about me. Are you okay?"

Three simple words, and yet, it somehow makes Jayden choke up on the other side. A small part of him hates seeing the concern and anxiousness across Troy's face, but another part is almost happy to see someone concerned for him.

He hates himself for that more than he'd like to admit as he swallows the small lump. His head is pounding from the music and alcohol, but hearing Troy's voice instantly makes him feel fuzzy inside. Weirdly enough, he can't find himself lying, not when it comes to him.

"It...could be better," Jayden signs with a half-shrug, a loopy smile on his face. "It is what it is with parents who don't care for you, or you'll never be good enough for them, am I right? Though I suppose that's my fault as well for Weston."

What? Whose...Weston?

Troy found himself frowning heavily on the other side of this completely new information.

However, there is a more important task at hand. "Where are you right now?"

"A bar downtown," he replies, though the signal is somewhat choppy wherever he is. He frowns, squinting his eyes momentarily as he tries to make an articulate thought before abandoning it. "Somewhere…near my place? I can't remember the name, if I'm honest."

Well, that doesn't help in the slightest.

"How many drinks have you had?" Troy asks, his brows knitting together as he sees Jayden's eyes turning hazy momentarily as if deep in thought. It makes him anxious to see Jayden like this, mainly because he was fine just before Coach Winter congratulated them.

In fact, he looked fine, so what changed?

"I think…five? Four or five shots," he answers. "Give or take, think five."

"*Shots*?"

"I've had more back in…" he trails off. His hand movements are now sloppy, and he looks so disoriented that Troy can't determine what he said. Troy knows that if he were to hang up right now, he would keep him up all night, so he quickly throws out the first solution that comes to him.

"Well, do you…want to hang out?" Troy finds himself signing. Just like when he drank, he didn't think he'd ever find any circumstances to which he would want to be around someone who was intoxicated. However, he finds himself brushing it aside when it comes to him.

"Right now?" he questions, his brows knit together.

"If you want, I can meet with you," he offers, and Jayden quickly turns it down.

"No, it's dangerous to walk at night," he objects, and for a moment, Troy resists the urge to scowl at him. While grateful he's so caring, it's not exactly what he wants to hear right now as he gets up and throws on a pair of sweat-pants before redirecting his attention back to his phone propped up.

This is probably the most impulsive thing he's done. Truthfully, he knows that aside from Quinn, he would never do this for another person. However, the look on his face seemed to tell him that Jayden needed someone there.

"Then I'll take an Uber to you," he answers. "Where are you?"

"I don't—"

"Check," he cuts off with a glare that even makes Jayden shut his mouth obediently. Once he signs the address, Troy tells him to stay still and that he will be there in fifteen minutes. He sighs as he orders an Uber, grabbing his wallet and keys just as Aston looks at him in confusion.

"Where are you going so late at night?" he signs with a slight frown.

"A friend needs me right now," he answers, not wanting to go too much into detail. It just seems like an invasion of privacy, as if it were him; he would want the person he chose to confine himself with to keep his secret. "Please don't wait up!"

With that, he hurries down just in time for his Uber to arrive.

He's already on edge, fiddling with the hem of his shirt as he checks the estimation time before he arrives. Time seems to be going too slow, and he doesn't answer despite texting Jayden. He tinkers for a moment when calling him, but the last thing he wants is to do anything that might 'persuade' Jayden to do something else entirely.

It happened a few times when he went to pick up Quinn after one too many drinks.

When the Uber drops him off, he bows his head as thanks before exiting.

He heads straight into the bar, already thinking of every possible situation and what to do to ensure he can get Jayden home safely. Whatever was going through his mind right now, it wasn't good. He can put that much together, at the very least.

Instantly, the blinding lights, smell of alcohol and sweat, and the vibration make him stiffen. It reminds him so much of the house party a few weeks ago and what happened a few years ago mixing together. He takes a deep breath, shaking away the thought as he looks for the counter where Jayden had called him from.

This time, he was more cautious in avoiding accidentally bumping into people.

It shouldn't be a shock to Troy that with one sweep around, he can quickly find Jayden slumped over on the table. Luckily, no one is around him, so he quickly walks over to lightly tap him on the shoulder.

Immediately, Jayden lifts his head with a scowl—almost like he's picking a fight.

It soon blooms into a full-on smile as he pulls Troy into a fight hug, practically knocking them both to the ground from sheer force. The younger man can already feel his face heating up, mainly because of Jayden hugging and nuzzling him and how adorable he looks right now.

Who would have thought he'd be such an affectionate drunk?

"Hi," Jayden signs after pulling away.

"Hi, let's get you home, okay?" Troy replies, not wanting to beat around the bush. He looked utterly wasted at this point, and something told him that if they were to stay just a bit longer, he would probably puke.

He should have known Jayden would put up a fight as he shakes his head. "You said we'll hang out."

"We will," he answers, using the same trick that usually works on Quinn. "At home. Now come on."

Thankfully, he still remembers where Jayden lives, and it's just a block away. Yet, it didn't deter Troy from thinking just how he'd be able to haul him back or the next problem that quickly arises when he shakes his head and has the audacity to pout.

"No, I don't want to go home. I want to stay here," he signs.

"You look like you were glaring at anyone who approached you from the looks of it," Troy retorts.

"That's because I wasn't having fun since they're not you," he responds, and his heart skips a beat before he quickly shakes the thought away and scolds himself. No, Troy, do not think about how happy that makes you because he meant as a close friend.

Do not try to think about or overanalyze why he decided to call you rather than anyone else.

Most importantly, do *not* think about why he smiled so brightly before he saw him.

Troy takes a deep breath as it seems he's going to have to toughen up when it comes to Jayden. Not just for the well-being of his heart but also to get his teammate to go in one piece and help him through whatever he's going through now.

"Well, I'm not having fun here," he tries instead, and that seems to sober him up ever so slightly.

"You're not?" he questions, and Troy shakes his head to drive home his point.

"No, you know I never like parties."

"Me either," Jayden signs. "I just…come here to forget. We can do something else then, like get a bagel."

While it seems good for him to eat in the morning, as carbs are the best hangover food from helping Quinn nurse one too many after her drinking, it certainly wouldn't be for today. Something tells him that if he disagrees at that moment, it will just lead to another tantrum, so he uses his hand to gesture for a check he has seen many times before.

Luckily, the bartender understands he's asking for the closing tab.

Grabbing the credit card and tucking it away for safekeeping, he turns to Jayden and shakes his head. "No, we're not going to get a bagel right now. We're going home so you can sleep this off, Advil, and have lots of water. You're going to thank me tomorrow, Jayden."

"You're mean," he whines, making a flamboyant gesture with his hands all the while.

Troy resists the urge to pinch his cheek as he helps Jayden sling one arm around his shoulder.

"I wouldn't have to be if you behaved," he signs in retaliation.

"I don't like to play Mr. Nice with you."

Somehow, Troy does know that from the bottom of his stomach.

He's seen how he acts with him compared to his teammates and strangers. His little façade doesn't seem to be in place when it comes to him, and again, Troy doesn't want to think too hard about it or read into it.

With one hand wrapped around his waist to help steady him, they slowly return to Jayden's apartment. The usually calm and aloof man seems to be an entirely different person now, babbling but not as if Troy can hear it.

Once they manage their way inside, only after Jayden drops his key twice and then signs a bunch of nonsensical things do they head inside. It should be no surprise that he starts to look green as he lets go of Troy.

He's one step away, just seconds away, from hurling onto the carpet before lunging into the toilet bowl. Troy winces, going to get a bottle of water from the fridge and back over to soothingly run his hands down his back.

He supposes that's to be expected from downing five shots so quickly.

"Feeling better?" Troy signs, handing him a bottle of water and the Advil that he manages to find after a little effort, seeing as the apartment isn't that large. Jayden gives a rather sour look, chugging the bottle, and Troy then caps it back. "Come on, let's get you to bed."

"I don't want to sleep," he signs, nose wrinkling.

"We'll talk on the bed," Troy wedges, and when Jayden still doesn't look convinced, he gives a small smile. "We're not sleeping; I just want to lie down and talk. You just threw up, so I want you to be comfortable."

Thankfully, that seems to fool him into following behind him. "Okay."

It takes everything in Troy not to laugh when he realizes Jayden has held onto the bottom hem of his shirt like a small child as they head into his room. When they get inside, Troy can feel his heart pounding nervously.

Excitement, he dares to say.

He really isn't making this any easier for Troy, who is trying to sizzle out this crush of his, that's for sure.

Especially when he realizes he shouldn't sleep in the same clothes he's been wearing since morning and he's almost positive that he might have puked a tad bit on. Troy looks away bashfully, trying to make things awkward as he signs, "I think you should change before sleeping."

Jayden frowns. "I'm not—"

"I meant laying in bed and talking," he quickly corrects himself. His face only gets redder by the second when he nods and then grabs the back of his shirt to sling it off in one motion. He's certain his heart stopped beating as he signs, "I'll turn. Can you tap me when you're done!"

God, why did this man have to be so hot?

Why did this man, who is literally his damn gay awakening, have to be so defenseless?

Troy starts to count to thirty when he feels a tap on his shoulder. He breaths out a sign of relief, only for his knees to almost give out when he sees him only in a pair of boxers with his hair all tousled. Jayden only smiles as if nothing is wrong. "Done."

"Why are you naked?" Troy questions as he watches him crawl into bed.

Rather than replying, he shuffles all the way to the corner and then signs, "I want a bagel tomorrow, please. Cream cheese and jelly, extra toasted just like the way you ordered it the other day and…coffee. I still like my coffee black."

Seriously? Why is he so obsessed with that?

He doesn't answer, just tucking him in before signing, "We can have it tomorrow."

"Promise?"

"Yes."

"Okay," he signs and scoots even inside so that his side is almost pressed near the wall. "Lie with me."

"I don't think that's…very smart."

"Why?" he questions in turn with a small pout. "We're just talking. You promised."

Bloody hell, this man really is trying to kill him, but he can't find himself to argue because, frankly, he's tired, and the last thing he wants is for Jayden to throw another tantrum. He bites his lips for a moment, willing his little friend not to act up before getting in.

With that, he crams himself right at the very edge of the bed but faces one another so they can still talk with one another. Though rather than doing that, Troy just finds himself completely lost in his eyes, wavering between asking or just talking about whatever comes to his mind as he swallows the lump in his throat.

"So…do you…want to talk about what happened?" he signs slowly so Jayden can follow along. For a moment, it looks as if the man being questioned isn't comfortable, and just as Troy is about to give him a way out, he beats him to it.

"It's because of today's dinner with my parents. My parents and I don't get along in the slightest. Not since my brother passed away because of me, because I chose to run away that night and he slipped and slammed his head into that rock. They…they don't see me, but they see him through me," he signs, the quickest he's ever done since he had scolded him for following and slipping into the water.

Well, *shit*.

That's…certainly something that he thought Jayden would suddenly spring onto him. Troy doesn't think he is holding this so closely as he takes everything in, trying to digest it. He fully knows that he won't remember any of this tomorrow in confessing this to him as he finds the right thing to sign.

After a moment, he slowly lifts his hands. "Have you ever spoken to them about this?"

"Do I even have the rights?" he says, his nose wrinkling. "I owe it to them because it was my recklessness that got him killed. I've…I've never told anyone before, but it's because of me that he died. It should have been me."

What can anyone say to that?

Truthfully, he has no idea of the full story regarding Jayden's family.

However, he can only speak for himself if it were him— if he were in his brother's shoes.

"Your brother...wouldn't want you to live like this, I think. I don't think your parents would as well if they knew you've been suffering for their sake," he signs. It suddenly hits Troy as to why there always seems to be a dark cloud that hangs from Jayden's head every Friday. He thought he was imagining it, but it seemed he had been right on the mark. "I'm not going to sit around and pretend I know the whole story because I don't, but...I know no parents would want their child to suffer."

Again, a heavy silence fills the air right before Troy sees Jayden's eyes slowly drooping.

"He...would have liked you," he quietly signs. "He's deaf but...he's like you. So positive and talkative."

Somehow in that moment, Jayden looks so lonely that Troy can't help but crawl over to him, nuzzling right onto his chest that seems to be practically made for him. Gently, he wraps his arms around him and in turn, Jayden does the same.

Laying a chaste kiss at the top of his forehead.

Although no words were exchanged, in that moment, it was enough for them.

CHAPTER THIRTY-ONE

If there's one thing Jayden always forgets until the day after any party or binge drinking until he blacks out, it is how lethargically sick he feels, like this very moment. He's confident his brain might very well be on the brink of splitting into two as he groans before wincing at how loud his voice sounds.

Feeling lost and dazed with a pounding in his head unlike any ever, he managed to crack open one eye.

Well, at least he's alive and back in his own room.

However, he can't exactly remember when or how he ended up back in his apartment.

Usually, when he's blacked out, he often ends up slumping in some twenty-four-hour diner or, one time, blacked out on the park's benches. When he's at a house party, often in someone else's bed or whoever threw the party's couch. The fact that he ended up back in his bed is certainly something he had least expected as he find himself frowning.

Well, that's a damn first.

Still trying to recollect himself and figure out what happened between them last night and the current time, he notices the sun's warmth on his face, signaling the start of a new day. Then, it's the chirping of birds just outside and loud, noisy honks from a nearby car.

It didn't help that the chirping and honking was like a boombox at max volume right next to his ears.

Also, he didn't understand just why it was so damn bright.

He squints his eyes and sees that the curtain has been drawn, which is strange because he could have sworn that he had them closed. In these moments, he's glad it's the weekend but hates nursing a hangover that often lasts the whole day.

"Argh," he groans again, much lower this time, while looking around as his brain tries to catch up on everything, like his name and just what year it is at this point. He's never drunk that much in one go for a while now as he takes a deep breath, trying to string together the jagged, broken memories.

Another strange occurrence is two Advil sitting alongside a water bottle on his nightstand.

Did he somehow do that last night?

Either way, he slowly pushes himself up, trying to ignore the nausea that slams into him as he finds himself gripping hard onto the blankets as the room spins temporarily. He takes the pill and quickly wash it down when he feels confident that he won't vomit.

Still feeling a bit disoriented, he barely heard the knock

until movements caught in front of his eyes; his eyes instantly widen as he stares at Troy in complete bafflement, a mixture of shock and disbelief if he's there or hallucinating.

Shit, did he take some drug offered to him? He can't even recall after his second or so shot.

His eyes drift down to the tray in his hand and the smell of what he presumed to be a raisin bagel with cream cheese and jelly and a cup of piping hot coffee. His stomach immediately starts growling, and his mouth starts to water. It certainly does feel real, especially his smile while walking over and placing the tray on his lap.

"Hi, morning," he signs, glancing over at the empty water bottle and Advil for a moment before his eyes refocus on him with a small, friendly smile. "Oh good, you ate the medicine! I'm sorry I used your kitchen; I hope that's okay. How are you feeling?"

He felt like shit when he had just awoken, but for some reason, upon seeing Troy, he was a tad better.

Maybe he's just hungry, but it doesn't answer why he's here.

He racks his brain, but still, it comes up empty of what happened the last eight to ten hours.

Hell, he doesn't even know what time it is, either.

For a moment, his face pales as he tries to feel if he's dressed. He sighs when he realizes he is but frowns for a moment as he could have sworn that he was wearing something else yesterday. When he realizes he's been quiet for too long, he quickly signs, "I'm fine, just a bit hungover, but nothing like water, medicine, and carbs can't fix. Thank you."

"No, it's okay! I've done this many times for Quinn before, so eat, eat," he instructs.

Not being able to hold back any longer, Jayden quickly digs in; he would rather eat now and try to piece the puzzle together than just gawk at him. The sweet taste of the cream cheese is in perfect harmony with the jelly, and he's working on chewing so he doesn't choke.

Strangely, he didn't realize he had been craving that until this very moment as he practically swallowed it down. Only after he had finished and washed it down with coffee did his head and stomach feel a tad better that he couldn't take the suspense anymore.

No matter how hard he tries raking the back of his brain, it comes off empty like a missing puzzle piece he can't seem to put together; seeing as Troy doesn't seem to be that awkward or running for the hills, he likes to take his chances.

"What happened last night?" he finally musters the courage to ask.

Troy pauses, barely noticeable if you didn't look hard enough, but Jayden did.

Suddenly, he can feel his stomach churning, but almost as if Troy can understand just what's on his mind, he immediately shakes his head and signs quickly to clear the miscommunication. "No, it's nothing bad in the slightest! Nothing like that!"

"What about my clothes?"

"You ended up changing before sleeping because you felt hot and sweaty," Troy replies, feeling his face only getting redder. Though Jayden did kiss him on the forehead, he's going to keep that to himself so as not to make things more awkward.

Jayden stares at him for a moment before feeling his shoulder sag slightly.

"Okay, but did I do or say anything weird last night?" he questions skeptically.

His lips pursed for a moment. Weird?

"Define that," he asks with his hands. "Actually, just how much do you remember from last night?"

He figures it might be easier to start there and see how much he can fill in from there. He didn't even want to get started on how he clung to him like a koala the entire night or his…thing poking him first thing in the morning.

Which is natural, so he can't exactly blame him!

"Not much, if I'm being honest," he acknowledges rather grimly. "I remember going to my parents for dinner, then to the bar before planning to head back home. Seeing as you're here now, I presume…I called you to come fetch me or something along those lines?"

"Or something along those lines," he affirms with a curt nod. "You drunk-dialed me."

"Shit, I'm so sorry," he expresses profoundly, his brows knit together.

"It's okay! I'm glad you did," he concurs, taking the tray to settle on the nightstand and watching how Jayden buries his face into the palms. "I mean, I'm happy you trust me enough to come get you when you were blackout drunk."

God, how sweet can this man be?

After a while, he straightens himself.

"How badly did I mess up?" he asks. "Be honest."

"Not too bad," Troy quickly amends, but when Jayden stares at him through pointed eyes, he can't help but sigh. He should have known nothing would get by when it came to Jayden reading him like an open book. "Okay, bad, but... not too bad, I promise!"

He even holds up his pinky to emphasize the word, 'bad.'

"Troy."

"You got blacked out drunk and ended up throwing up in the toilet as soon as we walked into your apartment. You might...had some on the floor and your clothes, but I managed to clean it up, so nothing too bad," he replies quickly.

However, he knows that he's hiding something bigger.

Troy debates momentarily about bringing it up but isn't faster than Jayden. "There's more, isn't there?"

He took a deep breath before lifting his hand once more to sign, much slower and sluggish now as he didn't want to lie, but he didn't exactly know how to bring it up. That kept him up the entire night, alongside how comfortable he felt in his arms.

"Well..." he trails off for a moment, looking away. "You...talked about your...family. Your...brother."

Ah.

Somehow, Jayden didn't feel at all surprised; even when he goes drinking and blacks out with Trevis or any of his teammates, he has never spoken about any of his family's troubles back at home before. If you were to ask why this particular binge drinking led to this, he wouldn't know how to answer.

What he can say for sure is that he feels like a weight has been lifted off his shoulders.

In fact, he feels pretty relieved, which surprises him as he is more than convinced that he would never tell another person about his brother and his family's lengthy history. Yet his body seems to say otherwise by seeming to relax now wholly.

Is it because he's finally able to find someone to confide in? Or is it *because* it's Troy?

"How much did I tell you?" he signs, rubbing his temples right after.

"Basically…the main gist," he retorts, feeling like it's already eating him alive. "I'm sorry."

"No, don't be. I mean…I guess it's only a matter of time anyway," Jayden says with a heavy sigh.

That causes him to bump his brows together in confusion. "It is?"

He can't help but laugh at how adorable he signs, which comes off between awkward and stiff from the shock. He only sits himself up more comfortably, leading on the headboard while patting the spacious room in front of him so Troy wouldn't have to sit on the edge of the bed and sign at an awkward angle that would just hurt him in the long term.

Troy immediately understands, getting more comfortable while looking at him peculiarly.

"I mean, weren't you always curious about why I knew sign language?" he asks in turn, tilting his head.

He thinks about it momentarily and realizes he didn't as he shakes his head.

"Not in particular," he counters, and when Jayden looks at him in perplexity, he tries to make his point across to the best of his abilities through rambling. "It's just…why should I dig into your life or make assumptions rather than enjoy and appreciate that we crossed paths and ended up where we are right now?"

After all, his parents had taught him that there are many people from all walks of life in this world.

There is without a shadow of a doubt that there will be times you might be sitting next to someone you never know is struggling for their next meal or someone who has more money than they know what to do with it.

The point is that many people are dealing with their own problems that you never know. Most of the time, you wouldn't know, and to make presumptions without knowing the full context never sat well with Troy when growing up.

It was why, when he was almost…sexually assaulted, he couldn't find himself wanting to hate the man, which only made him spiral further years ago for even making an excuse for a potential rapist, saying he was drunk and might not have known better since Troy couldn't speak up.

His therapist had taught him that all these feelings are valid and part of who he is.

However, it shouldn't excuse any person from throwing themselves onto a person, no matter what.

Drunk or not.

It was those words that helped him during those rough nights.

When Jayden finally lifts his hand, it snaps him back.

"I don't think I have ever met a person quite like you," he professes. "Is it really that simple?"

Troy grins with a half-shrug.

"You'll tell me what you want to. If you don't want to tell me all about it, that's fine too!"

"That's really it?" he asks again, and Troy nods.

"Yes, why should it be that complicated?" he retorts.

If someone doesn't want to say something, the last person who wants to force them is himself. He knew firsthand the detriments of pushing when someone isn't ready yet, and he wouldn't want to do that with someone else.

A silence stretches between them for a moment, comfortable and soothing. As Troy is about to get up and suggests Jayden get out of bed and walk to help with circulation, which might help his hangover rather than staying in bed, Jayden lifts his hands up to sign.

"I'm sure you know I have a brother, right?" he begins slowly, his eyes focused on his words in front of him rather than Troy. He can't even believe he's doing this, something he never thought he'd tell anyone. "He was...the younger of us two by just a minute and two seconds, something I always held over his head. Just like you, he was deaf. For him, it was due to a fever and infection shortly after he was born that caused him to be in the emergency room unit for months."

"If it's hard, you don't have to tell me," he quickly signs before waving his hands to drive home the point.

In turn, Jayden goes to shake his head.

"I know, but I want to," he retorts and then gives a small smile. "You know…if I'm being honest, I wanted to pair up with you because you reminded me so much of my brother. He's so damn brave, kind, and the best damn tennis player."

"He played tennis as well?" he asks, his mouth parting in shock.

What were the chances?

"He did," he affirms, a genuine smile appearing on his face at the recollection of his brother. No matter how long it's been and the heartache his death had brought, he loved his brother more than anything else in the world. "Best one at Little League Tennis. Always won games, brought home trophies, and even the coach had said he'll be big one day."

"What about you in Little League?" Troy ask curiously, wanting also to hear a bit regarding his childhood.

"Me? No, I wasn't even in the program. My parents signed us both up for classes, but I would often sneak off to do something else. Even Weston had a hard time tracking me down right because as soon as Mother dropped us off, I was out of there," he remarks with a laugh. "The number of instances where he went to cover my ass since we're twins was uncanny. Hell, he even went as me one time just so I wouldn't get kicked out for missed attendance, putting himself at risk for me. Father was furious when he found out because Weston didn't get that award for perfect attendance. I never once went to any of the practices or played in any event either. Always sitting out or hiding in the bathroom doing anything else."

What was it exactly? He can't even remember anymore.

He can't remember what he likes if it's outside of what Weston likes.

"What? But you're the best player on the team, though!" Troy exclaims through his hands energetically.

He gawks at Jayden, surprised. Is he just a natural?

"It wasn't until much later that I became a better player," he muses, seeing the different expression that crosses his face. "Actually, would you believe me if I were to tell you that as a child, I was like the devil's incarnation? That's what my father liked to call me when he thinks I'm not listening."

He frowns. "I wouldn't say a devil's incarnation, but... an adventurous person?"

Jayden chuckles, running his hands through his thick hair back before continuing to sign. "Yeah, but to my parents, Weston was the golden child. They liked to joke often that he must have taken everything good from me when we were in the womb, and I got all of his rowdiness."

What?

Troy frowns. "Or it can just be...your way of being seen and expressing yourself. It's just you."

He also used to think that because that's what he overheard his teachers saying. He's acting out to get his parent's attention. Somehow, he always seems to be in the wrong place, and that comment only fueled him further. However, he didn't want to lash out at his brother as well because he loves him, so he resorted to something else entirely.

From running away for a few hours, skipping classes, or getting into fights.

Anything that made him feel something, at the very least.

That made him much more than Weston's "bad" twin.

Yet through it all, the only person who truly did understand him had been his brother, and yet…

How did he repay him?

By making him worry and risk his life looking for him?

Ended up dying before even knowing if he was found safely?

"I wouldn't lie and say that really does feel like the case when I'm always living in his shadow despite me being the older one," he attests. Suddenly, he feels so tired as he lets out a sigh. "Either way…I realized just how harmful my…antics and actions were, but it was too late in the end."

"Too late? I mean…there's no such thing as too late so long as you're still alive, right?" he parrots with his hands, tilting his head to the side. Yet, at that moment, that look on Jayden's face made his stomach churn. After all, he had told him everything last night, and he had asked at the moment without thinking it through.

"That's true," he signs, suddenly feeling much more tired than he had yesterday, but it's too late to back down now as he looks Troy right in the eyes. "However, it's because of me that cost my brother his life. How can I repay someone that's not here anymore?"

CHAPTER THIRTY-TWO

A silence stretches once more from the bombshell of news. Jayden can feel his stomach gnawing, and he can't tell if it's due to him downing the bagel in four bites or dropping that upsetting news. To admit that he's essentially killed his brother is another thing he never thought he'd do.

Though that's what he is, isn't he?

A *murderer*.

It didn't make it better that, for once, he couldn't read the expression on Troy's face as they stared into one another's eyes. He can feel his palm getting sweaty and clammy by the second, his heart beating so hard that he can feel it in his eardrums.

Just like when Troy fell into the water or when that fucker grabbed him at the party.

Troy swallows, feeling like he's been put in the spotlight for his inconsiderate comment as he quickly tries to retrace. "That's not...exactly what I meant. I'm sorry it came out that way. I meant you changing now, and it's not too late to be better or be whoever you want to be."

"If only that's possible," he remarks, casting his head downward momentarily.

However, no one likes who he is.

From his tennis coach and teammates from Little League, teachers, and even his parents.

"Though I'm presuming you already know that much from the drunk me yesterday, huh?" Jayden signs and Troy tries not to wince at how obvious it must have been from his lack of shock. While he did tell him that he knew the general gist, it also felt like an invasion of privacy to have found out from a drunken confession.

"I did," he affirms with a slow nod.

"Then...you know how he died?" he asks. He presses his lips into a thin line, glancing down at his hand on how to start answering such a difficult question. For a moment, he can't help but contemplate if this is the equivalent version of getting tongue-tied.

In this case, would it be called hand-tied?

After a brief pause, he raises his arm, which almost feels like stiff, heavy boulders.

"You ran away that night," he starts. "He...slipped while looking for you."

"That's the basic idea of it, anyway," he acknowledges. "We lived in Western Australia, just near a nature reserve. It had been raining all morning, and I stormed off over my report card during dinner. Father asked why I couldn't be more like Weston, and I remember snapping that maybe he should be their only son then and decided to run out of the house."

God.

That was the last thing his brother had ever heard before his death.

"Jayden," he signs, finally finding his movement to start signing again.

"He ran after me, knowing what route I'd take because we'd had our little hideout there. You had to hike off a rocky off-trail path to get there, and he…tripped and slammed his head. He died on impact. He was just eleven, Troy."

Goosebumps break out through every inch of Troy's body at how empty he looks while signing. It's as if he's here but mentally, somewhere else entirely. It breaks his heart to see him like this, but most of all, to even try to comprehend and imagine the pain of losing someone you love.

He cannot even say he understands the feelings of a single child.

However, he knows how close Quinn is to her younger brother and would do anything for him. Whenever they went out together to the mall or to have lunch, she would always get something for him at the very least.

It's a bond that can't be broken, and the fact that they're twins, Troy cannot even start to imagine it.

"You don't have to—"

"It's funny," he concurs, almost on autopilot as he stares right into his eyes. "I remember…something not feeling right in my guts, twin intuition, or something like that, so I headed back. Only, I was greeted with sirens, officers, and my parents crushing me into their arms and crying their hearts out. It was the first time they've ever…*hugged* me. I remember the warmth of it right before they broke the news. When I saw him in his casket…it would hunt me even to this day because it should have been me. I saw *myself*."

Hearing Jayden's confession when he's sober hits Troy painfully hard in his chest.

Troy can't help it anymore and reaches forward to show support by placing a hand on Jayden's knee. While he would have taken his hand, it also seemed discourteous to cut him off as well. They stare at one another, almost in a trance.

Yet, for Troy, it's also an effort to tell Jayden he's there for him.

"Breath," he signs, moving his hands forward away from his chest and then back towards it.

Thankfully, he listens, inhales, and exhales slowly based on his instructions.

Only when it seems he's somewhat better that he continues, and Troy doesn't try to stop him. It's almost as if he knows he needs to get this out before he can chicken out, and he allows him to. His hand still goes to his knee as he continues.

"As I said before, my antics and actions cost my brother and broke my family's heart. We never…recovered after that. We ended up packing and moving here to start anew, but honestly, I feel like nothing has changed," he signs, his shoulder sagging. "It's why I'm trying to make it up to them."

Something about that statement didn't sit well with Troy in the slightest, and he frowned.

Only a short time later, it seemed to slam into him what was going on.

The way he tries to be the "Mr. Nice" around campus.

The way in which he tries to hide who he really is from everyone.

The way he plays tennis, and he's a pro, but whenever the team wins or loses, he doesn't care as much.

He might have collapsed in complete shock if he wasn't sitting down.

"Are you...trying to make it up to your parents by... *being* him?" he dares to sign, hoping that might very well *not* be the case. When Jayden doesn't try to deny it, he can feel a sharp stinging at the back of his eyes in complete shock while tremors overtake him.

"I mean, what else can I do?" he signs. "After all, I owe it to him, to them. By being what Weston should have been, it's killing two birds with one stone. Not only do they get the perfect son they always wanted, but I can make it up to Weston."

What kind of logic is that?

Troy can feel his head spinning.

It's not just messed up, but downright fucked up to be doing something like this—inhuman and cruel.

"I don't...know if I have the right to say this," Troy says, carefully thinking before he acts with his words. He could feel his hand shaking slightly at the thought of imposing, but something like this needed to be said as he looked him straight in the eyes. "However, I don't think Weston would have wanted that for his older brother."

How he wishes for those words to be, and he finds himself signing once more.

"Why do you think that?"

For Jayden to even ask is a start by Troy's standard as he quickly takes out his points based on the limited things he already knows. "Well, your brothers, for one. I don't think anyone would ever want that for their siblings."

"He must have hated me," he retorts. He can feel those words like punctures in her already bleeding heart, but he knows deep down it's what he deserves after everything he has put Weston through. "Always cleaning after his older brother's mess, covering for him when things go South. He probably considered me a nuisance, just like my parents."

Ah, that's when Troy realizes how wrong he is.

He finds himself shaking his head in disagreement.

"No, I don't think so. After all, he always covered for you so you wouldn't get in trouble, right? Rather than trying to dissociate himself from you, he went out of his way to cover for you. Someone who cares for you so deeply would do it in a heartbeat. I would," he retaliates, and when he realizes how it sounds, he feels himself blushing and quickly retraces his step. "Though that is beside the point. I know Weston would have wanted you to live and be happy."

"I am happy being his replacement. I mean, everyone likes me better this way anyway," he scowls.

"I don't! I like and want to know who Jayden is, not Weston's replacement. Why can't you see that you're amazing the way you are?" he angrily signs, his hand moving like a blur as he lets out a loud huff. It was like something else completely overtook his body momentarily as he hopped out of bed. He can feel his face getting redder and redder, but he can't hold it in any longer. "I'm tired of you putting yourself down. I get it; you're kicking yourself for what happened, but what makes it better than your parents when you're also stuck in the past? How can they move on when you don't want to?"

Jayden feels his breath hitching, his heart thumping erratically fast at his words.

Troy…is right.

He had always blamed his parents for always living in the past, and yet he was doing the same thing.

He's living as Weston and being the perfect son, denying who he is as a person because he thinks that's what he needs to do to atone for his sins of taking his younger brother's life. He knows of his mother's breakdown and his father's disappointment.

Yet, Isn't that just feeding into his parent's decision of not moving on when he refuses to?

What the hell?

How could I be so blind?

That's the only thing coming through Jayden's mind, and it's like Troy had suddenly taken a bucket of cold water and splashed it on his body. He can feel those words seeping into his bones, making up his entire existence because it's the truth.

"Troy," he begins, and he beats him to it this time.

"Sorry," he quickly signs, realizing how stuck up he might have sounded in the moment by speaking against his action without knowing his whole story. When he heard Jayden talking down on himself, his hand seemed to sign everything before he could think twice. "I didn't know what came over me, I didn't mean—"

"No," he cuts in, shaking his head firmly. "No, that's... what I needed to hear, actually."

It was something he had never thought about before.

He didn't dare to do such a thing.

For a moment, Troy felt slightly relieved that Jayden didn't seem to be lying, though another pressing question arose. "I did ask you yesterday, but I want to ask again if you plan to...tell your parents about this?"

"No, I don't think I *can*," he admits. Troy turns the whole thing on its head when he lets out what appears to be a snort as he rolls his eyes. Jayden gawks at him for a moment, completely dumbfounded by his actions, when Troy gives him a small smile.

"I didn't mean to laugh. It's just that I find it humorous since I think you can do whatever you want, Mr. Daredevil-Always-Living-on-the-Edge-Jayden-Harrington," he signs, leaning forward to punch him in the shoulder lightly. "There's no way someone who's always living on the edge can't do something like this."

Somehow, Jayden finds himself smiling. "Are you trying to cheer me up?"

"No, I'm just saying the man willing to do all these adrenaline-seeking things can do something like confronting your parents whenever you're ready," he adds. "I'll be here if you ever need anything, but I think the first healing process always starts with acceptance. Your...brother would have wanted his big brother and parents to be able to live and not be stuck in the past; I would think if you said I'm just like him."

Jayden can feel something pricking at the back of his eyes for some reason. "Thank you."

"Oh, you don't have to thank me. I think you already knew deep down that's what you and Weston wanted. After all, don't you know him better than anyone?" he ponders with a grin, and Jayden finds himself laughing.

God, it felt...good.

He felt so free knowing there had always been a third path for him, but he had been too blinded to see otherwise. He's naturally too stubborn regarding his viewpoint, only seeing straight when he's locked onto something.

It is something Weston always had to steer him clear of, and now, Troy had done the same.

"I guess I was too busy wallowing in my self-pity to realize it," he professes, slowly getting up from where he had been lying for the past twelve-plus hours. His body is entirely sore as he stretches. "You know that you can be quite mean sometimes."

"Sometimes, a little bit of brutal honesty is what someone needs when push comes to shove. Also, if your parents can't see you for the amazing person you are, that's their loss," he quips, huffing out his chest while crossing his arms before a question pops up. "Wait, if your brother was deaf and you learned sign language in Australia, how come you know American sign language then?"

"You know, after his death, and we moved here, I didn't talk for a while. I...the only thing I found comfort in was learning American sign language. As a way to start anew," he answers as he opens his door. He tries not to squint that all the window curtains are pulled upward, something he hasn't done in such a long time. "Did you eat yet?"

"No, not yet. I was going to after getting back to my dorm," he confesses.

"Did you have something to do today?" he asks as Troy follows him to the living room.

"Not exactly," he answers, tilting his head to the side. "Why?"

"I want to take you somewhere."

CHAPTER THIRTY-THREE

The Centennial Wheel.

An iconic part of Chicago's skyline, reaching over two hundred feet in the air.

For many people visiting Chicago, there are usually three top sightseeing sights to visit: from the Cloud Gate at Millennium Park, the museums, or the Navy Piers. Troy had thought about coming here one day when he first decided to attend college in the windy city.

He didn't think that day would exactly be today.

More importantly—why?

Troy's heart races erratically as he stands next to Jayden in line, waiting for their turn on the Ferris wheel.

Strangely enough, since coming to Chicago to study, he hasn't found the time to explore the city or anything touristy with his hectic schedule. Quinn, born and raised here, never considered bringing Troy to this place compared to the mall or any shopping establishment. So it wasn't something precisely on his radar either in doing these things alone.

So, for Jayden to bring him here after their brunch at a diner nearby, he can't help but feel a tad nervous and excited coming here. Even more so when Troy realizes that many visiting couples practically surround them.

Again, how did this happen?

Biting his lips, Troy slowly veers his attention towards Jayden and feels a jolt of electricity shoot through his body. It just so happens that it is the exact moment a soft breeze rushes through his tousled hair, making him even more handsome under the sunlight as he looks up at the Ferris wheel, which prompts him to do so.

As he looks up at the towering Ferris wheel, Troy can't help but feel a gust of excitement and nervousness. After all, the last time he's ever been on a Ferris wheel was when he was just a kid, and it was just at a small state fair.

Almost as if Jayden can sense his nervousness, he turns his attention back to him, cocking his head.

"Is everything okay?" he asks, his hands pointing up more to show emphasis.

"Oh, yes," he fumbles with his hand, his cheek flushing. "Sorry, it's just really…tall."

It's probably a dumb thing to say, stating the obvious, but it's a bit hard for Troy to focus correctly when he sees a couple kissing just behind Jayden. He swallows the lump in his throat as Jayden's frown deepens. "Are you afraid of heights?"

"Not exactly," he replies, pressing his lips thinly together. "Honestly, I'm not too sure. The last time I've been on a Ferris wheel was when I was a kid with my parents at the state fair. Besides that, I've never even been to any amusement park."

"You haven't?" he asks, his brows almost hitting his hairline to hear so.

"My parents worked all day, so we didn't have the time for things like vacationing," he explains.

As an only child who always knew he was different from others, he didn't frequently ask his parents for anything. The last thing he wanted was to make his parents go out of their way for him when they had already done so much to accommodate his needs.

It's why, so long as they were spending time together in some way, he was content. Even if he just said he stayed home or played tennis all summer alone in the courtyard while hearing about his classmates' returning trips from different countries to Disneyland.

He's happy, honestly.

It's the very reason why he never understood what his parents meant when they told him he could be more selfish regarding himself and what he wanted. It was something he had never comprehended what it meant until now.

Until he realized how he was rejecting a part of himself for other people's happiness.

"Does that mean this is your first-time riding anything this tall?" Jayden questions curiously

It leads him to a sheepish grin. "That and I've never gone to the Navy Piers either."

The look of complete shock is almost laughable, and even Troy knows how ridiculous that might sound, given how the college is just half an hour away on public transport or about a forty-five-minute walk. "You haven't?"

He shakes his head, rolling his eyes playfully. "I mean, you've met Quinn. Do you think she'd come here?"

They have been to the shopping mall nearby, so Troy knows its existence. However, by the time Quinn is done shopping, Troy's tired of being dragged around to do anything but head back to his dorm and crash.

Rinse and then repeat.

Jayden can't help but pause before signing.

"I see your point," he muses. "Well, I'm glad to be your first in something then."

Troy resists the urge to blush madly at how off the mark he was on *that* statement.

If only this man knew how many firsts he had already taken from Troy without realizing it. From his reckless action in jumping into the ocean to save him, then to his first *ever* kiss, to his first puppy love crush after coming to terms with his sexuality.

Needless to say, it's the damn understatement of the century.

Luckily, a couple was already getting off when a staff member was already ushering them in.

Jayden gets on the cart first, which is a short three-inch elevation upward.

What Troy didn't expect was for him to turn and then hold out his hand with a small smile.

Damn it, he was making it quite challenging to try moving on from him.

Taking his hand, Troy then pushes himself up as Jayden pulls him. In the last second, he still manages to trip somehow, in some freaking way. His eyes widen in shock, but he's cushioned right into a warm chest the next thing he notices. His heart flutters erratically as he quickly fumbles and pulls away, seeing how amused Jayden seems regarding the whole thing.

"Thank you," he signs with a small smile upon readjusting himself, still flustered that even when he had held Jayden's hand, he still managed to trip by some means. They each take a seat, and shortly after the ride starts, he comes to a revelation.

His body didn't go rigid when he fell, as if prepared for impact.

As if he had anticipated Jayden to catch him.

To distract himself and his poor heart, he looks out the window, but it doesn't take long until he becomes entirely fascinated by the view. He finds himself leaning closer, and his eyes widen at the breathtaking sight of the city.

"Oh, you can see all the Chicago skyline and the pier here. It's beautiful," Troy signs in excitement before refocusing on the sight behind him. Troy's eyes were completely fixated on the stunning view of the skyline.

He didn't think the city could ever look this beautiful with the sun high above the sky.

He feels a sense of awe as he looks down at the sprawling city below.

The city was alive with lights and sounds and the cool sea breeze blowing through the overhead department. The tall skyscrapers seemed to reach up and touch the sky, and he couldn't help but feel small in comparison, especially when he saw the people down below were no bigger than ants.

While it had always sounded cliché, he finally understood it at that very moment.

Troy leans forward to get a better view of the bustling streets and buildings, pressing his hands and forehead against it. Yet, while he's looking at the beautiful view laid out before him, Jayden's view is focused entirely on something else.

Someone else.

Wondering what it was about Troy makes his heart feel so damn *alive*.

As they reach the top of the Ferris wheel, the ride comes to a stop, leaving them suspended in the air.

Troy's in utter awe, turning to Jayden and wanting to ask if he's enjoying the view, only to find him hovering over him. His breath catches as they suddenly become close in an instant. His eyes are fixed on Jayden's, and he can feel his face heating up.

He can't help but notice how stunning Jayden looks in the moment, the bright blue sky in the back compared to Jayden's tanned skin. His hair flowed in the wind, and his eyes were fixed on the view before them.

"Oh, you're right; you can see everything," he signs, plopping down on the seat beside him. Sometimes, Troy can't help and wonder if he knows what he's doing to his poor damn heart. He can practically feel the heat radiating from his skin.

He swallows the lump, biting his lips as he nods.

"Yeah," he signs stiffly and hastily tries to find something to say. "You can also see Lake Michigan."

Jayden's eyes fall from the skyline in the back of Troy's for a moment and then to the other side where he had been sitting. Then, ever so slowly, he smiles. "Huh, I never would have thought I'd be here. Now that I think about it, it's funny."

At that, he blinks, a bit perplexed. "What is?"

"Just…how much more relaxed I've felt since this weight has been lifted this morning," he confesses, his eyes still trained outside. "I guess that since I met you, everything has been…different. I never got to thank you for that."

Thank me? For what?

"You don't have to," he tries to start, but he's cut off when Jayden crosses his flat, open hands across his chest, and releases them to shush him. Troy watches as Jayden releases a heavy sigh, racking his tousled hair back as he recollects himself.

"to be honest, I've practically spent almost half my life here in Chicago, but I've never gone on this Ferris wheel or the piers," he replies, and the news takes him by surprise. However, the following statement out of his mouth puts the whole thing on its head. "If I'm being honest, this is my first time *on* a Ferris wheel."

"So I'm your first?" Troy signs before he can stop himself.

When he realizes the little twinkle of amusement, he mentally kicks himself. Though thankfully, Jayden doesn't try to tease him too much as he nods at his question. "You are. I've been to many amusement parks before but never rose on a Ferris wheel."

"So…why now?"

It's a question Jayden doesn't even know the answer to. Why?

Truthfully, he just wanted to see the beautiful city with Troy because he just wanted to take everything in. When they're this high above, it makes him feel as if he can accomplish anything, especially with Troy by his side.

However, it wasn't as if he could voice that either, so he shrugged. He brings his hands up for a moment, trying to find the right words. "I thought you'd like it, so I figured we could go together. Like myself, I didn't expect this to be your first time either."

Which, in itself, isn't technically a lie.

"I do," he confirms, nodding eagerly. "But…as a thrill seeker and someone who seems like they'd want to ride just about everything and anything. Was there a reason why you didn't want to ride the Ferris wheel before?"

He didn't expect the entertained smile on his face to drop ever so slightly.

"If I'm being honest…I always had this…call to the void, I suppose."

Something about his statement didn't settle in the slightest with Troy as he parrots. "Call of the void?"

"The sudden urge or thought to jump from a rather high place," he informs him, and his eyes widen when Jayden's eyes drift over the doorway ever so slowly. "It wouldn't be that hard, I would think, to pry the door open and jump;

how easy it would be—the ultimate experience of sorts—as my last thrill-seeking ride. It's why I thought if I were to go, especially with my parents when I was a kid, I might have."

He was certain he would have.

Something about that look on his face, so devoid of emotions like he did whenever he acted on impulse alone, scared Troy. His stomach churns, and Jayden can't finish his statement before Troy reacts.

Getting up and practically holding him down to the best of his abilities despite him being twice his size.

"You can't," he exclaims with his hands before wedging his legs about his broad thigh, hoping to hold him down as he shakes his head repeatedly. For a moment, Jayden is utterly just stunned. After all, he wasn't *truly* going to do it, but something about Troy's strong reaction ultimately makes him freeze up.

Something in his heart thumps and beats painfully.

To know that someone cares so much.

To know that he matters to someone here.

To know that his existence meant something.

It was a different euphoria that beat all his other thrill-seeking adventures.

Why the hell was this emotion making his heart want to pound out of his chest?

As he stares down at Troy, who is gripping his shirt for dear life like he might actually—probably from all the things he had done in front of him—he finds something prick at the corner of his eyes. As he stares down at him, he can't help but feel as if he has just discovered a little treasure for him only.

A tiny little piece of heaven that calms his ever-wandering mind, especially after this morning.

He slowly holds Troy close, stroking his back while swallowing the lump in his throat. It is only when it seems he has calmed down enough that he cups his cheeks, bringing him away slightly so he can talk to him.

Only his heart almost shatters when he sees the tears brimming there.

Fuck.

When was the last time someone had cried for him besides his brother?

When did someone last cry for *Jayden* Harrington?

"Troy. Troy, calm down; I'm not going to jump," he signs, but if he was being honest, seeing him cry made him absolutely want to make some apology. When a tear slips free, Jayden swipes it away with his thumb, watching how he leans into his touch slightly and sniffles. "I was just saying. I don't...I don't want to die."

He looks at him skeptically, his brows bumped together. "Really?"

"Truly," he answers with his hands. "I'm sorry; I didn't mean to worry you. I'm just saying."

"Good," he signs, sniffling again.

Jayden can't help but wrap one arm around him, always realizing but never really considering how precious Troy is. As they looked into one another's eyes, it was almost as if something overpowered them at that moment.

Something they had never felt before.

A heady mix of desire, fear, and excitement, all swirling

together in a tumultuous storm inside them. Troy soon finds his pulse quickening and his palms growing damper when he sees what position they had accidentally found themselves in.

It seems Jayden's impulsive behavior is finally rubbing up on him after all.

He knew that he was falling harder and faster for Jayden, and it was a feeling that he couldn't deny.

Something he's trying so damn hard to do.

With every passing second, his emotions grew stronger until it felt like his very soul was on fire. Troy's attention soon falls over to his lips as he stares at him. For some reason, he knew that he would do anything to be with Jayden, feel his touch's warmth, and understand what it would feel like to steal just one more kiss.

Just one more of that high he's desperately chasing, even though he knew how wrong it was.

Then, Jayden makes the first move, signing ever so slowly so there would be no miscommunication:

"Can I kiss you?"

He doesn't try to hide how much he wants it, licking his parched lips and nodding.

That's all it takes for Jayden to grab him by the back of his neck, colliding his lips desperately and feverishly. It surprises Troy, especially because there's no initial tentative kissing. Instead, there's only intense crashing and pulling; strangely enough, it reminded Troy so much of Jayden.

Unlike before, something about this feels so damn right.

Like for the first time, it feels as if they can breathe again.

Unconsciously, he digs his nails into his broad chest, slowly rocking his hips down, and a shudder runs down his body when he feels his thickness nudging against his. Troy muffled a moan as shivers racked down his back when he felt Jayden nibbling at his swollen lips with nothing but powerful expertise.

When he tilts his head slightly, that's all Jayden needed to slip his tongue in. Troy readily accepts it despite feeling so light-headed and shy if he is even doing this right. Precum slowly gathers and strains his pants; all too soon, it's over as Jayden pulls away.

It leaves a thin saliva connecting the two before panic settles inside Troy's stomach.

"Did I do something wrong?" he asks, and Jayden shakes his head quickly.

"No, it's just that the ride is almost over, and the last thing I want is for others to see you like this," he signs, regret written all over his face. When Troy realizes they're about three carts from getting off, he quickly scrambles up and back to the other side of the seat.

Each of them was still panting, trying desperately to make themselves decent again before getting off.

Neither one of them knew what to say to the other.

Neither one of them believed just how intense that all was.

Troy realized he was feeling something he had never felt before as they got out, something he had long known. He tried to push the thought away, but it kept creeping back into his mind. There's no point denying that no matter how hard he's trying, he can't fight what his heart wants.

Unfortunately for him, he wanted Jayden.

He stole a glance at Jayden, wondering if he felt the same way, but he seemed lost in thought, with a far-off look in his eyes. If only he had known Jayden was just as conflicted with what happened in the Ferris wheel.

He had never felt such a strong connection with anyone before and didn't know how to express it. He didn't want to ruin their friendship by asking, especially if Troy didn't want to bring it up first. He also feels a sense of longing as he walks beside Troy—hand in hand—an emotion he never felt with anyone before.

It's now that both thought the same pressing question that they were too terrified to voice:

What the hell are we?

CHAPTER THIRTY-FOUR

"So…did you both finally kiss, made up, and are an official thing now or…?"

"Shut it," he growls, resisting the urge to flip Trevis off when he plops down beside his seat bench. His attention focused entirely on Troy, who was in the sunny courtyard as they'd be playing in their competitor's court today.

Playing the finals would decide their fate, whether they'll be playing in the championships or not.

Jayden watches him play, his eyes fixed on him like a hawk without even realizing it. Troy's movements are fluid and graceful; each racket swing would send the ball soaring across the court, with Benjamin barely having enough time to return it. As he moves, Jayden can't help but admire how his muscles ripple beneath his skin and how his hair falls in soft waves around his face.

How much he wants to kiss his lips until they're swollen again.

Until he's breathless and looking at him as if he's the holder of every answer in this universe.

Fuck, just the thought alone is already making him shift uncomfortably.

Since that kiss last Saturday, he's been thinking about it.

While they never speak about what happened, they certainly act as if they have between sneaky, flirtatious glances and kisses. Almost as if Troy can feel himself being stared at, he looks over and catches Jayden's eyes.

He flashes him a quick smile before returning his focus to the game. Jayden feels his heart skip at the sight of that smile, which lights up his face and makes him look even more *adorable*. He's more than confident this man is out for him.

As the game continues, Jayden can't help but be mesmerized by Troy's every move. He watches as he lunges for the ball, his body stretching to its limits, and he can't help but marvel at how strong and agile he is.

Despite the sun's heat bearing down on them, Jayden feels a shiver run down his spine as he watches him play. He can't deny his attraction towards him, and he finds himself lost in thought, imagining what it would be like to be with him.

Imagining what face he would make on the throne of his pleasure.

Yet for now, all he can do is watch and admire from afar, content to bask in the beauty of Troy's presence on the court as he warms up with Benjamin before their match in half an hour at the opposite end of the court.

His jawline ticks, his eye twitching in irritation to see them play so well together.

Mine.

He sighs, running his hand through his tousled hair as he leans back, wondering the same thing.

The million—*billion*—dollar question, if you will.

They have made up, and the past week has been amazing since he had come clean with himself, but he didn't even know what to do, much less what label should be put on them. Sure, they go on runs, sometimes watch a movie, go out more, and share kisses, but Jayden has never been more confused.

They act as he thinks a couple would, but what exactly were they?

Sometimes, Jayden would walk him to class.

Sometimes, Troy would bump his hands with his until Jayden took it.

Sometimes, Jayden would bring him to the university's campuses and kiss him until they were breathless.

So what the hell were they? He definitely knew it was nothing casual by any means.

Despite saying he only does casual flings, he hasn't even entertained the idea of others since Troy came into his life. Even old friends-with-benefits that had come up to him in the past few days, he had turned down without missing a beat.

Though, did he want a label?

Staring right at Benjamin, smiling while giving Troy a thumbs up, the answer couldn't have been more than evident. He wants everyone to know that he is his, but then the question comes down to where they would go from there.

How would he tell his parents if he were to come clean without the façade suddenly about his sexuality?

What would Weston have wanted me, as Jayden, to do?

What does Jayden Harrington want?

What does he want?

The question comes up whenever he thinks about what he's been wanting. It's still strange to think for a moment, seeing how he's been hiding behind a façade for so long, trying to live like Weston would that honestly—he's now just rediscovering who he was as a person.

All thanks to a certain someone.

"You know, it's not too late to call out of this bet."

Here it is again.

His scowl only intensified, his stomach churning for a moment at the bet he placed that now, he was starting to regret deeply. He glares at Trevis when he swings his arms around him on the bleachers. He elbows him, and he should have known he would only laugh. "Fuck off."

"Dude, seriously, how dense are you?" he throws back, rolling his eyes. When Jayden looks at him as if he had lost his mind, he only sighs heavily. "You're practically looking at Troy with the largest heart eyes I've ever seen on anyone right now."

"What, you'd know what it looks like?" Jayden scowls.

"It can't be more obvious than right in this moment," he counters. "I mean it. I brought it up as a joke, but I don't think we should go through with it. My sister has tormented me with their romance novel retelling hyper-fixation for me now. Suck up your pride and call it off, I mean it. Look, I'll even call off our original bet and consequences as well if you do."

Trevis swears that if looks can kill, he would have long been killed by the look on his face.

Yet, much to his absolute astonishment, Jayden gives a rather curt and stiff nod. "Fine."

He jolts his head so fast towards him that he almost gets whiplash. "What?"

After all, Jayden has got to be the most stubborn man to which Trevis has the pleasure of knowing. For him to agree so quickly, he almost feels he might have misheard it entirely. However, that was before Jayden managed to pry his eyes away to frown at him.

"What? I'm calling off the bet then," he affirms, and then when Trevis's jaw actually drops open, Jayden has the urge to push him off the bleacher if they didn't have a game in less than fifteen minutes. "You told me to call it off. Why are you so shocked?"

"I didn't think your stubborn ass would do it," he admits with a sheepish smile, rubbing at the back of his head. "I mean, I've known you for almost two years, and you've never exactly been the type to back out on anything."

He stares back at him, deadpanned. "Are you saying I shouldn't?"

Immediately, he shakes his head.

"No, not at all. It's just…he must be special then," he admits. Jayden chuckles at how understated that comment was, his attention turning back to Troy once again while Trevis sighs. "Shit, if I had known you'd agree so easily, I would have said our original deal was in place."

This time, Jayden doesn't bother trying to hide his

annoyance, flipping him off, but there's a smile on his face. It doesn't take long for the semi-final match to begin as Troy sits next to Jayden just as he sneakily kisses his forehead.

Something that makes Troy's heart skip a beat, long given up trying to suppress how deeply he has fallen for Jayden and taking whatever was thrown at him.

It was a beautiful day, and the crowds had gathered at the court to witness an intense match between two powerhouse universities. The match had been tied so far, and it didn't take long until all eyes were on the last two players—Jayden and Troy—who would now play the tiebreaker.

Somehow, Jayden didn't find it surprising in the slightest.

The sun beat down on the tennis court as Troy and Jayden stepped up to play against Dolan and Jake—their opponents from the last college that was standing between them going to the Conference Championships.

Needless to say, the tension was palpable as they shook hands and took their positions on opposite sides of the court. Jayden glances over at Troy for a moment, giving him a nod as he tucks the tennis bat under his arm.

"Are you ready?" he signs, and Troy gives a firm nod.

"Ready, let's do it," he signs back with a grin. "Just don't hold me back, okay?"

Jayden can't help but laugh at his mischievousness, something he's been having the great pleasure of finding out when Troy sticks out his tongue. They both knew they had to bring their best game forward if they wanted a chance at winning.

Though they were already off to a great start, with Troy serving an ace, Jayden quickly followed up with a forehand winner. They can see the other team was taken aback by their playstyle, quickly regrouping and launching a series of powerful shots that backed Troy and Jayden up to play defensive.

The first set was a nail-biter, with both teams trading points back and forth.

Troy and Jayden's teamwork was impeccable as usual, topped by how they've been practicing and training, with Troy taking charge at the net and Jayden playing a more defensive game from the baseline.

They communicated with each other using tennis jargon that only they could understand, making quick adjustments to their strategy as the game progressed. It should be duly noted that between sessions, it didn't take long until Troy and Jayden were able to come up with their own little language.

Formed between a series of eye contact and their own signing.

Jayden would get it from a nod or a slight head tilt, saying they'll go on defense.

It was all narrowed down and perfected because of Troy's impairment.

However, Dolan and Jake were equally skilled in their own way, making Troy and Jayden work for every point. They hit a series of malicious slice shots that spun the ball in unexpected directions, forcing Troy and Jayden to scramble to keep up.

They weren't going against them for a spot in the championship for nothing, after all.

However, Troy and Jayden quickly made up for the challenges, managing to hold out on their own, winning the first set 7-5. The chair umpire permits a short five-minute break, and Jayden grabs his water bottle, chugging it as he tosses Troy's.

They both collapse onto the bench, catching their breath after an exhausting first match.

They were both drenched in sweat, yet their minds were still racing with ideas for their next match. The pressure was mounting, as they knew they had to win against Dolan and Jake to secure their spot in the championship.

Easier said than done.

"Are you okay?" Troy signs, glancing over at Jayden while getting a towel to wipe the excessive sweat.

Jayden nods, taking a deep breath before answering. "Yeah, I'm good. Just a little tired."

Troy grins. "You and me both. Those guys really don't hold back, do they?"

He groans, shaking his head in disappointment at the amount of pressure already riding on them. Every muscle in his body was already protesting, but he sure as hell wasn't giving up yet. "They know how to make us work for it, huh?"

"That's what makes it fun, right?"

Leave it to Troy to think this would be fun, yet Jayden can't help but agree either.

"Absolutely. I mean, we're not here to play around. We're here to win," he answers, emphasizing the notion of winning by holding his gaze. Troy leans forward, his expression turning serious as he nods curtly to where Dolan and Jake are sitting.

"So? Any tactic should we do?"

Jayden thought for a moment before responding. "Well, we know Dolan has a killer serve, so maybe we should focus on returning it. He seems to have a blind spot regarding the ad court of the net, so we'll try striking there as necessary."

Troy nods, agreeing completely and thinking the same thing. "What about Jake? He's quick on his feet."

Jayden frowns, rubbing his temples.

That was another problem, and that was why they were able to put them on defense quickly; whereas Dolan was brute with his strength, Jack was quick to make up. "Yeah, that's true. Maybe we should try to keep him at the back of the court. Push him to no man's land."

"What about us? Should I do anything differently on the court?" he questions.

"I think we have a pretty good dynamic on the court. Just keep focus and don't get too cocky," he replies.

It only leads to Troy raising an eyebrow. "Who said anything about getting cocky?"

"Asked the one just before saying not to hold him back," he teases and rolls his eyes, nudging him playfully on the arm. "Other than that, we'll focus on returning Dolan's serve, keeping Jake at the back of the court, and trying to mess with their play dynamic."

Troy grins, huffing out his chest. "Sounds like a plan to me."

At that moment, the tennis umpire blows his whistle, and Jayden gets up, followed by Troy.

"Let's do this."

The second set was even more intense than the first—something neither thought would have been possible—with both teams playing at the top of their game. Dolan and Jake were determined to make a comeback, and their shots were more aggressive and precise than before when it came to serving.

Troy and Jayden found themselves struggling to keep up, barely able to make the swing in time.

As the games went back and forth, each team refused to give the other the inch they needed.

Troy and Jayden tried to maintain their momentum, but Dolan and Jake were relentless. They hit a series of drop shots that left Troy and Jayden scrambling, and they followed up with powerful volleys that forced Troy and Jayden to play defensively once again.

"Shit," Jayden curses, quickly struggling back up and refusing to be intimated.

Not when the score is currently tied at 5-5, and the tension is at an all-time high,

As the final games approached, Troy and Jayden had no choice but to dig deep, drawing on all their skills and experience to outmaneuver their opponents. It's undoubtedly challenging, especially with their play style.

In the end, they hit a series of cross-court shots that left Dolan and Jake floundering, and they followed up with a series of powerful serves that left them reeling. The score was 6-5 in their favor, and they knew that one more game would secure their spot in the championships.

The crowd is on their feet as the final game begins.

Troy serves, and Jake returns the ball with equal force, which Jayden has to quickly jump to serving back. The rallies were intense, with each team trying to gain the upper hand. The sun beat down relentlessly, but neither team showed any signs of slowing down.

Not when there's so much on the line.

Finally, after what felt like an eternity, they saw an opening.

Dolan and Jake had mistakenly spread their net too wide, leaving the center in the middle.

Troy and Jayden seize the opportunity with all their might. Their hearts racing, they charged forward, their racket swinging with deadly precision. They pushed forward with everything they had, determined to secure the final point and win the game.

Dolan and Jake quickly realize their error and try to close the gap, but it is too late.

Troy makes the final swing, and that's it.

The final point was theirs, and they had won the game. The crowd erupted into cheers, and Troy and Jayden collapsed onto the ground, exhausted but victorious.

It has been an intense battle that tested them to their limits. Yet in the end, they had emerged victorious, their determination and skill carrying them through as they basked in the glow of winning. Ever so slowly, Troy and Jayden look over at one another. A grin on their face as they bump their fists before Jayden signs high in the air for Troy to catch only.

"We're going to the championships, baby."

Baby.

What those words did to him.

CHAPTER THIRTY-FIVE

Could you somehow speed up time in exchange for a few seconds or minutes of your life?

If so, Troy wants to know how he was faced with the most unlikely friendship between his roommate and best friend. He didn't even recall the last time they'd been this friendly as they helped him back from his two-night trip.

He should have known something was off when Aston and Quinn, the night owls of the group who preferred to sleep in, decided to aid his packing. He sighs, brewing another cup of coffee and resisting the urge to rub his temple in dismay.

"Done yet?" he signs, arching a brow questionably as they rummage and double-check his duffel bag.

"Uniform, pajamas, and enough clothes for two nights," Quinn signs, nodding with each item ticked.

"Chargers, toiletries, and protein bars for your three-hour ride in case you get hungry," Aston chimes in next. He pushes up his glances and then looks to where Troy is leaning. "Do you have your wallet and keys?"

"Yes, in my pocket," he answers before pouring the much-needed coffee into his thermal for the ride. Once finishing, he caps it and squints his eyes warily at them. "Now, are you both ready and I believe I have packed everything I need? What is even the point of this again?"

"Actually," Quinn grins rather wickedly. "You forgot to pack two things."

"What?" Troy asks, lips pursed as he runs down his list mentally again.

"Troy, Troy, Troy," Quinn signs, shaking her head. "Typical Troy."

"I know," Aston signs in turn, and suddenly, Troy doesn't feel good about where this is going anymore. He watches how his best friend gets up from the bed, a mischievous grin on her face as she heads towards her tote bag.

Whatever it is in there, he doesn't have a good feeling about it.

It's confirmed when Quinn pulls out an all-familiar black box and blue tube that makes his face pale. She heads back to the bed, laying it out like it's something not to be ashamed of, but in all honesty, Troy is just about ready to leap from the window.

"You have happened to forget a box of condoms—XL— and a bottle of lube," she signs happily.

Troy didn't know if he should laugh or cry.

"Why would I need that?" he asks, completely *mortified*.

"Do you really need me to sign it out to you?" Quinn retaliates. All the while, she's already shoving the box and lube into his bag. Troy instantly strides over, but she's one step quicker, dodging and then having the audacity to leap and stand at the top of his bed. Duffel bag tucked in her arms, she scowls. "You'll be thanking me."

Like hell, he would!

"I don't need it," he signs, adding a few exclamation marks to drive home his point.

"Trust me, you do," Quinn throws back with a few dozen exclamations. She hops down, wagging her finger at him. "Look, Jayden obviously has the hots for you, and it's better to be safe than sorry. I've read enough books to know."

How does that even apply here?

Truthfully, even Troy knows that whatever is going on between him and Jayden is something more. They kissed, and after their game yesterday, they even went to have pizza together to celebrate without joining the huge after-party.

Jayden then walked him back to the dorm and kissed him again before waiting until he got inside to leave. However, Troy highly doubts that they'll find the time or energy to talk about their feelings while on the road—

It's much less going past second base itself.

Is this weird period between something more and dating supposed to be this complicated?

"You guys are exaggerating," he only signs, rubbing his temples in dismay.

"Dude, remember how I said your roommate did have a crush on you?"

Aston's eyes widen, whirling to her in disbelief. "*Really?*"

The fact that he didn't deny it only sells his point.

"Desperate times, desperate measures," she quips with

no remorse. "Point is, you're dense regarding people's feelings, Troy. No offense. Let me tell you that Jayden has a thing for you, and I know from the look on your face that you have a thing for him, too. Though, I don't blame you for it."

"Even so, why would you pack me these things?"

"Just in case," Quinn remarks, rolling her eyes. "You are very welcome."

Thank God he decided to pack in the morning.

He was confident he wouldn't have a wink of sleep if he were bombarded with all this information last night. However, he still cannot comprehend how it came to something like this. That was the one question circling like a vulture spinning overhead its prey or a vinyl record stuck after being scratched.

"You're both insane," he remarks before throwing his hands up in the air.

He watches as they grin before Quinn zips up his bag and hands it to him. Once her hands are free, she almost looks proud in how she puffs out her chest. "There you go. Now you're ready to take on the championships."

Did anyone hear how ridiculous that sounds?

"Which we're proud of," Aston throws in.

Troy doesn't even have the time to find the right words as his hands lay on his side. Not a second later, the little light installed at the doorway of the dorm room lights up, signaling that someone has rung it. Quinn turns to them both, brows furrowed. "Are either of you expecting anyone?"

"No," they sign as Quinn walks over.

Sure enough, she opens the door wide enough, and Troy's heart does little flip-flops.

He is a sight to behold from Jayden's messy, tousled hair, sweatpants, and a plain navy shirt that stretches across his chest. As Jayden flashes a charming smile, Troy can feel himself fighting off the grin while failing miserably.

"Hey, morning," Jayden signs, tilting his head to the side. "Seems there's a party first thing."

"Look who decided to get you," Quinn signs with a giant grin.

"What a gentleman," Aston chimes in next.

Kill him now.

"Sorry, I didn't know if you were awake and thought maybe you overslept. I texted you to ask if we can walk together to the bus," Jayden explains, and Troy is already darting out while resisting the urge to flip them both off.

"Yeah, we can. Sorry that I didn't reply; I was packing," he replies. "I'm ready to go right now."

"Have fun," Quinn remarks with a grin, and Troy ends up flipping them off this time.

Finally, outside the residency, Jayden looks at him with an arched brow, curious and amused. "Should I be concerned about what that look on Quinn's and Aston's faces was before? Much less why they're helping you pack first thing in the morning?"

If anything, they should drop this conversation altogether if you were to ask Troy.

"No, just ignore them. They're being idiots," he signs, rolling his eyes.

Jayden and Troy head onto the charter bus and make their way to the back seat. As they walk past the other passengers, Troy can't help but notice how exhausted everyone looks. Their eyes are baggy, and they seem to be pacing at death's front door.

It's clear to him that they've been partying all night long and probably hungover beyond belief. Troy feels sorry for them and wishes they had taken the party a little easier upon seeing how miserable everyone looks.

Yikes.

He hopes they get some rest on the bus ride ahead, preferably without someone retching.

"Glad we didn't go to the party, huh?" Jayden asks with a grin.

Truthfully, since what happened with Troy—

Jayden stopped going to parties and just about any invites to parties and random hookups.

He wants to try being someone worthy of Troy because he believes in someone like him.

Coach Winter soon boarded, giving a rather loud statement that makes just about everyone cringe at how booming his voice is, yet refusing to say anything because they all know it's only to make things worse.

Once the bus starts, Jayden leans in, his eyes sparkling with mischief.

Something that Troy comes to appreciate and love when he's not doing anything too crazy and reckless.

"So, Troy," he signs, his smirk ticking upward. "Do you have any plans for tonight?"

Troy grins, feeling his heart race.

There's something about the fact that only they know what the other is saying that makes his heart flutter. It's like they're in their own little world, and he never once would have presumed he would see his disability in such a certain light.

"Nothing in particular. I did all my homework assigned already," he replies. "What did you have in mind?"

Jayden shrugs, a mischievous glint in his eye as he slowly links their fingers together.

"I'm thinking we can hang out," he signs. "Maybe watch a movie or something in your room or mine."

Is Jayden somehow in cahoots with Quinn and Aston?

Despite how fast his heart is racing, he tries to keep his face composed because, for all he knows, maybe it's just that. He's internally cursing out his roommate and best friend for even planting these thoughts in his head as he nods.

After all, he did want to spend more time with Jayden.

"That sounds great," he answers.

As they talked among themselves, Jayden should have known it was only a matter of time before Travis decided to interject.

"Good morning," he signs to Troy, who quickly signs back in greeting with a grin. At first, Jayden did feel a bit pleased and pleasantly surprised. It seemed his friend had decided to take it upon himself to learn how to greet using ASL. However, it faded when he turned back to Jayden with a wicked grin. "You little *lovebirds*. Why don't you save it for off the court?"

Jayden shot Travis a look, arching a brow before coughing rather obnoxiously loud.

Instantly, Travis and a few others groan and shoot Jayden a glare.

"Blame Travis," Jayden remarks. "Something about his face and seeing it makes me cough intensely."

Trevis gawks at him. "Dude? Really? Do you have no heart?"

"Keep that up and see what happens," he declares, and Troy chuckles. Despite not knowing what they're saying, he can pick up some cues, like when Travis crosses his arm like a child and then rolls his eyes before wincing.

"You're an asshole," he huffs. "I'll get you back, mark my words."

With that, Travis backed off, looking a little defeated, but both knew it was not the end of him once he was over that hangover. Once Travis was gone, the two boys turned back to each other, the tension between them palpable.

"Be nice," Troy chides, still grinning.

"He asked for it," he remarks, pouting before pausing momentarily. "Oh, before I forget."

"What do you mean?"

Before Troy can think of what he meant by that comment, Jayden leans in and kisses his lips. His eyes widen in shock, his face heating up to be suddenly caught off guard. Yet because most of their teammate is either on their phones or trying to sleep their hangover away, Jayden decides to take the initiation.

For a moment, nothing else mattered but the two of them lost in the heat of the moment.

As they pull away, Jayden grins at Troy.

"You know, I've wanted to do that for a while since I picked you up, but I didn't know if you told Aston and Quinn just yet," he admits. Troy is still reeling between the kiss he thought he had misheard before biting his lips and bumping his arm against his.

"I'm glad you did," he admits.

They spent the rest of the bus ride lost in each other's company, chatting and laughing together. About an hour in, they make their way to their pit stop for a short break, and most end up getting a rather hearty brunch.

By the time they ended up at the hotel, what was supposed to be a three-hour journey had ended up being five hours due to a series of bad misfortunes. From engine problems when everyone huddled back into the charter bus to car accidents and deathly long detours off the main highway.

Everyone is tired and eager to check in so they can finally rest for a few hours, including Jayden and Troy. As everyone crashes into the lobby like a zombie, Travis lets out a huge groan. "I'm never drinking and smoking again right before our game for the rest of the season."

"Which is something you should have done from the start," Jayden snorts, handing him and a few of his teammates water bottles alongside Troy. Jayden can't help but narrow his eyes at how Troy and Benjamin communicate about Benajmin's limited knowledge of ASL.

However, Jayden tries not to dwell on it.

It's only a matter of time before, after the game, he will tell everyone.

He has decided that's what he wants—Jayden Harrington.

Even if it goes against his rules and everyone's expectations—even his parents.

He's done being Mr. Nice.

A few minutes later, Coach Winters assigns each person their hotel card key and room numbers with clear instructions not to do anything that would land them in hot water and can't play tomorrow.

Something the team knows it's honestly a lowkey death threat.

By the end, Jayden and Troy can't help but notice it's just the two of them left. They look at one another and then back at Couch Winter, whose lips are pressed into a thin line. It's something Jayden knows can't ever be good news as he clears his throat.

"Boys, we have a bit of a problem," Coach Winters says, his brow furrowed. "If you can translate to Troy later, that would be amazing, but it seems the hotel messed up our booking. Something with their system and the website's booking that I didn't realize. It seems we only have enough room for everyone but one member."

Jayden blinks once and then twice in disbelief at his words.

He'd also be lying if he said his heart didn't skip a beat, either.

"What?"

"Look, I know it's not ideal, but we don't have much choice with the cards we're dealt with," he sighs. "The hotel is fully booked, so they don't have an extra room. I figure it would be fine since it's you two, and you're both relatively close as teammates. Can you ask Troy how he feels regarding you both sharing a room for the next two nights?"

CHAPTER THIRTY-SIX

Seriously, were they living in some cliché romance Wattpad or Ao3 fanfiction?

Also, the one-bed trope of all things?

Who was setting them up?

Troy needed to know because if so, he wanted to wring the neck of the maker of his fate right now as he awkwardly followed Jayden into the hotel room they'd be staying in for the next two nights. Slowly settling his duffel bag on the floor, he turns to Jayden with a small, impish smile.

"So...this is awkward?" he signs leisurely, still in a mix of utter disbelief.

Jayden chuckles, putting his bag down on the table.

Although he appears to be calm, composed, and collected on the outside, he is freaking out on the inside. The memories of everything that happened this week, from the kiss on the Ferris wheel to admitting his feelings for someone to Trevis, are overwhelming him.

Something he didn't think was possible.

"We'll just have to make do, won't we?" he muses. "I mean, this would happen to us, huh?"

"I can't believe it either," Troy finds himself holding in a laugh at the irony of it all while surveying the area. It's the typical hotel room with one queen-sized bed smacked in the middle, a TV mounted on the wall, and a singular bathroom and shower alongside a little desk cramped into the corner space with the window. He tilts his head curiously before signing, "I can take the floor."

Jayden immediately freezes, turning with a slight frown from where he was adjusting the temperatures.

"Excuse me?" he signs slowly, arching up one brow his way.

"I'm fine taking the floor," he parrots once more, in clarification, not realizing Jayden questioned, not because he didn't understand the first time but for an entirely different reason. "I've slept over at Quinn's before, so I'm used to it. Just give me a few blankets and I'm good to go. Or I can ask the front desk if there's a cot they can lend and how much it would be."

Not to mention, Troy deducts Jayden needs it much more with his build compared to his lean physique.

"No, I meant why?" he articulates, showing emphases by the knit brow and the extra question marks thrown in. "The bed is big enough for the both of us to get in together without you having to sleep on the floor."

Jayden would sleep on the floor and fight him tooth and nail before allowing him to sleep on the floor.

At his remark, Troy freezes momentarily as he numbly signs as casually as he can muster.

"That's true."

Butterflies explode across his stomach, his heart leaping to his chest at how nonchalant he is.

Is this normal for him for him to be so *casual* about it?

Suddenly, his stomach churns at the thought of Jayden with someone else, even though he doesn't entirely know what they are. They act as Troy believes a couple would from kissing, going on dates, and texting a lot, but without the label.

What exactly does that mean for them?

If they sleep in the same bed, what happens if they accidentally kiss or go further?

His face flushes, the sudden discomfort and tightness in his cargo pants becoming something he's painfully aware of. Curling his toes, he quickly turns his body to the window because that's a better option than to expose where his brain is wondering.

If he had to blame someone, it must have been Aston and Quinn who planted these shameless thoughts in him. Unaware of how much his suggestion has affected Troy, Jayden heads back from the thermostat to flick on the lights at his side that he just called his own before looking over.

Only to then realize his comment may not have been the most appropriate.

Shit.

From the way Jayden is acting, you would have never believed he wasn't a damn virgin.

Yet this is how he knew Troy was different from anyone he knew or would come to know. Perhaps it's a gut feeling, but he knew deep in his very existence that Troy was the anomaly to his entire being. He waits patiently until he turns back before pressing his lips into a thin line. "Do you not feel comfortable?"

Troy shakes his head immediately. "No, not at all."

"Are you sure?" he asks, tilting his head. From how quickly he replied, Jayden wants to believe it, but knowing Troy, he could just be lying for the sake of him. It's one of the most endearing and frustrating things that Jayden cherishes with him. "If you are, I'm fine switching rooms as well with—"

"No," he cuts off, but when he realizes how frantic and eager he sounds, he quickly winces and tries to redo his own words. He swallows the lump in his throat, toes curling. "I mean...no, I'm just...surprised but not in a bad way! I'm more than comfortable with it; I mean, it's not like we haven't slept in the same space before and—"

This time, Jayden interjects by placing his hands on his chest, moving them away and back.

"*Breath*," he instructs.

Troy presses his lips into a thin line, wanting to hide under the bed in embarrassment. "Sorry."

"No, it's okay," he chuckles and then decides to be truthful. "If I'm being honest, I'm just as nervous."

He stares at him skeptically, squinting his eyes. "You are?"

After all, he certainly doesn't give off that impression as Jayden nods.

"Why wouldn't I be when it comes to you?" he counters.

He pauses for a moment. "Like…in…a good way?"

"Yes, in a good way," Jayden affirms. "Now relax. We will have a rough day tomorrow. If we want to keep advancing without any distraction, we need to be in our best shape, which means you shouldn't have even suggested sleeping on the floor in the first place."

"I know, I know," he signs with a loud huff. "Do you mind if I shower first?"

More importantly, he needed to take care of the problem between his legs, which he didn't want to talk about.

"Be my guest. I'll start unpacking some things first," he says.

Trying to calm his ever-growing nerves, Troy makes his way in first in hopes that a refreshing shower is exactly what he needs upon grabbing his pajamas. As he turns on the water, he can feel the steam filling the room and quickly jumps in.

Jayden, on the other hand, turns on the TV.

He sets the subtitles so Troy can follow along, flicking through the channel while getting his necessities out. As Troy steps out of the shower, he finally feels invigorated and energized after taking care of that problem. He reaches for his towel, dries himself off, and then throws on a comfy baggy shirt and sweats before stepping out.

"Your turn," he signs. "The water is just perfect, actually."

"Thank you."

Jayden can't help but notice how cute he looks and flashes him a smile as he heads towards the bathroom. Troy can't help but see the subtitles are automatically on as he settles to sit down, a small smile making its way to his face.

It's the little things for him, so how can he not have a crush on him?

He watches whatever is on, which happens to be some game show, until movement catches from the corner of his eyes. He then proceeds almost to have a damn heart attack when Jayden comes out with just a towel around his neck.

Water dripped from his abs as he stood in nothing but a pair of boxers.

"Do you…just sleep in your boxers?"

"Yeah," he sheepishly signs, plopping beside him on the bed. Troy can't help but stare before dragging his eyes elsewhere. "Plus, if I had known we would share a room, I would have packed sweatpants. Do you want me to wear my tennis shorts?"

"It's fine," he replies.

"What are you watching?"

"No clue, some game show," he remarks with a half-shrug, getting more comfy. "Though I have no idea what's going on. I never grew up watching much anyway compared to reading or doing something in between."

"Me either," he muses. "Do you have an appetite for dinner?"

"No, still too early, especially after our huge lunch," he comments. "Want to watch?"

At that, Troy nods and gets more comfortable.

Even with the TV on, they find themselves talking for hours about everything and anything. A feat that comes with being deaf is that he knows their voices wouldn't disturb any of their teammates just next door.

From their hobbies to their family, the conversation flows easily and endlessly between the two.

Almost as if making up for the lost time they couldn't due to their responsibilities as students and athletes alongside their rather messy and closed-off beginnings. However, as the night wore on, they decided they were much too tired and full to go out for dinner, and both started to feel sleepy from the long bus ride. Something that the rest of the team, who were still hungover and having the munchies, wouldn't understand.

Jayden yawns from where he's been lying. As the hours passed, both ended up in new positions under the covers. Pillows plopped on the headboard as they used for support, comfortably tucked into one another and cuddled up while they watched some thrilled-pack movie. Troy stretches out on the bed, his eyes drooping ever so slightly.

"Do you mind if I dim the lights?" Jayden asks.

"Not at all," Troy answers, shaking his head.

Jayden gets up to turn off the light, and as he makes his way back to the bed, he pauses for a moment, looking down at Troy. Suddenly, the ambiance seems much different than earlier, making Troy's body buzz as Jayden slowly crawls into bed.

Laying in bed, neither seems to be able to look away, and there's a certain buzz.

Ever so gently, Jayden raises his arm.

Slowly stroking the side of his face with the pad of his thumb, Troy lets out a small sigh.

Leaning into his touch, he's practically *humming*.

It is messing with his head in all the right places, making him feel utterly intoxicated in the best way. Without thinking, he leans down and presses his lips to Troy's, softly at first, then more urgently as Troy responds.

They break apart, both breathing heavily, and Jayden looks at Troy, his eyes dark with desire.

"I'm sorry," Jayden signs, pulling away enough for him to make out his words. It feels wrong to apologize, but at the same time, he knows what Troy has gone through. The last thing he wants is to make him hate him. The thought is enough to tear him up from the inside out. "I shouldn't have done that."

They both know they shouldn't be doing this. There wasn't any alcohol they could blame in the morning or the rush of adrenaline either. Troy knows deep down he didn't want a one-night stand or give his virginity up on the whim of the moment.

Yet when it comes to Jayden, it's like his body and mind didn't mind if it's him.

Troy knows he is hopeless, but he can't find himself caring.

With his mind made up, he smiles, reaching up to pull Jayden down for another kiss.

"Don't be sorry," he signs. "I wanted you to do that."

"Are you sure?" Jayden questions, his heart pounding recklessly in his chest. When Troy all but nods, he narrows his eyes, maneuvering so that he's now straddling over him. He can feel their half-hard lengths grinding on one another, and he stops himself from losing all control as he stares down at Troy. "I need a physical sign, Troy."

Really?

"Yes," he signs with a slight pout.

How much more obvious did this man want as an answer?

However, Jayden gawks at him in shock. "Are you sulking right now?"

"Do you realize how hard it is for me even to sign that?" he throws back. "It's *embarrassing*."

In fact, Troy can just about feel his face burning all the way down to his damn chest.

"You're so cute and too damn much for my heart," he confesses before he leans down, kissing Troy without a moment of hesitation. Troy's brain cannot handle nor comprehend his confession and what is happening.

Yet, neither of them can fight back their feelings any longer.

Then, Troy's brain finally starts registering what is happening.

Jayden's lips are surprisingly feathery soft, and luscious in every damn way that makes him flutter.

Gently, he coaxes his lips. He wastes no time in sliding his tongue into the small, delicate space between his lips and finding him instantly. A soft vibration escapes Troy's lips into their sizzling kiss as Jayden presses his lean and muscular body against his like a second skin.

Almost like shielding him from the world.

Instantly, Troy's hand becomes entangled into his, pulling him closer.

He wanted *more*, despite never doing anything past a

small peck on the lips with his prom date in high school. Their breathing becomes more intense with each moment, and their kiss grows more intense and passionate. As their lips start to move to adjust to one another, Jayden's short stubble brushes against Troy's skin, causing his cock to throb and *pulse.*

For a copious amount of precum to start sloshing down and stain his boxers.

It's everything Troy dreamt about and more.

Even though he's never kissed anyone before or done anything else with anyone, something about this feels right. A shudder racks down his back as Jayden's hand, which has been cupping his cheeks, slowly travels down his body before Jayden gets onto his knees.

"Are you sure about this, Troy?" he asks again, his nose flaring at how delectable he looks pinned underneath him. His eyes pierced his as they held onto one another's. "We're about to cross a thin line. I don't want you to get hurt if we go any further if you don't want this."

Troy's pupils are entirely dilated as he works on catching his panting breath.

But, rather than doing as he asks, the latter bites his somewhat swollen lips before hooking his fingers onto his boxers and sliding them off to the best of his abilities while being pinned down. Jayden's eyes widened, his mouth dry as Troy lay back down to look up at him. He slowly finds the right words, trying to get his hand to stop shaking out of nervousness. "I don't want you to stop either. Unless you... want to stop?"

"God, no," he signs as he takes in his words.

Their eyes seemed to comprehend what was at stake, yet they wanted to take the risk together.

With newfound knowledge of what they mean to one another, Jayden hurries to bring his lips back down onto his. By the time they pull away, they are both panting heavily with a smile on their face. Even though this was their first time doing so, it just felt right when it was them.

Something Jayden has never felt before.

A strange vibration in what Troy can only believe must be a weird moan escapes his lips when Jayden palms his erection before his eyes widen at the lewd sound tumbling out of his mouth. He quickly fumbles over his signing. "I—I'm sorry, I'm usually…I mean, I've never done this. Oh God, what is—"

Immediately, Jayden captures his hands to silence him.

"Troy," Jayden chuckles after pulling away and letting go. He nibbles and bites his lower lip gently before chuckling. "It's fine, don't worry and relax. I think it's cute and hot. Everything you do is perfect because it's *you*."

That seems to ease Troy's mind ever so slightly at his words.

Jayden releases a groan when Troy's hands start to wander around too—timid but experimentally.

He fiddles with the waistband of Jayden's boxers, fumbling ever so nervously. It doesn't take long before Jayden finally pulls his lips away to help remove his shirt. Once he pulls it off his head, his lips bear down onto his again.

Despite how impatient Jayden feels, he knows to go slow with Troy.

The last thing he wants is to ruin this moment and make it into something forgettable or lackluster.

Troy isn't just anyone, not one of those one-night stands he had many before. Jayden closes his eyes at the tenderness stirring inside his heart, trailing kisses along Troy's jaw before settling just over his ears.

He nibbles and suckles onto it, causing him to gasp and whimper.

Troy feels as if he's dreaming, his crush kissing and making his body buzz as they lay skin-to-skin.

He can feel Jayden's cock aching, rubbing up against his as he lays kisses and hickeys in the wake of where his lips go. A groan escapes their lips when pre-cum drips from both of their swollen tips and *mixes*.

Luckily for Troy, who didn't know what else to do, Jayden took charge.

A gasp escapes both their lips when Jayden gets a firm grip on his erection, the sensation almost too much. More pre-cum leaks out and all over his hands. The feelings were more than mutual as Jayden's bulbous tip leaked, making a mess in Jayden's hand.

Troy finds himself bucking his lips, groaning and mewling in the way Jayden's lips continue to trail downward. All rational thoughts left Troy's head when Jayden's warm mouth envelopes around his cock. He groans; the feeling of Jayden's mouth is like a piece of heaven, his mouth hot and so tight. Using Troy's grunts and tiny little jolts as guidance to see what he likes, Jayden soon finds a rhythm that causes Troy to grip hard onto his tousled hair and snap his hips upwards.

How is it possible for something to feel this good?

With a grunt, Jayden grips the base of his cock firmly as he savors and lapses up the taste of him.

Sucking gently on the head and tonguing at the slit.

Troy whimpers, his balls throbbing.

Taking a deep breath, he engulfs as much of his cock as he could manage and starts to suck him in earnest. Troy groans, and he can't help but thrust gently back into his mouth, which is now hollowed out—giving the perfect suction.

Troy spreads his legs as far as possible, giving himself entirely to Jayden.

Troy wasn't the only one enjoying it, as Jayden has started to pump his lengthy cock. Jayden has bobbed his head up and down enthusiastically as now and then, he grunts *happily*. As we got more into it, he's able to take more of him into his hot mouth.

It didn't help in Troy's situation when Jayden cupped his balls gently and kneaded them to make him repeat his name repeatedly, like a prayer inside his head. It causes his balls to tighten as Jayden sticks one finger into his mouth before getting back to work.

Troy's cock is tingling so much that he doesn't realize that Jayden's index finger is starting to trail toward his back entrance. It's then that his balls begin to contract as cum seems to be boiling in hopes of escaping his body.

It's when Jayden touches the opening of his entrance for the first time.

Troy's body starts to shake and quiver when he takes

his cock down his throat while plunging one finger into his ass. Troy cries out, orgasm erupting violently as cum squirts down Jayden's mouth. Shivers run down both of their back as Jayden welcomes every single drop he has to offer. When Troy finally regains control of his body, Jayden releases his cock and puts his head to rest on Troy's hips.

Neither said anything, recovering as Troy ran his fingers gently through Jayden's hair.

"You okay?" Jayden signs, and Troy nods.

"Yes. Oh, I...have some lube and a box of condoms if you want to use it in my bag," he answers drowsily. Jayden arches a brow, partially curious, while a more possessive side scowl at why he even has. Almost as if Troy can read his mind, he quickly fumbles. "Aston and Quinn packed it, saying I need it...with you...if the time comes. It's stupid."

Tension leaves Jayden slightly, and he finds himself grinning.

"So I guess everyone knows about my big, fat crush but us, huh?"

Troy can't even stop the way his heart flutters at his confession as Jayden pulls away to retrieve the box of condoms and lube from his bag. If what Jayden says is true and they're on the same page, then doesn't that mean this is something he can have hope in?

Maybe after this, they can be something more?

He decides to put a tack on the thought as he returns with what appears to be a stack of condoms and lube. Jayden then gently nudges his legs apart once more. Settling onto his knees between Troy's legs, he sucks his balls gently in his mouth, lolling them around before he heads south to suckle gently in the sweet spot right between his balls.

A whimper tumbles out of Troy's mouth again, his cock already hardening back.

This man has an insatiable appetite and a damn menace.

Once Jayden can get him half erect, he reaches over where his bottle of lube is at the side of the bed. It's then that Troy realizes just how long and thick his cock is. His eyes widen, wondering how he'll be able to fit that into his virgin hole as Jayden lathers his cock with lube, spreading it all around.

With the side of his head buried into the pillow, Jayden gently pries his ass for him, exposing himself completely. Gently, Jayden runs a finger lightly over his puckered entrance. Troy thought he would slowly nudge his cock and prob him open.

He didn't expect to feel Jayden lapse up his hole gently. In an instant, all fear and hesitation fly out the window as the tip of Jayden's tongue penetrates him. Troy moans loudly, and he can't help but push his ass back in an effort for him to go deeper.

This is it.

There's no turning back.

Troy's cock is pounding and leaking pre-cum almost inadequately onto his stomach in no time at all. He's panting hard as Jayden alternates between lapping at his opening and sticking his tongue as far up his ass as humanly possible.

Soon, Jayden's tongue is replaced with his fingers.

One and then another, stretching him open.

As he slides his long digits into his slick ass and hits a spot that makes Troy's cock drool more of pre-cum, his moans become louder. He continues until he can fit three fingers inside of him before he gets up to his knees and slathers more lube onto his cock upon rolling a condom on.

Slowly placing the bulbous cockhead at his loosened entrance.

At first, he makes sure to go slow and cautious, but he speeds up on his insertion when he realizes how much Troy enjoys this. It didn't take long until his cock is seated tightly into Troy's ass, his cock hitting the prostate.

It didn't take long until he grips hard onto Troy's hips and starts picking up the pace.

Driving them on the verge of utter insanity.

Jayden's short and hard stabs had Troy buried further into the bed. Troy can already feel himself being hurled into another intense orgasm. Jayden is already right behind him as Troy angles himself and thrusts back the best he can manage.

It didn't take long before an orgasm broke over Troy in great, washing waves. It sends nerve endings all over his body to tingle. His spasm and squeezing against Jayden's cock is enough to trigger him into a climax.

Jayden thrusts two more times before holding himself perfectly still inside of Troy. His entire body seems to clench as Jayden completely leaps over in intense currents. Jayden lets out a low groan, kissing his lips as he slowly pulls out.

Tying the condom, he gets up to throw it into the trash bin before coming back and pulling Troy into his chest. He's not the cuddling type in the slightest, but then again, no one made him feel the way Troy does.

Relaxing once more, Jayden hums quietly, gently pulling Troy tighter in his chest. Neither of them says anything, enjoying the intimate moment as they listen to one another's heartbeat and get drowsier. Nothing seems to be said, and it's more than loud enough, too.

There's no going back from here.

CHAPTER THIRTY-SEVEN

There's something *addicting* about just walking up.

You're not exactly sure what's going on yet, let alone your name or who you are. Your brain is racing to put everything together while you struggle to gain a footing in your environment after returning from the realm of dreams. It's like someone has dropped you into the middle of a puzzle without instructions but simultaneously given you unlimited time to solve it.

Yet,at least, that's what it feels like for the first few seconds, with all the time in the world.

Troy knows this feeling all too well as he gently sighs and snuggles into the warmest pillow he has ever felt. He is enveloped by the sweet scent of vanilla and spice, and for a moment, he imagines this is how a cat feels when lounging in a pile of freshly laundered clothes.

It must be.

However, he didn't recall ever having a weighted blanket before.

His brows furrowed gently, realizing it was not a

weighted blanket per se but something quite heavy draped around his stomach. Then, there's what appears to be a similar feeling, almost like a leg hooked onto his thighs, drawing Troy in closer.

Sticky.

However, it's not unpleasant or discomforting as he re-arranges himself, so he's now on his sides and snuggling deeper into this pillow. A blissful view of seconds of bathing in the moment before reality starts creeping up on him.

Slowly but ever so surely.

As Troy's brows furrowed with confusion, he felt his eyes drift open slowly; suddenly, the weight of reality came crashing down on him of everything that happened last night. His heart races as he tries to make sense of his surroundings, which is definitely *not* his dorm room.

Gradually, he began to piece together the fragments of his memory.

Coach asked him and Jayden to share a room because of a technical error in the booking.

Amidst it all, both tumbled into bed together while lost in one another's embrace.

The numerous times Jayden had been able to wring out multiple, ground-shaking orgasms from him throughout the night and why he feels so refreshed now. Well, except for figuring out where you and your tennis partner stand in all this.

Heart leaping to his throat, he gradually looks up only to find Jayden's eyes already staring down at him; then, he practically becomes completely blinded by how *bright* he is when he smiles.

"Good morning," he signs before laying a kiss on top of his forehead. It makes Troy's heart race as he swallows the lump in his throat. He had presumed it would be similar to how it was during the drunken kiss they shared, with it being awkward and stiff.

So it is anything but a pleasant surprise as he reaches his hand up to sign in turn.

"Morning. Have…you been watching me all morning?"

Jayden chuckles, shaking his head at his somewhat humorous question.

"No, just for about five minutes. Did you know you wiggle your nose a lot when you sleep?"

"Mm, do I?"

Stifling a yawn, he slowly sits up, only for his back to almost give out as he falls back onto the bed.

Well, today is certainly going to be a challenging game.

He internally chuckles, ready to tell Jayden, but doesn't get to before Jayden hovers over him like a worried mother hen. "How are you feeling? Are you okay? Do you need anything? Where does it hurt? Should I get you something? Water?"

To date, Troy has been almost positive no one in this world can beat Quinn regarding speed signing. Yet here Jayden is, moving his hand in rapid-fire that it becomes nothing more than a blur. Paired with the worry lines etched across his face, it disperses all the worry Troy has.

They're going to be okay.

"I'm okay, please don't worry, it's nothing too serious. However, my back was just a tad sore and took me by surprise," he informs him before frowning at his own words. "Probably not a good thing, seeing we have a game in less than two hours."

Upon helping him sit up on the bed, Jayden then places one fist proudly onto his chest before resuming his remark. "It's okay if you want to take it slow for today. I can pick up the slack for the both of us today."

Troy snorts, lightly shoving him on the shoulder. "I see you're overconfident as ever."

"After making my boyfriend come four times last night, who wouldn't?" he teases with a wink.

Boyfriend.

Upon hearing Jayden refer to him as his boyfriend, Troy feels a sudden rush of excitement and happiness. He had been hoping for more, wanting to be greedy but not knowing if it'd be reciprocated, and now, this declaration confirms that his feelings have returned.

Troy can't help but smile to himself, feeling a sense of contentment that he hasn't felt in a while.

"Boyfriend, huh?" he signs before bringing up the blankets to hide his flushed body.

Instantly, his face pales, thinking he had said something wrong. "Shit. Sorry, I thought—"

"I like it," he interjects. "I like the way my heart feels whenever I sign them."

Jayden's heart skips several beats as he looks at Troy's bright smile. It's a feeling he's never experienced before with anyone else. He can't resist the urge to pull Troy closer— Jayden's front to Troy's back— wrapping his arms around him from behind. He nestles his head into the crook of Troy's neck and starts to sign.

"Has anyone ever told you how freaking adorable and cute you are?"

Troy turns around to face him, his eyes shimmeringas he leans in for a kiss. "Actually, yes."

Jealousy sparks and runs like wildfire for a moment inside Jayden's heart, and he frowns.

"Is that right? Who?"

"My parents."

A silence stretches, and it doesn't take long until Troy finds himself throwing his head back, clapping and laughing. To think that Jayden, the university's playboy, and most sought-after man— would be so jealous of him is pretty endearing.

"I'm starting to think my boyfriend is a bully," Jayden remarks after Troy can catch his breath.

He grins, arching a brow playfully as he signs. "What are you going to do about it?"

The silent challenge is there, causing his nose to flare and his cock to jump. He lightly pinches him in the arm, his mouth nipping his neck playfully. "Don't tempt me first thing in the morning, Troy. You need to eat before our first game."

He pouts. "I'll be—"

"No," he interjects before placing his hand back onto Troy's high. "You need to eat; I'm not letting you play on an empty stomach, especially because you didn't eat last night either. However, you're free to come to sleep at my place once we return to campus."

His heart flutters at the invitation, and he nods in excitement. "Really?"

"Why wouldn't it be okay?" he questions in turn, and Troy responds with a small, half-shrug response.

"Well, I didn't think you'd be so sticky."

Sticky.

Jayden's heart skips a beat, and he tries his hardest not to laugh at how bones deep that comment hits home. If only Troy knew half of it. Whenever he is around him, he feels a rush of emotions that he hasn't known how to label until recently.

It is as though Troy had an extraordinary power over him, one that only he possessed.

His heart races quickly, and his palms grow clammy and sweaty.

It is as if he is experiencing everything for the first time and never wants it to end. He knows that if it were anyone else, he wouldn't even spare the time of day, but with Troy, he greedily wants more, whatever he is willing to give him.

Jayden can't help but think that something is enchanting when it comes to Troy. Maybe his infectious smile or how he looks at him makes him feel like the most important person in the world in ways no one ever tried.

Whenever they are together, Jayden feels alive, better than any wild, thoughtless high he can get—

Especially knowing how much it upsets Troy, something he hates.

Who would have thought it had been love? He, of all people.

By the time Jayden finds out he has fallen in love with Troy, there's no turning back. Every moment they spend together is a moment cherished, and this time, it's no different. Since he came into his life, he had only turned it for the better.

It made it so much brighter and easier to *breathe*.

"Just you, it seems," he muses, laying one more kiss on his temple. "Now, let's go."

"Oh, before then," he says before turning his body completely to face Jayden, a gentle smile spreading across his face. He can already feel his heart beating erratically before he cups his face and gathers all his courage to close the distance between them for a sweet, timid-like kiss.

With a groan that sends a shiver down Troy's spine, Jayden then hauls their body even closer.

Wanting to consume this man.

As they embrace each other, Troy's mind fills with memories of the moments they shared last night.

Wanting more.

Finally, as they break apart, both can barely control themselves.

If it weren't because Jayden is set on ensuring his partner—both on the field and off—is fed before their game, he would probably not let him leave until absolutely necessary. With much difficulty, he pulls away before helping him up as they head into the shower together.

Once finishing between a handful of kisses and touches, they head down for breakfast, where it seems everyone else is already there, shoving piles of all-you-can-eat continental breakfast down their throats like they've been starved for days.

"Well, look who decided to finally join us," Trevis remarks, wagging an eyebrow at Jayden, who only flips him off in return. Judging from the shit-faced grin, it didn't take a genius for Jayden to know he was already on them.

Typical.

"Fuck off," he snarls, flipping him off, and though Troy can't precisely hear, he's able to pick up the teasing nature relatively quickly. Sliding onto the table and between eating, they discuss the tennis match and game plan.

"Honestly, I don't know if I'm ready for this match today. The other team has some *really* strong players," Trevis sighs, allowing time for Jayden to sign it and then back to Troy. He then signs in return, and it takes everything in Trevis not to tease the two by the way he's smiling like an idiot entirely in love.

"Troy says we've been practicing hard all week, so we can definitely give them a run for their money."

"Your boyfriend sure is cocky," he says, just loud enough for them to hear while laughing. Trevis intended to tease Jayden, but to his surprise, Jayden doesn't deny it. Instead, he playfully rolls his eyes. Trevis can't help but become a bit shell-shocked at Jayden's reaction.

He notices a mischievous glint in Jayden's eyes as he translates it back to Troy, who only blushes.

Well, Trevis mused, he never thought he'd see this day come around.

Yet he's happy on his behalf of finding someone that pairs him so well.

They continued eating breakfast soon after, discussing different strategies they could use during the match. As they finish up, they gather their tennis gear, head out to their destination, and are ready to give it their all.

By the time they get to the university's tennis court, they quickly get changed, with Jayden and Troy going first in the program. As they step onto the tennis court, their eyes lock on the opposing team. They know this is going to be a tough match.

After all, this is the conference game now, but they are ready for whatever is thrown their way.

Suddenly, Troy can't help but feel his arrogance from earlier slipping just ever so slightly.

Every move they make, down to how they think and bring to the court, is crucial.

Even the slightest bit of nervousness can throw off their entire play and jeopardize their chances of success. One mistake could mean the difference between victory and defeat; both know they cannot afford to slip up.

Not when this is their first round.

The stakes are high, and failure is not an option.

As he steps onto the court, he can feel his stomach churning and his knees starting to buckle; he tries to take a deep breath and steady himself, but it's useless. The nerves have taken hold, and he can't shake the feeling of dread that's settling over him.

Troy takes his position on the baseline while Jayden stands at the net.

In fact, he can feel his heart pounding irrationally as

he looks out at the sea of faces in the stands, he can feel the sweat bead on his forehead, and his hands shake slightly. It's not just the number of people that's making him nervous; it's the fact that this is the biggest match he's ever played in.

He's used to playing in front of small crowds at local colleges, but this is a whole different level.

Despite his best efforts to stay focused and gear himself up, Troy can't help but feel squeamish and uneasy. Every time he looks up at the crowd, he feels like he's going to be sick. He tries to block out the noise and the distractions, but it's a losing battle.

All he can think about is how badly he wants to win and how much is riding on this one game. He takes a deep breath and steadies himself, trying to push aside the fear and anxiety that's threatening to overwhelm him.

Every so often, his eyes would linger on Jayden.

His *boyfriend*, what a strange sound it is.

Yet something about being paired with him, him being his teammate, and being able to trust and work with him so in sync helps his jumpiness of being on the field. Right now, it's just like practice, going against their teammates rather than it being a competition.

It's just practice.

And something about that mindset helps tremendously with his nerves.

The game starts slow, with both teams evenly matched. But as the game progresses, Troy and Jayden's teamwork becomes more and more evident. They move across the court, communicating without saying a word, anticipating each other's moves, and adjusting their own accordingly.

With each point, Troy feels a little more confident and in control. Though the nerves never completely go away, he manages to push through with a confident smile Jayden would flash every time they score. As the crowd watches in bated breath, the ball flies back and forth, each player pushing themselves to their limits.

It's not a conference champion game if it was easy.

Troy and Jayden are in sync, perfectly connected in ways they never thought possible before. They hit the ball with precision and force, refusing to let their opponents gain the upper hand. Troy and Jayden move with fluidity, their movements synchronized as if they share one mind.

The ball flies back and forth between them; each hit is calculated with precision and executed with force. They refuse to let their opponents gain the upper hand, constantly communicating and adjusting their strategy to maintain their lead. It's as if they are two halves of a whole, perfectly connected in ways they never thought possible before.

The tension on the court is palpable as the game soon reaches its climax.

Both knew that when it came down to them, of course, it would be a damn tie, with this game being the tiebreaker itself. In the end, Troy's powerful serve secures the win for them. The ball flies over the net at lightning speed, catching their opponents off-guard and ensuring the final point.

The crowd is cheering loudly, and although Troy cannot hear them, he can feel the excitement in the air. The energy is palpable, and it's clear that everyone is thoroughly enjoying themselves. Despite his hearing impairment, Troy can still soak up the atmosphere and revel in the joyous celebration.

Troy and Jayden, right before Troy, leap into his embrace.

The game was over all soon, with Columbia University having the chance to advance to the next round.

The team is riding on high, and it would have been the case for Jayden as well—

Had it not been for the message he received from his father asking to have dinner tomorrow.

Just freaking *great*.

As Troy and Jayden sat beside each other on the bus ride home to the university, it didn't take long for Troy to notice that something was off with Jayden. The signs are obvious, from his jaw ticking to his leg bouncing—like he has a lot of energy and no way of dispelling it.

As everyone is still riding that high or getting some much-needed sleep after the game, Troy reaches over to squeeze his hand, jolting Jayden to look back at him. A small, apologetic smile appears on Jayden's expression, but it's not going to pass by Troy, who can feel his frown only deepening.

"What's wrong?" he signs, tilting his head to the side. "Are you…not happy we won?"

Or…was it something else entirely?

Jayden shakes his head, letting out a sigh.

He should have known when it came to Troy; he would quickly notice something was off.

"My parents…want to have dinner with me tomorrow."

He had thought getting into the conference championship would mean missing Friday's mandatory dinner for a few weeks, but it seems his father had different plans for this year. Troy looks at him sympathetically, knowing how strained his relationship with his parents is and wishing he could do something about it.

"I'm sorry; I know how tough that can be," he retorts. "Is…there anything I can do to help, possibly?"

His mouth is ready to reassure Troy that he's going to be okay when he suddenly finds himself freezing.

A bizarre and probably crazy idea started formulating inside his head, yet…

He realizes he can't lie to his parents anymore nor feed into the high expectations they have set of being his twin's replacement. Frankly, he doesn't think he can do that anymore, not after what Troy taught him.

He wants to embrace himself, his sexuality, his life, and be *himself*.

He wants to find himself and his parents to learn who Jayden Harrington is.

He wants to be honest with himself and move on from the past they were all stuck in.

He wants, he wants, and *wants*.

After years, the burden of hiding his identity is becoming too heavy for him to carry. He has been living in fear of being rejected by his family and feeling as if he owed them for what happened, but he realizes that it's time to move on.

It was what Weston would have wanted.

He's sure about that because his brother is selfless, just like his boyfriend.

So, he takes a deep breath before turning to Troy with a small, impish-like smile.

"Do you…want to meet my parents tomorrow?"

CHAPTER THIRTY-EIGHT

Was it crazy to ask your partner to meet your parents less than forty-eight hours after making it official?

Probably.

Was Jayden also confident that this would be one of the craziest and most erratic things he's done?

Undoubtedly.

Was he also starting to become nervous for the first time in what seems to be a decade?

Certainly.

"What the hell am I doing?" he murmurs in dismay as he stares at himself in the mirror.

His jawline ticks with uncertainty as he stands in front of the mirror. He considers canceling tonight's dinner with his parents altogether at the thought of just what their re-action might be. While he *did* tell them last night that he was bringing a guest, he didn't specify in particular who he was.

Other than the fact that he is his teammate—who they happen to know is deaf.

He lets out a long-winded sigh, walking over to the bed and then collapsing onto it.

In the other room, he can hear water running as Troy prepares himself.

After arriving on campus last night, Troy and Jayden walked together to Troy's dorm room, where he collected some of his essentials—like an extra set of clothing that would make a good impression on meeting your partner's parents for the first time—before heading to Jayden's place.

Hand-in-hand through the relatively deserted campus.

During the walk, both were lost in thought about what the next day would hold. Despite Jayden giving Troy several opportunities to back out before he texted his parents back, Troy was determined to follow through with it.

To be there for *him*.

At the very end, they ended up cuddling and talking for the entire night, too exhausted from the game and anxious about tomorrow—though neither would admit it. For Jayden, he knew his parents well. He knew how heated it might get, and he selfishly wanted Troy there to get him through it.

Because he didn't think he'd be able to by himself.

Knowing that he owed them and yet wanting to end this vicious cycle.

Not to mention, it's been gnawing at his stomach about the bet he had taken with Trevis.

He has been intending to tell him about it so there wouldn't be any secret in the future, but with an unexpected obstacle suddenly appearing, he is uncertain when he will be able to do so. The situation has caused him to feel frustrated and unsure how to proceed.

Right now, Jayden is almost sure he must be freaking out as Troy steps out of the bathroom and offers a smile. He can't help but notice how cute and dashing Troy looks in his casual button-down shirt tucked into his slacks.

His hair is still a tad wet from the shower, and he runs his fingers through it as he approaches Jayden. The scent of his cologne is subtle but intoxicating, and Jayden can't help but feel a bit drunk in his presence.

"Nervous?" Troy signs, walking over to the bed just as Jayden sits up to lay a gentle peck on his lips.

"I should be asking you that," Jayden replies with a chuckle.

"Just a tad," he replies, and when he arches up a brow in disbelief, Troy rolls his eyes while pouting. "Okay, a whole lot of tad, but…I can't imagine not being there for you. You know I'll be there for you no matter what, right?"

"I don't know what I did to have deserved you," he states with a heavy sigh, and Troy grins.

"That should be the other way around. Now let's go."

Jayden and Troy leave the apartment holding hands, their fingers intertwined as they approach the elevator. They are both nervous, and the silence between them is palpable. Jayden presses the button for the lobby, and they stand side by side as they wait for the elevator to arrive.

When the doors opened, they stepped inside, and Jayden hit the button for the lobby. The elevator descends slowly, and neither of them says a word. They are lost in their thoughts, thinking about what the night might hold.

Of how terrible the night can really go.

As they exit the lobby, they make their way outside, waving down a cab; they climb into the back seat, Jayden sitting closest to the door and Troy beside him. They hold hands again, and neither says a word as they begin their journey.

The car ride is silent, and the only sound is the engine's hum as they make their way through the city. Jayden glances at Troy, who is staring out the window, lost in thought. He looks so handsome, and Jayden can't help but feel grateful that he has him by his side.

As they pull up to Jayden's house, he pays the driver, and they step out onto the sidewalk; Jayden leads the way up the front steps, still holding Troy's hand tightly. He takes a deep breath before ringing the doorbell, and before he knows it, the door swings open, and his dad is soon standing before him.

"Father," Jayden murmurs in greeting. "This is Troy. Troy Evans."

"Welcome," the father greets, extending his hand.

Troy shakes his hand firmly, pulling away to continue, then signing.

"It's a pleasure to meet you, Sir," he replies, trying to look confident, but internally, he's freaking out when Jayden's father then looks him up and down, staring him for a moment. Troy felt like he was just put on a scale to display, and the silence made him even more nervous.

"The pleasure is mine," he signs in return, opening the door wide. His eyes shift over to Jayden, arching a brow. "I must admit, I was taken aback. The first person you brought home after moving here was your teammate."

His jawline ticks as he arches a brow. "Is there a problem with my choices?"

"No, just presumed it would be your girlfriend," he retorts. Jayden can guess where this is going to go, mainly because he's planning to introduce Troy as his boyfriend during the dinner. As they head into the dining room, Jayden walks over to his mother, who is just setting the lasagna down and kisses her forehead.

"Mother," he says. "I'm home."

"Hi, Pumpkin," she smiles. Every time she says that nickname, Jayden can feel a part of himself withering because that had always been Weston's nickname. He swallows down the lump in his throat, can't even remember the last time she had even said his name. "Welcome home; I missed you. Come sit down. I heard you brought a guest."

"Yes, his name is Troy," he introduces just as Troy walks up in greeting.

"Hello. It's nice to meet you," he signs.

"Oh, he signs just like you," she remarks before placing the tray down. She then removed her mittens and set them on the counter before signing. "It's nice to meet you. Feel free to call me Peony. I've heard from Harvey that deaf. Were you always born deaf?"

"Mom," he hisses, and Troy doesn't need to hear to

understand the rising tension. Ever so slightly, he raises his hand and places it on Jayden's arm. Despite his anger, his body's tension eases up just somewhat in return.

"I was born deaf," he answers after withdrawing his hand.

"Oh, my son became deaf after getting sick," she replies, and Troy finds his brow knitting together.

"Jayden isn't deaf," he signs.

The tension in the air is so thick that both can feel it like a physical weight on their shoulders. Neither says a word, but Troy doesn't back down from his comment or look away. Jayden stares at his mother, begging quietly for her to correct herself.

To talk about Weston.

The intensity of their stare-down is suffocating until, finally—she smiles.

"Right," she signs with a soft smile that doesn't quite reach her eyes. "Slip of hand. Now let's eat."

They each take a seat, with Jayden and Troy across from his parents. They exchange small talk throughout dinner, though it's more than clear that Troy's comment from earlier did not exactly sit well with them. After an unhealthy amount of time, Jayden's father finally breaks it first as he finishes chewing.

"So, I heard you both played tremendously well yesterday at the conference playoffs."

"Yes, Troy is actually one of the best players I've played with," Jayden says with a smile before signing what his father said back to Troy, who grins in return and gives his thanks.

Though Jayden is slightly irritated about why his father didn't sign the entire way, he lets it slide.

Counting down the minutes until this is over or when is the perfect time to come out.

Might as well get it damn over with.

His father nods in agreement, sipping his wine. "Though it would be better if he were able to hear."

At this statement, Jayden stiffens, feeling a wave of frustration and anger wash over him. Troy tilts his head to the side, not hearing what Jayden's father just said, but sees how Jayden's tenses catch his attention.

"What the hell is wrong with you?" Jayden snaps, unable to contain his frustration any longer.

"Jayden," his mother scolds, her tone admonishing.

"You're getting quite defensive, don't you think?" his father questions, arching a brow. This isn't certainly how Jayden wanted to come out, but by the tense look in his eyes, he's confident he's already catching on. "Is there something you want to tell me?"

To hell with it.

Jayden hesitated momentarily before taking a deep breath and turning to Troy. Troy stares back, a bit concerned about what's going on, before he reaches for his hand, intertwining their fingers together. It was a small gesture, but it made him feel more comfortable.

More grounded.

"You already knew though, didn't you?" Jayden asks, his voice barely above a whisper.

"I was waiting to see how long you'd keep this charade

up," he quips, his tone cold. "Why don't you tell your mother, though? I'm sure she's more than curious to know what his perfect son has been up to this entire time."

Perfect.

How much he hates that word.

"What's wrong?" his mom interjects in confusion, her eyes dashing between everyone in the room. Jayden swallowed hard, his heart racing as he prepared to break the notion they had always had over him finally.

He's done being Mr. Perfect.

He's done being his dead brother's replacement.

"I'm dating Troy," he affirms.

The air is still and quiet, so much so you can hear a pin drop; the silence is so thick that it feels almost tangible, like a heavy blanket draped over the room. It's as if even the slightest sound would shatter the stillness, making the atmosphere almost palpably tense.

"What?" his mother gasps, clearly caught off-guard as she stands up.

Jayden didn't think seeing the shock and revulsion in his mother's face would hurt so much.

"So that's why you decided to bring him over," his dad chuckles, his eyes narrowing as his eyes waver from his son to Troy. "And for what exactly? Is it your rebellious phase? Are you not happy with something or want attention?"

"No, I'm in love with him," Jayden replies, his voice steady.

"But...what about kids? You always told me..." his mother

trails off, clearly struggling to come to terms with the news. The sight of her makes Jayden feel nauseous, and he fears that she might faint at any moment.

"Mother, *Weston* told you," Jayden maintains, frustration creeping into his voice. "Not me. Not Jayden."

It was the first time he had ever mentioned his name in years.

"Son," his father warned, his tone harsh. "You're confused."

Was he serious?

The room fell silent as his father's words hung in the air.

He felt a mix of fear, anger, sadness, and frustration. All he wanted was to be accepted for who he was, but he knew that might not be possible with his parents. Troy squeezes his hand reassuringly, letting him know that he is there for him no matter what.

"No, father. I'm *done*. I'm fucking done," Jayden growls, his voice rising. He lets go of Troy, slamming his hands down and standing up. "I'm done acting. I'm not Weston, and I never *will* be. I'm tired. I'm so damn fucking tired of hiding it now. I feel terrible for what I did that night, for being the reason your precious son isn't here, but I'm not him. I *can't* be him. Weston is gone."

He hates the way his mother runs out of the room in tears.

He hates how his father looks like he might jump across the table and punch him.

More than anything else, he hates how relieved he finally feels—like a large boulder has been lifted.

"Get the hell out," he snarls. "Don't ever fucking come back."

"With pleasure," he grits out before looking over at Troy. "Let's go."

To hell with them.

The ride back to the apartment is not better than the ride there.

Returning to the apartment, they climb out of the car and return inside. They collapse onto the couch, holding each other tightly. Neither needed to say a word, and truthfully, there was something about the silence that Jayden appreciated. Troy didn't need to lie about it getting better because no one knew, nor did he need to offer any sympathy either.

He was just there for him whenever he was ready.

Jayden feels slightly lighter in his next air intake for the first time in years.

CHAPTER THIRTY-NINE

"**Y**ou sly, sly foxes! I knew something was up! Details! I need the details now!"

Troy fights the urge to flip his phone over or end the call as soon as his best friend's face appears on the screen, grinning from ear to ear. Somehow, Troy is almost sure that if he did, Quinn might actually show up at Jayden's in less than thirty minutes flat before barreling down the door for the "tea," as she calls it.

He already knew it was a bad idea when she proceeded to drop her phone *twice* in disbelief upon hearing the news before being able to prop the phone up on the gooseneck phone stand—with shaky hands—to sign back.

Yet, despite his embarrassment, Troy can't help but chuckle at her reaction.

"Details? Whatever do you mean?" Jayden signs teasingly with a loop smile, and Troy elbows him.

"Don't egg her on," Troy remarks while rolling his eyes.

However, there's no stopping the rapid fire of questions that soon spews from Quinn's hand rapid fire.

"Nope, it's too late," she counters before turning to Jayden. "You have to give me the details, and I mean everything! Who confessed first? How did this happen? Why did you both decide to tell me so late? Does anyone else know?"

"Just our parents," Jayden begins. "Actually, we just told them right before we called you. We only started going out two days ago, so we were still figuring things out before deciding to tell anyone, so it's not that late."

Troy nods in agreement but refrains from divulging what happened at his parents' house the day before. He understands that it is unnecessary to share the information and that Jayden is still upset about it despite his claims that he is not bothered.

"Okay then, did this happen?" she demanded next without missing a beat. From the looks of it, she looks practically ready to reach out from the phone and hold them both hostage until they both spill everything. "Details! Stop keeping me waiting! How? How?!"

Whenever Troy thinks Quinn can't sign any faster, he's proven wrong by how quickly she's throwing up those exclamations and question marks. As Troy racks his brain to find out the best way to tell her, he should have known Jayden would have beat him to the punch.

"I guess when we were forced to share a bed because of a technical error with the room bookings?" Jayden replies with a half-shrug, putting his head onto Troy's shoulder. Troy is almost sure Quinn might have a nosebleed soon because of how red her face gets.

"One bed?!"

"Yeah," Jayden nods, followed by him wincing, and Troy can only presume she is squealing at the top of her lungs. He recalls his parents having to explain it's like a loud piercing rattle inside your eardrum, and he reaches to pat Troy's thighs supportively.

They were mentally exhausted when they both could get Quinn to hang up with the promise of her not showing up at Jayden's apartment, demanding more answers almost *two* hours later. It didn't help that they had a fierce practice this morning and midterms soon, too.

"That went way better than I expected," Troy muses, turning over to Jayden.

He grins, leaning over to place a peck on Troy's temple that still makes butterflies flutter around in his stomach. While he heard this was the beginning of the honeymoon phase, something in his guts told him that he would never get tired of this.

Never get tired of him, really.

"Yeah, but…it's…" he trails off for a moment, his hands lingering in the air as he tries to grasp the right words. When he finally can settle on one, he gives a small, sheepish smile for his lack of a better word. "Strange, I guess? Not in a bad way, but certainly not what I expected."

Troy sits up a bit straighter, tilting his head towards the side. "What do you mean?"

"How…" he lingers his hands for a moment. "I suppose how accepting they are."

"They?" he parrots with his hands, brows furrowing together. "Wait, you mean Quinn?"

"Not just Quinn, but everyone else, especially your parents," he admits.

Jayden can't help but feel overwhelmed by the acceptance and kindness shown by Troy's parents during their video call. As he listens to Troy's father express his happiness and excitement for them, Jayden's mind races with thoughts of his own parents, who have never accepted him for who he is—

Who only saw him as a replacement to date.

The contrast between the two sets of parents is striking, filling Jayden with mixed emotions.

On the one hand, he is grateful for Troy's parents and the love they have shown him, something he has never felt before with his own parents. He feels a sense of relief, knowing that people in his life accept him for who he is.

Yet, on the other hand, he can't help but feel a sense of sadness and frustration when he thinks about his own parents. Despite how *free* he feels, it also feels like a stab that no matter what, he would never be good enough for *them*. Nothing would probably ever be for a mistake he made as a child who only wanted attention in the only way he knew how.

By acting out.

He wishes they could be as accepting as Troy's parents, but he knows that is unlikely to happen.

At least, not any time soon that he can anticipate.

Initially, he didn't want to trouble Troy with his insecurities and doubts. He didn't want to burden him with his inner turmoil. However, the contrast between the two sets of parents weighs heavily on his mind, and he can't help himself in the end.

Just like a selfish child.

Yet Troy didn't seem upset; it was quite the opposite.

He turns his body to face Jayden, slowly cupping his cheek gently to ensure he has his full attention. Only then does he take his hands away to sign slowly, making his message evident and clear. "Your parents, they'll come around."

"What if they don't?" Jayden questions, in turn, his eyes drooping downward at the thought.

He hated how much he wanted them to.

He hated how much he wanted things to be different, even now.

He hated how they didn't even reach out to say anything, and more importantly, he hated that he cared.

"Then we'll get through it together when the time comes," Troy signs, giving him a small, encouraging smile. "Give them time and space to process everything. It's a lot to take in, but I know they will because you're their son. Don't focus on what ifs; focus on what is already."

Troy knows it's a lot of talk for someone who barely went through what Jayden went through to say something like that. Yet, he can only hope that, in the end, he can comfort him and remind him that he's not alone.

He's never alone from now on.

Almost as if Jayden knows what he's thinking, he grins wildly.

"I like that quote."

"You were the one that taught me that," he admits, and Jayden only scrunches his face in confusion.

"What? I don't remember saying that," he signs.

Troy rolls his eyes, finding it unironic and something that would be what he would do.

"It was during that party. I have to admit I don't remember much, but I remember your words' impact on me that night," he replies, smiling at his own words as he recalls the memories. "When you told me to not look at my disability as...well, a disability."

"It's because it's not," he remarks quickly, hauling him into his lap and holding him closely.

Troy finds himself chuckling at his remark and nodding in agreement.

"Yeah. You told me to look at myself as an inspiration for others and focus on what is rather than anything that it could have been if I'm not," he remarks, leaning comfortably with his back to Jayden's front as he continues proudly. "I'm deaf and gay. If you don't like it, deal with it."

If you were to ask Troy just a year prior, he certainly wouldn't have said it as arrogantly as he did now.

Troy feels a sudden shaking motion behind him and turns around, only to see Jayden laughing uncontrollably with his head thrown back. It warms Troy's heart to see his partner so carefree and happy, even though he's slightly confused about what he said to have gotten him to laugh.

Yet he takes in how Jayden's eyes crinkle at the corners, and his cheeks are flushed with joy. Troy can't help but smile at the sight, feeling grateful to have someone like him in his life without even realizing it. Despite being deaf, Troy can sense the joy emanating from Jayden's laughter, which also fills him with happiness.

It's only when he's done catching his breath that Troy huffs, crossing his arms and snuffing him playfully.

"Sorry, sorry. I didn't mean to laugh," he signs after playing his hands in front for Troy to see.

"Yes, you did," he huffs, trying not to shudder when he feels Jayden nuzzling into the crook of his neck. He peppers kisses alongside his neck teasingly and softly, grinning at how Troy shifts and wiggles as he kisses his cheek.

"Aw, is my baby pouting? Why?" he questions, knowing fully well he's just playing into his tantrum.

He never thought he could find such joy in such a simple way of being around another person, yet here he is, feeling complete and content in Troy's embrace. With every passing day since Saturday, he can't help but feel greedy for more time with his beloved.

Beloved, who would have thought he'd ever call someone that?

Someone who never wanted commitment because he wants to be free to do whatever he wanted without being chained now. He was content with spending forever alone or marrying someone his parents approved of because that was what Weston would have done.

Yet now, every morning, he wakes up longing to spend the entire day with Troy.

Every night, he falls asleep with the hope that tomorrow will bring more moments of togetherness.

He likes to wake up with the same person he saw before sleeping.

This desire to have someone constant in his life is something new to him, and he feels grateful to be able to express this want *openly*, as Jayden Harrington wants. It makes him feel a sense of security and comfort, knowing he has someone he trusts and adores to start his day with.

He feels like a child again because of Troy.

This very person who had freed him from his own hell.

"You know why," Troy signs, narrowing his eyes and swatting him away.

It only makes Jayden smile wider.

"Sorry, I just found you so dang cute. I didn't think someone like you secretly had claws," he grins, and even if he tried, Troy knows from the bottom of his heart that he can't precisely stay mad at him for too long.

"I didn't think I had any either until I met you," he remarks. "I am so grateful to you for giving me the courage to pursue my dream of playing professionally. You have inspired me to be more comfortable in myself and to show others that even with disabilities, anyone can achieve greatness."

Jayden can't help but kiss him on the lips.

"You are going to be the world's best tennis player. I knew from the moment I saw you play," he admits. Even thinking about it now still gave him goosebumps. His movements were fluid and precise, unlike any other player he'd seen to date.

The way Troy plants his feet and positions his body just before each serve and keeps his eyes focused on the ball throughout the entire rally. Jayden could still see that Troy had a fierce backhand, delivering powerful shots quickly. He admired the way Troy moved on the court, gliding effortlessly from one side to the other.

To find out that he wasn't able to hear either yet moved with such precision?

It was the damn cherry on top.

"Same with you," Troy signs, and Jayden hums for a moment before responding.

"Truthfully, I don't know if I really want to get scouted and sign with a major league or...am I playing because I'm expected to follow Weston's footsteps my entire life? After all, this was his hobby, but...I don't even know if it's his dream. He was just a child," he admits.

At that, Troy nods.

He recalls that when he was a child, he wanted to be a veterinarian, and as he got older, he realized he couldn't stand the thought of putting a beloved pet down or the sight of blood itself. Now that Jayden can be himself and rediscover himself outside the façade of his departed brother, it makes sense for him to be confused about who he is.

Much less what he wants to do, and that's okay.

"Just take it one day at a time. Whatever it is you want to do at the end, I know everyone on the team will support you," Troy signs before reaching out to squeeze his thighs supportively. That's the beautiful thing about being a human is that everyone is expected to grow and change.

What we may like now might be something of the past tomorrow.

"Even you?" Jayden asks, and something about his childishness makes Troy chuckle.

He bites his lips to stop himself from laughing, not wanting to be a hypocrite by laughing now and nods.

"Especially me," he remarks.

Jayden sighs contently, nuzzling into the crook of his neck again to hide how flustered he feels inside. It's still strange to have someone support him so openly and actually mean it from the very bottom of their heart.

"You spoil me too much," he concurs, and Troy ruffles his hair before signing in return.

"Isn't that a good thing?"

"Yeah, I'm so glad I fell in love with you," he states.

How freeing that statement makes him feel to have it out in the open.

How nice it is to know that the world's best and most beautiful thing can't be heard or seen but felt with the heart. Love doesn't expect anything in return but brings joy, happiness, and fulfillment to the giver and the receiver.

How beautiful and wonderful is that?

"Me too," he replies. "I'm…really glad to have met you, Jayden."

Jayden is almost sure his heart is moments from combusting.

He never understood why people come to "like" or what it even means to "love" someone all his life. Growing up and being compared to his twin before causing the indirect cause of his death had jaded how he viewed what love meant.

For him, he vowed never to like anybody.

At least, he will never like anybody too much because that's no different than putting a collar and leash on yourself. He would know firsthand in trying to chase his parents' love. It's the reason why he tried so hard to be liked by others but also kept a reasonable distance from them as the campus's Mr. Nice.

He never wants to be attached emotionally to anyone.

Yet, in the end, he realizes he ended up eating his own words but not regretting it one bit, either.

Jayden can say he's happy for the first time and means it from the bottom of his heart.

So tell him then if you're confident of your love.

Jayden can feel his heart squeezing at the sudden thought of what's been holding him back.

Just tell him the truth.

Just tell him about the bet.

Yeah, easier said than damn done.

It sits at the edge of his fingertips, unsure if he even has it in him to sign it out loud. If he doesn't tell him now, he may never get the chance again. The thought of someone bringing it up casually and shattering the one thing he has left after Weston's death is unbearable. Every fiber of his being urges him to tell him, yet he can't shake the feeling that this is his last chance to keep his heart from breaking all over again.

Especially when he had just discovered what it means to be in love with someone wholeheartedly again.

How cruel is that?

While he knows he can tell the team never to mention

it again, it didn't sit right to lie to his boyfriend regarding the bet Jayden had initially taken on when he didn't know better. He needed to tell him because, at the very least, he felt as if he owned him that much.

Jayden feels his jawline ticking, and unconsciously, he holds Troy tighter. It doesn't go unnoticed by the latter, who slowly turns towards him with curiosity and confusion. Troy tilts his head, allowing his head to nuzzle into the crook of his lover's shoulder just as Jayden then sighs.

"Actually…there's something I think you should know," he begins solemnly, like a man about to be placed on death's row. It quickly catches Troy's attention, concern plastered across his heart like a plague at the sudden shift over what he had said.

Troy turns to face Jayden, giving him his full attention. He can't help but notice the tense expression on Jayden's face and the way his eyes dart around nervously. As Jayden lifts his hands, Troy's concern mounts.

He can sense that whatever Jayden wants to say is important, and he braces himself for the worst. Troy can see the agony in his eyes, as if he's physically carrying the weight of whatever he's about to reveal.

Despite his own unease, Troy remains calm and attentive. "What's wrong?"

"I…I really fucked up, Troy," he admits gravely, knowing there's no turning back now.

He blinks a few times, brows knitting together. "What? What do you mean? Why?"

Jayden presses his lips together into a thin line, trying

to put together how he can best word it without sounding horrible. However, no matter how hard he tried inside his head, anything and everything sounded equally terrible because it was.

"I just want you to know that it's selfish of me to say this now after telling everyone, but I don't think keeping it from you would be any better going forth," he signs quickly, looking away as he continues painfully. "However, I...I respect if you don't want to be with me anymore, too."

Troy is terrified at this point. "Jayden, what is it? You're scaring me."

He can feel his heart racing as he waits in anticipation for Jayden's response.

His palms are sweaty, and he can feel his throat tightening. The fear of losing Jayden, the one person he has fallen in love with since coming to terms with himself, is overwhelming. Troy's mind races with worst-case scenarios, and his anxiety only intensifies with each passing moment.

He tries to remain calm for Jayden's sake, but his body is betraying him.

Troy looks at him with pleading eyes, hoping for a positive response, but the fear of what he might say hangs heavy in the air. Jayden breaks the silence between them after what feels close to an eternity.

"I took a bet a few months back with Trevis."

The silence that stretches isn't just deafening for Troy—something he didn't think was even possible for him, but unnerving and suffocating as well. They stare at one another for a few seconds before he finally gets his hands to work again.

"A....bet?" he parrots, adding a few question marks to emphasize his confusion of where this is headed.

He stiffly nods, rubbing the back of his neck for a moment before continuing. "Trevis had placed a bet that I would sleep with you in the very beginning when we first were assigned to be teammates. If I did, I would break my vow that I will never sleep or date anyone on the same team because it'll just cause issues and troubles down the line."

Oh.

The strings are slowly starting to click together.

"I see," he slowly answers. "And you said..."

"I said I wouldn't," he concurs. "I took on the bet because I knew I would win. It was supposed to be like any other bet because I have a strict rule of not getting involved with teammates, as it can go south quickly."

"Okay," he replies with a curt nod.

Jayden can only swallow the lump in his throat, feeling his hands grow clammier and shakier by the second. "However, as soon as I realized I'd started to have feelings for you, I called it off. Before I slept with you before I realized how important you were to me, before anything else."

"What was on the line if he won?" Troy questions, his face so expressionless and stoic that it's *terrifying*.

"If he won, cleaning the toilets for a whole year. If I won..." he trails off, and only then does he find himself chuckling to himself as a new realization hits him.

"Truthfully, I don't think I even answered Trevis back of what was on the line if I did win the bet."

Perhaps because he knew from the start that he would have lost.

He wanted an excuse not to fall for him because he knew that Troy was different from others internally.

Now, it's coming to bite him once more tenfold.

Troy's unnervingly calm reaction only intensifies his panic with every word he signs.

He had been expecting Troy to storm out in a fit of rage, but instead, he stands there, looking stoic and indifferent. Jayden can feel the weight of his statement hanging in the air, and his mind races with all the worst-case scenarios.

Maybe he shouldn't have said anything.

Maybe he should have kept it to himself and let things continue as they were.

However, it's too late now, and all he can do is wait for Troy's response, no matter how terrifying it might be. Ultimately, Jayden would respect his decision because he knew he deserved it. Whatever memories he was given in the short time together, he would treasure it forever.

He then watches as Troy takes a deep breath before signing slowly. "Then it doesn't matter."

Jayden can feel his entire body going rigid.

"What? What do you...mean?" he asks, his fingers slow and tense. "It...doesn't matter?"

"It doesn't," Troy verifies with a nod. "You clearly regret it and didn't go through with it at the end. You called it off as soon as you could before it became big, and you told me about it rather than keeping it a secret and me having to find out from someone else. How can I be that upset?"

For a moment, he thinks he must be hallucinating because it seems impossible that someone could say something like that so *casually* after hearing how awful he is as a person. He blinks a few times, but Troy doesn't flinch away or move his hands to correct his statement.

There are no "buts" added in.

There's no waiting for the other shoe to drop.

Instead, Troy's calm and relaxed demeanor only intensifies Jayden's confusion.

He wonders how someone could be so collected in such a bizarre situation. Jayden tries to compose himself and thinks of asking Troy again if he understood what he just signed. However, Troy looks at him calmly, with an almost serene expression on their face as if he has made peace with it.

It makes him feel like he's stuck in a dream, but he knows he's very wide awake.

"But...you are upset?" Jayden finally finds the courage to ask because he doesn't believe it.

How can anyone, after putting their partner through such a thing?

"Okay, I am. Though it's just a tad..." he remarks, trailing off before narrowing his eyes slightly up in his direction. "I mean, nothing happened at the end, right? Can you swear that there's nothing else you're keeping from me?"

"Nothing, I swear," he remarks with no hesitation. "I still owe you an apology, though. I didn't mean to."

"I know," Troy concurs, craning his neck to kiss his

cheek. He can tell already by how guilty he looks and the reason why; even though he's a little bit hurt, he's not precisely fuming either. "I wouldn't change anything that got us to where we are now. Would you?"

"No, never," he signs, shaking his head.

"Then there we are," he reassures. "Plus, I already had a hunch something was wrong. In the beginning, Benjamin told me to be careful and not trust you for some reason. I'm starting to understand why he said that now that I'm connecting all the dots."

At the gesture of Benjamin's name, Jayden snorts, nose scrunching together.

"Of course he did. Why am I not surprised?"

As Jayden spews out his venomous words, and despite being deaf, Troy can sense the toxicity of their anger. He chuckles and adjusts his position, wrapping his legs tightly around his boyfriend's waist, and turns to face him.

"Are you jealous?" he ponders with a grin despite already knowing the answer.

"Why wouldn't I be?" he pouts. Troy's laughter is infectious, causing Jayden's face to light up with a wide grin at how much he trusts him to laugh in his presence without shying away. He's almost in awe that Troy doesn't even notice how much joy he brings to someone like him without even trying. "Shit, what did I do to deserve you?"

At his question, Troy lightly swats at his chest, shaking his head.

"You didn't have to do anything. You're amazing just the way you are," he attests.

Jayden can't help but smile, feeling a sense of warmth spreading throughout his body.

He knows that he doesn't have to do anything to earn Troy's love and affection, and that knowledge fills him with a deep sense of comfort and security. At this moment, he feels truly blessed to be with someone as amazing as Troy, and he can't imagine his life without him.

Yet...

"Still," he starts, bumping his nose with his. "I still want to make it up for you somehow?"

Opening his mouth, Troy is ready to shoot down his statement when an idea suddenly pops up. It makes his heart skip several beats as he bites his lips, his eyes hovering over Jayden's lips as he signs rather shyly, "I mean...I can...maybe think of one?"

Eagerly, Jayden finds himself nodding. "What is it?"

Suddenly, the latter doesn't know how to bring it up. Troy can feel his face flusher as he looks away, resisting the urge to abruptly get off his lap and possibly find a hiding place. "Do you really need me to sign it?"

Silence follows for a few seconds, and when Jayden can finally connect the dots, he bursts out laughing. He immediately intertwines his fingers behind Troy, hauling him closer before getting up with him in tow and straight into the bedroom, where he'll definitely be proving his apology for the rest of the night.

CHAPTER FORTY

As soon as they stumble through the bedroom, hungry lips latch on quickly to hungrier lips.

Their kiss is feverish and maddening, their hands roaming eagerly and quickly everywhere they can find in blind desperation—as if they were in a drought and the only saving grace would be one another. Troy can't help but wonder if that's just something that would ever go away or something permanent.

Troy hopes it's the latter because he doesn't know if he can live without this man who has breathed so much life and joy into his life. If only he knew that internally, Jayden would feel the same way, seeing his other half as his savior and his chance of finding happiness.

He alone can satisfy his insatiable craving for thrill-seeking and recklessness. He doesn't seek the thrill of feeling alive anymore because all that satisfaction comes with making Troy happy. He's come to realize these dare-devilish stunts make his heart race, and his adrenaline surges aren't the adrenaline he sought—

It was to feel alive.

He feels alive just being with him.

Their greedy, soul-devouring kisses didn't break until Jayden slammed him against the wall behind the door. Troy gasps in surprise, pulling his swollen, plump lips away to look at Jayden, whose eyes are full of hunger, affection, and mischievousness.

"You did that on purpose," he signs with a pout, making sure to wrap his legs tightly around his waist so as not to fall while simultaneously trying to ignore the thickened bulge digging right beneath him. Jayden only laughs, kissing his nose as he pulls away to answer him quickly.

"Yeah, you were too cute not to tease," he retorts with a smirk.

"You're so mean," he quips playfully, rolling his eyes. "A big fat meanie, by the way."

He chuckles, coyly tilting his head to the side. "Yeah, but you love me."

"You sure do love saying that," he retorts, and honestly, Jayden can't even lie. He has never truthfully fallen in love before Troy. Now that he has and knows how addictive it is, he doesn't know if he'd ever stop saying it or asking for confirmation.

"Yeah, I really do," he whispers before diving in one more, kissing alongside his jawline up to his collarbone. He lays a pepper of kisses wherever his mouth can reach, leaving small hickeys rather possessively in their place.

Every time Troy gasps or whines, bucking unconsciously onto his thickened length, it drives Jayden wild.

"Mm," Troy moans, tugging on Jayden's hair, hips jerking wildly when his teeth scrap a particularly sensitive spot just under his throat. In an instant, he rips Troy away from the wall, towing him to the bed, and as soon as he falls, Jayden wastes no time in crawling right over him.

Instinctively, Troy slowly starts to grind upward, almost feeling like he is back in middle school again and just going through puberty. Their hands explore one another more slowly and then more determinedly as time passes.

The bed soon starts to creak louder and faster as Troy whines and moans, drawing a growl out of Jayden. The latter can't help but growl, sinking his teeth into Troy's bottom lips while grinding him harder into the mattress.

They're panting, thoroughly entertained with one another sweetly and stickily.

Jayden hesitantly approaches to massage the small of Troy's back, lowering it until he can firmly grasp his partner's plump buttock. In response, Troy jolts before practically melting under his touch as they leisurely rub their lower halves on one another.

Almost as if they have all the time in the world.

Grunting in response, it didn't take long until Jayden picked up the pace, rubbing their thighs until he could feel their cocks touching and caressing one another through the light fabric of their boxers as they were having a relatively lazy day.

They are both throbbing, pulsating with need, fully engorged, and precum staining rapidly across their article of clothing. If Troy is being honest, he almost feels as if he is going to combust into flames at this point, his need for Jayden completely overtaking him.

In fact, his heart is thumping so fast he's more than sure Jayden can hear it, too.

Troy is disappointed when Jayden finally breaks away from their passionate, heated kiss, though it doesn't last long as he slowly trails his kisses over his jawline and neck again. However, Jayden doesn't stop, kissing up to his collarbone to then yank the shirt off.

It doesn't stop until both of them are completely naked and exposed to one another.

"Are you okay?" Jayden signs, asking for confirmation.

Troy can only muster enough to nod frantically in response, his hands shaky and his face flushed red. Jayden trails kiss downward, admiring how Troy's cock is up against his chest when he settles onto his nipples, straining, making his cock even harder.

He has to squeeze his eyes closed for a moment, concentrating on not coming just yet.

Christ, only Troy would be able to make him feel like this.

Without another word between them, Jayden latches onto one of his puckered, puffy nipples with a growl, drawing onto it hungrily. He's lapping it up with dirty grunts that fill his small apartment space, circling that pebbled bud over and over until Troy's wiggling and wiggling in pure frustration under him.

Jayden's other hand went to palm the other, pitching and tweaking while giving it undivided attention. Finally, he opened his eyes as their eyes locked while Jayden continued to lap up his nipple over and over.

"More," he signs before tugging Jayden's hair to bring him closer while arching his back, practically demanding he serve him. Neither of them can honestly think straight anymore; they are wholly lost in one another's embrace.

Troy only knew how to rock his thickness against him, hoping to find any relief from what Jayden was doing to his nipple. The way he sucks, nibbles, and lapses it up is everything and more he's been looking for.

Right now, they're no different than kerosene and a burning match itself.

It doesn't help that Troy's groans are driving Jayden out of his fucking mind.

"You want more, baby?" Jayden questions upon pulling away to ask him. Troy only nodded in return to his question, trying to catch his breath as Jayden then proceeded to assault his nipples and skin, placing new hickeys everywhere he could put his mouth on.

Troy didn't realize just how much he actually loved them.

In honesty, Troy feels as if he is still dreaming at times, the love of his life kissing him as they lay skin-to-skin without anything between them. He could feel Jayden's cock throbbing, rubbing up against his as he lays kisses and hickeys in the wake of where his lips go.

Down, down, down—right until Jayden's face settles over Troy's thickened member.

The sight of Troy's cock caused a feral noise to tumble

from Jayden's mouth. Jayden could feel his descent slipping into madness itself. Though more than anything else, Jayden wants to please Troy, wanting to feel his own lips around his lover's member. A droplet of pre-cum had gathered around Troy's thick cock already for what's to come.

As Jayden stares at Troy's cock—taking in the sight of him now that they're not in the dark—the tip, wet, glistening with pre-cum becomes even more prominent. Jayden can feel the heat building in his stomach, an overwhelming desire to consume and taste this beautiful man and please this man lying below him.

Mine, mine, mine.

Without hesitation, he leaned and darted his tongue at the bulbous tip as he unconsciously pushed more of his length into his tight mouth.

A gasp escaped both their lips when Jayden got a firm grip on his erection, the sensation almost too much for Troy. He is so sensitive that it shocked Jayden, loving the moans tumbling out of Troy's parted mouth.

More pre-cum trickled out and all over his hands.

Slowly, he pulls away enough to spit onto his head, allowing his saliva and his pre-cum to mix together for a better glide as Troy grips hard onto the pillow, thrusting upwards eagerly in response. Troy almost lost it when he pressed the pad of his thumbs onto the opening, rubbing the sensitive tip downward.

"Jayden," Troy finds enough willpower to sign.

"More?" he questions, licking his lips eagerly as he nods in affirmation. All conscious thoughts left Troy's head when his lover's hot mouth enveloped his cock. He groaned; the feeling of Jayden's mouth was like a piece of heaven, his mouth hot and so tight.

So fucking good.

Using Troy's groans and grunts to see what he liked, Jayden soon found a rhythm that caused Troy to grip hard onto the pillow and Jayden's hair and snap his hips upwards. It doesn't take long until Troy's toes curl in the overwhelming sensation.

With a grunt, Jayden grips the base of his cock firmly as he savors and lapses up the salty and sweet taste of him. Sucking gently on the head and tonguing at the slit, Jayden grunts in appreciation before he releases his cock from his mouth with a loud pop—only to do it all over again.

He tastes as beautiful as he looked.

That was the only thing going through Jayden's mind as he pushed his head deeper, taking much of his cock down his mouth to the best of his abilities. Frothy saliva ran down Jayden's mouth as he flicked his tongue across the bulbous mushroom head.

He licks his cock like a starved man on his last death row meal, savoring it as if it was his favorite flavored lollipop. Then, finally, Troy spreads his legs as far as he can go, giving himself entirely to Jayden and being at his complete mercy.

It felt so good that Troy couldn't help but be disappointed when Jayden's hand traveled towards his puckered little back hole. It caused his balls to tighten as Jayden proceeded to stick one finger into his hole after gathering enough slickness from how much he was oozing before getting back to work.

Only when he's satisfied with working three fingers in

does Jayden pull away, licking his lips as he slowly grabs the back of Troy's legs and works his length inward. Troy bites his lips, never realizing how erotic the whole scene looks.

The improvised lube helped immensely as he felt his tightness gripping Jayden's mushroom head as he fed every inch into him. At first, he tightened up until Jayden started to coo at him, giving him encouraging words with his hands that only added to his ecstasy as he slowly pushed past the muscles, trying to keep his lover out of his puckered back entrance.

"So good, baby."

"That's it. Push me back out and then pull me back in."

"You're such a good boy, Troy. So *perfect* for me."

Only when Jayden is seated at the hilt does he hiss at Troy's tightness, perfectly enveloping him like a glove. Sweat trickles down his face as Troy tries to get used to feeling so full and stretched out simultaneously.

It took everything in Jayden not to come right there and then lose his mind, allowing Troy to get used to it as he slowly wiggled around. They stared at one another as Jayden slowly leaned forward, pressing a kiss to Troy's lips, starting to rock his cock in and off him, enjoying his stiff shaft between his ass cheek and choking his asshole.

"Are you okay?" Jayden questions, rolling his forehead on top of his.

"Yeah, it feels…really good," Troy signs, letting out a shuddering breath. "I think…you can move now?"

"I will," he nods. "I love you."

Those three words alone make Troy's heart skip a beat as he reaches to cup his cheek for a moment.

"I love you too."

Groaning, Jayden is overwhelmed by how tight he is, as his sphincter muscles tighten and reluctantly let him go with each outward stroke before slamming back home. Once Troy is comfortable enough, Jayden wastes no time picking up the pace quickly and eagerly inside of his boyfriend.

Troy has his legs completely spread out as Jayden pumps into him hard and fast, his free hand wrapped around Troy's cock, stroking him reluctantly. In fact, Jayden would feel Troy's tightness clamping down harder on his cock with each passing second.

Troy is *completely* lost in pleasure, his hands going onto Jayden's broad shoulders and gripping them hard for strength as Jayden practically nails him to the bed. Every time Jayden's fingers would then flick onto his nipple, it makes Troy whimper, and his tightness squeezes even harder.

Groaning, Jayden decides to flick Troy's taut nipple, causing him to cry out again as his other hand reaches down to take his member into his hand. Jayden slowly begins to pump his cock in rhythm to how he's slamming his thickness in return.

It does not take long until Troy's eyes start to close, completely lost in pleasure. His mouth starts to curl upward into a delirious-like smile as sweat trickles down his body. Their grunts and moans become one as Jayden keeps pumping his cock deeper and faster into him.

Higher and higher, they bright each other to a pleasurable state of no return. Troy loves how Jayden dirty talks with his hand, praising how good and tight he is, asking if he likes it, and telling him how close he is.

It was all it took as, not before long, an orgasm broke completely, blinding Troy as he spurts all over his chest. He is clenching hard onto the pillow he was lying on, his body still spasming from the intensity of his orgasm.

The sight alone pushes Jayden over the edge as he pumps a copious thick amount of come into his boyfriend, filling him up to the brim with his seed. Jayden then grabs Troy's cheeks and crashes his lips down onto his as they swallow one another's moan.

Troy feels electricity coursing through his entire body as he feels his thick cum erupting from Jayden's cock as he shoots into his tightness, coating his insides with his thick, white potent seed. He keeps grinding onto Jayden, riding him in an attempt to draw out every last remnant of his spurt as their tongues battle passionately.

Only after they pulled away, a thin saliva connecting one another for a moment.

No one could say anything as Jayden collapsed on top of him, nuzzling into him as Troy moaned.

After a while, Jayden rolls to his side in front of Troy, grinning at him.

"How's that for forgiveness?" he teasingly asks, loving how Troy doesn't stop laughing.

"One more round," Troy signs back eagerly and truly. Deep down, they know whatever life throws at them, they'll be able to get through it together. So long as they're holding one another's hand, they can focus on what *is*.

Them.

EPILOGUE

Jayden was dying.

The room suddenly feels as if it is closing in, making him feel uneasy.

He loosens his tie, realizing it is a tad too stuffy for his liking. With each passing moment, he feels more suffocated and uncomfortable. He takes a deep breath to calm his nerves, but the air feels thin and stifling.

"Dude, are you really freaking out right now? You? You, of all people?"

He scowls, throwing daggers at Trevis in the mirror, who only grins back in turn.

His fingers twitch in his seat, and it takes everything in him not to sock his closest friend, no matter how *punchable* his face looks right now. If it weren't because today was such a busy freaking day, and he promised Troy not to punch him, he would have.

"Shut up," he scowls.

"What are you going to do?" he laughs, wagging his brow. "Punch me?"

"Tempting, I'll make a note to do it later," he wagers, finding great joy in the way his cockiness and smile dropped. After all, they both know he'd not only remember but pay it back tenfold for his *lovely* friend's suggestion. However, he can't help but feel his heart growing somewhat nervous. "I mean…what if…he doesn't show up?"

Damn it.

He hates how frightened he sounds right now, his hands growing clammier at the thought.

When you're genuinely in love and trust them completely, you're not afraid of them cheating.

No, you're terrified of them leaving you because he knew deep down he got lucky with Troy.

So damn fucking lucky.

"Are you serious right now?" Trevis asks, flabbergasted. "Say you're kidding. Do you even hear yourself?"

"Thanks for the comfort, ass wipe," he glares at him through the mirror. "Two punches, let's just add on."

"Woah, woah, you don't have to go that far. Come on, dude! We can handle this like adults. I…I was joking anyway, really, but if you're going to punch me, please don't hit my face," he stammers out when Jayden finally gets up from where he had been sitting in front of the large vanity mirror. "I have an interview this weekend! Come on!"

"Perfect, then you can tell them it's because you're trying to give me pre-wedding jitters."

"Dude, you want me to call you out like that on national TV for the world to see?" he remarks.

"Second thought, three punches and a black eye, so you definitely won't try attending that interview now. Thanks for the heads up, buddy," he retorts with a bright smile as he cocks his fist. It causes him to yelp, trying to duck.

"But why are you even nervous in the first place?" he spatters, throwing his hands up and then deciding to shield his face. It's funny that things don't change. "You and I both know you guys are practically made for one another. Plus, it's not as if you guys aren't already married technically. This is just a make-up now that you both have the capability!"

"You wouldn't understand," he remarks, crossing his arm while rolling his eyes.

"How? I'm married myself," he concurs, squinting his eyes in turn while Jayden snaps his finger.

"Oh yeah."

"I hate you so much," he grumbles, causing him to laugh.

It helps…somewhat.

However, his hands are still clammy as ever, his heart pounding recklessly.

Even though they were already married back in college, which consisted of them going to the city clerk only, this was their first actual wedding, and family and friends would surround them. It made everything feel more real, and Jayden was scared that Troy might not feel the same way now that the reality of their marriage was settling in.

It didn't help that he'll be walking down in fifteen minutes to the love of his life, and he's already freaking out that this might come crashing down onto Troy that he deserves to marry someone who's so much better than him.

God, he deserves the fucking world.

Someone who doesn't have so many…issues.

Someone who's making minimum wage compared to a two-time tennis gold medalist and the first gay and deaf ITF tournament and Deaflympics winner. While he's so proud—so damn proud—with how far Troy had come, he sometimes felt as if he deserved so much better.

However, he was also a selfish bastard, too.

Don't focus on what-ifs; focus on what is.

"It's just…what if he realizes now that he could do so much better?" he questions softly.

"That's ridiculous," he chuckles, patting him on his shoulder with a loopy smile. "Come on, relax and have more confidence in yourself, would you? What happened to the daredevil, adrenaline-chasing guy I knew in college?"

He snorts, rolling his eyes.

"The last daredevil, adrenaline-racing thing I've done the past few years was trying fries with ice cream."

"Scandalous," he teases before clearing his throat again. "Seriously, have more confidence in yourself and Troy, would you? If you can't believe in yourself, believe in him. He really does love you. I've never seen him even glance at another person. You guys came a long way together."

At that, Jayden can't help but agree.

They certainly have, and he only came this far in life— so happy and content—because of him.

It's the reason why today has to be perfect.

"Thanks, Trevis," he remarks and awkwardly pulls him in for a hug.

"Ew, don't get sappy on me. That's so damn weird coming from—ouch! You motherfucker," he groans when Troy decides to punch him in the side after all. He flips him off, and suddenly, it feels as if they're back in college again.

"Two more to go," he notes, fixing his suit's cuff and ensuring everything is to his standard.

After all, he will walk down the aisle to the love of his life.

"You're a dick," he grumbles, storming out the door while continuing to hold his middle finger up.

"See you at the after party; you had better watch yourself. You never know what will accidentally come for you when you're least expecting it as payback," he calls after him, making him groan like a whale once more.

"Fuck you!"

"You wish," he laughs. "Speaking of which, did you ever tell your girl that we shared a ki—"

"Hey!" Trevis exclaims before quickly storming back with his entire face red. "Did you tell Troy?"

"Of course, we have no secrets," he proudly replies. It makes his friend make a gagging face and proceed to flip him off on the way out. He can't help but continue to grin, thankful for him to drop by as a surprise.

Taking a few breaths, he was able to calm himself down enough before making his way out and where his parents would be meeting him to walk him towards the alter. Even the thought of this day happening seems foreign to him.

He's becoming more comfortable around them, who are trying to come around and make a conscious effort to get to know Jayden, though it still feels awkward and tense at times. He supposes it makes sense, trying to undo the years of trauma between them.

Yet, they're trying to get to know him, which is a good step forward, as they try to have dinner every week at Jayden's discretion rather than vice versa. However, some conversations get a tad stalled as if they always have the same discussion repeatedly—as if those questions were the only ones they felt safe asking without potentially ruining their fragile relationship.

He supposes it makes sense.

After cutting him off for two years, they suddenly decided to come around again after the initial shock of it all, as Troy had predicted. His mother finally went to see a therapist; his father is still coming around with his sexuality, and little by little—they decided to go to family counseling together.

It's uncomfortable as hell, but...he sees them finally coming around and moving forward.

Just last year, they even suggested spending Christmas with Troy.

The thought of his husband—fuck, he'd never get tired of that word—makes him smile.

It's hard to imagine it's been four years since they decided to tie the knot.

Is it probably crazy they decided to get married on their first anniversary?

In fact, it was probably the dumbest decision on a

technicality. They were both in school, barely even adults, when they decided to fly to Vegas and tie the knot after one too many champagnes as a celebration.

For Troy, a couple of scouts were interested in recruiting him and his application to the Deaflympics.

For Jayden, it was pursuing his newfound dream in coaching, thanks to Coach Winter.

When they returned home after spring break, everyone practically exploded on them. If Jayden closes his eyes, he can still hear Quinn screeching and almost lunging at him for not inviting her.

However, when has Jayden ever been the planner?

Neither of them says a word, but it means everything.

They're still here—they're trying.

That's all he asks for, really.

Jayden finds himself smiling genuinely as they reach the front, surrounded by his college and family friends. His ring finger twitches, and the tattoo with Troy's name over his chest, which he got as a surprise last year, seems to pulse as everyone stands for the ceremony as his husband walks down the aisle.

Troy looks stunning in his suit, eyes locked onto Jayden's as he walks towards him. Just as the first time their eyes met when they had bumped into one another, everything seemed to disappear. Suddenly, he realizes there's no reason for his nervousness.

Because he and Troy?

They're meant to be together—in this life, the next, and every single one after.

Milton Keynes UK
Ingram Content Group UK Ltd.
UKHW041830201024
449814UK00004B/292